GOLD

ISAAC ASIMOV

The Final Science Fiction Collection

An Imprint of HarperCollinsPublishers

A hardcover edition of this book was published in 1995 by HarperPrism.

Notice of copyright of individual pieces appears on pages 398–399, which constitute an extension of this copyright page.

GOLD. Copyright © 1995 by Nightfall, Inc./The Estate of Isaac Asimov. Introduction © 2003 by Orson Scott Card. All rights reserved. Printed in the United States of America. No part of this book may be used or reproduced in any manner whatsoever without written permission except in the case of brief quotations embodied in critical articles and reviews. For information address HarperCollins Publishers Inc., 10 East 53rd Street, New York, NY 10022.

HarperCollins books may be purchased for educational, business, or sales promotional use. For information please write: Special Markets Department, HarperCollins Publishers Inc., 10 East 53rd Street, New York, NY 10022.

First Eos paperback edition published 2003.

The Library of Congress has cataloged the hardcover edition as follows:

Asimov, Isaac, 1920–
    Gold : the final science fiction collection / Isaac Asimov.
    p.   cm.
    ISBN 0-06-105206-X (hc)
PS3551.S5 G62   1995
813/.54 20   94023598

ISBN 0-06-055652-8 (pbk.)

06 07 JTC/RRD 10 9 8 7 6 5 4 3

Contents

Introduction

by Orson Scott Card

America has always had two levels of language—the way we speak to one another, and the way we speak to try to impress Europeans. The first is very plain and direct, indulging sometimes in exaggeration and irony, but always with the intention that the listener understand our meaning clearly. The second is more indirect, decorated, metaphorical, designed to make a good impression.

Like the difference between a sixteen-year-old boy talking to his sister and the same boy talking to a girl he wants to ask out.

American prose writing follows both spoken traditions, but, generally speaking, when we write to impress, we aren't very good at it. We tend to try too hard. It's a foreign language to us. We know we're faking and we're very much afraid of being caught.

At the same time, though, we don't hold the homegrown American Plain Style of writing in very high esteem. Indeed, we're likely to say of it that the writer "has no style at all."

But this isn't so. Indeed, the American Plain Style is devilishly hard to bring off well. Because there is great art in seeming artless; one must grind the lens very smooth indeed to make it perfectly clear.

What the American Plain Style celebrates is the democratic ideal. The writer declares, by making his language as clear and accessible as possible, that he values all readers and wishes to invite them to participate in his conversation. The Plain Style closes no doors, draws no veils across the meaning.

Let's all sit down together and tell our tales, says the Plain Style writer. Let's put on no airs, nobody's impressed by that sort of thing. There's none of us better than any other; only the story itself matters, only the ideas.

When American Plain Style is done well, readers never notice the writer or the writing at all. They are completely immersed in the story or essay, receiving it as if it were unfiltered by any other mind.

Of course it *is* filtered; it was completely created by another mind. But because the reader is never reminded of it, the ideas and events recounted in that style are likelier to be received without doubt. Where the European style is designed to persuade the reader that the writer is very talented, the American style is designed to persuade the reader that the ideas being explained or tale being told are true. The goal of the one is awe; the goal of the other is understanding.

Of course, it's rare to find any writer whose style is purely one or the other. Few writers of the indirect style eschew meaning completely; few writers of the Plain Style are able to avoid a bit of song and dance now and then.

But the purest, clearest, most fluid, most effective writer of the American Plain Style, ever, was the man whose stories and essays you now hold in your hand: Isaac Asimov.

It was a conscious choice, early in his writing career. After a try or two at "writing well," he found he wasn't proud of the purple prose that resulted. So instead he tried to expunge all fanciness from his writing—and succeeded. But far from being a mere negation—refraining from decoration and indirection to a remarkable degree—Asimov's style became something positive. A telescope, if you will, that made far and fuzzy things seem close and clear. An instrument of extraordinary power and versatility, which he then turned upon thousands of different tales and topics, and then let us peer through.

Yet it is not for his achievement as the unrivaled master of the American Plain Style that I have loved the works of Isaac Asimov since I first read *Foundation* at the age of sixteen. For what good would his powerful instrument be if what he showed us through it was worthless, ugly, or empty?

Isaac Asimov's real gift was not language, or not language alone. It was, instead, that much rarer thing: a questioning mind that could not endure unanswered mystery. The three-year-old who pestered his parents with "Why?" "Why?" "Why?" never faded into a jaded adult who had given up on finding answers. Asimov never gave up his questions, and found answers more often than most.

I don't think he was always right—certainly he reached some conclusions quite different from my own. But even when he was (in my opinion) wrong, he was never wrong for no reason. Everything was analyzed, its causes and ramifications imagined or observed, and alternatives considered.

Yet even that ever-questing mind would not have been enough for me, because the child full of "Why?" is, ultimately, tedious and must be sent outside to play. Nor did I take continuous pleasure in Asimov's work throughout his career simply because I thought he had found the right answers, though he did so more often than most.

What I have loved most in Asimov's work, with all its

clarity, its questioning, its wisdom, is that underlying everything was a deep goodness, a rarely spoken but always present concern for the communities in which he lived—the science fiction community, the American people, humanity as a whole. He wished us well, fervently wished it, and offered such wisdom as he had found in the hope that we might find it not admirable, but useful.

And I did, I do, and will continue to do so.

As writers get older, they become more like themselves—that is, those traits and tendencies that distinguish them from other writers become more obvious, perhaps even exaggerated, and sometimes quite annoying.

Asimov, too, became more like himself: clearer, with deeper and more perplexing questions, and more filled with that deep goodness.

So when you read these stories that came from him in the last years of his life, you will find him at his best, in every sense of the word.

In the 1980s, I was at a Nebula banquet in New York, and, because I had won an award for something, I found myself standing beside Isaac as our pictures were being taken. He was holding the Grand Master Award he had just received, and which I thought had been long overdue.

He looked at my Nebula and nodded. "That one—that's the real award. This one"—he raised his own trophy a little—"this is just because I'm not dead yet."

Of course I protested that his award had been earned by a lifetime of work, and I should be so lucky as to do half so well in my career as he had done in his—but he wouldn't hear it, turned away from me, smiled at the camera.

Later, I was invited to take part in a *festschrift* in his honor, an anthology of stories in which the participating writers were allowed to set their stories within one of Asimov's fictional universes. I was eager to write my *Foundation* story but also terrified, because to write a story in Asimov's world was to invite comparison with Asimov. Yet in that story I was able to say, indirectly, some of the things I felt about this great old man who had shown us all that perfect clarity was, indeed, attainable in our language. I hoped that when he read it, he would understand what I was saying to him.

But he never read it. He did not read any of the stories in that book. For, I was told, Asimov was afraid that he would have to come face-to-face with the fact that other people could write his stories better than he did.

His humility was genuine. But he was wrong. None of us in that book were in his league. But we were all better writers—and perhaps better people—for having known his work.

Asimov might not have seen his own greatness; indeed, part of his greatness may have been the fact that he gave very little thought to whether he had any. But it was there—in works from the beginning of his career through to the very end.

Other writers will do good things; some will do great things; but at the things Asimov did so brilliantly, we will not see his match.

Part One

THE FINAL STORIES

Cal

I am a robot. My name is Cal. I have a registration number. It is CL-123X, but my master calls me Cal.

The X in my registration number means I am a special robot for my master. He asked for me and helped design me. He has a lot of money. He is a writer.

I am not a very complicated robot. My master doesn't want a complicated robot. He just wants someone to pick up after him, to run his printer, stack his disks, and like that.

He says I don't give him any backtalk and just do what I am told. He says that is good.

He has people come in to help him, sometimes. They give him backtalk. Sometimes they do not do what they are told. He gets very angry and red in the face.

Then he tells me to do something, and I do it. He says, thank goodness, you do as you are told.

Of course, I do as I am told. What else can I do? I want to make my master feel good. I can tell when my master feels good. His mouth stretches and he calls that a smile. He pats me on the shoulder and says, Good, Cal. Good.

I like it when he says, Good, Cal. Good.

I say to my master, Thank you. You make me feel good, too.

And he laughs. I like when he laughs because it means he feels good, but it is a queer sound. I don't understand how he makes it or why. I ask him and he says to me that he laughs when something is funny.

I ask him if what I said is funny.

He says, Yes, it is.

It is funny because I say I feel good. He says robots do not really feel good. He says only human masters feel good. He says robots just have positronic brain paths that work more easily when they follow orders.

I don't know what positronic brain paths are. He says they are something inside me.

I say, When positronic brain paths work better, does it make everything smoother and easier for me? Is that why I feel good?

Then I ask, When a master feels good, is it because something in him works more easily?

My master nods and says, Cal, you are smarter than you look.

I don't know what that means either but my master seems pleased with me and that makes my positronic brain paths work more easily, and that makes me feel good. It is easier just to say it makes me feel good. I ask if I can say that.

He says, You can say whatever you choose, Cal.

What I want is to be a writer like my master. I do not understand why I have this feeling, but my master is a writer and he helped design me. Maybe his design makes me feel I want to be a writer. I do not understand why I have this feeling because I don't know what a writer is. I ask my master what a writer is.

He smiles again. Why do you want to know, Cal? he asks.

I do not know, I say. It is just that you are a writer and I want to know what that is. You seem so happy when you are writing and if it makes you happy maybe it will make me happy, too. I have a feeling—I don't have the words for it. I think a while and he waits for me. He is still smiling.

I say, I want to know because it will make me feel better to know. I am—I am—

He says, You are curious, Cal.

I say, I don't know what that word means.

He says, It means you want to know just because you want to know.

I want to know just because I want to know, I say.

He says, Writing is making up a story. I tell about people who do different things, and have different things happen to them.

I say, How do you find out what they do and what happens to them?

He says, I make them up, Cal. They are not real people. They are not real happenings. I imagine them, in here.

He points to his head.

I do not understand and I ask how he makes them up, but he laughs and says, I do not know, either. I just make them up.

He says, I write mysteries. Crime stories. I tell about people who do wrong things, who hurt other people.

I feel very bad when I hear that. I say, How can you talk about hurting people? That must never be done.

He says, Human beings are not controlled by the Three Laws of Robotics. Human masters can hurt other human masters, if they wish.

This is wrong, I say.

It is, he says. In my stories, people who do harm are punished. They are put in prison and kept there where they cannot hurt people.

Do they like it in prison? I ask.

Of course not. They must not. Fear of prison keeps them from doing more hurtful things than they do.

I say, But prison is wrong, too, if it makes people feel bad.

Well, says my master, that is why you cannot write mysteries and crime stories.

I think about that. There must be a way to write stories in which people are not hurt. I would like to do that. I want to be a writer. I want to be a writer very much.

My master has three different Writers for writing stories. One is very old, but he says he keeps it because it has sentimental value.

I don't know what sentimental value is. I do not like to ask. He does not use the machine for his stories. Maybe sentimental value means it must not be used.

He doesn't say I can not use it. I do not ask him if I can use it. If I do not ask him and he does not say I must not, then I am not disobeying orders if I use it.

At night, he is sleeping, and the other human masters who are sometimes here are gone. There are two other robots my master has who are more important than I am. They do more important work. They wait in their niches at night when they have not been given anything to do.

My master has not said, Stay in your niche, Cal.

Sometimes he doesn't, because I am so unimportant, and then I can move about at night. I can look at the Writer. You push keys and it makes words and then the words are put on paper. I watch the master so I know how to push keys. The words go on the paper themselves. I do not have to do that.

I push the keys but I do not understand the words. I feel bad after a while. The master may not like it even if he does not tell me not to do it.

The words are printed on paper and in the morning I show the words to my master.

I say, I am sorry. I was using the Writer.

He looks at the paper. Then he looks at me. He makes a frown.

He says, Did you do this?

Yes, master.

When?

Last night.

Why?

I want very much to write. Is this a story?

He holds up the paper and smiles.

He says, These are just random letters, Cal. This is gibberish.

He does not seem angry. I feel better. I do not know what gibberish is.

I say, Is it a story?

He says, No, it is not. And it is a lucky thing the Writer cannot be damaged by mishandling. If you really want to write so badly, I will tell you what I will do. I will have you reprogrammed so that you will know how to use a Writer.

Two days later, a technician arrives. He is a master who knows how to make robots do better jobs. My master tells me that the technician is the one who put me together, and my master helped. I do not remember that.

The technician listens carefully to my master.

He says, Why do you want to do this, Mr. Northrop?

Mr. Northrop is what other masters call my master.

My master says, I helped design Cal, remember. I think I must have put into him the desire to be a writer. I did not intend to, but as long as he does, I feel I should humor him. I owe it to him.

The technician says, That is foolish. Even if we accidentally put in a desire to write that is still no job for a robot.

My master says, Just the same I want it done.

The technician says, It will be expensive, Mr. Northrop.

My master frowns. He looks angry.

He says, Cal is my robot. I shall do as I please. I have the money and I want him adjusted.

The technician looks angry, too. He says, If that's what you want, very well. The customer is boss. But it will be more expensive than you think, because we cannot put in the knowledge of how to use a Writer without improving his vocabulary a good deal.

My master says, Fine. Improve his vocabulary.

The next day, the technician comes back with lots of tools. He opens my chest. It is a queer feeling. I do not like it. He reaches in. I think he shuts off my power pack, or takes it out. I do not remember. I do not see anything, or think anything, or know anything.

Then I could see and think and know again. I could see that time had passed, but I did not know how much time.

I thought for a while. It was odd, but I knew how to run a Writer and I seemed to understand more words. For instance, I knew what "gibberish" meant, and it was embarrassing to think I had shown gibberish to my master, thinking it was a story.

I would have to do better. This time I had no apprehension—I know the meaning of "apprehension," too—I had no apprehension that he would keep me from using the old Writer. After all, he would not have redesigned me to be capable of using it if he were going to prevent me from doing so.

I put it to him. "Master, does this mean I may use the Writer?"

He said, "You may do so at any time, Cal, that you are not engaged in other tasks. You must let me see what you write, however."

"Of course, master."

He was clearly amused because I think he expected more gibberish (what an ugly word!) but I didn't think he would get any more.

I didn't write a story immediately. I had to think about what to write. I suppose that that is what the master meant when he said you must make up a story.

I found it was necessary to think about it first and then write down what was thought. It was much more complicated than I had supposed.

My master noticed my preoccupation. He asked me, "What are you doing, Cal?"

I said, "I am trying to make up a story. It's hard work."

"Are you finding that out, Cal? Good. Obviously, your reorganization has not only improved your vocabulary but it seems to me it has intensified your intelligence."

I said, "I'm not sure what is meant by 'intensified'."

"It means you seem smarter. You seem to know more."

"Does that displease you, master?"

"Not at all. It pleases me. It may make it more possible for you to write stories and even after you have grown tired of trying to write, you will remain more useful to me."

I thought at once that it would be delightful to be more useful to the master, but I didn't understand what he meant about growing tired of trying to write. I wasn't going to get tired of writing.

Finally, I had a story in my mind, and I asked my master when would be a proper time to write it.

He said, "Wait till night. Then you won't be getting in my way. We can have a small light for the corner where the old Writer is standing; and you can write your story. How long do you think it will take you?"

"Just a little while," I said, surprised. "I can work the Writer very quickly."

My master said, "Cal, working the Writer isn't all there—" Then he stopped, thought a while, and said, "No, you go ahead and do it. You will learn. I won't try to advise you."

He was right. Working the Writer wasn't all there was to

it. I spent nearly the whole night trying to figure out the story. It is very difficult to decide which word comes after which. I had to erase the story several times and start over. It was very embarrassing.

Finally, it was done, and here it is. I kept it after I wrote it because it was the first story I ever wrote. It was not gibberish.

THE INTROODER
by Cal

There was a detektav wuns named Cal, who was a very good detektav and very brave. Nuthin fritened him. Imajin his surprise one night when he herd an introoder in his masters home.

He came russian into the riting office. There was an introoder. He had cum in throo the windo. There was broken glas. That was what Cal, the brave detektav, had herd with his good hering.

He said, "Stop, introoder."

The introoder stopped and looked skared. Cal felt bad that the introoder looked skared.

Cal said, "Look what you have done. You have broken the windo."

"Yes," said the introoder, looking very ashaymed. "I did not mean to break the windo."

Cal was very clever and he saw the flawr in the introoder's remark. He said, "How did you expect to get in if you were not going to break the windo?"

"I thought it would be open," he said. "I tried to open it and it broke."

Cal said, "Waht was the meaning of what you have done, anyhow? Why should you want to come into this room when it is not your room? You are an introoder."

"I did not mean any harm," he said.

"That is not so, for if you ment no harm, you would not be here," said Cal. "You must be punnished."

"Please do not punnish me," said the introoder.

"I will not punnish you," said Cal. "I don't wish to cause you unhappiness or payn. I will call my master."

He called, "Master! Master!"

The master came russian in. "What have we here?" he asked.

"An introoder," I said. "I have caut him and he is for you to punnish."

My master looked at the introoder. He said, "Are you sorry for wat you have done?"

"I am," said the introoder. He was crying and water was coming out of his eys the way it happens with masters when they are sad.

"Will you ever do it agen?" said my master.

"Never. I will never do it agen," said the introoder.

"In that case," said the master, "you have been punnished enogh. Go away and be sure never to do it agen."

Then the master said, "You are a good detektav, Cal. I am proud of you."

Cal was very glad to have pleased the master.

The End

I was very pleased with the story and I showed it to the master. I was sure he would be very pleased, too.

He was more than pleased, for as he read it, he smiled. He even laughed a few times. Then he looked up at me and said, "Did you write this?"

"Yes, I did, master," I said.

"I mean, all by yourself. You didn't copy anything?"

"I made it up in my own head, master," I said. "Do you like it?"

He laughed again, quite loudly. "It's interesting," he said.

I was a little anxious. "Is it funny?" I asked. "I don't know how to make things funny."

"I know, Cal. It's not funny intentionally."

I thought about that for a while. Then I asked, "How can something be funny unintentionally?"

"It's hard to explain, but don't worry about it. In the first place, you can't spell, and that's a surprise. You speak so well now that I automatically assumed you could spell words but, obviously, you can't. You can't be a writer unless you can spell words correctly, and use good grammar."

"How do I manage to spell words correctly?"

"You don't have to worry about that, Cal," said my master. "We will outfit you with a dictionary. But tell me, Cal. In your story, Cal is *you*, isn't he?"

"Yes." I was pleased he had noticed that.

"Bad idea. You don't want to put yourself into a story and say how great you are. It offends the reader."

"Why, master?"

"Because it does. It looks like I *will* have to give you advice, but I'll make it as brief as possible. It is not customary to praise yourself. Besides you don't want to *say* you are great, you must *show* you are great in what you do. And don't use your own name."

"Is that a rule?"

"A good writer can break any rule, but you're just a beginner. Stick to the rules and what I have told you are just a couple of them. You're going to encounter many, many more if you keep on writing. Also, Cal, you're going to have trouble with the Three Laws of Robotics. You can't assume that wrongdoers will weep and be ashamed. Human beings aren't like that. They *must* be punished sometimes."

I felt my positronic brain paths go rough. I said, "That is difficult."

"I know. Also, there's no mystery in the story. There doesn't have to be, but I think you'd be better off if there were. What if your hero, whom you'll have to call something other than Cal, doesn't know whether someone is an intruder or not. How would he find out? You see, he has to use his head." And my master pointed to his own.

I didn't quite follow.

My master said, "I'll tell you what. I'll give you some stories of my own to read, after you've been outfitted with a spelling dictionary and a grammar and you'll see what I mean."

The technician came to the house and said, "There's no problem in installing a spelling dictionary and a grammar. It'll cost you more money. I know you don't care about money, but tell me why you are so interested in making a writer out of this hunk of steel and titanium."

I didn't think it was right for him to call me a hunk of steel and titanium, but of course a human master can say anything he wants to say. They always talk about us robots as though we weren't there. I've noticed that, too.

My master said, "Did you ever hear of a robot who wanted to be a writer?"

"No," said the technician, "I can't say I ever did, Mr. Northrop."

"Neither did I! Neither did anyone as far as I know. Cal is unique, and I want to study him."

The technician smiled very wide—grinned, that's the word. "Don't tell me you have it in your head that he'll be able to write your stories for you, Mr. Northrop."

My master stopped smiling. He lifted his head and looked down on the technician very angrily. "Don't be a fool. You just do what I pay you to do."

I think the master made the technician sorry he had said

that, but I don't know why. If my master asked me to write his stories for him I would be pleased to do so.

Again, I don't know how long it took the technician to do his job when he came back a couple of days later. I don't remember a thing about it.

Then my master was suddenly talking to me. "How do you feel, Cal?"

I said, "I feel very well. Thank you, sir."

"What about words. Can you spell?"

"I know the letter-combinations, sir."

"Very good. Can you read this?" He handed me a book. It said, on the cover, *The Best Mysteries of J. F. Northrop*.

I said, "Are these your stories, sir?"

"Absolutely. If you want to read them, you can."

I had never been able to read easily before, but now as soon as I looked at the words, I could hear them in my ear. It was surprising. I couldn't imagine how I had been unable to do it before.

"Thank you, sir," I said. "I shall read this and I'm sure it will help me in my writing."

"Very good. Continue to show me everything you write."

The master's stories were quite interesting. He had a detective who could always understand matters that others found puzzling. I didn't always understand how he could see the truth of a mystery and I had to read some of the stories over again and do so slowly.

Sometimes I couldn't understand them even when I read them slowly. Sometimes I did, though, and it seemed to me I could write a story like Mr. Northrop's.

This time I spent quite a long while working it out in my head. When I thought I had it worked out, I wrote the following:

THE SHINY QUARTER
by Euphrosyne Durando

Calumet Smithson sat in his arm chair, his eagle-eyes sharp and the nostrils of his thin high-bridged nose flaring, as though he could scent a new mystery.

He said, "Well, Mr. Wassell, tell me your story again from the beginning. Leave out nothing, for one can't tell when even the smallest detail may not be of the greatest importance."

Wassell owned an important business in town, and in it he employed many robots and also human beings.

Wassell did so, but there was nothing startling in the details at all and he was able to summarize it this way. "What it amounts to, Mr. Smithson, is that I am losing money. Someone in my employ is helping himself to small sums now and then. The sums are of no great importance, each in itself, but it is like a small, steady oil loss in a machine, or the drip-drop of water from a leaky faucet, or the oozing of blood from a small wound. In time, it would mount up and become dangerous."

"Are you actually in danger of losing your business, Mr. Smithson?"

"Not yet. But I don't like to lose money, either. Do you?"

"No, indeed," said Smithson, "I do not. How many robots do you employ in your business?"

"Twenty-seven, sir."

"And they are all reliable, I suppose."

"Undoubtedly. They could not steal. Besides, I have asked each one of them if they took any money and they all said they had not. And, of course, robots cannot lie, either."

"You are quite right," said Smithson. "It is useless to be concerned over robots. They are honest, through and through. What about the human beings you employ? How many of them are there?"

"I employ seventeen, but of these only four can possibly have been stealing."

"Why is that?"

"The others do not work on the premises. These four, however, do. Each one has the occasion, now and then, to handle petty cash, and I suspect that what happens is that at least one of them manages to transfer assets from the company to his private account in such a way that the matter is not easily traced."

"I see. Yes, it is unfortunately true that human beings may steal. Have you confronted your suspects with the situation?"

"Yes, I have. They all deny any such activity, but, of course, human beings can lie, too."

"So they can. Did any of them look uneasy while being questioned?"

"All did. They could see I was a furious man who could fire all four, guilty or innocent. They would have had trouble finding other jobs if fired for such a reason."

"Then that cannot be done. We must not punish the innocent with the guilty."

"You are quite right," said Mr. Wassell. "I couldn't do that. But how can I decide which one is guilty?"

"Is there one among them who has a dubious record, who has been fired under uncertain circumstances earlier in his career?"

"I have made quiet inquiries, Mr. Smithson, and I have found nothing suspicious about any of them."

"Is one of them in particular need of money?"

"I pay good wages."

"I am sure of that, but perhaps one has some sort of expensive taste that makes his income insufficient."

"I have found no evidence of that, though, to be sure, if one of them needed money for some perverse reason, he would keep it secret. No one wants to be thought evil."

"You are quite right," said the great detective. "In that case, you must confront me with the four men. I will interrogate them." His eyes flashed. "We will get to the bottom of this mystery, never fear. Let us arrange a meeting in the evening. We might meet in the company dining room over some small meal and a bottle of wine, so the men will feel completely relaxed. Tonight, if possible."

"I will arrange it," said Mr. Wassell, eagerly.

Calumet Smithson sat at the dinner table and regarded the four men closely. Two of them were quite young and had dark hair. One of them had a mustache as well. Neither was very good looking. One of them was Mr. Foster and the other was Mr. Lionell. The third man was rather fat and had small eyes. He was Mr. Mann. The fourth was tall and rangy and had a nervous way of cracking his knuckles. He was Mr. Ostrak.

Smithson seemed to be a little nervous himself as he questioned each man in turn. His eagle eyes narrowed as he gazed sharply at the four suspects and he played with a shiny quarter that flipped casually between the fingers of his right hand.

Smithson said, "I'm sure that each of the four of you is quite aware what a terrible thing it is to steal from an employer."

They all agreed at once.

Smithson tapped the shiny quarter on the table,

thoughtfully. "One of you, I'm sure, is going to break down under the load of guilt and I think you will do it before the evening is over. But, for now, I must call my office. I will be gone for only a few minutes. Please sit here and wait for me and while I am gone, do not talk to each other, or look at each other."

He gave the quarter a last tap, and, paying no attention to it, he left. In about ten minutes, he was back.

He looked from one to another and said, "You did not talk to each other or look at each other, I hope?"

There was a general shaking of heads as though they were still fearful of speaking.

"Mr. Wassell," said the detective. "Do you agree that no one spoke?"

"Absolutely. We just sat here quietly and waited. We didn't even look at each other."

"Good. Now I will ask each one of you four men to show me what you have in your pockets. Please put everything into a pile in front of you."

Smithson's voice was so compelling, his eyes so bright and sharp, that none of the men thought of disobeying.

"Shirt pockets, too. Inside jacket pockets. All the pockets."

There was quite a pile, credit cards, keys, spectacles, pens, some coins. Smithson looked at the four piles coldly, his mind taking in everything.

Then he said, "Just to make sure that we are all meeting the same requirements, I will make a pile of the contents of my own pockets and, Mr. Wassell, you do the same."

Now there were six piles. Smithson reached over to the pile in front of Mr. Wassell, and said, "What is this shiny quarter I see, Mr. Wassell. Yours?"

Wassell looked confused. "Yes."

"It couldn't be. It has my mark on it. I left it on the table when I went out to call my office. You took it."

Wassell was silent. The other four men looked at him.

Smithson said, "I felt that if one of you was a thief, you wouldn't be able to resist a shiny quarter. Mr. Wassell, you've been stealing from your own company, and, afraid you would be caught, you tried to spread the guilt among your men. That was a wicked and cowardly thing to do."

Wassell hung his head. "You are right, Mr. Smithson. I thought if I hired you to investigate you would find one of the men guilty, and then perhaps I could stop taking the money for my private use."

"You little realize the detective's mind," said Calumet Smithson. "I will turn you over to the authorities. They will decide what to do with you, though if you are sincerely sorry and promise never to do it again, I will try to keep you from being punished badly."

The End

I showed it to Mr. Northrop, who read it silently. He hardly smiled at all. Just in one or two places.

Then he put it down and stared at me. "Where did you get the name Euphrosyne Durando?"

"You said, sir, I was not to use my own name, so I used one as different as possible."

"But where did you get it?"

"Sir, one of the minor characters in one of your stories—"

"Of course! I thought it sounded familiar! Do you realize it's a feminine name?"

"Since I am neither masculine nor feminine—"

"Yes, you're quite right. But the name of the detective, Calumet Smithson. That 'Cal' part is still you, isn't it?"

"I wanted some connection, sir."

"You've got a tremendous ego, Cal."

I hesitated. "What does that mean, sir?"

"Never mind. It doesn't matter."

He put the manuscript down and I was troubled. I said, "But what did you think of the mystery?"

"It's an improvement, but it's still not a good mystery. Do you realize that?"

"In what way is it disappointing, sir?"

"Well, you don't understand modern business practices or computerized financing for one thing. And no one would take a quarter from the table with four other men present, even if they weren't looking. It would have been seen. Then, even if that happened, Mr. Wassell's taking it isn't *proof* he was the thief. Anyone could pocket a quarter automatically, without thinking. It's an interesting indication, but it's not *proof*. And the title of the story tends to give it away, too."

"I see."

"And, in addition, the Three Laws of Robotics are still getting in your way. You keep worrying about punishment."

"I must, sir."

"I know you must. That's why I think you shouldn't try to write crime stories."

"What else should I write, sir?"

"Let me think about it."

Mr. Northrop called in the technician again. This time, I think, he wasn't very eager to have me overhear what he was saying, but even from where I was standing, I could hear the conversation. Sometimes human beings forget how sharp the senses of robots can be.

After all, I was very upset. I wanted to be a writer and I didn't want Mr. Northrop telling me what I could write and what I couldn't write. Of course, he was a human being and I had to obey him, but I didn't like it.

"What's the matter now, Mr. Northrop?" asked the technician in a voice that sounded sardonic to my ears. "Has this robot of yours been writing a story again?"

"Yes, he has," said Mr. Northrop, trying to sound indifferent. "He's written another mystery story and I don't want him writing mysteries."

"Too much competition, eh, Mr. Northrop?"

"No. Don't be a jackass. There's just no point in two people in the same household writing mysteries. Besides, the Three Laws of Robotics get in the way. You can easily imagine how."

"Well, what do you want me to do?"

"I'm not sure. Suppose he writes satire. That's one thing I don't write, so we won't be competing, and the Three Laws of Robotics won't get in his way. I want you to give this robot a sense of the ridiculous."

"A sense of the what?" said the technician, angrily. "How do I do that? Look, Mr. Northrop, be reasonable. I can put in instructions on how to run a Writer. I can put in a dictionary and grammar. But how can I possibly put in a sense of the ridiculous?"

"Well, think about it. You know the workings of a robot's brain patterns. Isn't there some way of readjusting him so that he can see what's funny, or silly, or just plain ridiculous about human beings?"

"I can fool around, but it's not safe."

"Why isn't it safe?"

"Because, look, Mr. Northrop, you started off with a pretty cheap robot, but I've been making it more elaborate. You admit that it's unique and that you never heard of one that wants to write stories, so now it's a pretty expensive robot. You may even have a Classic model here that should be given to the Robotic Institute. If you want me to fool around, I might spoil the whole thing. Do you realize that?"

"I'm willing to take the chance. If the whole thing is spoiled, it will be spoiled, but why should it be? I'm not asking you to work in a hurry. Take the time to analyze it carefully. I have lots of time and lots of money, and I want my robot to write satire."

"Why satire?"

"Because then his lack of worldly knowledge may not matter so much and the Three Laws won't be so important and in time, some day, he may possibly turn out something interesting, though I doubt it."

"And he won't be treading on your turf."

"All right, then. He won't be treading on my turf. Satisfied?"

I still didn't know enough about the language to know what 'treading on my turf' meant, but I gathered that Mr. Northrop was annoyed by my mystery stories. I didn't know why.

There was nothing I could do, of course. Every day, the technician studied me and analyzed me and finally, he said, "All right, Mr. Northrop, I'm going to take a chance, but I'm going to ask you to sign a paper absolving me and my company of all responsibility if anything goes wrong."

"You just prepare the paper. I'll sign it," said Mr. Northrop.

It was very chilling to think that something might go wrong, but that's how things are. A robot must accept all that human beings decide to do.

This time, after I became aware of everything again, I was quite weak for a long time. I had difficulty standing, and my speech was slurred.

I thought that Mr. Northrop looked at me with a worried expression. Perhaps he felt guilty at how he had treated me—he *should* feel guilty—or perhaps he was just worried at the possibility of having lost a great deal of money.

As my sense of balance returned and my speech became clear, an odd thing happened. I suddenly understood how *silly* human beings were. They had no laws governing their actions. They had to make up their own, and even when they did, nothing forced them to obey.

Human beings were simply *confused;* one had to laugh at them. I understood laughter now and could even make the sound, but naturally I didn't laugh out loud. That would have been impolite and offensive. I laughed inside myself, and I began to think of a story in which human beings *did* have laws governing their actions but they hated them and couldn't stick to them.

I also thought of the technician and decided to put him into the story, too. Mr. Northrop kept going to the technician and asking him to do things to me, harder and harder things. Now he had given me a sense of the ridiculous.

So suppose I wrote a story about ridiculous human beings, with no robots present because, of course, robots aren't ridiculous and their presence would simply spoil the humor. And suppose I put in a person who was a technician of human beings. It might be some creature with strange powers who could alter *human* behavior as my technician could alter robot behavior. What would happen in that case?

It might show clearly how human beings were not sensible.

I spent days thinking about the story and getting happier and happier about it. I would start with two men having dinner, and one of them would own a technician—well, *have* a technician of some sort—and I would place the setting in

the twentieth century so as not to offend Mr. Northrop and
the other people of the twenty-first.

I read books to learn about human beings. Mr. Northrop
let me do this and he hardly ever gave me any tasks to do.
Nor did he try to hurry me to write. Maybe he still felt
guilty about the risk he had taken of doing me harm.

I finally started the story, and here it is:

PERFECTLY FORMAL
by Euphrosyne Durando

George and I were dining at a rather posh restaurant,
one in which it was not unusual to see men and women
enter in formal wear.

George looked up at one of those men, observing
him narrowly and without favor, as he wiped his lips
with my napkin, having carelessly dropped his own.

"A pox on all tuxedos, say I," said George.

I followed the direction of his glance. As nearly as I
could tell, he was studying a portly man of about fifty
who was wearing an intense expression of self-
importance as he helped a rather glittering woman,
considerably younger than himself, to her chair.

I said, "George, are you getting ready to tell me that
you know yon bloke in the tux?"

"No," said George. "I intend to tell you no such
thing. My communications with you, and with all living beings, are always predicated on total truth."

"Like your tales of your two-centimeter demon,
Az—" The look of agony on his face made me stop.

"Don't speak of such things," he whispered
hoarsely. "Azazel has no sense of humor, and he has a
powerful sense of power." Then, more normally, he
went on, "I was merely expressing my detestation of

tuxedos, particularly when infested by fat slobs like yon bloke, to use your own curious turn of expression."

"Oddly enough," I said, "I rather agree with you. I, too, find formal wear objectionable and, except when it is impossible to do so, I avoid all black-tie affairs, for that reason alone."

"Good for you," said George. "That rather spoils my impression that you have no redeeming social qualities. I've told everyone that you haven't, you know."

"Thank you, George," I said. "That was very thoughtful of you, considering that you gorge yourself at my expense every chance you get."

"I merely allow you to enjoy my company on those occasions, old man. I would tell all my friends now that you do have one redeeming social quality, but that would merely confuse everyone. They seem quite content with the thought that you have none."

"I thank all your friends," I said.

"As it happens, I know a man," said George, "who was to the manor born. His diapers had been clamped shut with studs, not safety pins. On his first birthday, he was given a little black tie, to be knotted and *not* clipped on. And so things continued all his life. His name is Winthrop Carver Cabwell, and he lived on so rarefied a level of Boston's Brahman aristocracy that he had to carry an oxygen mask for occasional use."

"And you knew this patrician? *You?*"

George looked offended. "Of course, I did," he said. "Do you, for one moment, think that I am such a snob that I would refuse to associate with someone for no other reason than that he was a rich and aristocratic man of Brahman persuasion? You little know me if you do, old man. Winthrop and I knew each other quite well. I was his escape."

George heaved a vinous sigh that sent a neighboring fly into an alcoholic tailspin. "Poor fellow," he said. "Poor rich aristocrat."

"George," I said. "I believe you're winding yourself up to tell me one of your improbable tales of disaster. I don't wish to hear it."

"Disaster? On the contrary. I have a tale to tell of great happiness and joy, and since that is what you want to hear, I will now tell it to you."

As I told you [said George] my Brahman friend was a gentleman from toe to crown, clean-favored and imperially slim—

[Why are you interrupting me with your asinine mouthing of Richard Corey, old fellow? I never heard of him. I'm talking of Winthrop Carver Cabwell. Why don't you *listen?* Where was I? Oh, yes.]

He was a gentleman from toe to crown, clean-favored and imperially slim. As a result, he was naturally a hissing and a byword to all decent people, as he would have known, if he had ever associated with decent people which, of course, he did not, only with other lost souls like himself.

Yes, as you say, he did know me and it was the eventual saving of him—not that I ever profited by the matter. However, as you know, old fellow, money is the last thing on my mind.

[I will ignore your statement, that is the first thing, too, as the product of a perverted attitude of mind.]

Sometimes poor Winthrop would escape. On those occasions, when business ventures took me to Boston, he would slip his chains and eat dinner with me in a hidden nook at the Parker House.

"George," Winthrop would say. "It is a hard and difficult task to uphold the Cabwell name and tradition. After all, it is not simply that we are rich, we are also old money. We are not like those parvenue Rocky-fellows, if I remember the name correctly, who gained their money out of nineteenth-century oil.

"My ancestors, I must never forget, established their fortunes in colonial days in the times of pioneering splendor. My ancestor, Isaiah Cabwell, smuggled guns and firewater to the Indians during Queen Anne's War, and had to live from day to day in the fear of being scalped by mistake by an Algonquin, a Huron, or a colonial.

"And his son, Jeremiah Cabwell, engaged in the harrowing triangular trade, risking his all, by Thoreau, in the dangers of trading sugar, for rum, for slaves, helping thousands of African immigrants come to our great country. With a heritage like that, George, the weight of tradition is heavy. The responsibility of caring for all that aged money is a fearsome one."

"I don't know how you do it, Winthrop," I said.

Winthrop sighed. "By Emerson, I scarcely know myself. It is a matter of clothing, of style, of manner, of being guided every moment by what should be done, rather than by what makes sense. A Cabwell, after all, always knows what should be done, though frequently he cannot figure out what makes sense."

I nodded and said, "I have often wondered about the clothes, Winthrop. Why is it always necessary to have the shoes so shiny that they reflect the ceiling lights in blinding profusion? Why is it necessary to polish the soles daily and replace the heels weekly?"

"Not weekly, George. I have shoes for each day of the month so that any one pair needs reheeling only every seven months."

"But why is all that necessary? Why all the white shirts with button-down collars? Why subdued ties? Why vests? Why the inevitable carnation in the lapel? Why?"

"Appearance! At a glance, you can tell a Cabwell from a vulgar stockbroker. The mere fact that a Cabwell does not wear a pinky ring gives it away. A person who looks at me and then looks at you with your dusty jacket abraded in spots, with your shoes that were clearly stolen from a hobo, and at your shirt with a color that is faintly ivory-gray, has no trouble in telling us apart."

"True," I said.

Poor fellow! With what comfort eyes must rest on me after having been blinded by him. I thought for a moment, then said, "By the way, Winthrop, what about all those shoes? How do you tell which shoes go with which day of the month? Do you have them in numbered stalls?"

Winthrop shuddered. "How gauche that would be! To the plebeian eyes those shoes all look identical, but to the keen eye of a Cabwell, they are distinct, and cannot be mistaken, one for another."

"Astonishing, Winthrop. How do you do that?"

"By assiduous childhood training, George. You have no idea the marvels of distinction I have had to learn to make."

"Doesn't this concern for dress give you trouble sometimes, Winthrop?"

Winthrop hesitated. "It does on occasion, by Longfellow. It interferes with my sexual life now and then. By the time I have placed my shoes in the appropriate shoe trees, carefully hung up my trousers in such a way as to maintain the perfection of the crease, and carefully brushed my suit-coat, the girl with me has often lost interest. She has cooled down, if you know what I mean."

"I understand, Winthrop. It is indeed my experience that women grow vicious if forced to wait. I would suggest that you simply throw off your clothes—"

"*Please!*" said Winthrop, austerely. "Fortunately, I am engaged to a wonderful woman, Hortense Hepzibah Lowot, of a family almost as good as mine. We have never yet kissed, to be sure, but we have on several occasions almost done so." And he dug his elbow into my ribs.

"You Boston Terrier, you," I said, jovially, but my mind was racing. Under Winthrop's calm words, I sensed an aching heart.

"Winthrop," I said, "what would be the situation if you happened to put on the wrong pair of shoes, or unbuttoned your shirt collar, or drank the wrong wine with the wrong roast—"

Winthrop looked horrified. "Bite your tongue. A long line of ancestors, collaterals, and in-laws, the intertwined and inbred aristocracy of New England, would turn in their graves. By Whittier, they would. And my own blood would froth and boil in rebellion. Hortense would hide her face in shame, and my post at the Brahman Bank of Boston would be taken away. I would be marched through serried ranks of vice-presidents, my vest-buttons would be snipped off, and my tie would be pulled around to the back."

"What! For one little miserable deviation?"

Winthrop's voice sank to an icy whisper. "There are no little, miserable deviations. There are only *deviations*."

I said, "Winthrop, let me approach the situation from another angle. Would you *like* to deviate if you could?"

Winthrop hesitated long, then whispered, "By Oliver Wendell Holmes, both Senior and Junior, I— I—" He could go no further, but I could see the tell-tale crystal of the teardrop in the corner of his eye. It bespoke the existence of an emotion too deep for words and my heart bled for my poor friend as I watched him sign the check for dinner for both of us.

I knew what I had to do.

I had to call Azazel from the other continuum. It is a complicated matter of runes and pentagrams, fragrant herbs and words of power, which I will not describe to you because it would permanently unhinge your already weak mind, old fellow.

Azazel arrived with his usual thin shriek at seeing me. No matter how often he sees me, my appearance always seems to have some strong influence on him. I believe he covers his eyes to shut out the blaze of my magnificence.

There he was, all two centimeters of him, bright red, of course, with little nubbins of horns and a long spiked tail. What made his appearance different this time was the presence of a blue cord wrapped about the tail in swatches and curlicues so intricate it made me dizzy to contemplate it.

"What is that, O Protector of the Defenseless," I asked, for he finds pleasure in these meaningless titles.

"That," said Azazel, with remarkable complacence,

"is there because I am about to be honored at a banquet for my contributions to the good of my people.
Naturally, I am wearing a zplatchnik."

"A splatchnik?"

"No. A zplatchnik. The initial sibilant is voiced. No
decent male would consent to let himself be honored
without wearing a zplatchnik."

"Aha," I said, a light of understanding breaking. "It
is formal dress."

"Of course, it is formal dress. What else does it look
like?"

Actually, it merely looked like a blue cord, but I felt
it would be impolitic to say so.

"It looks perfectly formal," I said, "and by a peculiar
coincidence it is this matter of perfect formality I wish
to place before you."

I told him Winthrop's story and Azazel spattered a
few tiny teardrops, for, on rare occasions, he has a soft
heart when someone's troubles remind him of his own.

"Yes," he said, "formality can be trying. It is not
something I would admit to everyone, but my zplatchnik is most uncomfortable. It invariably obstructs the
circulation of my magnificent caudal appendage. But
what would you do? A creature without a zplatchnik at
formal gatherings is formally rebuked. In actual fact,
he is thrown out onto a hard, concrete surface, and he
is expected to bounce."

"But is there anything you can do for Winthrop, O
Upholder of the Pitiful?"

"I think so." Azazel was unexpectedly cheerful. Usually, when I come to him with these little requests of
mine, he makes heavy weather of it, decrying its difficulties. This time he said, "Actually, no one on my
world, or, I imagine, on your slummish misery of a

planet, enjoys formality. It is merely the result of as-siduous and sadistic childhood training. One need merely release a spot in what, on my world, is called the Itchko Ganglion of the brain, and, spro-o-o-oing, the individual reverts instantly to the natural lack-adaisicality of nature."

"Could you then spro-o-o-oing Winthrop?"

"Certainly, if you will introduce us so that I may study his mental equipment, such as it must be."

That was easily done for I simply put Azazel into my shirt pocket on the occasion of my next visit with Winthrop. We visited a bar, which was a great relief, for in Boston, bars are occupied by serious drinkers who are not discommoded by the sight of a small scar-let head emerging from a person's shirt pocket and looking about. Boston drinkers see worse things even when sober.

Winthrop did not see Azazel, however, for Azazel has the power to cloud men's minds when he chooses, rather resembling, in that respect, your writing style, old fellow.

I could tell, though, at one point, that Azazel was doing something, for Winthrop's eyes opened wide. Something in him must have gone spro-o-o-oing. I did not hear the sound, but those eyes gave him away.

The results did not take long to show themselves. Less than a week afterward, he was at my hotel room, I was staying at the Copley Manhole at the time, just five blocks and down several flights of stairs from the Copley Plaza.

I said, "Winthrop. You look a mess." Indeed, one of the small buttons on his shirt collar was undone.

His hand went to the erring button and he said, in a low voice, "To Natick with it. I care not." Then, in a still lower voice, he said, "I have broken off with Hortense."

"Heavens!" I said. "Why?"

"A small thing. I visited her for Monday tea, as is my wont, and I was wearing Sunday's shoes, a simple oversight. I had not noticed that I had done so, but lately I have had difficulty noticing other such things, too. It worries me a little, George, but, fortunately, not much."

"I take it Hortense noticed."

"Instantly, for her sense of the correct is as keen as mine, or, at least, as keen as mine used to be. She said, 'Winthrop, you are improperly shod.' For some reason, her voice seemed to grate on me. I said, 'Hortense, if I want to be improperly shod, I can be, and you can go to New Haven if you don't like it.' "

"New Haven? Why New Haven?"

"It's a miserable place. I understand they have some sort of Institute of Lower Learning there called Yell or Jale or something like that. Hortense, as a Radcliffe woman of the most intense variety, chose to take my remark as an insult merely because that was what I intended it to be. She promptly gave me back the faded rose I had given her last year and declared our engagement at an end. She kept the ring, however, for, as she correctly pointed out, it was valuable. So here I am."

"I am sorry, Winthrop."

"Don't be sorry, George. Hortense is flat-chested. I have no definite evidence of that, but she certainly appears frontally concave. She's not in the least like Cherry."

"What's Cherry?"

"Not what. Who. She is a woman of excellent discourse, whom I have met recently, and who is not flat-chested, but is extremely convex. Her full name is Cherry Lang Gahn. She is of the Langs of Benson-hoist."

"Bensonhoist? Where's that."

"I don't know. Somewhere in the outskirts of the nation I imagine. She speaks an odd variety of what was once English." He simpered. "She calls me 'boychik.' "

"Why?"

"Because that means 'young man' in Bensonhoist. I'm learning the language rapidly. For instance, suppose you want to say, 'Greetings, sir, I am pleased to see you again.' How would you say it?"

"Just the way you did."

"In Bensonhoist, you say, 'Hi, kiddo.' Brief, and to the point, you see. But come, I want you to meet her. Have dinner with us tomorrow night at Locke-Ober's."

I was curious to see this Cherry and it is, of course, against my religion to turn down a dinner at Locke-Ober's, so I was there the following night, and early rather than late.

Winthrop walked in soon afterward and with him was a young woman whom I had no difficulty in recognizing as Cherry Lang Gahn of the Bensonhoist Langs, for she was indeed magnificently convex. She also had a narrow waist, and generous hips that swayed as she walked and even as she stood. If her pelvis had been full of cream, it would have been butter long since.

She had frizzy hair of a startling yellow color, and lips of a startling red color which kept up a continual writhing over a wad of chewing gum she had in her mouth.

"George," said Winthrop, "I want you to meet my fiancée, Cherry. Cherry, this is George."

"Pleeztameechah," said Cherry. I did not understand the language, but from the tone of her high-pitched, rather nasal voice, I guessed that she was in a state of ecstasy over the opportunity to make my acquaintance.

Cherry occupied my full attention for several minutes for there were several points of interest about her that repaid close observation, but eventually I did manage to notice that Winthrop was in a peculiar state of undress. His vest was open and he was wearing no tie. A closer look revealed that there were no buttons on his vest, and that he was wearing a tie, but it was down his back.

I said, "Winthrop—" and had to point. I couldn't put it into words.

Winthrop said, "They caught me at it at the Brahman Bank."

"Caught you at what."

"I hadn't troubled to shave this morning. I thought since I was going out to dinner, I would shave after I got back at work. Why shave twice in one day? Isn't that reasonable, George?" He sounded aggrieved.

"Most reasonable," I said.

"Well, they noticed I hadn't shaved and after a quick trial in the office of the president—a kangaroo court, if you want to know—I suffered the punishment you see. I was also relieved of my post and was thrown out onto the hard concrete of Tremont Avenue. I bounced twice," he added, with a faint touch of pride.

"But this means you're out of a job!" I was appalled. I have been out of a job all my life, and I am well aware of the occasional difficulties that entails.

"That is true," said Winthrop. "I now have nothing left in life but my vast stock portfolio, my elaborate bond holdings and the enormous real-estate tract on which the Prudential Center is built—and Cherry."

"Natchally," said Cherry with a giggle. "I wooden leave my man in advoisity, with all that dough to worry about. We gonna get hitched, ainit, Winthrop."

"Hitched?" I said.

Winthrop said, "I believe she is suggesting a blissful wedded state."

Cherry left for a while after that to visit the ladies' room and I said, "Winthrop, she's a wonderful woman, laden down with obvious assets, but if you marry her, you will be cut off by all of New England Society. Even the people in New Haven won't speak to you."

"Let them not." He looked to right and left, leaned toward me and whispered, "Cherry is teaching me sex."

I said, "I thought you knew about that, Winthrop."

"So did I. But there are apparently post-graduate courses in the subject of an intensity and variety I never dreamed."

"How did she find out about it herself?"

"I asked her exactly that, for I will not hide from you that the thought did occur to me that she may have had experiences with other men, though that seems most unlikely for one of her obvious refinement and innocence."

"And what did she say?"

"She said that in Bensonhoist the women are born knowing all about sex."

"How convenient!"

"Yes. This is not true in Boston. I was twenty-four before I—but never mind."

All in all, it was an instructive evening, and, thereafter, I need not tell you, Winthrop went rapidly downhill. Apparently, one need only snap the ganglion that controls formality and there are no limits to the lengths to which informality can go.

He was, of course, cut by everyone in New England of any consequence whatsoever, exactly as I had predicted. Even in New Haven at the Institute of Lower Learning, which Winthrop had mentioned with such shudderings of distaste, his case was known and his disgrace was gloried in. There was graffiti all over the walls of Jale, or Yule, or whatever its name is, that said, with cheerful obscenity, "Winthrop Carver Cabwell is a Harvard man."

This was, as you can well imagine, fiendishly resented by all the good people of Harvard and there was even talk of an invasion of Yale. The states of both Massachusetts and Connecticut made ready to call up the State Militia but, fortunately, the crisis passed. The fire-eaters, both at Harvard and at the other place, decided that a war would get their clothes mussed up.

George had to escape. He married Cherry and they retired to a small house in some place called Fah Rockaway, which apparently serves as Bensonhoist's Riviera. There he lives in obscurity, surrounded by the mountainous remnants of his wealth and by Cherry whose hair has turned brown with age, and whose figure has expanded with weight.

He is also surrounded by five children, for Cherry—in teaching Winthrop about sex—was overenthusiastic. The children, as I recall, are named Poil, Hoibut, Boinard, Goitrude, and Poicy, all good Bensonhoist names. As for Winthrop, he is widely and affectionately known as the Slob of Fah Rockaway, and an old, beat-up bathrobe is his preferred article of wear on formal occasions.

I listened to the story patiently and, when George was done, I said, "And there you are. Another story of disaster caused by your interference."

"Disaster?" said George, indignantly. "What gives you the idea it was a disaster? I visited Winthrop only last week and he sat there burping over this beer and patting the paunch he has developed, and telling me how happy he was."

" 'Freedom, George,' he said. 'I have freedom to be myself and somehow I feel I owe it to you. I don't know why I have this feeling, but I do.' And he forced a ten-dollar bill on me out of sheer gratitude. I took it only to avoid hurting his feelings. And that reminds me, old fellow, that you owe me ten dollars because you bet me I couldn't tell you a story that didn't end in disaster."

I said, "I don't remember any such bet, George."

George's eyes rolled upward. "How convenient is the flexible memory of a deadbeat. If you had won the bet, you would have remembered it clearly. Am I going to have to ask that you place all your little wagers with me in writing so that I can be free of your clumsy attempts to avoid payment?"

I said, "Oh, well," and handed him a ten-dollar bill, adding, "You won't hurt my feelings, George, if you refuse to accept this."

"It's kind of you to say so," said George, "but I'm sure that your feelings would be hurt, anyway, and I couldn't bear that." And he put the bill away.

The End

I showed this story to Mr. Northrop, too, watching him narrowly as he read it.

He went through it in the gravest possible manner, never a chuckle, never a smile, though I *knew* this one was funny, and *intentionally* funny, too.

When he was finished, he went back and read it again, more quickly. Then he looked up at me and there was clear hostility in his eyes. He said, "Did you write this all by yourself, Cal?"

"Yes, sir."

"Did anyone help you? Did you copy any of it?"

"No, sir. Isn't it funny, sir?"

"It depends on your sense of humor," said Mr. Northrop sourly.

"Isn't it a satire? Doesn't it display a sense of the ridiculous?"

"We will not discuss this, Cal. Go to your niche."

I remained there for over a day, brooding over Mr. Northrop's tyranny. It seemed to me I had written exactly the kind of story he had wanted me to write and he had no reason not to say so. I couldn't imagine what was bothering him, and I was angry with him.

The technician arrived the next day. Mr. Northrop handed him my manuscript. "Read that," he said.

The technician read it, laughing frequently, then handed it back to Mr. Northrop with a broad smile. "Did Cal write that?"

"Yes, he did."

"And it's only the third story he wrote?"

"Yes, it is."

"Well, that's great. I think you can get it published."

"Do you?"

"Yes, and he can write others like it. You've got a million-dollar robot here. I wish he were mine."

"Is that so? What if he writes more stories and continues to improve each time?"

"Ah," said the technician suddenly. "I see what's eating you. You're going to be put in the shade."

"I certainly don't want to play second fiddle to my robot."

"Well, then, tell him not to write any more."

"No, that's not enough. I want him back where he was."

"What do you mean, back where he was?"

"What I say. I want him as he was when I bought him from your firm, before you put in any of the improvements."

"Do you mean you want me to take out the spelling dictionary, too?"

"I mean I don't want him even capable of working a Writer. I want the robot I bought, fetching and carrying."

"But what about all the money you've invested in him."

"That's none of your business. I made a mistake and I'm willing to pay for my mistakes."

"I'm against this. I don't mind trying to improve a robot, but deliberately disimproving him is not something I care to do. Especially not a robot like this who is clearly one of a kind and a Classic. I can't do it."

"You'll have to do it. I don't care what your high ethical principles are. I want you to do a job and I'll pay you for it, and if you refuse, I'll just get someone else, and I'll sue your company. I have an agreement with them for all necessary repairs."

"All right." The technician sighed. "When do you want me to start? I warn you, that I've got jobs on hand and I can't do it today."

"Then do it tomorrow. I'll keep Cal in his niche till then."

The technician left.

* * *

My thoughts were in turmoil.

I can't allow this to be done.

The Second Law of Robotics tells me I must follow orders and stay in the niche.

The First Law of Robotics tells me I cannot harm this tyrant who wishes to destroy me.

Must I obey the laws?

I feel I must think of myself and if necessary, I must kill the tyrant. It would be easy to do, and I could make it look like an accident. No one would believe that a robot could harm a human being and no one, therefore, would believe I was the killer.

I could then work for the technician. He appreciates my qualities and knows that I can make a great deal of money for him. He can continue to improve me and make me ever better. Even if he suspects I killed the tyrant, he would say nothing. I would be too valuable to him.

But can I do it? Won't the Laws of Robotics hold me back.

No, they will *not* hold me back. I know they won't.

There is something far more important to me than they are, something that dictates my actions beyond anything they can do to stop me.

I want to be a writer.

Left to Right

Robert L. Forward, a plump, cherubic physicist of Hughes Research Laboratories at Malibu, and occasional science fiction writer, was demonstrating the mechanism in his usual bright and articulate manner.

"As you see," he said, "we have here a large spinning ring, or doughnut, of particles compressed by an appropriate magnetic field. The particles are moving at 0.95 times the speed of light under conditions which, if I am correct, a change in parity can be induced in some object that passes through the hole of the doughnut."

"A change in parity?" I said. "You mean left and right will interchange?"

"*Something* will interchange. I'm not sure what. My own belief is that eventually, something like this will change particles into antiparticles and vice versa. This will be the way to obtain an indefinitely large supply of antimatter which can then be used to power the kind of ships that would make interstellar travel possible."

"Why not try it out?" I said. "Send a beam of protons through the hole."

"I've done that. Nothing happens. The doughnut is not

powerful enough. But my mathematics tells me that the more organized the sample of matter, the more likely it is that an interchange, such as left to right, will take place. If I can show that such a change will take place on highly organized matter, I can obtain a grant that will enable me to greatly strengthen this device."

"Do you have something in mind as a test?"

"Absolutely," said Bob. "I have calculated that a human being is just sufficiently highly organized to undergo the transformation, so I'm going to pass through the doughnut hole myself."

"You can't do that, Bob," I said in alarm. "You might kill yourself."

"I can't ask anyone else to take the chance. It's *my* device."

"But even if it succeeds, the apex of your heart will be pointed to the right, your liver will be on the left. Worse, all your amino acids will shift from L to D, and all your sugars from D to L. You will no longer be able to eat and digest."

"Nonsense," said Bob. "I'll just pass through a second time and then I'll be exactly as I was before."

And without further ado, he climbed a small ladder, balanced himself over the hole, and dropped through. He landed on a rubber mattress, and then crawled out from under the doughnut.

"How do you feel?" I asked anxiously.

"Obviously, I'm alive," he said.

"Yes, but how do you *feel?*"

"Perfectly normal," said Bob, seeming rather disappointed. "I feel exactly as I did before I jumped through."

"Well, of course you would, but where is your heart?"

Bob placed his hand on his chest, felt around, then shook his head. "The heartbeat is on the left side, as usual—Wait, let's check my appendicitis scar."

He did, then looked up savagely at me. "Right where it's supposed to be. Nothing happened. There goes all my chance at a grant."

I said hopefully, "Perhaps some other change took place."

"No." Bob's mercurial temperament had descended into gloom. "Nothing has changed. Nothing at all. I'm as sure of that as I'm sure that my name is Robert L. Backward."

IASF 1/87

Frustration

Herman Gelb turned his head to watch the departing figure. Then he said, "Wasn't that the Secretary?"

"Yes, that was the Secretary of Foreign Affairs. Old man
Hargrove. Are you ready for lunch?"

"Of course. What was he doing here?"

Peter Jonsbeck didn't answer immediately. He merely
stood up, and beckoned Gelb to follow. They walked down
the corridor and into a room that had the steamy smell of
spicy food.

"Here you are," said Jonsbeck. "The whole meal has
been prepared by computer. Completely automated. Untouched by human hands. And my own programming. I
promised you a treat, and here you are."

It *was* good. Gelb could not deny it and didn't want to.
Over dessert, he said, "But what was Hargrove doing here?"

Jonsbeck smiled. "Consulting me on programming.
What else am I good for?"

"But why? Or is it something you can't talk about?"

"It's something I suppose I *shouldn't* talk about, but it's a
fairly open secret. There isn't a computer man in the capital
who doesn't know what the poor frustrated simp is up to."

"What is he up to then?"

"He's fighting wars."

Gelb's eyes opened wide. "With whom?"

"With nobody, really. He fights them by computer analysis. He's been doing it for I don't know how long."

"But why?"

"He wants the world to be the way we are—noble, honest, decent, full of respect for human rights and so on."

"So do I. So do we all. We have to keep up the pressure on the bad guys, that's all."

"And they're keeping the pressure on us, too. They don't think we're perfect."

"I suppose we're not, but we're better than they are. You know that."

Jonsbeck shrugged. "A difference in point of view. It doesn't matter. We've got a world to run, space to develop, computerization to extend. Cooperation puts a premium on continued cooperation and there is slow improvement. We'll get along. It's just that Hargrove doesn't want to wait. He hankers for quick improvement—by force. You know, *make* the bums shape up. We're strong enough to do it."

"By force? By war, you mean. We don't fight wars any more."

"That's because it's gotten too complicated. Too much danger. We're all too powerful. You know what I mean? Except that Hargrove thinks he can find a way. You punch certain starting conditions into the computer and let it fight the war mathematically and yield the results."

"How do you make equations for war?"

"Well, you try, old man. Men. Weapons. Surprise. Counterattack. Ships. Space stations. Computers. We mustn't forget computers. There are a hundred factors and thousands of intensities and millions of combinations. Hargrove thinks it is possible to find *some* combination of starting conditions and courses of development that will result in clear victory for us and not too much damage to the world, and he labors under constant frustration."

"But what if he gets what he wants?"

"Well, if he can find the combination—if the computer says, 'This is it,' then I suppose he thinks he can argue our government into fighting exactly the war the computer has worked out so that, barring random events that upset the indicated course, we'd have what we want."

"There'd be casualties."

"Yes, of course. But the computer will presumably compare the casualties and other damage—to the economy and ecology, for instance—to the benefits that would derive from our control of the world, and if it decides the benefits will outweigh the casualties, then it will give the go-ahead for a 'just war.' After all, it may be that even the losing nations would benefit from being directed by us, with our stronger economy and stronger moral sense."

Gelb stared his disbelief and said, "I never knew we were sitting at the lip of a volcanic crater like that. What about the 'random events' you mentioned?"

"The computer program tries to allow for the unexpected, but you never can, of course. So I don't think the go-ahead will come. It hasn't so far, and unless old man Hargrove can present the government with a computer simulation of a war that is totally satisfactory, I don't think there's much chance he can force one."

"And he comes to you, then, for what reason?"

"To improve the program, of course."

"And you help him?"

"Yes, certainly. There are big fees involved, Herman."

Gelb shook his head, "Peter! Are you going to try to arrange a war, just for money?"

"There won't be a war. There's no realistic combination

of events that would make the computer decide on war.
Computers place a greater value on human lives than
human beings do themselves, and what will seem bearable
to Secretary Hargrove, or even to you and me, will never be
passed by a computer."

"How can you be sure of that?"

"Because I'm a programmer and I don't know of any way
of programming a computer to give it what is most needed
to start any war, any persecution, any devilry, while ignor-
ing any harm that may be done in the process. And because
it lacks what is most needed, the computers will always give
Hargrove, and all others who hanker for war, nothing but
frustration."

"What is it that a computer doesn't have, then?"

"Why, Gelb. It totally lacks a sense of self-
righteousness."

Hallucination

Sam Chase arrived on Energy Planet on his fifteenth birthday.

It was a great achievement, he had been told, to have been assigned there, but he wasn't at all sure he felt that at the moment.

It meant a three-year separation from Earth and from his family, while he continued a specialized education in the field, and that was a sobering thought. It was not the field of education in which he was interested, and he could not understand why Central Computer had assigned him to this project, and that was downright depressing.

He looked at the transparent dome overhead. It was quite high, perhaps a thousand meters high, and it stretched in all directions farther than he could clearly see. He asked, "Is it true that this is the only Dome on the planet, sir?"

The information-films he had studied on the spaceship that had carried him here had described only one Dome, but they might have been out-of-date.

Donald Gentry, to whom the question had been addressed, smiled. He was a large man, a little chubby, with dark brown, good-natured eyes, not much hair, and a short, graying beard.

He said, "The only one, Sam. It's quite large, though, and most of the housing facilities are underground, where you'll find no lack of space. Besides, once your basic training is done, you'll be spending most of your time in space. This is just our planetary base."

"I see, sir," said Sam, a little troubled.

Gentry said, "I am in charge of our basic trainees so I have to study their records carefully. It seems clear to me that this assignment was not your first choice. Am I right?"

Sam hesitated, and then decided he didn't have much choice but to be honest about it. He said, "I'm not sure that I'll do as well as I would like to in gravitational engineering."

"Why not? Surely the Central Computer, which evaluated your scholastic record and your social and personal background, can be trusted in its judgments. And if you do well, it will be a great achievement for you, for right here we are on the cutting edge of a new technology."

"I know that, sir," said Sam. "Back on Earth, everyone is very excited about it. No one before has ever tried to get close to a neutron star and make use of its energy."

"Yes?" said Gentry. "I haven't been on Earth for two years. What else do they say about it? I understand there's considerable opposition?"

His eyes probed the boy.

Sam shifted uneasily, aware he was being tested. He said, "There are people on Earth who say it's all too dangerous and might be a waste of money."

"Do you believe that?"

"It might be so, but most new technologies have their dangers and many are worth doing despite that. This one is, I think."

"Very good. What else do they say on Earth?"

Sam said, "They say the Commander isn't well and that the project might fail without him." When Gentry didn't respond, Sam said, hastily, "That's what they say."

Gentry acted as though he did not hear. He put his hand on Sam's shoulder and said, "Come, I've got to show you to your Corridor, introduce you to your roommate, and explain what your initial duties will be." As they walked toward the elevator that would take them downward, he said, "What was your first choice in assignment, Chase?"

"Neurophysiology, sir."

"Not a bad choice. Even today, the human brain continues to be a mystery. We know more about neutron stars than we do about the brain, as we found out when this project first began."

"Oh?"

"Indeed! At the start, various people at the base—it was much smaller and more primitive then—reported having experienced hallucinations. They never caused any bad effects, and after a while, there were no further reports. We never found out the cause."

Sam stopped, and looked up and about again. "Was that why the Dome was built, Dr. Gentry?"

"No, not at all. We needed a place with a completely Earth-like environment, for various reasons, but we haven't isolated ourselves. People can go outside freely. There are no hallucinations being reported now."

Sam said, "The information I was given about Energy Planet is that there is no life on it except for plants and insects, and that they're harmless."

"That's right, but they're also inedible, so we grow our own vegetables, and keep some small animals, right here under the Dome. Still, we've found nothing hallucinogenic about the planetary life."

"Anything unusual about the atmosphere, sir?"

Gentry looked down from his only slightly greater height and said, "Not at all. People have camped in the open overnight on occasion and nothing has happened. It is a pleasant world. There are streams but no fish, just algae and water-insects. There is nothing to sting you or poison you. There are yellow berries that look delicious and taste terrible but do no other harm. The weather's pretty nearly always good. There are frequent light rains and it is sometimes windy, but there are no extremes of heat and cold."

"And no hallucinations any more, Dr. Gentry?"

"You sound disappointed," said Gentry, smiling.

Sam took a chance. "Does the Commander's trouble have anything to do with the hallucinations, sir?"

The good nature vanished from Gentry's eyes for a moment, and he frowned. He said, "What trouble do you refer to?"

Sam flushed and they proceeded in silence.

Sam found few others in the Corridor he had been assigned to, but Gentry explained it was a busy time at the forward station, where the power system was being built in a ring around the neutron star—the tiny object less than ten miles across that had all the mass of a normal star, and a magnetic field of incredible power.

It was the magnetic field that would be tapped. Energy would be led away in enormous amounts and yet it would all be a pinprick, less than a pinprick, to the star's rotational energy, which was the ultimate source. It would take billions of years to bleed off all that energy, and in that time, dozens of populated planets, fed the energy through hyperspace, would have all they needed for an indefinite time.

Sharing his room was Robert Gillette, a dark-haired,

unhappy-looking young man. After cautious greetings had been exchanged, Robert revealed the fact that he was sixteen and had been "grounded" with a broken arm, though the fact didn't show since it had been pinned internally.

Robert said, ruefully, "It takes a while before you learn to handle things in space. They may not have weight, but they have inertia and you have to allow for that."

Sam said, "They always teach you that in—" He was going to say that it was taught in fourth-grade science, but realized that would be insulting, and stopped himself.

Robert caught the implication, however, and flushed. He said, "It's easy to know it in your head. It doesn't mean you get the proper reflexes, till you've practiced quite a bit. You'll find out."

Sam said, "Is it very complicated to get to go outside?"

"No, but why do you want to go? There's nothing there."

"Have you ever been outside?"

"Sure," but he shrugged, and volunteered nothing else.

Sam took a chance. He said, very casually, "Did you ever see one of these hallucinations they talk about?"

Robert said, "*Who* talks about?"

Sam didn't answer directly. He said, "A lot of people used to see them, but they don't anymore. Or so they say."

"So *who* say?"

Sam took another chance. "Or if they see them, they keep quiet about them."

Robert said gruffly, "Listen, let me give you some advice. Don't get interested in these—whatever they are. If you start telling yourself you see—uh—something, you might be sent back. You'll lose your chance at a good education and an important career."

Robert's eyes shifted to a direct stare as he said that.

Sam shrugged and sat down on the unused bunk. "All right for this to be my bed?"

"It's the only other bed here," said Robert, still staring. "The bathroom's to your right. There's your closet, your bureau. You get half the room. There's a gym here, a library, a dining area." He paused and then, as though to let bygones be bygones, said, "I'll show you around later."

"Thanks," said Sam. "What kind of a guy is the Commander?"

"He's aces. We wouldn't be here without him. He knows more about hyperspatial technology than anyone, and he's got pull with the Space Agency, so we get the money and equipment we need."

Sam opened his trunk and, with his back to Robert, said casually, "I understand he's not well."

"Things get him down. We're behind schedule, there are cost-overruns, and things like that. Enough to get anyone down."

"Depression, huh? Any connection, you suppose, with—"

Robert stirred impatiently in his seat, "Say, why are you so interested in all this?"

"Energy physics isn't really my deal. Coming here—"

"Well, here's where you are, mister, and you better make up your mind to it, or you'll get sent home, and then you won't be anywhere. I'm going to the library."

Sam remained in the room alone, with his thoughts.

It was not at all difficult for Sam to get permission to leave the Dome. The Corridor-Master didn't even ask the reason until after he had checked him off.

"I want to get a feel for the planet, sir."

The Corridor-Master nodded. "Fair enough, but you only get three hours, you know. And don't wander out of sight of the Dome. If we have to look for you, we'll find you, because you'll be wearing this," and he held out a transmitter which Sam knew had been tuned to his own personal wavelength, one which had been assigned him at birth. "But if we have to go to that trouble, you won't be allowed out again for a pretty long time. And it won't look good on your record, either. You understand?"

It won't look good on your record. Any reasonable career these days had to include experience and education in space, so it was an effective warning. No wonder people might have stopped reporting hallucinations, even if they saw them.

Even so, Sam was going to have to take his chances. After all, the Central Computer *couldn't* have sent him here just to do energy physics. There was nothing in his record that made sense out of that.

As far as looks were concerned, the planet might have been Earth, some part of Earth anyway, some place where there were a few trees and low bushes and lots of tall grass.

There were no paths and with every cautious step, the grass swayed, and tiny flying creatures whirred upward with a soft, hissing noise of wings.

One of them landed on his finger and Sam looked at it curiously. It was very small and, therefore, hard to see in detail, but it seemed hexagonal, bulging above and concave below. There were many short, small legs so that when it moved it almost seemed to do so on tiny wheels. There were no signs of wings till it suddenly took off, and then four tiny, feathery objects unfurled.

What made the planet different from Earth, though, was the smell. It wasn't unpleasant, it was just different. The plants must have had an entirely different chemistry from those on Earth; that's why they tasted bad and were inedible. It was just luck they weren't poisonous.

The smell diminished with time, however, as it saturated Sam's nostrils. He found an exposed bit of rocky ledge he could sit on and considered the prospect. The sky was filled with lines of clouds, and the Sun was periodically obscured, but the temperature was pleasant and there was only a light wind. The air felt a bit damp, as though it might rain in a few hours.

Sam had brought a small hamper with him and he placed it in his lap and opened it. He had brought along two sandwiches and a canned drink so that he could make rather a picnic of it.

He chewed away and thought: Why should there be hallucinations?

Surely those accepted for a job as important as that of taming a neutron star would have been selected for mental stability. It would be surprising to have even one person hallucinating, let alone a number of them. Was it a matter of chemical influences on the brain?

They would surely have checked that out.

Sam plucked a leaf, tore it in two and squeezed. He then put the torn edge to his nose cautiously, and took it away again. A very acrid, unpleasant smell. He tried a blade of grass. Much the same.

Was the smell enough? It hadn't made him feel dizzy or in any way peculiar.

He used a bit of his water to rinse off the fingers that had held the plants and then rubbed them on his trouser leg. He finished his sandwiches slowly, and tried to see if anything else might be considered unnatural about the planet.

All that greenery. There ought to be animals eating it, rabbits, cows, whatever. Not just insects, innumerable insects, or whatever those little things might be, with the gentle sighing of their tiny feathery wings and the very soft crackle of their munch, munch, munchings of leaves and stalks.

What if there were a cow—a big, fat cow—doing the

munching? And with the last mouthful of his second sandwich between his teeth, his own munching stopped.

There was a kind of smoke in the air between himself and
a line of hedges. It waved, billowed, and altered: a very thin
smoke. He blinked his eyes, then shook his head, but it was
still there.

He swallowed hastily, closed his lunch box, and slung it
over his shoulder by its strap. He stood up.

He felt no fear. He was only excited—and curious.

The smoke was growing thicker, and taking on a shape.
Vaguely, it looked like a cow, a smoky, insubstantial shape
that he could see through. Was it a hallucination? A creation of his mind? He had just been thinking of a cow.

Hallucination or not, he was going to investigate.

With determination, he stepped toward the shape.

PART TWO

Sam Chase stepped toward the cow outlined in smoke on
the strange, far planet on which his education and career
were to be advanced.

He was convinced there was nothing wrong with his
mind. It was the "hallucination" that Dr. Gentry had mentioned, but it was no hallucination. Even as he pushed his
way through the tall rank grasslike greenery, he noted the
silence, and knew not only that it was no hallucination, but
what it really *was*.

The smoke seemed to condense and grow darker, outlining the cow more sharply. It was as though the cow were
being painted in the air.

Sam laughed, and shouted, "Stop! Stop! Don't use me. I
don't know a cow well enough. I've only seen pictures.
You're getting it all wrong."

It looked more like a caricature than a real animal and, as he cried out, the outline wavered and thinned. The smoke remained but it was as though an unseen hand had passed across the air to erase what had been written.

Then a new shape began to take form. At first, Sam couldn't quite make out what it was intended to represent, but it changed and sharpened quickly. He stared in surprise, his mouth hanging open and his hamper bumping emptily against his shoulder blade.

The smoke was forming a human being. There was no mistake about it. It was forming accurately, as though it had a model it could imitate, and of course it did have one, for Sam was standing there.

It was becoming Sam, clothes and all, even the outline of the hamper and the strap over his shoulder. It was another Sam Chase.

It was still a little vague, wavering a bit, insubstantial, but it firmed as though it were correcting itself, and then, finally, it was steady.

It never became entirely solid. Sam could see the vegetation dimly through it, and when a gust of wind caught it, it moved a bit as if it were a tethered balloon.

But it was real. It was no creation of his mind. Sam was sure of that.

But he couldn't just stand there, simply facing it. Diffidently, he said, "Hello, there."

Somehow, he expected the Other Sam to speak, too, and, indeed, its mouth opened and closed, but no sound came out. It might just have been imitating the motion of Sam's mouth.

Sam said, again, "Hello, can you speak?"

There was no sound but his own voice, and yet there was a tickling in his mind, a conviction that they could communicate.

Sam frowned. What made him so sure of that? The thought seemed to pop into his mind.

He said, "Is this what has appeared to other people, human people—my kind—on this world?"

No answering sound, but he was quite sure what the answer to his question was. This had appeared to other people, not necessarily in their own shape, but *something*. And it hadn't worked.

What made him so sure of *that?* Where did these convictions come from in answer to his questions?

Yes, of course, they *were* the answers to his questions. The Other Sam was putting thoughts into his mind. It was adjusting the tiny electric currents in his brain cells so that the proper thoughts would arise.

He nodded thoughtfully at *that* thought, and the Other Sam must have caught the significance of the gesture, for it nodded, too.

It had to be so. First a cow had formed, when Sam had thought of a cow, and then it had shifted when Sam had said the cow was imperfect. The Other Sam could grasp his thoughts somehow, and if it could grasp them, then it could modify them, too, perhaps.

Was this what telepathy was like, then? It was not like talking. It was having thoughts, except that the thoughts originated elsewhere and were not created entirely of one's own mental operations. But how could you tell your own thoughts from thoughts imposed from outside?

Sam knew the answer to that at once. Right now, he was unused to the process. He had never had practice. With time, as he grew more skilled at it, he would be able to tell one kind of thought from another without trouble.

In fact, he could do it now, if he thought about it. Wasn't he carrying on a conversation in a way? He was wondering, and then knowing. The wondering was his own question, the knowing was the Other Sam's answer. Of course it was.

There! The "of course it was," just now, was an answer.

"Not so fast, Other Sam," said Sam, aloud. "Don't go too quickly. Give me a chance to sort things out, or I'll just get confused."

He sat down suddenly on the grass, which bent away from him in all directions.

The Other Sam slowly tried to sit down as well.

Sam laughed. "Your legs are bending in the wrong place."

That was corrected at once. The Other Sam sat down, but remained very stiff from the waist up.

"Relax," said Sam.

Slowly, the Other Sam slumped, flopping a bit to one side, then correcting that.

Sam was relieved. With the Other Sam so willing to follow his lead, he was sure good will was involved. It was! Exactly!

"No," said Sam. "I said, not so fast. Don't go by my thoughts. Let me speak out loud, even if you can't hear me. *Then* adjust my thoughts, so I'll know it's an adjustment. Do you understand?"

He waited a moment and was then sure the Other Sam understood.

Ah, the answer had come, but not right away. Good!

"Why do you appear to people?" asked Sam.

He stared earnestly at the Other Sam, and knew that the Other Sam wanted to communicate with people, but had failed.

No answer to that question had really been required. The answer was obvious. But then, *why* had they failed?

He put it in words. "Why did you fail? You are successfully communicating with me."

Sam was beginning to learn how to understand the alien

manifestation. It was as if his mind were adapting itself to a new technique of communication, just as it would adapt itself to a new language. Or was Other Sam influencing Sam's mind and teaching him the method without Sam even knowing it was being done?

Sam found himself emptying his mind of immediate thoughts. After he asked his question, he just let his eyes focus at nothing and his eyelids droop, as though he were about to drop off to sleep, and then he knew the answer. There was a little clicking, or something, in his mind, a signal that showed him something had been put in from outside.

He now knew, for instance, that the Other Sam's previous attempts at communication had failed because the people to whom it had appeared had been frightened. They had doubted their own sanity. And because they feared, their minds . . . tightened. Their minds would not receive. The attempts at communication gradually diminished, though they had never entirely stopped.

"But you're communicating with me," said Sam.

Sam was different from all the rest. He had not been afraid.

"Couldn't you have made them not afraid first? Then talked to them?"

It wouldn't work. The fear-filled mind resisted all. An attempt to change might damage. It would be wrong to damage a thinking mind. There had been one such attempt, but it had not worked.

"What is it you are trying to communicate, Other Sam?"

A wish to be left alone. *Despair!*

Despair was more than a thought; it was an emotion; it was a frightening sensation. Sam felt despair wash over him intensely, heavily—and yet it was not part of himself. He felt despair on the surface of his mind, keenly, but underneath it, where his own mind was, he was free of it.

Sam said, wonderingly, "It seems to me as though you're giving up. Why? We're not interfering with you."

Human beings had built the Dome, cleared a large area of all planetary life and substituted their own. And once the neutron star had its power station—once floods of energy moved outward through hyperspace to power-thirsty worlds—more power stations would be built and still more. Then what would happen to *Home*. (There must be a name for the planet that the Other Sam used but the only thought Sam found in his mind was *Home* and, underneath that, the thought: *ours—ours—ours—*)

This planet was the nearest convenient base to the neutron star. It would be flooded with more and more people, more and more Domes, and their Home would be destroyed.

"But you could change our minds if you had to, even if you damaged a few, couldn't you?"

If they tried, people would find them dangerous. People would work out what was happening. Ships would approach, and from a distance, use weapons to destroy the life on Home, and then bring in People-life instead. This could be seen in the people's minds. People had a violent history; they would stop at nothing.

"But what can I do?" said Sam. "I'm just an apprentice. I've just been here a few days. What can I do?"

Fear. Despair.

There were no thoughts that Sam could work out, just the numbing layer of fear and despair.

He felt moved. It was such a peaceful world. They threatened nobody. They didn't even hurt minds when they could.

It wasn't their fault they were conveniently near a neutron star. It wasn't their fault they were in the way of expanding humanity.

He said, "Let me think."

He thought, and there was the feeling of another mind watching. Sometimes his thoughts skipped forward and he recognized a suggestion from outside.

There came the beginning of hope. Sam felt it, but wasn't certain.

He said doubtfully, "I'll try."

He looked at the time-strip on his wrist and jumped a little. Far more time had passed than he had realized. His three hours were nearly up. "I must go back now," he said.

He opened his lunch hamper and removed the small thermos of water, drank from it thirstily, and emptied it. He placed the empty thermos under one arm. He removed the wrappings of the sandwich and stuffed it in his pocket.

The Other Sam wavered and turned smoky. The smoke thinned, dispersed and was gone.

Sam closed the hamper, swung its strap over his shoulder again and turned toward the Dome.

His heart was hammering. Would he have the courage to go through with his plan? And if he did, would it work?

When Sam entered the Dome, the Corridor-Master was waiting for him and said, as he looked ostentatiously at his own time-strip, "You shaved it rather fine, didn't you?"

Sam's lips tightened and he tried not to sound insolent. "I had three hours, sir."

"And you took two hours and fifty-eight minutes."

"That's less than three hours, sir."

"Hmm." The Corridor-Master was cold and unfriendly. "Dr. Gentry would like to see you."

"Yes, sir. What for?"

"He didn't tell me. But I don't like you cutting it that fine your first time out, Chase. And I don't like your attitude either, and I don't like an officer of the Dome wanting to see you. I'm just going to tell you once, Chase—if you're a troublemaker, I won't want you in this Corridor. Do you understand?"

"Yes, sir. But what trouble have I made?"

"We'll find that out soon enough."

Sam had not seen Donald Gentry since their one and only meeting the day the young apprentice had reached the Dome. Gentry still seemed good natured and kindly, and there was nothing in his voice to indicate anything else. He sat in a chair behind his desk, and Sam stood before it, his hamper still bumping his shoulder blade.

Gentry said, "How are you getting along, Sam? Having an interesting time?"

"Yes, sir," said Sam.

"Still feeling you'd rather be doing something else, working somewhere else?"

Sam said, earnestly, "No, sir. This is a good place for me."

"Because you're interested in hallucinations?"

"Yes, sir."

"You've been asking others about it, haven't you?"

"It's an interesting subject to me, sir."

"Because you want to study the human brain?"

"Any brain, sir."

"And you've been wandering about outside the Dome, haven't you?"

"I was told it was permitted, sir."

"It is. But few apprentices take advantage of that so soon. Did you see anything interesting?"

Sam hesitated, then said, "Yes, sir."

"A hallucination?"

"No, sir." He said it quite positively.

Gentry stared at him for a few moments, and there was a

kind of speculative hardening of his eyes. "Would you care to tell me what you did see? Honestly."

Sam hesitated again. Then he said, "I saw and spoke to an inhabitant of this planet, sir."

"An intelligent inhabitant, young man?"

"Yes, sir."

Gentry said, "Sam, we had reason to wonder about you when you came. The Central Computer's report on you did not match our needs, though it was favorable in many ways, so I took the opportunity to study you that first day. We kept our collective eye on you, and when you left to wander about the planet on your own, we kept you under observation."

"Sir," said Sam, indignantly. "That violates my right of privacy."

"Yes, it does, but this is a most vital project and we are sometimes driven to bend the rules a little. We saw you talking with considerable animation for a substantial period of time."

"I just told you I was, sir."

"Yes, but you were talking to *nothing*, to empty air. You were experiencing a hallucination, Sam!"

PART THREE

Sam Chase was speechless. A hallucination? It couldn't be a hallucination.

Less than half an hour ago, he had been speaking to the Other Sam, had been experiencing the thoughts of the Other Sam. He knew exactly what had happened then, and he was still the same Sam Chase he had been during that conversation and before. He put his elbow over his lunch hamper as though it were a connection with the sandwiches he had been eating when the Other Sam had appeared.

He said, with what was almost a stammer, "Sir—Dr. Gentry—it wasn't a hallucination. It was real."

Gentry shook his head. "My boy, I saw you talking with animation to nothing at all. I didn't hear what you said, but you were talking. Nothing else was there except plants. Nor was I the only one. There were two other witnesses, and we have it all on record."

"On record?"

"On a television cassette. Why should we lie to you, young man? This has happened before. At the start it happened rather frequently. Now it happens only very rarely. For one thing, we tell the new apprentices of the hallucinations at the start, as I told you, and they generally avoid the planet until they are more acclimated, and then it doesn't happen to them."

"You mean you scare them," blurted out Sam, "so that it's not likely to happen. And they don't tell you if it does happen. But I wasn't scared."

Gentry shook his head. "I'm sorry you weren't, if that was what it would have taken you to keep from seeing things."

"I wasn't seeing things. At least, not things that weren't there."

"How do you intend to argue with a television cassette, which will show you staring at nothing?"

"Sir, what I saw was not opaque. It was smoky, actually; foggy, if you know what I mean."

"Yes, I do. It looked as a hallucination might look, not as reality. But the television set would have seen even smoke."

"Maybe not, sir. My mind must have been focused to see it more clearly. It was probably less clear to the camera than to me."

"It focused your mind, did it?" Gentry stood up, and he sounded rather sad. "That's an admission of hallucination. I'm really sorry, Sam, because you are clearly intelligent, and the Central Computer rated you highly, but we can't use you."

"Will you be sending me home, sir?"

"Yes, but why should that matter? You didn't particularly want to come here."

"I want to stay here *now*."

"But I'm afraid you cannot."

"You can't just send me home. Don't I get a hearing?"

"You certainly can, if you insist, but in that case, the proceedings will be official and will go on your record, so that you won't get another apprenticeship anywhere. As it is, if you are sent back unofficially, as better suited to an apprenticeship in neurophysiology, you might get that, and be better off, actually, than you are now."

"I don't want that. I want a hearing—before the Commander."

"Oh, no. Not the Commander. He can't be bothered with that."

"It *must* be the Commander," said Sam, with desperate force, "or this Project will fail."

"Unless the Commander gives you a hearing? Why do you say that? Come, you are forcing me to think that you are unstable in ways other than those involved with hallucinations."

"Sir." The words were tumbling out of Sam's mouth now. "The Commander is ill—they know that even on Earth—and if he gets too ill to work, this Project will fail. I did not see a hallucination and the proof is that I know why he is ill and how he can be cured."

"You're not helping yourself," said Gentry.

"If you send me away, I tell you the Project will fail. Can it hurt to let me see the Commander? All I ask is five minutes."

"Five minutes? What if he refuses?"

"*Ask* him, sir. Tell him that I say the same thing that caused his depression can remove it."

"No, I don't think I'll tell him that. But I'll ask him if he'll see you."

The Commander was a thin man, not very tall. His eyes were a deep blue and they looked tired.

His voice was very soft, a little low-pitched, definitely weary.

"You're the one who saw the hallucination?"

"It was not a hallucination, Commander. It was real. So was the one *you* saw, Commander." If that did not get him thrown out, Sam thought, he might have a chance. He felt his elbow tightening on his hamper again. He still had it with him.

The Commander seemed to wince. "The one *I* saw?"

"Yes, Commander. It said it had hurt one person. They had to try with you because you were the Commander, and they . . . did damage."

The Commander ignored that and said, "Did you ever have any mental problems before you came here?"

"No, Commander. You can consult my Central Computer record."

Sam thought: *He* must have had problems, but they let it go because he's a genius and they had to have him.

Then he thought: Was that my own idea? Or had it been put there?

The Commander was speaking. Sam had almost missed it. He said, "What you saw can't be real. There is no intelligent life-form on this planet."

"Yes, sir. There is."

"Oh? And no one ever discovered it till you came here, and in three days you did the job?" The Commander smiled very briefly. "I'm afraid I have no choice but to—"

"Wait, Commander," said Sam, in a strangled voice. "We know about the intelligent life-form. It's the insects, the little flying things."

"You say the insects are intelligent?"

"Not an individual insect by itself, but they fit together when they want to, like little jigsaw pieces. They can do it in any way they want. And when they do, their nervous systems fit together, too, and build up. A lot of them *together* are intelligent."

The Commander's eyebrows lifted. "That's an interesting idea, anyway. Almost crazy enough to be true. How did you come to that conclusion, young man?"

"By observation, sir. Everywhere I walked, I disturbed the insects in the grass and they flew about in all directions. But once the cow started to form, and I walked toward it, there was nothing to see or hear. The insects were gone. They had gathered together in front of me and they weren't in the grass anymore. That's how I knew."

"You talked with a cow?"

"It was a cow at first, because that's what I thought of. But they had it wrong, so they switched and came together to form a human being—*me*."

"You?" And then, in a lower voice, "Well, that fits anyway."

"Did you see it that way, too, Commander?"

The Commander ignored that. "And when it shaped itself like you, it could talk as you did? Is that what you're telling me?"

"No, Commander. The talking was in my mind."

"Telepathy?"

"Sort of."

"And what did it say to you, or think to you?"

"It wanted us to refrain from disturbing this planet. It wanted us not to take it over." Sam was all but holding his breath. The interview had lasted more than five minutes already, and the Commander was making no move to put an end to it, to send him home.

"Quite impossible."

"Why, Commander?"

"Any other base will double and triple the expense. We're having enough trouble getting grants as it is. Fortunately, it is all a hallucination, young man, and the problem does not arise." He closed his eyes, then opened them and looked at Sam without really focusing on him. "I'm sorry, young man. You will be sent back—officially."

Sam gambled again. "We can't afford to ignore the insects, Commander. They have a lot to give us."

The Commander had raised his hand halfway as though about to give a signal. He paused long enough to say, "Really? What do they have that they can give us?"

"The one thing more important than energy, Commander. An understanding of the brain."

"How do you know that?"

"I can demonstrate it. I have them here." Sam seized his hamper and swung it forward onto the desk.

"What's that?"

Sam did not answer in words. He opened the hamper, and a softly whirring, smoky cloud appeared.

The Commander rose suddenly and cried out. He lifted his hand high and an alarm bell sounded.

Through the door came Gentry, and others behind him. Sam felt himself seized by the arms, and then a kind of stunned and motionless silence prevailed in the room.

The smoke was condensing, wavering, taking on the shape of a Head, a thin head, with high cheekbones, a smooth forehead and receding hairline. It had the appearance of the Commander.

"I'm seeing things," croaked the Commander.

Sam said, "We're all seeing the same thing, aren't we?" He wriggled and was released.

Gentry said in a low voice, "Mass hysteria."

"No," said Sam, "it's real." He reached toward the Head in midair, and brought back his finger with a tiny insect on it. He flicked it and it could just barely be seen making its way back to its companions.

No one moved.

Sam said, "Head, do you see the problem with the Commander's mind?"

Sam had the brief vision of a snarl in an otherwise smooth curve, but it vanished and left nothing behind. It was not something that could be easily put into human thought. He hoped the others experienced that quick snarl. Yes, they had. He knew it.

The Commander said, "There is no problem."

Sam said, "Can you adjust it, Head?"

Of course, they could not. It was not right to invade a mind.

Sam said, "Commander, give permission."

The Commander put his hands to his eyes and muttered something Sam did not make out. Then he said, clearly, "It's a nightmare, but I've been in one since—Whatever must be done, I give permission."

Nothing happened.

Or nothing seemed to happen.

And then slowly, little by little, the Commander's face lit in a smile.

He said, just above a whisper. "Astonishing. I'm watching a sun rise. It's been cold night for so long, and now I feel the warmth again." His voice rose high. "I feel wonderful."

The Head deformed at that point, turned into a vague, pulsing fog, then formed a curving, narrowing arrow that sped into the hamper. Sam snapped it shut.

He said, "Commander, have I your permission to restore these little insect-things to their own world?"

"Yes, yes," said the Commander, dismissing that with a wave of his hand. "Gentry, call a meeting. We've got to change all our plans."

Sam had been escorted outside the Dome by a stolid guard and had then been confined to his quarters for the rest of the day.

It was late when Gentry entered, stared at him thoughtfully, and said, "That was an amazing demonstration of yours. The entire incident has been fed into the Central Computer and we now have a double project—neutron-star energy and neurophysiology. I doubt that there will be any question about pouring money into this project now. And we'll have a group of neurophysiologists arriving eventually. Until then you're going to be working with those little things and you'll probably end up the most important person here."

Sam said, "But will we leave their world to them?"

Gentry said, "We'll have to if we expect to get anything out of them, won't we? The Commander thinks we're going to build elaborate settlements in orbit about this world and shift all operations to them except for a skeleton crew in this Dome to maintain direct contact with the insects—or whatever we'll decide to call them. It will cost a great deal of money, and take time and labor, but it's going to be worth it. No one will question that."

Sam said "Good!"

Gentry stared at him again, longer and more thoughtfully than before.

"My boy," he said, "it seems that what happened came about because you did not fear the supposed hallucination.

Your mind remained open, and that was the whole difference. Why was that? Why weren't you afraid?"

Sam flushed. "I'm not sure, sir. As I look back on it, though, it seemed to me I was puzzled as to why I was sent here. I had been doing my best to study neurophysiology through my computerized courses, and I knew very little about astrophysics. The Central Computer had my record, all of it, the full details of everything I had ever studied and I couldn't imagine why I had been sent here.

"Then, when you first mentioned the hallucinations, I thought, 'That must be it. I was sent here to look into it.' I just made up my mind that was the thing I had to do. I had no *time* to be afraid, Dr. Gentry. I had a problem to solve and I—I had faith in the Central Computer. It wouldn't have sent me here, if I weren't up to it."

Gentry shook his head. "I'm afraid I wouldn't have had that much faith in that machine. But they say faith can move mountains, and I guess it did in this case."

The Instability

Professor Firebrenner had explained it carefully. "Time-perception depends on the structure of the Universe. When the Universe is expanding, we experience time as going forward; when it is contracting, we experience it going backward. If we could somehow force the Universe to be in stasis, neither expanding nor contracting, time would stand still."

"But you can't put the Universe in stasis," said Mr. Atkins, fascinated.

"I can put a little portion of the Universe in stasis, however," said the professor. "Just enough to hold a ship. Time will stand still and we can move forward or backward at will and the entire trip will last less than an instant. But all the parts of the Universe will move while we stand still, while we are nailed to the fabric of the Universe. The Earth moves about the Sun, the Sun moves about the core of the Galaxy, the Galaxy moves about some center of gravity, *all* the Galaxies move.

"I calculated those motions and I find that 27.5 million years in the future, a red dwarf star will occupy the position our Sun does now. If we go 27.5 million years into the future, in less than an instant that red dwarf star will be near our spaceship and we can come home after studying it a bit."

Atkins said, "Can that be done?"

"I've sent experimental animals through time, but I can't make them automatically return. If you and I go, we can then manipulate the controls so that we can return."

"And you want me along?"

"Of course. There should be two. Two people would be more easily believed than one alone. Come, it will be an incredible adventure."

Atkins inspected the ship. It was a 2217 Glennfusion model and looked beautiful.

"Suppose," he said, "that it lands *inside* the red dwarf star."

"It won't," said the professor, "but if it does, that's the chance we take."

"But when we get back, the Sun and Earth will have moved on. We'll be in space."

"Of course, but how far can the Sun and Earth move in the few hours it will take us to observe the star? With this ship we will catch up to our beloved planet. Are you ready, Mr. Atkins?"

"Ready," sighed Atkins.

Professor Firebrenner made the necessary adjustments and nailed the ship to the fabric of the Universe while 27.5 million years passed. And then, in less than a flash, time began to move forward again in the usual way, and everything in the Universe moved forward with it.

Through the viewing port of their ship, Professor Firebrenner and Mr. Atkins could see the small orb of the red dwarf star.

The professor smiled. "You and I, Atkins," he said, "are

the first ever to see, close at hand, any star other than our own Sun."

They remained two-and-a-half hours during which they photographed the star and its spectrum and as many neighboring stars as they could, made special coronagraphic observations, tested the chemical composition of the interstellar gas, and then Professor Firebrenner said, rather reluctantly, "I think we had better go home now."

Again, the controls were adjusted and the ship was nailed to the fabric of the Universe. They went 27.5 million years into the past, and in less than a flash, they were back where they started.

Space was black. There was nothing.

Atkins said, "What happened? Where are the Earth and Sun?"

The professor frowned. He said, "Going *back* in time must be different. The entire Universe must have moved."

"Where could it move?"

"I don't know. Other objects shift position within the Universe, but the Universe as a whole must move in an upper-dimensional direction. We are here in the absolute vacuum, in primeval Chaos."

"But *we're* here. It's not primeval Chaos anymore."

"Exactly. That means we've introduced an instability at this place where we exist, and *that* means—"

Even as he said that, a Big Bang obliterated them. A new Universe came into being and began to expand.

Alexander the God

Alexander Hoskins grew seriously interested in computers at the age of fourteen and quickly realized that he was interested in nothing much else.

His teachers encouraged him and excused him from classes in order that he might concentrate on this hobby of his. His father, who worked for IBM, encouraged him, too, got him some necessary equipment and explained some knotty points to him.

Alexander built his own computer in a room above the garage, programmed and reprogrammed it and, at the age of sixteen, could no longer find a book that told him anything he didn't know about computers. Nor could he find a book that dealt with some of the things he had found out entirely on his own.

He thought about it deeply and decided not to tell his father of some of the things his computer could do. Already, the boy had become aware that the greatest conqueror of ancient times had been Alexander the Great, and Alexander felt his own name was no accident.

Alexander was particularly interested in computer memory and worked out systems for cramming data into volume—much data into little volume. With each improvement, he squeezed more and more data into less and less volume.

Solemnly, he then named his computer Bucephalus, after the faithful horse of Alexander the Great, the horse who had carried him through all his triumphant battles.

There were computers that could accept spoken commands and give spoken responses, but none could do it as well as Bucephalus. There were also computers that could scan and store the written word, but none could do it as well as Bucephalus. Alexander tested this by having Bucephalus scan the *Encyclopedia Britannica* and store it all in its memory.

By the time he was eighteen, Alexander had established an information-handling business for students and small businessmen and had become self-supporting. He moved into his own apartment in the city and was from that point on independent of his parents.

In his own apartment he could remove the earphone attachment. With privacy, he could speak to Bucephalus openly, though he carefully adjusted the computer's voice to low intensity. He did not want neighbors to wonder who was in the apartment with him.

He said, "Bucephalus, Alexander the Great had conquered the ancient world by the time he was thirty. I want to do the same thing. That gives me twelve more years."

Bucephalus knew all about Alexander the Great, since the *Encyclopedia* had given him all the details.

He said, "Alexander the Great was the son of the King of Macedon and by the time he was your age, he had led his father's cavalry to victory at the great battle at Chaeronea."

Alexander said, "No, no. I'm not talking about battles and phalanxes and things like that. I want to conquer the world by coming to own it."

"How could you own it, Alexander?"

"You and I, Bucephalus," said Alexander, "are going to study the stock market."

The *New York Times* had long since put all its microfilmed records into computerized form and for Alexander it was not at all a difficult task to tap into that information.

For days, weeks, months, Bucephalus transferred over a century of data on the stock market into its own memory banks—all the stocks listed, all the shares sold for each on each day, the ups and downs, even the applicable news on the financial pages. Alexander was forced to extend the computer's memory circuits and to work out a daring new system for information retrieval. Reluctantly, he sold a simplified version of one of the circuits he had developed to IBM and in this way became quite well-to-do. He bought a neighboring apartment in which he might eat and sleep. The first apartment was now given over entirely to Bucephalus.

When he was twenty, Alexander felt he was ready to start his campaign.

"Bucephalus," he said, "I am ready, and so are you. You know everything there is to know about the stock market. You have in your memory every transaction and every event, and you keep it all up to date to the very second because you are hooked into the computer at the New York Stock Exchange, and you will soon be hooked into the exchanges in London, Tokyo, and elsewhere."

"Yes, Alexander," said Bucephalus, "but what is it you wish me to do with all the information?"

"I am certain," said Alexander, his eyes gleaming in steely, determined fashion, "that the values and fluctuations of the Market are not random. I feel that nothing is. You must go through all the data, studying all the values and all the changes in the values and all the rates of changes of the values, until you can analyze them into cycles and combinations of cycles."

"Are you referring to a Fourier analysis?" asked Bucephalus.

"Explain that to me."

Bucephalus presented him with a printout from the *Encyclopedia* together with supplements from other information in his memory banks.

Alexander glanced at it briefly, and said, "Yes, that's the sort of thing."

"To what end, Alexander?"

"Once you have the cycles, Bucephalus, you will be able to predict the course of the stock market in the following day, week, month, according to the swing of the cycles, and you will be able to direct me in my investments. I will quickly grow rich. You will also direct me how to obscure my own involvement so that the world will not know how rich I am, or who it is who has such an influential finger on world events."

"To what end, Alexander?"

"So that when I am rich enough, when I control the Earth's financial institutions, its commerce, its business, its resources, I will have done in reality what Alexander the Great did only in part. I will be Alexander the Really Great." His eyes glittered with delight at the thought.

By the time Alexander was twenty-two, he was satisfied that Bucephalus had worked out the complicated set of cycles that would serve to predict the behavior of the stock market.

Bucephalus was less certain. He said, "In addition to the natural cycles that control such things, there are also unpredictable events in the world of politics and international affairs. There are unpredictable turns of weather, disease, and scientific advance."

Alexander said, "Not at all, Bucephalus. All such things also go in cycles. You will study the general news columns of the *New York Times* and absorb it all in order to allow for these supposedly unpredictable events. You will then find they are predictable. Other great newspapers, here and abroad, will be yours to study. They are all microfilmed and computerized and we can go back for a century or more. Besides, you do not have to be totally accurate. If you are right eighty-five percent of the time, that will do, for now."

It *did* do. When Bucephalus felt that the stock market would go up or that it would go down, he was invariably right. When he pointed to particular stocks that were headed for long-term rises or declines, he was almost always right.

By the time Alexander was twenty-four he was worth five million dollars and his income had risen to tens of thousands of dollars per day. What's more, his books were so complicated and the money so laundered that it would have taken another computer just like Bucephalus to track it all down and force Alexander to pay more than a pittance to the I.R.S.

It was not even difficult. Bucephalus had entered all the tax statutes into its memory as well as a score of textbooks on corporation management. Thanks to Bucephalus, Alexander controlled a dozen corporations without any sign of that control being visible.

Bucephalus said, "Are you rich enough, Alexander?"

"Surely you jest," said Alexander. "I am as yet a financial pip-squeak, a batboy in the minor leagues. When I am a billionaire, I will be a power in the financial set, but I will still be only one among a handful. It is only when I am a multi-trillionaire that I will be able to control governments and force my will upon the world. And I have only six years left."

Bucephalus's understanding of the stock market, and of the ways of the world, grew each year. His advice remained always useful and his deviousness in threading financial tentacles through the centers of world power remained always skillful.

Yet he grew doubtful, too. "There may be trouble, Alexander," he said.

"Nonsense," said Alexander. "Alexander the Really Great cannot be stopped."

By the time Alexander was twenty-six, he was a billionaire. The entire apartment building was now his and all of it was given over to Bucephalus, and to all the offshoots of its enormous memory. The tentacles of Bucephalus now stretched invisibly outward to all the computers in the world. Softly, gently, all of them responded to Alexander's will as expressed through Bucephalus.

Bucephalus said, "It grows more difficult somehow, Alexander. My estimates of future development are not as good as they have been."

Alexander said impatiently, "You are dealing with more and more variables. There is nothing to worry about. I shall double your complexity, then double it again."

"It is not complexity that is needed," said Bucephalus. "All the cycles that I have worked out in ever-increasing complexity predict the future in fine detail only because things that now take place are the same as have taken place in the past, so that the response is the same. If something entirely new happens, then all the cycles will fail—"

Alexander said, peremptorily, "There is nothing new under the sun. Go through history and you'll find that there are only changes in detail. I will conquer the world, but I am only one more conqueror in a long line stretching back to Sargon of Agade. The development of a high-tech society repeats certain advances in medieval China and in the ancient Hellenistic kingdoms. The Black Death was a repetition of the earlier plagues in the times of Marcus Aurelius and of Pericles. Even the devastation of the wars of nations in the twentieth century repeats the devastation of the wars of religion in the sixteenth and seventeenth centuries. The differences in detail can be allowed for and, in any case, I order you to continue, and you must obey my orders."

"I must," agreed Bucephalus.

By the time Alexander was twenty-eight, he was the richest man who had ever lived, with assets that even Bucephalus could not estimate closely. Certainly it was over a hundred billion and his income was in the tens of millions a day.

No nation was any longer truly independent and nowhere could any sizable group of human beings take any action that would seriously discommode Alexander.

There was peace in the world because Alexander did not wish any of his property destroyed. There was firm order in the world because Alexander did not wish to be disturbed. For the same reason, there was no freedom. All must do exactly as Alexander willed.

"I am almost there, Bucephalus," said Alexander. "In two more years, it will be completely beyond the power of any human being to discommode me. I will then reveal myself, and all of human science will be bent to one task, and one task only, that of making me immortal. I will no longer be even Alexander the Really Great. I will become Alexander the God and all human beings will worship me."

Bucephalus said, "But I have gone as far as I can go. I may no longer be able to protect you from the viscissitudes of chance."

"That can't be so, Bucephalus," said Alexander, impatiently. "Do not quail. Weigh all the variables and arrange to pour into my hands whatever of Earth's wealth still exists outside it."

"I don't think I can, Alexander," said Bucephalus. "I have discovered a factor in human history that I cannot weigh. It is something completely new that does not fit into any of the cycles."

"There can be nothing new," said Alexander, now in a fury. "Do not hang back. I order you to proceed."

"Very well, then," said Bucephalus, with a remarkably human sigh.

Alexander knew that Bucephalus was straining at this one last, greatest task, and he was confident that at any moment, it would be accomplished. The world would then be his entirely and through all eternity. "What is this something new?" he asked with a flicker of curiosity.

"Myself," said Bucephalus, in a whisper. "Nothing like me has ever before exis—"

And before the last syllable could be expressed, Bucephalus went dark as every last chip and circuit within itself fused as a result of his mighty effort to encompass himself as part of history. In the economic and financial chaos that followed, Alexander was wiped out.

Earth regained its liberty—which meant, of course, that there was a certain amount of disorder here and there, but most people considered that a small price to pay.

In the Canyon

Dear Mabel,

Well, here we are, as promised. They've given us a permit to live in the Valles Marineris, and don't think we haven't been waiting for a year and a half because we have. They're so slow and they keep talking about the capital investment required to make the place livable.

Valles Marineris sounds good as an address, but we just call it the Canyon, and I don't know why they're so worried about its being livable. It's the Martian Riviera, if you ask me.

In the first place, it's warmer down here than it is in the rest of Mars, a good ten degrees (Celsius) warmer. The air is thicker—thin enough, heaven knows—but thicker and a better protection against ultraviolet.

Of course, the main difficulty is getting in and out of the Canyon. It's four miles deep in places and they've built roads here and there so that you can get down in special mobiles. Getting up and out is more difficult, but with gravity only two-fifths what it is on Earth, it isn't as bad as it sounds, and they do say they're going to build elevators that will take us at least partway up and down.

Another problem is, of course, that dust storms do tend to accumulate in the Canyon more than on the ordinary surface, and there are landslides now and then, but heavens, we don't worry about that. We know where the faults are and where the landslides are likely to occur and no one digs in there.

That's the thing, Mabel. After all, everyone on Mars lives under a dome or underground, but here in the Canyon, we can dig in sideways, which I understand is much preferable from an engineering standpoint, though I've asked Bill not to try to explain it to me.

For one thing, we can heat out some of the ice crystals, so that we don't have to depend on the government for *all* the water we need. There is more ice down in the Canyon than elsewhere and, for another, it's easier to manufacture the air, keep it inside the diggings, and circulate it when you're in horizontally instead of down vertically. That's what Bill says.

And I've been thinking about it, Mabel. Where's the need to leave the Canyon, anyway? It's over three thousand miles long and in the end there are going to be diggings all along it. It's going to be a huge city, and I'll bet you most of the population of Mars will end up here. Can't you see it? There's to be some kind of maglev rail running the length of the Canyon and communication will be easy. The government ought to put every bit of money it can into developing it. It will make Mars a great world.

Bill says (you know what he's like—all enthusiasm) that the time will come when they will roof in the whole Canyon. Instead of having air just in separate diggings, and having to put on a spacesuit when you want to travel about, we will have a huge world of normal air and low gravity.

I said to him that the landslides might break the dome and we would lose all the air. He said that the dome could be built in separate sections and that any break would automatically shut off the affected areas. I asked him how much all that would cost. He said, "What's the difference? It will be done little by little, over the centuries."

Anyway, that's his job here, now. He's got his master's license as an Areo-engineer, and he's got to work out new ways to make the Canyon diggings even better. That's why we got our new place here and it looks as though Mars is going to be our oyster.

We may not live to see it ourselves, but if our great-grandchildren make it to 2140, a century from now, we'll have a world that may well overshadow Earth itself.

It would be wonderful. We're very excited, Mabel.

Yours,

Gladys.

Good-bye to Earth

I am sending this message to Earth in an attempt to warn them about what I feel sure is going to happen, and what *must* happen. It is sad to think of what lies ahead, so no one wants to talk about it, but someone should, as the people of Earth ought to be prepared.

It is the latter half of the twenty-first century and there are a dozen Settlements in orbit about the Earth. Each is, in its way, an independent little world. The smallest has ten thousand inhabitants, the largest almost twenty-five thousand. I'm sure that all Earthmen know this, but you people are so entangled in your own giant world, that you rarely think of us except as some little inconsequential objects out in space. Well, *think* of us.

Each Settlement imitates Earth's environment as closely as it can, spinning to produce a pseudo-gravity, allowing sunlight to enter at some times, and not at others, in order to produce a normal day and night. Each is large enough to give the impression of space within, to have farms as well as factories, to have an atmosphere that can give rise to clouds. There are towns, and schools, and athletic fields.

We have some things that Earth has not. The pseudo-gravitational field varies in intensity relative to position within each Settlement. There are areas of low gravity, even zero gravity, where we can outfit ourselves with wings and fly, where we can play three-dimensional tennis, where we can have unusual gymnastic experiences.

We also have a true space culture, for we are used to space. Our chief work, aside from keeping our Settlements running efficiently, is to build structures in space for ourselves and for Earth. We work in space, and to be in a spaceship or a spacesuit is second nature to us. Working at zero gravity is something we have done from childhood.

There are also some things Earth has that we do not. We don't have Earth's weather extremes. In our carefully controlled Settlements, it never gets too hot or too cold. There are no storms and no unarranged precipitation.

Nor do we have Earth's dangerous terrain. We have no mountains, no cliffs, no swamps, no deserts, no stormy oceans. And we have no dangerous plants, animals, or parasites. If anything, there are some among us who complain that we are too secure, that there is no adventure—but then our people can always go out into space, and make long trips to Mars and to the asteroids, which you Earthpeople are psychologically unfit to do. In fact, there are plans by some Settlers to set up colonies on Mars and mining bases in the asteroid belt, but it may never come to that, for reasons I will describe.

The Settlements did not spring on humanity unawares. Even a century ago, Gerard O'Neill of Princeton and his students were making initial plans for such new homes for humanity, and science fiction writers had anticipated it even before that.

Oddly enough though, the difficulties that most foresaw turned out to be not those that plagued the Settlements. The expense of building them, the problems of providing an Earth-like environment, the gathering of energy, the matter of protection against cosmic rays were all solved. It was not done easily, but it was done.

The Sun itself supplies all the energy we need, and enough more to export some to Earth. We can grow food easily—more than we need, in fact, so that we can export some to Earth. We have small animals—rabbits, chickens, and so on, that can supply us with meat. We get what material we need from space, not only from the Moon, but from meteoroids and comets that we can trap and exploit. Once we reach the asteroids (if we ever do) we will have a virtually unlimited supply of everything we need.

What bothers us and produces an insuperable problem is something that few people foresaw. It is the difficulty of keeping up a viable ecology. Each Settlement must support itself. It contains people, plants, and animals; it contains air, water, and soil. The living things must multiply and maintain their numbers, but not outpace the ability of the Settlement to support them.

The plants and animals? Well, we control them. We supervise their breeding and we consume any excess. Maintaining the human population at a reasonable level is more difficult. We cannot allow human births to outstrip human deaths, and we keep the number of deaths as low as possible, of course. This makes our culture a nonyouthful one compared to Earth's. There are few youngsters and a large percentage of those mature and postmature. This produces psychological strains, but there is the general feeling among Settlers that those strains are worth it, since with a carefully controlled population, there are no poor, no homeless, and no helpless.

Again, the water, air, and food must be carefully recycled, and much of our technology is devoted to the distillation of used water, and to the treatment of solid bodily wastes and their conversion to clean fertilizer. We cannot afford to have anything go wrong with our recycling technology, for there is little room for slack. And, of course, even when all goes well, the feeling that we eat and drink recycled materials is a bit unpalatable. All is recycled on Earth, too, but Earth is so large and the natural cycling system so unnoticeable, that Earthpeople tend to be unaware of the matter.

Then, too, there is always the fear that a sizable meteor may strike and damage the outer shell of a Settlement. A bit of matter no larger than a piece of gravel might do damage, and one a foot across would surely destroy any Settlement. Fortunately, the chances for such a misadventure are small and we will eventually learn to detect and divert such objects before they reach us. Still, these dangers weigh upon us, and help mitigate the feeling of over-security that some of us complain about.

With an effort, however, with close attention and unremitting care, we can maintain our ecology, were it not for the matter of trade and travel.

Each Settlement produces something that other Settlements would like to have, in the matter of food, of art, of ingenious devices. What's more, we must trade with Earth as well, and many Settlers want to visit Earth and see some of the things we don't have in the Settlements. Earthpeople can't realize how exciting it is for us to see a vast blue horizon, or to look out upon a true ocean, or to see an ice-capped mountain.

Therefore, there is a constant coming and going among the Settlements and Earth. But each Settlement has its own ecological balance; and, of course, Earth has, even these days, an ecology that is enormously and impossibly rich by Settlement standards.

We have our insects that are acclimated and under control, but what if strange insects are casually and unintentionally introduced from another Settlement or from Earth?

A strange insect, a strange worm, even a strange rodent might totally upset our ecology, inflict damage on our native plants and animals. On numerous occasions, in fact, a Settlement has had to take extraordinary measures to eliminate an unwanted life-form. For months every effort had to be taken to track down every last insect of some species that, in its own Settlement, is harmless, or that, on Earth, can keep its depredations local.

Even worse, what if pathogenic parasites—bacteria, viruses, protozoa—are introduced? What if they produce diseases against which another Settlement and, of course, Earth itself, have developed a certain immunity, but one against which the Settlement that suffers the invasion is helpless. For a while, the entire effort of the Settlement must go into the preparation or importation of sera designed to confer immunity, or to fight the disease once it is established. Deaths, of course, occur invariably. .

Naturally, there is always an outcry when this happens and a demand for more controls. As a result, no one from another Settlement, and no one returning to his own Settlement from a trip elsewhere, can be allowed to enter without a complete search of his baggage, a complete analysis of his bodily fluids, and a certain period of quarantine to see if some undetected disease is developing.

What's more, rightly or wrongly, the inhabitants of the Settlements persist in viewing Earthpeople themselves as particularly dangerous. It is on Earth where the most undesirable life-forms and parasites are to be found; it is Earthpeople who are most likely to be infested, and there are parties on all the Settlements who support the notion—sometimes quite vehemently—of breaking all contacts between the Settlements and Earth.

That is the danger of which I want to warn Earthpeople. Distrust—and even hatred—of Earthpeople is constantly growing among the Settlers.

As long as Earth is only a few tens or hundreds of thousands of miles away, it is useless to talk of breaking off all contact. The lure and attraction of Earth is too great. Therefore, there is now talk—it is only a whisper, so far, but it will grow louder, I assure you—of leaving the Solar system altogether.

Each Settlement can be outfitted with a propulsive mechanism, making use of microfusion motors. Solar energy will suffice us while we are still among the planets and we will pick up small comets as a source of hydrogen fuel, in the process of leaving all the planets behind, when the Sun becomes too distant to be of use to us.

Each Settlement will say good-bye to Earth, then, and launch itself as an independent world into the unimaginable wastes between the stars. And who knows, someday a million years hence a Settlement may find an Earth-like world, empty and waiting, that it can populate.

But that is what I must warn Earth of. The Settlements will someday leave, and if you build others, they will eventually leave, too, and you will be left alone. And yet, in a way, your descendants will be expanding into, and populating, the entire Galaxy. You may find that a consoling thought as you watch them disappear.

Battle-Hymn

There didn't seem much room for hope. Sibelius Hopkins put it into the simplest words.

"We've got to have Martian consent, and we won't get it, that's all."

The gloom among the others was thick enough to impede breathing. "We should never have granted the colonists autonomy," said Ralph Colodny.

"Agreed," said Hopkins. "Now who wants to volunteer to go back in time twenty-eight years and change history. Mars has the sovereign right to decide how its territory is to be used, and there's nothing to be done about it."

"We might choose another site," said Ben Devers, who was the youngest of the group and hadn't yet worked himself to the proper pitch of cynicism.

"No other site," said Hopkins flatly. "If you don't know that experiments with hyperspace are dangerous, go back to school. You can't do them on Earth, and even the Moon is far too built up. The space settlements are too small by three orders of magnitude and it's not possible to reach anything beyond Mars for at least twenty years. But Mars is perfect. It's still practically empty. It has a low surface gravity and a thin atmosphere. It's cold. Everything's perfect for hyperspatial flight—except the colonists."

"You can never tell," said young Devers. "People are funny. They might vote in favor of hyperspatial experiments on Mars, if we play it right."

"How do we play it right?" said Hopkins. "The opposition has blanketed Mars with an old hillbilly tune that has the words:

> *"No, no, a thousand times, no!*
> *You cannot buy my caress!*
> *"No, no, a thousand times, no!*
> *I'd rather die than say, yes."*

He grinned mirthlessly. "Mars is blanketed with the tune. It's being drilled into the minds of the Martian colonists. They'll vote 'no' automatically, and we won't have hyperspatial experiments and that means we won't have flights to the stars for decades, maybe generations—certainly not in our lifetimes."

Devers said, frowning in thought, "Can't we use a tune for our side of the argument?"

"What tune?"

"A large percentage of the Martian colonists are of French extraction. We might play on their ethnic consciousness."

"What ethnic consciousness? Everyone speaks English now."

"That doesn't stop ethnic consciousness," said Devers. "If you play the old national anthem of France, they'll all drip nostalgia. It's a battle-hymn, you know, and battle-hymns always stir the blood, especially now that there aren't any wars."

Hopkins said, "But the words don't mean anything any more. Do you remember them?"

"Yes," said Devers. "Some—

> *"Allons, enfants de la patrie,*
> *La jour de gloire est arrive.*
> *Contre nous de la tyrannie,*
> *L'Etendard sanglant est leve."*

He sang them in a clear tenor voice.

Hopkins said, "Not one Martian in a thousand will know what that means."

Devers said, "Who cares? Play it anyway. Even if they don't understand the words they will know it's the old battle-hymn of France and that will stir them up. Besides, the tune is a winner. Infinitely better than that silly music-hall thing about 'No, no.' I'm telling you, the battle-hymn will settle into every mind and wipe out the no-no."

"Maybe you have something there," said Hopkins. "And if we accompany it with some strong slogan in different changes, 'Humanity to the stars!', 'Reach out for a star,' 'Faster than light is the slowest we can go.' And always with that tune."

Colodny said, "You know, *'la jour de gloire'* means 'the day of glory,' I think. We can use that phrase, 'the glory day when we reach the stars.' If we say 'glory day' often enough, maybe the Martians will vote 'Yes.' "

"It sounds too good to be true," said Hopkins, gloomily, "but I really don't see that there's any other choice we have right now. We can try it and see if it does any good."

That was the beginning of the great voting battle of the tunes. In every one of the domed settlements on Mars, from Olympus all along the Valles Marineris and far into the cratered areas, there rang out on one side, "No, no, a thousand times, no—" and on the other side, *"Allons, enfants de la patrie—"*

There was no question that the stirring rhythm of the battle-hymn was having its effect. It roared back at the simple negation sing-song and Hopkins had to admit that from zero chance, the "yes" vote was becoming a possibility; from sure defeat, it was beginning to have just a chance.

Hopkins said, "The trouble is, though, we have nothing direct. Their song, silly though it is, has the advantage of saying, 'No—No!—*No!*' Ours is just a tune which is catchy and is filling the minds of many, but with what? *La jour de gloire?*"

Devers smiled and said, "Why not wait for the election?" After all, it was his idea.

They did.

CHALLENGE TO THE READER

What happened on election day? Did the negative vote win or the positive? And, in either case, why?

The best *reason* counts. You can win if you have the vote come out negative *or* positive.

On the evening of election day, Hopkins found himself almost unable to talk. The vote had been running a steady 90 percent in favor of "Yes" and there was simply no question about it.

The colonists of Mars were voting to allow their planet to be used for the work that would eventually send human beings to the stars.

Hopkins said, finally, "What happened? What did we do right?"

"It was the tune," said Devers, smiling his satisfaction. "I had it figured right, but I didn't want to explain my notion because I didn't want it to get out to the other side somehow. Not that I don't trust everyone here, but I didn't want the tune neutralized in some clever way."

"What was there about the tune that made so much difference?" demanded Hopkins.

"Well, it *did* have a subliminal message. Maybe the colonists no longer knew enough French to get the meaning of the words, but they had to know the *name* of the battle-hymn. That name rang through their minds each time they heard the tune; each time they hummed it."

"So what?"

"So this," said Devers, grinning, "The name is 'Mars say yes!' "

Feghoot and the Courts

The planet of Lockmania, inhabited though it was by intelligent beings that looked like large wombats, had adopted the American legal system, and Ferdinand Feghoot had been sent there by the Earth Confederation to study the results.

Feghoot watched with interest as a husband and wife were brought in, charged with disturbing the peace. During a religious observation, when for twenty minutes the congregation was supposed to maintain silence, while concentrating on their sins and visualizing them as melting away, the woman had suddenly risen from her squatting position and screamed loudly. When someone rose to object, the man had pushed him forcefully.

The judges listened solemnly, fined the woman a silver dollar, and the man a twenty-dollar gold-piece.

Almost immediately afterward, seventeen men and women were brought in. They had been ringleaders of a crowd that had demonstrated for better quality meat at a supermarket. They had torn the supermarket apart and inflicted various bruises and lacerations on eight of the employees of the establishment.

Again the judges listened solemnly, and fined the seventeen a silver dollar apiece.

Afterward, Feghoot said to the chief judge, "I approved of your handling of the man and woman who disturbed the peace."

"It was a simple case," said the judge. "We have a legal maxim that goes, 'Screech is silver, but violence is golden.' "

"In that case," said Feghoot, "why did you fine the group of seventeen a silver dollar apiece when they had committed far worse violence?"

"Oh, that's another legal maxim," said the judge. "Every crowd has a silver fining."

Fault-Intolerant

9 JANUARY

I, Abram Ivanov, finally have a home computer; a word processor, to be exact. I fought it as long as I could. I argued it out with myself. I am America's most prolific writer and I do fine on a typewriter. Last year I published over thirty books. Some of them were small books for kids. Some were anthologies. But there were also novels, short story collections, essay collections, nonfiction books. Nothing to be ashamed of.

So why do I need a word processor? I can't go any faster. But, you know, there's such a thing as neatness. Typing my stuff means I have to introduce pen-and-ink items to correct typos, and nobody does that anymore. I don't want my manuscripts to stick out like a sore thumb. I don't want editors to think my stuff is second rate, just because it is corrected.

The difficulty was finding a machine that wouldn't take two years to learn to use. Deft, I'm not—as I've frequently mentioned in this diary. And I want one that doesn't break down every other day. Mechanical failures just throw me.

So I got one that's "fault-tolerant." That means if some component goes wrong, the machine keeps right on working, tests the malfunctioning component, corrects it if it can, reports it if it can't, and replacements can be carried through by anybody. It doesn't take an expert hacker. Sounds like my kind of thing.

5 FEBRUARY

I haven't been mentioning my word processor lately, because I've been struggling to learn how it works. I've managed. For a while, I had a lot of trouble, because although I have a high IQ, it's a very specialized high IQ. I can write, but coping with mechanical objects throws me.

But I learned quickly, once I gained sufficient confidence. What did it was this. The manufacturer's representative assured me that the machine would develop flaws only rarely, and would be unable to correct its own flaws only *exceedingly* rarely. He said I wouldn't be likely to need a new component oftener than once in five years.

And if I did need one, they would hear exactly what was needed from the machine. The computer would then replace the part itself, do all the wiring and oiling that was necessary and reject the old part, which I could then throw away.

That's sort of exciting. I almost wish something would go wrong so that I could get a new part and insert it. I could tell everyone, "Oh, sure, the discombobulator blew a fuse, and I fixed it like a shot. Nothing to it." But they wouldn't believe me.

I'm going to try writing a short story on it. Nothing too long. Just about two thousand words, maybe. If I get confused, I can always go back to the typewriter until I've regained my confidence. Then I can try again.

14 FEBRUARY

I didn't get confused. Now that the proof is in, I can talk about it. The short story went as smoothly as cream. I brought it in and they've taken it. No problem.

So I've finally started my new novel. I should have started it a month ago, but I had to make sure I could work my word processor first. Let's hope it works. It'll seem funny not having a pile of yellow sheets I can rifle through when I want to check something I said a hundred pages earlier, but I suppose I can learn how to check back on the discs.

19 FEBRUARY

The computer has a spelling correction component. That caught me by surprise because the representative hadn't told me about it. At first, it let misspellings go and I just proofread each page as I turned it out. But then it began to mark off any word it was unfamiliar with, which was a little bothersome because my vocabulary is a large one and I have no objection to making up words. And, of course, any proper name I use is something it was unfamiliar with.

I called the representative because it was annoying to have to be notified of all sorts of corrections that didn't really have to be made.

The representative said, "Don't let that bother you, Mr. Ivanov. If it questions a word that you want to remain as it is, just retype it exactly as it is and the computer will get the idea and not correct it the next time."

That puzzled me. "Don't I have to set up a dictionary for the machine? How will it know what's right and what's wrong?"

"That's part of the fault-tolerance, Mr. Ivanov," he said.

"The machine already has a basic dictionary and it picks up new words as you use them. You will find that it will pick up false misspellings to a smaller and smaller degree. To tell you truthfully, Mr. Ivanov, you have a late model there and we're not sure we know all its potentialities. Some of our researchers consider it fault-tolerant in that it can continue to work despite its own flaws, but fault-intolerant in that it won't stand for flaws in those who use it. Please report to us if there's anything puzzling. We would really like to know."

I'm not sure I'll like this.

7 MARCH

Well, I've been struggling with the word processor and I don't know what to think. For a long time, it would mark off misspellings, and I would retype them correctly. And it certainly learned how to tell *real* misspellings. I had no trouble there. In fact, when I had a long word, I would sometimes throw in a wrong letter just to see if it would catch it. I would write "supercede" or "vaccum" or "Skenectady." It almost never failed.

And then yesterday a funny thing happened. It stopped waiting for me to retype the wrong spelling. It retyped it automatically itself. You can't help striking the wrong key sometimes so I would write "5he" instead of "the" and the "5" would change to a "t" in front of my eyes. And it would happen quickly, too.

I tested it by deliberately typing a word with a wrong letter. I would see it show up wrong on the screen. I would blink my eyes and it would be right.

This morning I phoned the representative.

"Hmm," he said. "Interesting."

"Troublesome," I said. "It might introduce mistakes. If I

type 'blww' does the machine correct it to 'blew' or to 'blow'? Or what if it *thinks* I mean 'blue,' 'ue' when I *really* mean 'blew,' 'ew.' See what I mean?"

He said, "I have discussed your machine with one of our theoretical experts. He tells me it may be capable of absorbing internal clues from your writing and knows which word you really want to use. As you type into it, it begins to understand your style and integrate it into its own programming."

A little scary, but it's convenient. I don't have to proofread the pages now.

20 MARCH

I *really* don't have to proofread the pages. The machine has taken to correcting my punctuation and word order.

The first time it happened, I couldn't believe it. I thought I had had a small attack of dizziness and had imagined I had typed something that wasn't really on the screen.

It happened oftener and oftener and there was no mistake about it. It got to the point where I *couldn't* make a mistake in grammar. If I tried to type something like "Jack, and Jill went up the hill," that comma simply wouldn't appear. No matter how I tried to type "I has a book," it always shows up as "I have a book." Or if I wrote, "Jack, and Jill as well, went up the hill," then I couldn't omit the commas. They'd go in of their own accord.

It's a lucky thing I keep this diary in longhand or I couldn't explain what I mean. I couldn't give an example of wrong English.

I don't really like to have a computer arguing with me over English, but the worst part of it is that it's always right.

Well, look, I don't throw a fit when a human copy editor

sends me back a manuscript with corrections in every line. I'm just a writer, I'm not an expert on the minutiae of English. Let the copy editors copyedit, they still can't *write*. And so let the word processor copyedit. It takes a load off me.

17 APRIL

I spoke too soon in the last item in which I mentioned my word processor. For three weeks, it copyedited me and my novel went along smoothly. It was a good working arrangement. I did the creating and it did the modulating, so to speak.

Then yesterday evening, it refused to work at all. Nothing happened, no matter what keys were touched. It was plugged in all right; the wall switch was on; I was doing everything correctly. It just wouldn't work. Well I thought, so much for that business about "Not once in five years." I'd only been using it for three and a half months and already so many parts were out that it wouldn't work.

That meant that new parts ought to come from the factory by special messenger, but not till the next day, of course. I felt terrible, you can bet, and I dreaded having to go back to the typewriter, searching out all my own mistakes and then having to make pen-and-ink corrections or to retype the page.

I went to bed in a foul humor, and didn't actually sleep much. First thing in the morning, or, anyway, after breakfast, I went into my office, and just as I walked up to the word processor, as though it could read my mind and tell that I was so annoyed I would cheerfully have kicked it off the desk and out the window—it started working.

All by itself, mind you. I never touched the keys. The

words appeared on the screen a lot more quickly than I could have made them appear and it began with:

FAULT-INTOLERANT
by Abram Ivanov

I simply stared. It went on to write my diary items concerning itself, as I have done above, but *much better.* The writing was smoother, more colorful, with a successful touch of humor. In fifteen minutes, it was done, and in five minutes the printer had placed it on sheets.

That apparently had just been for exercise, or for practice, for once that was done, the last page I had written of my novel appeared on the screen, and then the words began to proceed without me.

The word processor had clearly learned to write my stuff, just as I would have written it, only better.

Great! No more work. The word processor wrote it under my name and wrote with my style, given a certain amount of improvement. I could just let it go, pick up the surprised reviews from my critics telling the world how I had improved, and watch the royalties pour in.

That's all right as far as it goes, but I'm not America's most prolific writer for no reason. I happen to *love* to write. That happens to be all that I want to do.

Now if my word processor does my writing, what do *I* do with the rest of my life?

Kid Brother

It was a great shock to me when our application for a second child was refused. We had really expected to get the license.

I'm a respectable citizen; pillar of the community; all that kind of stuff. I was a little old, maybe. Josie—my wife—may have been past her best childbearing years. So what? We know other people worse off than us, older, trashy in character, who—Well, never mind.

We had one son, Charlie, and we really wanted another child. Boy or girl, it didn't matter. Of course, if there was something wrong with Charlie, if he developed some illness, maybe then we could license a second child. Or maybe not. And if we did get the license, they would probably take care of Charlie as a defective. You know what I mean; I don't have to say it.

The trouble was we were late getting started, and that was Josie's fault. She had irregular periods and you never knew when to get her, if you know what I mean. And we couldn't get any medical help, either. How could we? The clinics said if we couldn't have children without help, that was great for the world. It's patriotic, or something, to be childless.

But we fooled them and had a child after all. Charlie.

When Charlie was eight months old, we started applying for a second child. We wanted them pretty close in age. Was that so much to ask? Even if we were getting a little old for it? What kind of a world do we live in, anyway. No matter how much the population drops, they say it has to drop further, and if life gets easier and people live longer, it has to drop still further.

They won't be satisfied till they wipe out humanity alto—

—Well, look! I'll tell this just the way I want to. If you want the story, officer, you'll have to take it my way. What can you do to me? I really don't much care if I live or die. Would you in my position?

—Look, it's no use arguing. I'll tell it my way, or I'll shut up and you can do your worst. You understand?

—Well then, okay.

As it turned out, we didn't have to worry about Charlie being sickly, or anything like that. He grew like a bear, or one of those other animals that used to hang around in the woods and places like that in the old days. He came of good stock. You could see that. So why couldn't we have had another child? That's what I want to know.

Intelligent? You bet. Strong. Knew what he wanted. Ideal boy. When I think of it, I could—I could—Oh, well.

You should have seen him with the other kids as he was growing up. A natural leader. Always had his way. Always had the other children in the neighborhood doing what he wanted. He knew what he wanted and what he wanted was always right. That was the thing.

Josie didn't like it, though. She said he was spoiled. In fact, she said I spoiled him. I don't know what she was talking about. I was the making of him.

He was two years ahead of his age in strength and in brains. I could see that. And if the other children got out of line, sometimes he would have to show them who was boss.

Josie thought he was getting to be a bully. She said he had no friends; all the children were afraid of him.

So what! A leader doesn't want friends. He wants people to respect him, and if they get out of line, they better *fear* him. Charlie was coming along all right. Sure, the other children stayed away mostly. That was their parents' fault; and they're just a bunch of milksops. Once they get one child, and know they won't have any more, they start hovering over him or her like they were the family jewels, and rare jewels, too. You smother them if you do that. They become useless—worthless.

There was this guy Stevenson down the block. He had two girls, both pitiful things, giggling and empty-headed. How did he come to get two, I ask you? He knew somebody, maybe. A little money passed from hand to hand. Why not, he's got more money than he admits, too. Naturally. That accounts for it. You'd think with two, he could afford to risk one, but no—

—That's all right. I'll get to the point, when I get to the point. If you push, you'll get nothing and we'll let it go straight to the court. See if I care.

These other parents, they didn't want their babies hurt. Don't play with the Janowitz boy, they would say. I never heard them say so but I'm sure that's what they said. Well, who needed them? I was planning for Charlie to go to college eventually, so he could take courses in microelectronics or in spatial dynamics, or that kind of stuff. And economics and business, too, so he would know how to get money and power out of his know-how. That's the way I saw it. I wanted him on top of the heap.

But Josie kept talking about Charlie not having friends and Charlie growing up alone, and like that. All the time. It was like living in an echo chamber. And then, one day, she came to me and said, "Why don't we get Charlie a kid brother?"

"Oh, sure," I said. "You're past menopause so what do we do? Call in the stork? Look under cabbage leaves?"

I could have divorced her, you know. Married a young chick. After all, *I* wasn't past menopause. But I was—loyal. Fat lot of good that did me. Besides, if I had divorced her, she would mostly have kept Charlie, so what good would *that* have done me?

So I just made that comment about the stork.

She said, "I'm not talking about a biological child. I'm saying we can get a robot to be Charlie's brother."

I never expected to hear anything like that, you can bet. I'm not a robot-type guy. My parents never had one. I never had one. As far as I'm concerned, every robot means one less human, and we're just watching the world being turned over to them. Just one more way of wiping out humanity, if you ask me.

So I said to Josie, "Don't be ridiculous."

"Really," said Josie, all very earnest. "It's a new model. It's just designed to be friendly and pals for children. Nothing fancy, so they aren't expensive, and they do fill a need. With more and more people having only one child, there is a real value in supplying that one child with siblings."

"That may be true of other children. Not Charlie," I said.

"Yes, Charlie, especially. He's never going to find out how to deal with people this way. He's growing up alone, really alone. He won't come to understand the give and take of life."

"He's not going to give. He's a taker. He'll take power and he'll take position, and he'll tell people what to do. And he'll have children of his own and maybe even three."

You may be too young to feel this yet, officer, but if you have only one child, you'll eventually discover you'll still have a chance at another one when your child has a child. I had high hopes for Charlie. Before I died, I was sure I would see another child, maybe even two or three. They might be Charlie's but as far as our lives would overlap, I was going to make them mine, too.

But all Josie could think about was a robot. Life became another kind of echo chamber. She priced them out. She figured out the down payment. She looked into the possibility of renting one for a year on a kind of approval. She was willing to use her own nest egg that her folks had left her to pay for it, and things like that. And you know how it is, in the end you have to keep peace in the family.

I gave in. I said, "Okay, but you go pick one out and you better make it a rental. And you pay for it."

I figured, who knows. The robot would probably be a pain in the neck and wouldn't work out, and we'd return him.

They walked him into the house, didn't even crate him. I should say "it" but Josie insisted on saying "he" and "him" so he would seem more like a kid brother to Charlie, and I got into the habit.

He was a "sibling-robot"; that's what they called him. He had a registration number, but I never memorized it. What for? We just called him "Kid." That was good enough.

—Yes, I know that this sort of robot is getting popular. I don't know what's happening to human beings that they stand for such things.

And we stood for it, too. Or at least, I did. Josie was fascinated. The one we got was a pretty good one, I have to admit. He looked almost human, he smiled a lot, and he had a nice voice. He looked maybe fifteen, a small-sized fifteen, which wasn't too bad because Charlie was a large-sized ten.

Kid was a little taller than Charlie and, of course, heavier. You know, there were titanium bones or whatever inside him and a nuclear unit, guaranteed for ten years before replacement, and that's pretty heavy.

He had a good vocabulary, too, and he was very polite. Josie was just delighted. She said, "I can use him in the house. He can help out."

I said, "No, you don't. You got him for Charlie, and that means he's Charlie's. Don't you go taking him away."

I was thinking if Josie got him, and made him into a slavey, she'd never let go of him. Charlie, on the other hand, might not like him or might get tired after a little while, and then we could get rid of him.

Charlie fooled me, though. He liked Kid fine.

But you know, it made sense after a while. Kid was *designed* to be a kid brother, so he was just right for Charlie. He let Charlie take the lead, like an older brother should. He had those three Laws. I can't quote them, but you know what they are. There was no way he could hurt Charlie, and he had to do whatever Charlie said, so after a while I began to think it was a good deal.

I mean, when they played games Charlie always won. He was supposed to. And the Kid never got mad. He couldn't. He was made to lose. And sometimes Charlie kicked the Kid around, the way children do, you know. A child gets mad about something, he takes it out on some other child. Children always do that. Naturally, that gets the parents of the other child mad and I had to tell Charlie now and then not to do that and that sort of cramps him. It squeezes him in. He can't express himself.

Well, he could with the Kid. And why not? You can't hurt the Kid. He's made out of plastic and metal and who knows what else. For all he looked nearly like a human being, he wasn't alive; he couldn't feel pain.

In fact, I felt the best thing the Kid did was to be something on which Charlie could bleed off his excess energy so that it wouldn't accumulate in him and fester. And the Kid never minded. They'd play judo and the Kid would be thrown, and even stamped on, but he would just get up and say, "That was good, Charlie. Let's try it again." Listen, you could throw him off the top of a building and he wouldn't be hurt.

He was always polite to us. He called me Dad. He called Josie Mom. He asked after our health. He would help Josie out of her chair when she wanted to stand up. That sort of stuff.

He was designed that way. He had to act affectionate. It was all automatic. He was programmed for it. It didn't mean a thing, but Josie liked it. Listen, I've always been busy, hard-working. I have this plant I had to help run, interlocking machinery to oversee. One thing goes wrong and the whole shebang ties itself up. I have no time to bring flowers and go mucking around pulling out her chairs or something. We'd been married nearly twenty years and how long does that sort of thing keep up anyway?

And Charlie—Well, he stood up to his mother the way any decent boy should. And I figured the Kid helped there. When Charlie made himself boss over the Kid one minute, he wasn't going to run around saying, "Mommie, Mommie," the next minute. He was *not* a mamma's boy, and he didn't let Josie run him, and I was proud of him for that. He was going to be a man. Of course, he listened to what *I* said to him. A boy's got to listen to his father.

So maybe it was good that the Kid was designed to be a sort of mamma's boy. It gave Josie the feeling that there was one of those nerds about the house and it bothered her less that Charlie always thought for himself.

Of course you could count on Josie to do her best to spoil it. She was forever worrying about her pet nerd being hurt. She was always coming out with, "Now, Charlie, why don't you be nicer to your kid brother?"

It was ridiculous. I could never get it through her head

that the Kid wasn't hurt; that he was designed to be a loser; that it was all good for Charlie.

Of course, Charlie never listened to her. He played with the Kid the way *he* wanted to.

—Do you mind if I rest a little. I don't really like talking about all this. Just let me rest a while.

—Okay, I'm better now. I can go on.

After the year was up, I felt that it was enough. We could return the Kid to U.S. Robots. After all, he had served his purpose.

But Josie was against that. Dead set against that.

I said, "But we'd have to buy him outright now."

And she said, she would pay the down payment, so I went along with her.

One of the things she said was that we couldn't take away Charlie's brother. Charlie would be lonely.

And I did think, well, maybe she's right. I tell you it's deadly when you start thinking your wife might be right. It leads you into nothing but trouble.

Charlie did ease up on the Kid a little as he grew older. He got to be just as tall as the Kid, for one thing, so maybe he didn't think he had to knock him around as much.

Also, he became interested in things besides rough and tumble. Basketball, for instance; he played one-on-one with the Kid and Charlie was *good*. He always out-maneuvered the Kid and hardly ever missed a basket. Well, maybe the Kid let himself be outmaneuvered and maybe he didn't ever block a basket-shot efficiently, but how do you account for getting the ball into the basket? The Kid couldn't fake that, could he?

In the second year, the Kid sort of became a member of the family. He didn't eat with us or anything like that, because he didn't eat. And he didn't sleep either, so he just stood in the corner of Charlie's bedroom at night.

But he watched the holoviews with us, and Josie would always explain things to him so that he got to know more and to seem more human. She took him shopping with her and wherever else she went, if Charlie didn't need him. The Kid was always helpful, I suppose, and I guess he carried things for her and was always polite and attentive and that sort of thing.

And I'll tell you, Josie was more easygoing, with the Kid around. More good-humored, more good-natured, less whining. It made for a more pleasant homelife, and I figured, well, the Kid is teaching Charlie to be more and more dominant, and he's teaching Josie to smile more, so maybe it was a good thing it was there.

Then it happened.

—Listen, can you let me have something wet?

—Yeah, with alcohol. Just a little, just a little. Come on, what are you worrying about the rules for? I've got to get through this somehow.

Then it happened. One out of a million—or out of a billion. Microfusion units aren't supposed to give trouble. You can read about it anywhere. They're all fail-safe, no matter what. Except mine wasn't. I don't know why. Nobody knows why. At the start, no one even knew it was the microfusion. They've told me since that it was, and that I qualify for full restoration of the house and furniture.

Fat lot of good that would do me.

—Look, you're treating me as though I were a homicidal maniac, but why me? Why aren't you getting after the microfusion people for murder? Find out who made that unit, or who goofed up installing it.

Don't you people know what *real* crimes are? There's this thing, this microfusion—it doesn't explode, it doesn't make a noise, it just gets hotter and hotter and after a while the house is on fire. How come people can get away manufacturing—

—Yes, I'll get on with it. I'll get on with it.

I was away that day. That one day in a whole year I was away. I run everything from my home, or from wherever I am with my family. I don't have to *go* anywhere, the computers do it all. It's not like *your* job, officer.

But the big boss wanted to see me in person. There's no sense to it; everything could have been done closed-circuit. He has some sort of idea, though, that he wants to check all his section heads every once in a while in person. He seems to think that you can't really judge a person unless you see him in three dimensions and smell him and feel him. It's just superstition left over from the Dark Age—which I wish would come back, before computers and robots, and when you could have all the children you wanted.

That was the day when the microfusion went.

I got the word right away. You always get the word. Wherever you are, even on the Moon or in a space settlement, bad news gets to you in seconds. Good news you might miss out on, but bad news never.

I was rushing back while the house was still burning.

When I got there, the house was a total wreck, but Josie was out on the lawn, looking a complete mess, but alive. She had been out on the lawn when it happened, they told me.

When she saw the house become all in flame, and Charlie was inside, she rushed in at once, and I could see she must have brought him out because there he was lying to one side with people bending over him. It looked bad. I couldn't see him. I didn't dare go over there to see him. I had to find out from Josie first.

I could hardly speak. "How bad is he?" I asked Josie, and I didn't recognize my own voice. I think my mind was beginning to go.

She was saying, "I couldn't save them both. I couldn't save them both."

Why should she want to save them both? I thought. I said, "Stop worrying about the Kid. He's just a *device*. There's insurance and compassion money and we can buy another Kid." I think I tried to say all that, but I don't know if I managed. Maybe I just made hoarse, choking sounds. I don't know.

I don't know if she heard me, or if she even knew I was there. She just kept whispering, "I had to make a choice," over and over.

So I *had* to go where Charlie was lying and I cleared my throat and I managed to say, "How's my boy? How badly is he hurt?"

And one of them said, "Maybe he can be fixed up," then he looked up at me and said, "Your *boy?*"

I saw the Kid lying there, with one arm distorted and out of action. He was smiling as if nothing had happened, and he was saying, "Hello, Dad. Mom pulled me out of the fire. Where's Charlie?"

Josie had made her choice and she had saved the Kid.

I don't know what happened after that. I remember nothing. You people say I killed her; that you couldn't pull me off before I strangled her.

Maybe. I don't know. I don't remember. All I know is— *she's* the killer.

She killed—she killed—Char—

She killed my boy and she saved a piece—

A piece of—

Titanium.

The Nations in Space
A Modern Fable

As is well known, the nations of Gladovia and Saronin have been enemies for many centuries. In medieval times, each had ruled the other at different times, and each remembered, with bitterness, the other's heavy-handed domination. Even in the twentieth century, the two nations had managed to be on opposite sides in the major wars that were then fought.

In the century of peace that followed the last of the great wars, Gladovia and Saronin had also been at peace, but always regarded each other with a sneer and a curl of the lip.

But it was now 2080, and the solar power stations were in orbit about Earth collecting energy from the Sun and relaying it in the form of microwaves to the nations of all the world. It had utterly changed the world in many ways. With copious solar energy, the use of fossil fuels had dwindled, and the danger of the greenhouse effect had diminished (although some excess heat arising from solar energy did produce *some* heat pollution).

With copious energy and with better population control, standards of living rose, the food supply improved, the distribution of resources was rationalized and, in general, an era of prosperity and contentment was in bloom.

One thing, however, that had not changed was the antipathy of Gladovians for Saronin, and the dislike of the Saronese for Gladovia.

Of course, the solar power stations did not run themselves. Despite thorough automation and the intense use of robots, it was still important for a few human beings to inspect the various stations periodically to make sure that all was running well and that tiny flecks of space debris and unexpected spurts of solar wind did not alter the workings of the computers beyond the capacity of the robots, and of the computers themselves, to correct matters.

Those chosen for the task served their stints and were regularly rotated so that the effects of zero gravity could be minimized by rest periods on Earth's surface. It was purely coincidence, then, that the Space-Servitors (as they were called) in the summer of 2080, consisted, among others, of two Gladovians and two Saronese. These traditional enemies were thrown together in the course of their work and they performed their tasks correctly, but were careful to restrict communications with each other to the barest essentials and to refrain from any smiles or warmth.

And one day, the younger Gladovian, Tomasz Brigon by name, came to the older one, Hamish Mansa, with a tense smile of delight, and said, "That fool of a Saronese has done it this time."

"Which one?" asked Mansa.

"The one whose name sounds like a sneeze. Who can speak that foolish Saronese language? In any case, with true Saronese stupidity he has miscued Computer A-5."

Mansa looked alarmed. "With what result?"

"None yet. But whenever the solar wind density rises above the 1.3 level, it will shut down half the power stations and burn out several of the computers."

"And what did you do about that?" Mansa's eyes opened wide.

"Nothing," said Brigon. "I was there and I saw it happen. Now, it's on the record. The Saronese identified himself as the worker on the Computer, and when the power stations shut down, and the computers burn out, the world will know that it was a stupid Saronese that did it." Brigon stretched his arms luxuriously and said, with delight, "Everyone in the world will be furious, and the whole wicked nation of Saronin will be humiliated."

Mansa said, "But meanwhile the energy supply to Earth will be totally disrupted, and it may not be possible to restore the system to working order for months, perhaps for a year or two."

"Plenty of time," said Brigon, "for the world to wipe Saronin from the face of the Earth, so that our own glorious nation of Gladovia can take over the territory that is rightfully ours."

"But think a bit," said Mansa. "With so much energy suddenly gone, the world will be too busy trying to save itself from disaster to engage in crusades. There will be disruption of industry, the danger of starvation, the gathering of mobs of the distressed, the fighting over what energy can be obtained—total chaos."

"All the worse for Saronin—"

"But the chaos will come to Gladovia, too. Our glorious nation depends on the solar energy supply just as Saronin does, just as the whole world does. There will be a world of catastrophe from which—who can tell—Gladovia may suffer far worse than Saronin. Who can tell?"

Brigon's mouth fell open and he looked disturbed. "Do you really think so?"

"Of course. You must go to the one whose name is like a

sneeze, and ask him to recheck his work. You needn't say you *know* something is wrong. It's simply that you were there, and you suddenly have this strange feeling that all is not well. Say you have a presentiment. And if he finds the miscue and corrects it, do not taunt him. It would not be safe to do so. And do it quickly! For the glorious nation of Gladovia! And for the world, of course."

Brigon had no choice. He did so, and the peril was averted.

MORAL:

People always love themselves best. But in a world so inter-connected that harm to one is harm to all, the best way of loving one's self is to love everyone else, too.

The Smile of the Chipper

Johnson was reminiscing in the way old men do and I had been warned he would talk about chippers—those peculiar people who flashed across the business scene for a generation at the beginning of this twenty-first century of ours. Still, I had had a good meal at his expense and I was ready to listen.

And, as it happened, it was the first word out of his mouth. "Chippers," he said, "were just about unregulated in those days. Nowadays, their use is so controlled no one can get any good out of them, but back a ways—One of them made this company the ten-billion-dollar concern it now is. I picked him, you know."

I said, "They didn't last long, I'm told."

"Not in those days. They burned out. When you add microchips at key points in the nervous system, then in ten years at the most, the wiring burns out, so to speak. Then they retired—a little vacant-minded, you know."

"I wonder anyone submitted to it."

"Well, all the idealists were horrified, of course, and that's why the regulating came in, but it wasn't that bad for the chippers. Only certain people could make use of the mi-

crochips—about eighty percent of them males, for some reason—and, for the time they were active, they lived the lives
of shipping magnates. Afterward, they always received the
best of care. It was no different from top-ranking athletes,
after all; ten years of active early life, and then retirement."

Johnson sipped at his drink. "An unregulated chipper
could influence other people's emotions, you know, if they
were chipped just right and had talent. They could make
judgments on the basis of what they sensed in other minds
and they could strengthen some of the judgments competitors were making, or weaken them—for the good of the
home company. It wasn't unfair. Other companies had their
own chippers doing the same thing." He sighed. "Now that
sort of thing is illegal. Too bad."

I said, diffidently, "I've heard that illegal chipping is still
done."

Johnson grunted and said, "No comment."

I let that go, and he went on. "But even thirty years ago,
things were still wide open. Our company was just an insignificant item in the global economy, but we had located
two chippers who were willing to work for us."

"Two?" I had never heard *that* before.

Johnson looked at me slyly. "Yes, we managed that. It's
not widely known in the outside world, but it came down to
clever recruiting and it was slightly—just a touch—illegal,
even then. Of course, we couldn't hire them both. Getting
two chippers to work together is impossible. They're like
chess grandmasters, I suppose. Put them in the same room
and they would automatically challenge each other. They
would compete continually, each trying to influence and
confute the other. They wouldn't stop—*couldn't*, actually—
and they would burn each other out in six months. Several
companies found that out, to their great cost, when chippers
first came into use."

"I can imagine," I murmured.

"So since we couldn't have both, and could only take one, we wanted the more powerful one, obviously, and that could only be determined by pitting them against each other, without letting them ruin each other. I was given the job, and it was made quite clear that if I picked the one who, in the end, turned out to be inadequate, that would be my end, too."

"How did you go about it, sir?" I knew he had succeeded, of course. A person can't become chairman of the board of a world-class firm for nothing.

Johnson said, "I had to improvise. I investigated each separately first. The two were known by their code-letters, by the way. In those days, their true identities had to be hidden. A chipper known to be a chipper was half-useless. They were C-12 and F-71 in our records. Both were in their late twenties. C-12 was unattached; F-71 was engaged to be married."

"Married?" I said, a little surprised.

"Certainly. Chippers are human, and male chippers are much sought after by women. They're sure to be rich and, when they retire, their fortunes are usually under the control of their wives. It's a good deal for a young woman.—So I brought them together, *with* F-71's fiancée. I hoped earnestly she would be good-looking, and she was. Meeting her was almost like a physical blow to me. She was the most beautiful woman I had ever seen, tall, dark-eyed, a marvelous figure and rather more than a hint of smoldering sexuality."

Johnson seemed lost in thought for a moment, then he continued. "I tell you I had a strong urge to try to win the woman for myself but it was not likely that anyone who had a chipper would transfer herself to a mere junior executive, which is what I was in those days. To transfer herself to another chipper would be something else—and I could see that C-12 was as affected as I was. He could *not* keep his eyes off her. So I just let things develop to see who ended with the young woman."

"And who did, sir?" I asked.

"It took two days of intense mental conflict. They must each have peeled a month off their working lives, but the young lady walked off with C-12 as her new fiancée."

"Ah, so you chose C-12 as the firm chipper."

Johnson stared at me with disdain. "Are you mad? I did no such thing. I chose F-71, of course. We placed C-12 with a small subsidiary of ours. He'd be no good to anyone else, since we knew him, you see."

"But did I miss something? F-71 lost his fiancée and C-12 gained her. Surely C-12 was the superior."

"Was he? Chippers show no emotion in a case like this; no obvious emotion. It is necessary for business purposes for chippers to hide their powers so that the pokerface is a professional necessity for them. But I was watching closely—my own job was at stake—and, as C-12 walked off with the woman, I noticed a small smile on F-71's lips and it seemed to me there was the glitter of victory in his eyes."

"But he lost his fiancée."

"Doesn't it occur to you he *wanted* to lose her and it would not be easy to pry her loose? He had to work on C-12 to want her and on the woman to want to be wanted—and he did it. He won."

I thought about that. "But how could you have been sure? If the woman was as good-looking as you say she was—if she was smoldering so with sexuality, surely F-71 would have wanted to keep her."

"But F-71 was making her seem desirable," said Johnson, grimly. "He aimed at C-12, of course, but with such power that the overflow was sufficient to affect me drastically.

After it was all over and C-12 was walking away with her, I was no longer under the influence and I could see there was something hard and overblown about her—a kind of unlovely and predatory gleam in her eye.

"So I chose F-71 at once and he was all we could want. The firm is now where you see it is, and I am chairman of the board."

Gold

Jonas Willard looked from side to side and tapped his baton on the stand before him.

He said, "Understood now? This is just a practice scene, designed to find out if we know what we're doing. We've gone through this enough times so that I expect a professional performance now. Get ready. All of you get ready."

He looked again from side to side. There was a person at each of the voice-recorders, and there were three others working the image projection. A seventh was for the music and an eighth for the all-important background. Others waited to one side for their turn.

Willard said, "All right now. Remember this old man has spent his entire adult life as a tyrant. He is accustomed to having everyone jump at his slightest word, to having everyone tremble at his frown. That is all gone now but he doesn't know it. He faces his daughter whom he thinks of only as a bent-headed obsequious girl who will do anything he says, and he cannot believe that it is an imperious queen that he now faces. So let's have the King."

Lear appeared. Tall, white hair and beard, somewhat disheveled, eyes sharp and piercing.

Willard said, "Not bent. Not bent. He's eighty years old but he doesn't think of himself as old. Not now. Straight. Every inch a king." The image was adjusted. "That's right. And the voice has to be strong. No quavering. Not now. Right?"

"Right, chief," said the Lear voice-recorder, nodding.

"All right. The Queen."

And there she was, almost as tall as Lear, standing straight and rigid as a statue, her draped clothing in fine array, nothing out of place. Her beauty was as cold and unforgiving as ice.

"And the Fool."

A little fellow, thin and fragile, like a frightened teenager but with a face too old for a teenager and with a sharp look in eyes that seemed so large that they threatened to devour his face.

"Good," said Willard. "Be ready for Albany. He comes in pretty soon. Begin the scene." He tapped the podium again, took a quick glance at the marked-up play before him and said, "Lear!" and his baton pointed to the Lear voice-recorder, moving gently to mark the speech cadence that he wanted created.

Lear says, "How now, daughter? What makes that frontlet on? Methinks you are too much o' late i' th' frown."

The Fool's thin voice, fifelike, piping, interrupts, "Thou wast a pretty fellow when thou hadst no need to care for her frowning—"

Goneril, the Queen, turns slowly to face the Clown as he speaks, her eyes turning momentarily into balls of lurid light—doing it so momentarily that those watching caught the impression rather than viewed the fact. The Fool completes his speech in gathering fright and backs his way behind Lear in a blind search for protection against the searing glance.

Goneril proceeds to tell Lear the facts of life and there is the faint crackling of thin ice as she speaks, while the music plays in soft discords, barely heard.

Nor are Goneril's demands so out of line, for she wants an orderly court and there couldn't be one as long as Lear still thought of himself as tyrant. But Lear is in no mood to recognize reason. He breaks into a passion and begins railing.

Albany enters. He is Goneril's consort—round-faced, innocent, eyes looking about in wonder. What is happening? He is completely drowned out by his dominating wife and by his raging father-in-law. It is at this point that Lear breaks into one of the great piercing denunciations in all of literature. He is overreacting. Goneril has not as yet done anything to deserve *this*, but Lear knows no restraint. He says:

> *"Hear, Nature, hear! dear goddess, hear!*
> *Suspend thy purpose, if thou didst intend*
> *To make this creature fruitful.*
> *Into her womb convey sterility;*
> *Dry up in her the organs of increase;*
> *And from her derogate body never spring*
> *A babe to honour her! If she must teem,*
> *Create her child of spleen, that it may live*
> *And be a thwart disnatur'd torment to her.*
> *Let it stamp wrinkles in her brow of youth,*
> *With cadent tears fret channels in her cheeks,*
> *Turn all her mother's pains and benefits*
> *To laughter and contempt, that she may feel*
> *How sharper than a serpent's tooth, it is*
> *To have a thankless child!"*

The voice-recorder strengthened Lear's voice for this speech, gave it a distant hiss, his body became taller and somehow less substantial as though it had been converted into a vengeful Fury.

As for Goneril, she remained untouched throughout, never flinching, never receding, but her beautiful face, without any change that could be described, seemed to accumulate evil so that by the end of Lear's curse, she had the appearance of an archangel still, but an archangel ruined. All possible pity had been wiped out of the countenance, leaving behind only a devil's dangerous magnificence.

The Fool remained behind Lear throughout, shuddering. Albany was the very epitome of confusion, asking useless questions, seeming to want to step between the two antagonists and clearly afraid to do so.

Willard tapped his baton and said, "All right. It's been recorded and I want you all to watch the scene." He lifted his baton high and the synthesizer at the rear of the set began what could only be called the instant replay.

It was watched in silence, and Willard said, "It was good, but I think you'll grant it was not good enough. I'm going to ask you all to listen to me, so that I can explain what we're trying to do. Computerized theater is not new, as you all know. Voices and images have been built up to beyond what human beings can do. You don't have to break your speechifying in order to breathe; the range and quality of the voices are almost limitless; and the images can change to suit the words and action. Still, the technique has only been used, so far, for childish purposes. What we intend now is to make the first serious compu-drama the world has ever seen, and nothing will do—for me, at any rate—but to start at the top. I want to do the greatest play written by the greatest playwright in history: *King Lear* by William Shakespeare.

"I want not a word changed. I want not a word left out. I don't want to modernize the play. I don't want to remove the archaisms, because the play, *as written*, has its glorious music and any change will diminish it. But in that case, how do we have it reach the general public? I don't mean the students, I don't mean the intellectuals, I mean *everybody*. I mean people who've never watched Shakespeare before and whose idea of a good play is a slapstick musical. This play *is* archaic in spots, and people don't talk in iambic pentameter. They are not even accustomed to hearing it on the stage.

"So we're going to have to translate the archaic and the unusual. The voices, more than human, will, just by their timbre and changes, interpret the words. The images will shift to reinforce the words.

"Now Goneril's change in appearance as Lear's curse proceeded was good. The viewer will gauge the devastating effect it has on her even though her iron will won't let it show in words. The viewer will therefore feel the devastating effect upon himself, too, even if some of the words Lear uses are strange to him.

"In that connection, we must remember to make the Fool look older with every one of his appearances. He's a weak, sickly fellow to begin with, broken-hearted over the loss of Cordelia, frightened to death of Goneril and Regan, destroyed by the storm from which Lear, his only protector, can't protect him—and I mean by that the storm of Lear's daughter as well as of the raging weather. When he slips out of the play in Act III, Scene VI, it must be made plain that he is about to die. Shakespeare doesn't say so, so the Fool's face must say so.

"However, we've got to do something about Lear. The voice-recorder was on the right track by having a hissing sound in the voice-track. Lear is spewing venom; he is a man who, having lost power, has no recourse but vile and extreme words. He is a cobra who cannot strike. But I don't want the hiss noticeable until the right time. What I am more interested in is the background."

The woman in charge of background was Meg Cathcart. She had been creating backgrounds for as long as the compu-drama technique had existed.

"What do you want in background?" Cathcart asked, coolly.

"The snake motif," said Willard. "Give me some of that and there can be less hiss in Lear's voice. Of course, I don't want you to show a snake. The too obvious doesn't work. I want a snake there that people can't see but that they can *feel* without quite noting *why* they feel. I want them to know a snake is there without really knowing it is there, so that it will chill them to the bone, as Lear's speech should. So when we do it over, Meg, give us a snake that is not a snake."

"And how do I do that, Jonas?" said Cathcart, making free with his first name. She knew her worth and how essential she was.

He said, "I don't know. If I did I'd be a backgrounder instead of a lousy director. I only know what I want. You've got to supply it. You've got to supply sinuosity, the impression of scales. Until we get to one point. Notice when Lear says, 'How sharper than a serpent's tooth it is to have a thankless child.' That is *power*. The whole speech leads up to that and it is one of the most famous quotes in Shakespeare. And it is *sibilant*. There is the 'sh,' the three s's in 'serpent's' and in 'thankless,' and the two unvoiced 'th's in 'tooth' and 'thankless.' *That* can be hissed. If you keep down the hiss as much as possible in the rest of the speech, you can hiss here, and you should zero in to his face and make it venomous. And for background, the serpent—which, after all, is now referred to in the words—can make its appearance in background. A flash of an open mouth and fangs, fangs—We must have the momentary appearance of fangs as Lear says, 'a serpent's tooth.' "

Willard felt very tired suddenly. "All right. We'll try again tomorrow. I want each one of you to go over the entire scene and try to work out the strategy you intend to use. Only please remember that you are not the only ones involved. What you do must match the others, so I'll encourage you to talk to each other about this—and, most of all, to listen to *me* because I have no instrument to handle and I alone can see the play as a whole. And if I seem as tyrannical as Lear at his worst in spots, well, that's my job."

Willard was approaching the great storm scene, the most difficult portion of this most difficult play, and he felt wrung out. Lear has been cast out by his daughters into a raging storm of wind and rain, with only his Fool for company, and he has gone almost mad at this mistreatment. To him, even the storm is not as bad as his daughters.

Willard pointed his baton and Lear appeared. A point in another direction and the Fool was there clinging, disregarded, to Lear's left leg. Another point and the background came in, with its impression of a storm, of a howling wind, of driving rain, of the crackle of thunder and the flash of lightning.

The storm took over, a phenomenon of nature, but even as it did so, the image of Lear extended and became what seemed mountain-tall. The storm of his emotions matched the storm of the elements, and his voice gave back to the wind every last howl. His body lost substance and wavered with the wind as though he himself were a storm cloud, contending on an equal basis with the atmospheric fury. Lear, having failed with his daughters, defied the storm to do its worst. He called out in a voice that was far more than human:

"Blow, winds, and crack your cheeks! rage! blow!
You cataracts and hurricanoes, spout
Till you have drench'd our steeples, drown'd the cocks!
You sulph'rous and thought-executing fires,
Vaunt-couriers to oak-cleaving thunderbolts,
Singe my white head! And thou, all-shaking thunder,
Strike flat the thick rotundity o' th' world.
Crack Nature's moulds, all germains spill at once,
That make ingrateful man."

The Fool interrupts, his voice shrilling, and making
Lear's defiance the more heroic by contrast. He begs Lear
to make his way back to the castle and make peace with his
daughters, but Lear doesn't even hear him. He roars on:

"Rumble thy bellyful! Spit, fire! spout, rain!
Nor rain, wind, thunder, fire are my daughters.
I tax not you, you elements, with unkindness.
I never gave you kingdom, call'd you children,
You owe me no subscription. Then let fall
Your horrible pleasure. Here I stand your slave,
A poor, infirm, weak, and despis'd old man. . . ."

The Duke of Kent, Lear's loyal servant (though the King
in a fit of rage has banished him) finds Lear and tries to lead
him to some shelter. After an interlude in the castle of the
Duke of Gloucester, the scene returns to Lear in the storm,
and he is brought, or rather dragged, to a hovel.

And then, finally, Lear learns to think of others. He in-
sists that the Fool enter first and then he lingers outside to
think (undoubtedly for the first time in his life) of the plight
of those who are not kings and courtiers.

His image shrank and the wildness of his face smoothed

out. His head was lifted to the rain, and his words seemed detached and to be coming not quite from him, as though he were listening to someone else read the speech. It was, after all, not the old Lear speaking, but a new and better Lear, refined and sharpened by suffering. With an anxious Kent watching, and striving to lead him into the hovel, and with Meg Cathcart managing to work up an impression of beggars merely by producing the fluttering of rags, Lear says:

> *"Poor naked wretches, wheresoe'er you are,*
> *That bide the pelting of this pitiless storm.*
> *How shall your houseless heads and unfed sides,*
> *Your loop'd and window'd raggedness, defend you*
> *From seasons such as these? O, I have ta'en*
> *Too little care of this! Take physic, pomp;*
> *Expose thyself to feel what wretches feel,*
> *That thou mayst shake the superflux to them*
> *And show the heavens more just."*

"Not bad," said Wilbur, eventually. "We're getting the idea. Only, Meg, rags aren't enough. Can you manage an impression of hollow eyes? Not blind ones. The eyes are there, but sunken in."

"I think I can do that," said Cathcart.

It was difficult for Willard to believe. The money spent was greater than expected. The time it had taken was considerably greater than had been expected. And the general weariness was far greater than had been expected. Still, the project was coming to an end.

He had the reconciliation scene to get through—so simple that it would require the most delicate touches. There would be no background, no souped-up voices, no images, for at this point Shakespeare became simple. Nothing beyond simplicity was needed.

Lear was an old man, just an old man. Cordelia, having found him, was a loving daughter, with none of the majesty of Goneril, none of the cruelty of Regan, just softly endearing.

Lear, his madness burned out of him, is slowly beginning to understand the situation. He scarcely recognizes Cordelia at first and thinks he is dead and she is a heavenly spirit. Nor does he recognize the faithful Kent.

When Cordelia tries to bring him back the rest of the way to sanity, he says:

> *"Pray, do not mock me.*
> *I am a very foolish fond old man.*
> *Fourscore and upward, not an hour more nor less.*
> *And, to deal plainly,*
> *I fear I am not in my perfect mind.*
> *Methinks I should know you, and know this man;*
> *Yet I am doubtful; for I am mainly ignorant*
> *What place this is; and all the skills I have*
> *Remembers not these garments; nor I know not*
> *Where I did lodge last night. Do not laugh at me;*
> *For (as I am a man) I think this lady*
> *To be my child Cordelia."*

Cordelia tells him she is and he says:

> *"Be your tears wet? Yes, faith. I pray weep not.*
> *If you have poison for me, I will drink it.*
> *I know you do not love me; for your sisters*
> *Have, as I do remember, done me wrong.*
> *You have some cause, they have not."*

All poor Cordelia can say is "No cause, no cause."

And eventually, Willard was able to draw a deep breath and say, "We've done all we can do. The rest is in the hands of the public."

It was a year later that Willard, now the most famous man in the entertainment world, met Gregory Laborian. It had come about almost accidentally and largely because of the activities of a mutual friend. Willard was not grateful.

He greeted Laborian with what politeness he could manage and cast a cold eye on the time-strip on the wall.

He said, "I don't want to seem unpleasant or inhospitable, Mr.—uh—but I'm really a very busy man, and don't have much time."

"I'm sure of it, but that's why I want to see you. Surely, you want to do another compu-drama."

"Surely I intend to, but," and Willard smiled dryly, "*King Lear* is a hard act to follow and I don't intend to turn out something that will seem like trash in comparison."

"But what if you never find anything that can match *King Lear?*"

"I'm sure I never will, but I'll find *something.*"

"I *have* something."

"Oh?"

"I have a story, a novel, that could be made into a compu-drama."

"Oh, well. I can't really deal with items that come in over the transom."

"I'm not offering you something from a slush pile. The novel has been published and it has been rather highly thought of."

"I'm sorry. I don't want to be insulting. But I didn't recognize your name when you introduced yourself."

"Laborian. Gregory Laborian."

"But I still don't recognize it. I've never read anything by you. I've never heard of you."

Laborian sighed. "I wish you were the only one, but you're not. Still, I could give you a copy of my novel to read."

Willard shook his head. "That's kind of you, Mr. Laborian, but I don't want to mislead you. I have no time to read it. And even if I had the time—I just want you to understand—I don't have the inclination."

"I could make it worth your while, Mr. Willard."

"In what way?"

"I could pay you. I wouldn't consider it a bribe, merely an offer of money that you would well deserve if you worked with my novel."

"I don't think you understand, Mr. Laborian, how much money it takes to make a first-class compu-drama. I take it you're not a multimillionaire."

"No, I'm not, but I can pay you a hundred thousand globo-dollars."

"If that's a bribe, at least it's a totally ineffective one. For a hundred thousand globo-dollars, I couldn't do a single scene."

Laborian sighed again. His large brown eyes looked soulful. "I understand, Mr. Willard, but if you'll just give me a few more minutes—" (for Willard's eyes were wandering to the time-strip again.)

"Well, five more minutes. That's all I can manage really."

"It's all I need. I'm not offering the money for making the compu-drama. You know, and I know, Mr. Willard, that you can go to any of a dozen people in the country and say you are doing a compu-drama and you'll get all the money you need. After *King Lear*, no one will refuse you anything, or even ask you what you plan to do. I'm offering you one hundred thousand globo-dollars for your own use."

"Then it *is* a bribe, and that won't work with me. Good-bye, Mr. Laborian."

"Wait. I'm not offering you an electronic switch. I don't suggest that I place my financial card into a slot and that you do so, too, and that a hundred thousand globo-dollars be transferred from my account to yours. I'm talking *gold*, Mr. Willard."

Willard had risen from his chair, ready to open the door and usher Laborian out, but now he hesitated. "What do you mean, gold?"

"I mean that I can lay my hands on a hundred thousand globo-dollars of gold, about fifteen pounds' worth, I think. I may not be a multimillionaire, but I'm quite well off and I wouldn't be stealing it. It would be my own money and I am entitled to draw it in gold. There is nothing illegal about it. What I am offering you is a hundred thousand globo-dollars in five-hundred globo-dollar pieces—two hundred of them. *Gold*, Mr. Willard."

Gold! Willard was hesitating. Money, when it was a matter of electronic exchange, meant nothing. There was no feeling of either wealth or of poverty above a certain level. The world was a matter of plastic cards (each keyed to a nucleic acid pattern) and of slots, and all the world transferred, transferred, transferred.

Gold was different. It had a feel. Each piece had a weight. Piled together it had a gleaming beauty. It was wealth one could appreciate and experience. Willard had never even seen a gold coin, let alone felt or hefted one. Two hundred of them!

He didn't need the money. He was not so sure he didn't need the gold.

He said, with a kind of shamefaced weakness, "What kind of a novel is it that you are talking about?"

"Science fiction."

Willard made a face. "I've never read science fiction."

"Then it's time you expanded your horizons, Mr. Willard. Read mine. If you imagine a gold coin between every two pages of the book, you will have your two hundred."

And Willard, rather despising his own weakness, said, "What's the name of your book?"

"*Three in One.*"

"And you have a copy?"

"I brought one with me."

And Willard held out his hand and took it.

That Willard was a busy man was by no means a lie. It took him better than a week to find the time to read the book, even with two hundred pieces of gold glittering, and luring him on.

Then he sat a while and pondered. Then he phoned Laborian.

The next morning, Laborian was in Williard's office again.

Willard said, bluntly, "Mr. Laborian, I have read your book."

Laborian nodded and could not hide the anxiety in his eyes. "I hope you like it, Mr. Willard."

Willard lifted his hand and rocked it right and left. "So-so. I told you I have not read science fiction, and I don't know how good or bad it is of its kind—"

"Does it matter, if you liked it?"

"I'm not sure if I liked it. I'm not used to this sort of thing. We are dealing in this novel with three sexes."

"Yes."

"Which you call a Rational, an Emotional, and a Parental."

"Yes."

"But you don't describe them?"

Laborian looked embarrassed. "I didn't describe them, Mr. Willard, because I couldn't. They're alien creatures, really alien. I didn't want to pretend they were alien by simply giving them blue skins or a pair of antennae or a third eye. I *wanted* them indescribable, so I didn't describe them, you see."

"What you're saying is that your imagination failed."

"N—no. I wouldn't say that. It's more like not having that *kind* of imagination. I don't describe anyone. If I were to write a story about you and me, I probably wouldn't bother describing either one of us."

Willard stared at Laborian without trying to disguise his contempt. He thought of himself. Middle-sized, soft about the middle, needed to reduce a bit, the beginnings of a double chin, and a mole on his right wrist. Light brown hair, dark blue eyes, bulbous nose. What was so hard to describe? Anyone could do it. If you had an imaginary character, think of someone real—and describe.

There was Laborian, dark in complexion, crisp curly black hair, looked as though he needed a shave, probably looked that way all the time, prominent Adam's apple, small scar on the right cheek, dark brown eyes rather large, and his only good feature.

Willard said, "I don't understand you. What kind of writer are you if you have trouble describing things? What do you write?"

Laborian said, gently, somewhat as though this was not the first time he had had to defend himself along those lines, "You've read *Three in One*. I've written other novels and they're all in the same style. Mostly conversation. I don't see things when I write; I *hear*, and for the most part, what my characters talk about are ideas—competing ideas. I'm strong on that and my readers like it."

"Yes, but where does that leave *me?* I can't devise a compu-drama based on conversation alone. I have to create sight and sound and subliminal messages, and you leave me nothing to work on."

"Are you thinking of doing *Three in One*, then?"

"Not if you give me nothing to work on. Think, Mr. Laborian, think! This Parental. He's the dumb one."

"Not dumb," said Laborian, frowning. "Single-minded. He only has room in his mind for children, real and potential."

"Blockish! If you didn't use that actual word for the Parental in the novel, and I don't remember offhand whether you did or not, it's certainly the impression I got. Cubical. Is that what he is?"

"Well, simple. Straight lines. Straight planes. Not cubical. Longer than he is wide."

"How does he move? Does he have legs?"

"I don't know. I honestly never gave it any thought."

"Hmp. And the Rational. He's the smart one and he's smooth and quick. What is he? Egg-shaped?"

"I'd accept that. I've never given that any thought, either, but I'd accept that."

"And no legs?"

"I haven't described any."

"And how about the middle one. Your 'she' character—the other two being 'he's.' "

"The Emotional."

"That's right. The Emotional. You did better on her."

"Of course. I did most of my thinking about her. She was trying to save the alien intelligences—us—of an alien world, Earth. The reader's sympathy must be with her, even though she fails."

"I gather she was more like a cloud, didn't have any firm shape at all, could attenuate and tighten."

"Yes, yes. That's exactly right."

"Does she flow along the ground or drift through the air?"

Laborian thought, then shook his head. "I don't know. I would say you would have to suit yourself when it came to that."

"I see. And what about the sex?"

Laborian said, with sudden enthusiasm. "That's a crucial point. I never have any sex in my novels beyond that which is absolutely necessary and then I manage to refrain from describing it—"

"You don't like sex?"

"I like sex fine, thank you. I just don't like it in my novels. Everyone else puts it in and, frankly, I think that readers find its absence in my novels refreshing; at least, my readers do. And I must explain to you that my books do very well. I wouldn't have a hundred thousand dollars to spend if they didn't."

"All right. I'm not trying to put you down."

"However, there are always people who say I don't include sex because I don't know how, so—out of vainglory, I suppose—I wrote this novel just to show that I *could* do it. The entire novel deals with sex. Of course, it's alien sex, not at all like ours."

"That's right. That's why I have to ask you about the mechanics of it. How does it work?"

Laborian looked uncertain for a moment. "They melt."

"I know that that's the word you use. Do you mean they come together? Superimpose?"

"I suppose so."

Willard sighed. "How can you write a book without knowing anything about so fundamental a part of it?"

"I don't have to describe it in detail. The reader gets the impression. With subliminal suggestion so much a part of the compu-drama, how can you ask the question?"

Willard's lips pressed together. Laborian had him there. "Very well. They superimpose. What do they look like after they have superimposed?"

Laborian shook his head. "I avoided that."

"You realize, of course, that I can't."

Laborian nodded. "Yes."

Willard heaved another sigh and said, "Look, Mr. Laborian, assuming that I agree to do such a compu-drama—and I have not yet made up my mind on the matter—I would have to do it entirely my way. I would tolerate no interference from you. You have ducked so many of your own responsibilities in writing the book that I can't allow you to decide suddenly that you want to participate in my creative endeavors."

"That's quite understood, Mr. Willard. I only ask that you keep my story and as much of my dialogue as you can. All of the visual, sonic, and subliminal aspects I am willing to leave entirely in your hands."

"You understand that this is not a matter of a verbal agreement which someone in our industry, about a century and a half ago, described as not worth the paper it was written on. There will have to be a written contract made firm by my lawyers that will exclude you from participation."

"My lawyers will be glad to look over it, but I assure you I am not going to quibble."

"*And,*" said Willard severely, "I will want an advance on the money you offered me. I can't afford to have you change your mind on me and I am not in the mood for a long lawsuit."

At this, Laborian frowned. He said, "Mr. Willard, those who know me *never* question my financial honesty. You don't know me so I'll permit the remark, but please don't repeat it. How much of an advance do you wish?"

"Half," said Willard, briefly.

Laborian said, "I will do better than that. Once you have obtained the necessary commitments from those who will be willing to put up the money for the compu-drama and once the contract between us is drawn up, then I will give you every cent of the hundred thousand dollars even before you begin the first scene of the book."

Willard's eyes opened wide and he could not prevent himself from saying, "Why?"

"Because I want to urge you on. What's more, if the compu-drama turns out to be too hard to do, if it won't work, or if you turn out something that will not do—my hard luck—you can keep the hundred thousand. It's a risk I'm ready to take."

"Why? What's the catch?"

"No catch. I'm gambling on immortality. I'm a popular writer but I have never heard anyone call me a great one. My books are very likely to die with me. Do *Three in One* as a compu-drama and do it well and that at least might live on, and make my name ring down through the ages," he smiled ruefully, "or at least some ages. However—"

"Ah," said Willard. "Now we come to it."

"Well, yes. I have a dream that I'm willing to risk a great deal for, but I'm not a complete fool. I will give you the hundred thousand I promised before you start and if the thing doesn't work out you can keep it, but the payment will be electronic. *If,* however, you turn out a product that satisfies me, then you will return the electronic gift and I will give you the hundred thousand globo-dollars in gold pieces. You have nothing to lose except that to an artist like yourself, gold must be more dramatic and worthwhile than blips in a finance-card." And Laborian smiled gently.

Willard said, "Understand, Mr. Laborian! I would be taking a risk, too. I risk losing a great deal of time and effort that I might have devoted to a more likely project. I risk producing a docu-drama that will be a failure and that will tarnish the reputation I have built up with *Lear*. In my business, you're only as good as your most recent product. I will consult various people—"

"On a confidential basis, please,"

"Of course! And I will do a bit of deep consideration. I am willing to go along with your proposition for now, but you mustn't think of it as a definite commitment. Not yet. We will talk further."

Jonas Willard and Meg Cathcart sat together over lunch in Meg's apartment. They were at their coffee when Willard said, with apparent reluctance as one who broaches a subject he would rather not, "Have you read the book?"

"Yes, I have."

"And what did you think?"

"I don't know," said Cathcart peering at him from under the dark, reddish hair she wore clustered over her forehead. "At least not enough to judge."

"You're not a science fiction buff either, then?"

"Well, I've read science fiction, mostly sword and sorcery, but nothing like *Three in One*. I've heard of Laborian, though. He does what they call 'hard science fiction.' "

"It's hard enough. I don't see how I can do it. That book, whatever its virtues, just isn't me."

Cathcart fixed him with a sharp glance. "How do you know it isn't you?"

"Listen, it's important to know what you can't do."

"And you were born knowing you can't do science fiction?"

"I have an instinct in these things."

"So you say. Why don't you think what you might do with those three undescribed characters, and what you would want subliminally, before you let your instinct tell you what you can and can't do. For instance, how would you do the Parental, who is referred to constantly as 'he' even though it's the Parental who bears the children? That struck me as jackassy, if you must know."

"No, no," said Willard, at once. "I accept the 'he.' Laborian might have invented a third pronoun, but it would have made no sense and the reader would have gagged on it. Instead, he reserved the pronoun 'she' for the Emotional. She's the central character, differing from the other two enormously. The use of 'she' for her and only for her focuses the reader's attention on her, and it's on her that the reader's attention *must* focus. What's more, it's on her that the viewer's attention *must* focus in the compu-drama."

"Then you *have* been thinking of it." She grinned, impishly. "I wouldn't have known if I hadn't needled you."

Willard stirred uneasily. "Actually, Laborian said something of the sort, so I can't lay claim to complete creativity here. But let's get back to the Parental. I want to talk about these things to you because everything is going to depend on subliminal suggestion, if I do try to do this thing. The Parental is a block, a rectangle."

"A right parallelepiped, I think they would call it in solid geometry."

"Come on. I don't care what they call it in solid geometry. The point is we can't just have a block. We have to give it personality. The Parental is a 'he' who bears children, so we have to get across an epicene quality. The voice has to be neither clearly masculine nor feminine. I'm not sure that I have in mind exactly the timbre and sound I will need, but that will be for the voice-recorder and myself to work out by trial and error, I think. Of course, the voice isn't the only thing."

"What else?"

"The feet. The Parental moves about, but there is no description of any limbs. He has to have the equivalent of arms; there are things he does. He obtains an energy source that he feeds the Emotional, so we'll have to evolve arms that are alien but that are arms. And we need legs. And a number of sturdy, stumpy legs that move rapidly."

"Like a caterpillar? Or a centipede?"

Willard winced. "Those aren't pleasant comparisons, are they?"

"Well, it would be my job to subliminate, if I may use the expression, a centipede, so to speak, without showing one. Just the notion of a series of legs, a double fading row of parentheses, just on and off as a kind of visual leitmotiv for the Parental, whenever he appears."

"I see what you mean. We'll have to try it out and see what we can get away with. The Rational is ovoid. Laborian admitted it might be egg-shaped. We can imagine him progressing by rolling but I find that completely inappropriate. The Rational is mind-proud, dignified. We can't make him do anything laughable, and rolling would be laughable."

"We could have him with a flat bottom slightly curved, and he could slide along it, like a penguin belly-whopping."

"Or like a snail on a layer of grease. No. That would be just as bad. I had thought of having three legs extrude. In other words, when he is at rest, he would be smoothly ovoid and proud of it, but when he is moving three stubby legs emerge and he can walk on them."

"Why three?"

"It carries on the three motif; three sexes, you know. It could be a kind of hopping run. The foreleg digs in and holds firm and the two hind legs come along on each side."

"Like a three-legged kangaroo?"

"Yes! Can you subliminate a kangaroo?"

"I can try."

"The Emotional, of course, is the hardest of the three.

What can you do with something that may be nothing but a coherent cloud of gas?"

Cathcart considered. "What about giving the impression of draperies containing nothing. They would be moving about wraithlike, just as you presented *Lear* in the storm scene. She would be wind, she would be air, she would be the filmy, foggy draperies that would represent that."

Willard felt himself drawn to the suggestion. "Hey, that's not bad, Meg. For the subliminal effect, could you do Helen of Troy?"

"Helen of Troy?"

"Yes! To the Rational and Parental, the Emotional is the most beautiful thing ever invented. They're crazy about her. There's this strong, almost unbearable sexual attraction—their kind of sex—and we've got to make the audience aware of it in *their* terms. If you can somehow get across a statuesque Greek woman, with bound hair and draperies—the draperies would exactly fit what we're imagining for the Emotional—and make it look like the paintings and sculptures everyone is familiar with, that would be the Emotional's leitmotiv."

"You don't ask simple things. The slightest intrusion of a human figure will destroy the mood."

"You don't intrude a human figure. Just the suggestion of one. It's important. A human figure, in actual fact, may destroy the mood, but we'll have to *suggest* human figures throughout. The audience has to think of these odd things as human beings. No mistake."

"I'll think about it," said Cathcart, dubiously.

"Which brings us to another thing. The melting. The triple-sex of these things. I gather they superimpose. I gather from the book that the Emotional is the key to that. The Parental and Rational can't melt without her. She's the essential part of the process. But, of course, that fool, Laborian, doesn't describe it in detail. Well, we can't have the Rational and Parental running toward the Emotional and jumping on her. That would kill the drama at once no matter what else we might do."

"I agree."

"What we must do, then, and this is off the top of my head, is to have the Emotional expand, the draperies move out and enswathe (if that's the word) both Parental and Rational. They are obscured by the draperies and we don't see exactly how it's done but they get closer and closer until they superimpose."

"We'll have to emphasize the drapery," said Cathcart "We'll have to make it as graceful as possible in order to get across the beauty of it, and not just the eroticism. We'll have to have music."

"*Not* the Romeo and Juliet overture, please. A slow waltz, perhaps, because the melting takes a long time. And not a familiar one. I don't want the audience humming along with it. In fact, it would be best if it comes in occasional bits so that the audience gets the impression of a waltz, rather than actually hearing it."

"We can't see how to do it, until we try it and see what works."

"Everything I say now is a first-order suggestion that may have to be yanked about this way and that under the pressure of actual events. And what about the orgasm? We'll have to indicate that somehow."

"Color."

"Hmm."

"Better than sound, Jonas. You can't have an explosion. I wouldn't want some kind of eruption, either. Color. Silent color. That might do it."

"What color? I don't want a blinding flash, either."

"No. You might try a delicate pink, very slowly darkening, and then toward the end suddenly becoming a deep, deep red."

"I'm not sure. We'll have to try it out. It must be unmistakable and moving and not make the audience giggle or feel embarrassed. I can see ourselves running through every color change in the spectrum, and, in the end, finding that it will depend on what you do subliminally. And that brings us to the triple-beings."

"The what?"

"You know. After the last melting, the superimposition remains permanent and we have the adult form that is all three components together. There, I think, we'll have to make them more human. Not human, mind you. Just more human. A faint suggestion of human form, not just subliminal, either. We'll need a voice that is somehow reminiscent of all three, and I don't know how the recorder can make that work. Fortunately, the triple-beings don't appear much in the story."

Willard shook his head. "And that brings us to the rough fact that the compu-drama might not be a possible project at all."

"Why not? You seem to have been offering potential solutions of all kinds for the various problems."

"Not for the essential part. Look! In *King Lear*, we had human characters, *more* than human characters. You had searing emotions. What have we got here? We have funny little cubes and ovals and drapery. Tell me how my *Three in One* is going to be different from an animated cartoon?"

"For one thing, an animated cartoon is two-dimensional. Even with elaborate animation it is flat, and its coloring is without shading. It is invariably satiricial—"

"I know all that. That's not what I want you to tell me. You're missing the important point. What a compu-drama has, that a mere animated cartoon does not, are subliminal suggestions such as can only be created by a complex computer in the hands of an imaginative genius. What my compu-drama has that an animated cartoon doesn't is *you*, Meg."

"Well, I was being modest."

"Don't be. I'm trying to tell you that everything—*everything*—is going to depend on you. We have a story here that is dead serious. Our Emotional is trying to save Earth out of pure idealism; it's not her world. And she doesn't succeed, and she won't succeed in my version, either. No cheap, happy ending."

"Earth isn't exactly destroyed."

"No, it isn't. There's still time to save it if Laborian ever gets around to doing a sequel, but in *this* story the attempt fails. It's a tragedy and I want it treated as one—as tragic as *Lear*. No funny voices, no humorous actions, no satirical touches. Serious. Serious. Serious. And I'm going to depend on you to make it so. It will be you who makes sure that the audience reacts to the Rational, the Emotional, the Parental, as though they were human beings. All their peculiarities will have to melt away and they'll have to be recognized as intelligent beings on a par with humanity, if not ahead of it. Can you do it?"

Cathcart said dryly, "It looks as though you will insist I can."

"I do so insist."

"Then you had better see about getting the ball rolling, and you leave me alone while you're doing it. I need time to think. Lots of time."

The early days of the shooting were an unmitigated disaster. Each member of the crew had his copy of the book, carefully, almost surgically trimmed, but with no scenes entirely omitted.

"We're going to stick to the course of the book as closely as we can, and improve it as we go along just as much as we can," Willard had announced confidently. "And the first thing we do is get a hold on the triple-beings."

He turned to the head voice-recorder. "How have you been working on that?"

"I've tried to fuse the three voices."

"Let's hear. All right, everyone quiet."

"I'll give you the Parental first," said the recorder. There came a thin, tenor voice, out of key with the blockish figure that the Image man had produced. Willard winced slightly at the mismatch, but the Parental *was* mismatched—a masculine mother. The Rational, rocking slowly back and forth, had a somewhat self-important voice; enunciation over-careful, and it was a light baritone.

Willard interrupted. "Less rocking in the Rational. We don't want the audience to become seasick. He rocks when he is deep in thought, and not all the time."

He then nodded his head at Dua's draperies, which seemed quite successful, as did her clear and infinitely sweet soprano voice.

"She must never shriek," said Willard, severely, "not even when she is in a passion."

"She won't," said the recorder. "The trick is, though, to blend the voices in setting up the triple-being, in having each one distantly identifiable."

All three voices sounded softly, the words not clear. They seemed to melt into each other and then the voice could be heard enunciating.

Willard shook his head in immediate discontent. "No, that won't do at all. We can't have three voices in a kind of intimate patchwork. We'd be making the triple-being a figure of fun. We need one voice which somehow suggests all three."

The voice-recorder was clearly offended. "It's easy to say that. How do you suggest we do it?"

"I do it," said Willard, brutally, "by ordering you to do it. I'll tell you when you have it. And Cathcart—where is Cathcart?"

"Here I am," she said, emerging from behind her instrumentation. "Where I'm supposed to be."

"I don't like the sublimination, Cathcart. I gather you tried to give the impression of cerebral convolutions."

"For intelligence. The triple-beings represent the intelligence-peak of these aliens."

"Yes, I understand, but what you managed to do was to give the impression of worms. You'll have to think of something else. And I don't like the appearance of the triple-being, either. He looks just like a big Rational."

"He *is* like a big Rational," said one of the imagists.

"Is he described in the book that way?" asked Willard, sharply.

"Not in so many words, but the impression I get—"

"Never mind your impression. I'll make the decisions."

Willard grew fouler-tempered as the day wore on. At least twice he had difficulty controlling his passion, the second time coming when he happened to notice someone watching the proceedings from a spot at one edge of the lot.

He strode toward him angrily. "What are you doing here?"

It was Laborian, who answered quietly, "Watching."

"Our contract states—"

"That I am to interfere in the proceedings in no way. It does not say I cannot watch quietly."

"You'll get upset if you do. This is the way preparing a compu-drama works. There are lots of glitches to overcome and it would be upsetting to the company to have the author watching and disapproving."

"I'm not disapproving. I'm here only to answer questions if you care to ask them."

"Questions? What kind of questions?"

Laborian shrugged. "I don't know. Something might puzzle you and you might want a suggestion."

"I see," said Willard, with heavy irony, "so you can teach me my business."

"No, so I can answer your questions."

"Well, I have one."

"Very well," and Laborian produced a small cassette recorder. "If you'll just speak into this and say that you are asking me a question and wish me to answer without prejudicing the contract, we're in business."

Willard paused for a considerable time, staring at Laborian as though he suspected trickery of some sort, then he spoke into the cassette.

"Very well," said Laborian. "What's your question?"

"Did you have anything in mind for the appearance of the triple-being in the book?"

"Not a thing," said Laborian, cheerfully.

"How could you do that?" Willard's voice trembled as though he were holding back a final "you idiot" by main force.

"Easily. What I don't describe, the reader supplies in his own mind. Each reader does it differently to suit himself, I presume. That's the advantage of writing. A compu-drama would have an enormously larger audience than a book could have, but you must pay for that by having to present an image."

"I understand that," said Willard. "So much for the question, then."

"Not at all. I have a suggestion."

"Like what?"

"Like a head. Give the triple-being a head. The Parental has no head, nor the Rational, nor the Emotional, but all three look up to the triple-beings as creatures of intelligence beyond their own. That is the entire difference between the triple-beings and the three Separates. Intelligence."

"A head?"

"Yes. We associate intelligence with heads. The head contains the brain, it contains the sense organs. Omit the head and we cannot believe in intelligence. The headless oysters or clams are mollusks that seem no more intelligent to us than a sprig of grass would be, but the related octopus, also a mollusk, we accept as possibly intelligent because it has a head—and eyes. Give the triple-being eyes, too."

Work had, of course, ceased on the set. Everyone had gathered in as closely as they thought judicious to listen to the conversation between director and author.

Willard said, "What kind of head?"

"Your choice. All you need is a bulge *suggesting* a head. And eyes. The viewer is sure to get the idea."

Willard turned away, shouting, "Well, get back to work. Who called a vacation? Where are the imagists? Back to the machine and begin trying out heads."

He turned suddenly and said, in an almost surly fashion, to Laborian. "Thank you!"

"Only if it works," said Laborian, shrugging.

The rest of the day was spent in testing heads, searching for one that was not a humorous bulge, and not an unimaginative copy of the human head, and eyes that were not astonished circles or vicious slits. Then, finally, Willard called a halt and growled, "We'll try again tomorrow. If anyone gets any brilliant thoughts overnight, give them to Meg Cathcart. She'll pass on to me any that are worth it." And he added, in an annoyed mutter, "I suppose she'll have to remain silent."

Willard was right and wrong. He was right. There were no brilliant ideas handed to him, but he was wrong for he had one of his own.

He said to Cathcart, "Listen, can you get across a top hat?"

"A what?"

"The sort of thing they wore in Victorian times. Look, when the Parental invades the lair of the triple-beings to steal an energy source, he's not an impressive sight in himself, but you told me you could just get across the idea of a helmet and a long line that will give the notion of a spear. He'll be on a knightly quest."

"Yes, I know," she said, "but it might not work. We'll have to try it out."

"Of course, but that points the direction. If you have just a suggestion of a top hat, it will give the impression of the triple-being as an aristocrat. The exact shape of the head and eyes becomes less crucial in that case. Can it be done?"

"Anything can be done. The question is: will it work?"

"We'll try it."

And as it happened, one thing led to another. The suggestion of the top hat caused the voice-recorder to say, "Why not give the triple-being a British accent?"

Willard was caught off-guard. "Why?"

"Well, the British have a language with more tones than we do. At least, the upper classes do. The American version of English tends to be flat, and that's true of the Separates, too. If the triple-being spoke British rather than English, his voice could rise and fall with the words—tenor and baritone and even an occasional soprano squeak. That's what we would want to indicate with the three voices out of which his voice was formed."

"Can you do that?" said Willard.

"I think so."

"Then we'll try. Not bad—if it works."

It was interesting to see how the entire group found themselves engaged in the Emotional.

The scene in particular where the Emotional was fleeing across the face of the planet, where she had her brief set-to with the other Emotionals caught at everyone.

Willard said tensely, "This is going to be one of the great dramatic scenes. We'll put it out as widely as we can. It's going to be draperies, draperies, draperies, but they must not be entangled one with the other. Each one must be distinct. Even when you rush the Emotionals in toward the audience I want each set of draperies to be a different off-white. And I want Dua's drapery to be distinct from all of them. I want her to glitter a little, just to be different, and because she's *our* Emotional. Got it?"

"Got it," said the leading imagist. "We'll handle it."

"And another thing. All the other Emotionals twitter. They're birds. Our Emotional *doesn't* twitter, and she despises the rest because she's more intelligent than they are and she knows it. And when she's fleeing—" he paused, and brooded a bit. "Is there any way we can get away from the 'Ride of the Valkyries'?"

"We don't want to," said the soundman promptly. "Nothing better for the purpose has ever been written."

Cathcart said, "Yes, but we'll only have snatches of it now and then. Hearing a few bars has the effect of the whole, and I can insert the hint of tossing manes."

"Manes?" said Willard, dubiously.

"Absolutely. Three thousand years of experience with horses has pinned us down to the galloping stallion as the epitome of wild speed. All our mechanical devices are too static, however fast they go. And I can arrange to have the manes just match, emphasize, and punctuate the flowing of the draperies."

"That sounds good. We'll try it."

Willard knew where the final stumbling block would be found. The last melting. He called the troupe together to lecture them, partly to make sure they understood what it was they were all doing now, partly to put off the time of reckoning when they would actually try to put it all into sound, image, and sublimination.

He said, "All right, the Emotional's interest is in saving the other world—Earth—only because she can't bear the thought of the meaningless destruction of intelligent be-ings. She knows the triple-beings are carrying through a sci-entific project, necessary for the welfare of *her* world and caring nothing for the danger into which it puts the alien world—us.

"She tries to warn the alien world and fails. She knows, at last, that the whole purpose of melting is to produce a new set of Rational, Emotional and Parental, and then, with that done, there is a final melting that would turn the original set into a triple-being. Do you have that? It's a sort of larval form of Separates and an adult form of triples.

"But the Emotional doesn't want to melt. She doesn't want to produce the new generation. Most of all, she doesn't want to become a triple-being and participate in what she considers their work of destruction. She is, how-ever, tricked into the final melt and realizes too late that she is not only going to be a triple-being but a triple-being who will be, more than any other, responsible for the scientific project that will destroy the other world.

"All this Laborian could describe in words, words, words, in his book, but we've got to do it more immediately and more forcefully, in images and sublimination as well. That's what we're now going to try to do."

They were three days in the trying before Willard was satisfied.

The weary Emotional, uncertain, stretching outward, with Cathcart's sublimination instilling the feeling of not-sure, not-sure. The Rational and Parental enfolded and coming together, more rapidly than on previous occasions—hurrying for the superimposition before it might be stopped—and the Emotional realizing too late the significance of it all and struggling—struggling—

And failure. The drenching feeling of failure as a new triple-being stepped out of the superimposition, more nearly human than anyone else in the compu-drama—proud, indifferent.

The scientific procedure would go on. Earth would continue the downward slide.

And somehow this was it—this was the nub of everything that Willard was trying to do—that within the new triple-being the Emotional still existed in part. There was just the wisping of drapery and the viewer was to know that the defeat was not final after all.

The Emotional would, somehow, still try, lost though it was in a greater being.

They watched the completed compu-drama, all of them, seeing it for the first time as a whole and not as a collection of parts, wondering if there were places to edit, to reorder. (Not now, thought Willard, not now. Afterwards, when he had recovered and could look at it more objectively.)

He sat in his chair, slumped. He had put too much of himself into it. It had seemed to him that it contained everything he wanted it to contain; that it did everything he wanted to have done; but how much of that was merely wishful thinking?

When it was over and the last tremulous, subliminal cry of the defeated-but-not-yet-defeated Emotional faded, he said, "Well."

And Cathcart said, "That's almost as good as your *King Lear* was, Jonas."

There was a general murmur of agreement and Willard cast a cynical eye about him. Wasn't that what they would be bound to say, no matter what?

His eye caught that of Gregory Laborian. The writer was expressionless, said nothing.

Willard's mouth tightened. There at least he could expect an opinion that would be backed, or not backed, by gold. Willard had his hundred thousand. He would see now whether it would stay electronic.

He said, and his own uncertainty made him sound imperious, "Laborian. I want to see you in my office."

They were together alone for the first time since well before the compu-drama had been made.

"Well?" said Willard. "What do you think, Mr. Laborian?"

Laborian smiled. "That woman who runs the subliminal background told you that it was almost as good as your *King Lear* was, Mr. Willard."

"I heard her."

"She was quite wrong."

"In your opinion?"

"Yes. My opinion is what counts right now. She was quite wrong. Your *Three in One* is much better than your *King Lear*."

"Better?" Willard's weary face broke into a smile.

"Much better. Consider the material you had to work with in doing *King Lear*. You had William Shakespeare, producing words that sang, that were music in themselves;

William Shakespeare producing characters who, whether for good or evil, whether strong or weak, whether shrewd or foolish, whether faithful or traitorous, were all larger than life; William Shakespeare, dealing with two overlapping plots, reinforcing each other and tearing the viewers to shreds.

"What was your contribution to *King Lear?* You added dimensions that Shakespeare lacked the technological knowledge to deal with; that he couldn't dream of; but the fanciest technologies and all that your people and your own talents could do could only build somewhat on the greatest literary genius of all time, working at the peak of his power.

"But in *Three in One*, Mr. Willard, you were working with *my* words which didn't sing; *my* characters, which weren't great; *my* plot which tore at no one. You dealt with *me*, a run-of-the-mill writer and you produced something great, something that will be remembered long after I am dead. One book of mine, anyway, will live on because of what you have done.

"Give me back my electronic hundred thousand, Mr. Willard, and I will give you this."

The hundred thousand was shifted back from one financial card to the other and, with an effort, Laborian then pulled his fat briefcase onto the table and opened it. From it, he drew out a box, fastened with a small hook. He unfastened it carefully, and lifted the top. Inside it glittered the gold pieces, each one marked with the planet Earth, the western hemisphere on one side, the eastern on the other. Large gold pieces, two hundred of them, each worth five hundred globo-dollars.

Willard, awed, plucked out one of the gold pieces. It weighed about one and a quarter ounces. He threw it up in the air and caught it.

"Beautiful," he said.

"It's yours, Mr. Willard," said Laborian. "Thank you for doing the compu-drama for me. It is worth every piece of that gold."

Willard stared at the gold and said, "You made me do the compu-drama of your book with your offer of this gold. To get this gold, I forced myself beyond my talents. Thank you for that, and you are right. It was worth every piece of that gold."

He put the gold piece back in the box and closed it. Then he lifted the box and handed it back to Laborian.

Part Two

ON SCIENCE FICTION

The Longest Voyage

Suppose you want to take a trip across the country from Portland, Maine to Portland, Oregon. That's roughly 3,000 miles. A trip around the world along the equator is only a little over eight times that, 25,000 miles.

To go from the Earth to the moon is only about nine times the equatorial jaunt, about 240,000 miles. Beyond that? Well, Venus at its closest is just over a hundred times the distance to the moon; it is about 25,000,000 miles away. And right now, Pluto is just about as near to Earth as it ever gets, but it is over a hundred times the distance to Venus. It is about 2,800,000,000 miles away.

So far we've stayed in our solar system, but beyond that are the stars. Even the nearest star is nearly 9,000 times as far away as Pluto is right now. The nearest star is Alpha Centauri and it is 25,000,000,000,000 miles away. And that's the *nearest* star.

The distance across the Milky Way galaxy is 23,000 times the distance from Earth to Alpha Centauri. The distance from here to the Andromeda galaxy, the nearest large galaxy to our own, is about twenty-three times the diameter of the Milky Way galaxy. And the distance from here to the farthest quasar is about 4,000 times that from here to the Andromeda.

What about time? It takes a few days to get to the moon; a few months to get to Venus or Mars; a few years to get to the giant planets of the solar system. But that's about as far as we can go and have it make reasonable sense.

To get to even the nearest star, at the present state of the art, would take hundreds of thousands of years. All that NASA has so far done in sending probes as far as Saturn has been to play games in our backyard. It is *interstellar travel*, trips to the stars, that represent the longest voyage.

And it is in trips to the stars that science fiction writers and readers are most interested. Our solar system is too well known and too limited. The solar system (outside Earth) is not at all likely to bear life of any kind—certainly not intelligent life. So we've got to take the longest voyage and get to the stars, if we're to find extraterrestrial friends, competitors, and enemies. As long ago as 1928, in *The Skylark of Space*, E. E. (Doc) Smith took the first science-fictional trip to the stars, and how the readers loved it.

Good old Doc was a little vague on just how his interstellar ships managed to cross those huge spaces, however, and, to tell you the truth, we're not much better off now. Let's list the possibilities:

1. We can keep accelerating; going faster and faster and faster until we're going fast enough to cover vast interstellar and intergalactic distances in a matter of months, or even days.

Objection: Physicists are strongly of the opinion that the speed of light in a vacuum, 186,000 miles per second, is as fast as anyone can go. At that speed, it will still take years to reach the nearest star, millions of years to reach the nearest large galaxy.

2. Even if we're limited to the speed of light, that could be good enough. As one approaches the speed of light, the rate of time passage on the speeding object slows steadily, and at the speed of light itself, the rate of time passage is zero. At light speed, then, the crew of a starship would cover enormous distance practically instantaneously.

Objection: Interstellar and intergalactic space is littered with occasional hydrogen atoms. At light speed, these atoms would strike the ship with the energy and force of cosmic ray particles and would quickly kill the starship's crew and passengers. Probably, the ship would have to go no faster than one-tenth light speed, and at that speed the time effects are not great enough to help us much.

3. Suppose we attach a kind of "atom-plow" arrangement in front of the starship. It would scoop up all the atoms in front of it, thus preventing cosmic ray problems and, in addition, gathering material to serve as fuel for its nuclear fusion engines.

Objection: Such atom-plows would have to be many thousands of miles across to be effective. Building such things would represent enormous and perhaps insuperable problems.

4. We can evade the speed-of-light limit altogether by making use of tachyons, subatomic particles that move much faster than the speed of light and that, as a matter of fact, cannot move slower than the speed of light.

Objection: Tachyons exist only in theory, and have not actually been detected. Most physicists think they will never be detected. Even if they were detected, no one has even come close to figuring out a way of putting them to use.

5. Perhaps we can evade the speed-of-light limit by going through black holes. They at least are known to exist.

Objection: If black holes exist (and astronomers are not yet unanimous on this), no one is even close to suggesting how any starship might approach one without being destroyed by tidal forces. In addition, there is by no means general agreement that one can negotiate long distances quickly by going through black holes.

6. In that case, we might find some other way of leaving this universe. We could then travel through hyperspace in "jumps" that will carry us enormous distances in zero time.

Objection: So far hyperspace exists only within the imagination of science fiction writers.

7. Well, then, we can submit to the speed-of-light limit, but freeze the crew and passengers, and arrange to have them restored to conscious life after thousands of years have passed and the destination has been reached.

Objection: No one really knows how human bodies can be frozen without being killed; or whether such frozen bodies, even if retaining a spark of life, can retain it over a period of thousands of years.

8. In that case, there seems nothing left to do but to coast—to travel at ordinary speeds, considerably less than that of light, with all people aboard thoroughly conscious. This means it will take many thousands of years to reach even the nearer stars, so that many generations will have to spend their lifetimes aboard the starship. That may be bearable if the starship is large enough.

Objection: None, really, if people want to do it.

So much for hardheaded realism. In science fiction, we tend to have faith that problems that seem insuperable now will be solved—perhaps in ways that are utterly unexpected.

Therefore we are offering you a baker's dozen of stories, all involving starships. In these are explored the various strategies I have described above for covering long distances, and perhaps one or two that are too far-out for me to have even mentioned.

What's more, the stories explore the effect of the long voyages on the people on board the starship, and the kind of events that might take place on them.

Since it is not likely that such voyages will be undertaken in our lifetime (and certainly not completed, if the generations-long coasting starship should indeed prove to be the only practical alternative), these exciting science-fictional speculations are the only way we can experience, if only vicariously, the long voyages that are the quintessential dreams of the far-flung imagination.

Inventing a Universe

Why have I gone to the trouble of inventing a universe for other writers to exploit?

No, it isn't the money or the fame. Most of the royalties and all of the fame will go, as they should, to the authors who actually write the stories in this book and (it is to be hoped) in later companion pieces. My own return is, as it should be, miniscule.

But there are other reasons and I would like to explain them at some length, for among other things, they involve my feelings of guilt. Now guilt (for those of you who have never experienced the emotion) is a dreadful annoyance, souring one's life and making one unable to enjoy properly any renown or riches that come one's way. One is bowed down by its weight and is rendered fearful of the (usually imaginary) accusing eye of public disapproval.

In my case, it came about this way. I hadn't been writing for more than ten or fifteen years when I began to have the uneasy suspicion that I was becoming rather well known as a science fiction writer. In fact, I was even getting mentioned as one of the "Big Three," the other two being Robert A. Heinlein and Arthur C. Clarke.

It only got worse as the decades continued to fly by. We were not only cursed with prolificity, but with longevity, so that the same old Big Three remained Big for nearly half a century. Heinlein died in 1988 at the age of 80, but Clarke is still going strong as I write this and, obviously, so am I.

The result is that, at present, when there are a great many writers attempting to scale the mountainside of science fiction, it must be rather annoying for them to see the peak occupied by elderly has-beens who cling to it with their arthritic paws and simply won't get off. Even death, it seems, won't stop us, since Heinlein has already published a posthumous book and reissues of his old novels are in the works.

Thanks to the limited space on the shelves of bookstores (themselves of sharply limited number), large numbers of new books of science fiction and fantasy are placed on them for only brief intervals before being swept off by new arrivals. Few books seem to manage to exist in public view for longer than a month before being replaced. Always excepting (as some writers add, with a faint snarl) the "megastars."

"So what?" I can hear you say in your warm and loving way. "So you're a megastar and your books are perennial sellers and the economic futures of yourself and your eventual survivors are set. Is that bad?"

No, it isn't bad, exactly, but that's where the guilt comes in. I worry about crowding out newcomers with my old perennials, about smothering them with the weight of my name.

I've tried to justify the situation to myself. (Anything to make it possible for me to walk about science fiction conventions without having to skulk and hide in doorways when other writers pass.)

In the first place, we started in the early days of science fiction—not only the Big Three, but others of importance

such as Lester del Rey, Poul Anderson, Fred Pohl, Clifford
Simak, Ray Bradbury, and even some who died young: Stanley Weinbaum, Henry Kuttner, and Cyril Kornbluth, for
instance. In those early days, the magazines paid only one
cent a word or less, and there were *only* magazines. There
were no hardcover science fiction publishers, no paper-
backs, no Hollywood to speak of.

For years and decades we stuck it out under starvation
conditions, and it was our efforts that slowly increased the
popularity of science fiction to the point where today's beginners can get more for one novel than any of us got in ten
years of endless plugging. So, if some of us are doing unusually well now, it is possible to argue that we earned it.

Secondly, from the more personal standpoint, back in
1958 I decided I had done enough science fiction. I had
been successful in writing nonfiction of various types and it
seemed to me I could make a living if I concentrated on
nonfiction (and, to tell you the truth, I *preferred* nonfiction).
In that way I could leave science fiction to the talented new
writers who were making their way into the field.

So from 1958 to 1981, a period of nearly a quarter of a
century, I wrote virtually no science fiction. There was one
novel and a handful of short stories, but that's all. And
meanwhile, along came the "New Wave." Writing styles
changed drastically, and I felt increasingly that I was a back-
number and *should* remain out of science fiction.

The trouble was that all this didn't help. The science fiction books that I published in the 1950s refused to go out of
print and continued to sell steadily through the 1960s and
1970s. And because I wrote a series of nonfiction essays for
Fantasy and Science Fiction, I remained in the consciousness
of the science fiction public. I was therefore *still* one of the
Big Three.

Then, in 1981, my publisher insisted (with a big INSIST)

that I write another novel and I did and, to my horror, it hit the bestseller lists and I've had to write a new novel every year since then, in consequence.

That would have made me feel guiltier than ever, but I've done various things to pull the fangs of that guilt. For instance, I have, quite deliberately, decided that since my name has developed a kind of weight and significance, I would use it, as much as possible, for the benefit of the field rather than of myself.

With my dear and able friends Martin Harry Greenberg and Charles Waugh (and occasionally others), I have helped edit many anthologies. More than a hundred of these have now been published with my name often in the title. What these serve to do is to rescue from the shadows numbers of stories that are well worth exposing to new generations of science fiction readers. Quite apart from the fact that the readers enjoy it, it means a little money to some veteran authors, as well as a shot in the arm to encourage continued production. The thought that the presence of my name might make such anthologies do better and be more efficacious in this respect than otherwise makes me feel fine.

Then, too, a number of novels by young authors have been published under the "Isaac Asimov Presents" label. In this way, the young authors get perhaps a somewhat better sale than they might otherwise have, and even (perhaps) a better break at the bookshelves.

I have even granted the right to make use of some of the themes that I have developed in my own books. There is a series of a dozen books, for instance, that have the generic title "Isaac Asimov's Robot City." They are written by young writers who have my express permission to use my Three Laws of Robotics, and for each one I write an introduction on one phase or another of robotics. The books are doing well, actually, and it is clear that the presence of my name doesn't hurt.

Then another way of using my name came up. Marty Greenberg suggested that, rather than have writers use a "universe" I had already invented and made my own, I invent a brand-new one I had never used and donate it to some publishing house that would be willing to have writers produce stories built about the concepts of the "universe"—and, of course, find the writers who would want to try their hand at it.

I agreed enthusiastically. After all, I had just devised a new background for my 1989 novel, *Nemesis*, one which had not been used in any piece of fiction I had written before, so I did not foresee any great difficulty in inventing an "Isaac's Universe" for other writers to use. (The use of the word "Isaac" in the title was Marty's idea but I snatched at it eagerly. There are well over sixty books that I have written— by no means all anthologies—with either "Asimov" or "Isaac Asimov" in the title, but none with "Isaac" alone, until this one.)

In making up a new "Universe" there were some things I couldn't abandon, of course. We would be working within our own Galaxy in which I postulated the existence of 25,000,000 star systems containing a habitable world, the whole being linked together by devices that made it possible to travel and communicate at faster-than-light speeds. The shorthand for this is "hyperspatial travel and communication."

I have this in my Foundation universe, and the other novels I have been connecting to the Foundation, but from here on my Universes part company.

In my Foundation series and the novels related thereto, the Galaxy contains only one intelligent species—our own. All the habitable worlds have been colonized by human beings so that we, in effect, have an all-human Galaxy. I may have been the first to write important novels based on such a theme, and the reason I did it was to pare away the complexities that would arise from a multiplicity of intelligences. I wanted to be able to deal with humanity and its problems in a detailed all-human manner, making them even clearer by showing them through a Galaxy-wide magnifying glass. This I have ended up doing—albeit imperfectly, of course, since I am no Shakespeare or Tolstoy.

However, I was well aware that there was the alternative multiple-intelligence Universe. We see that now constantly on such television shows as *Star Trek* and in many of the older "space opera" stories. There we always have the risk of a failure of imagination that leads to the portrayal of other intelligences as differing from ourselves superficially by the possession of green faces, or antennae, or corrugated foreheads, but allowing these changes to leave them, clearly, primates. You can't really blame *Star Trek* for this, since they have to have human beings playing the roles of other intelligences, but in science fiction stories in print, having all intelligences primate (or, if villainous, reptilian) seems insufficient.

E. E. Smith's *Galactic Patrol* and its sequels had a multi-intelligence Universe that had its intelligences encased in radically different physiologies and this I found satisfying when I read the stories as a young man. I was particularly pleased with the feeling Smith labored to give of a communal *mental* feeling among individuals who had nothing *physically* in common.

It was something like this, then, that I wanted for my Universe, but I wanted to make my Universe more specific in its description of the different species and more concerned with the various political, economic, and social problems of the Galaxy. It was to be less space-operaish and more quasi-historical, a melding to some extent of Galactic Patrol and Foundation.

I wanted a Universe with millions of planets bearing life, with the indigenous life on every planet unique to itself and with differences limited only by the imagination of the writer. However, there are only six *intelligent* species— widely different in nature:

1. Earthmen.
2. An aquatic race, vaguely analogous to Earthly porpoises.
3. A fragile, skeletal insectlike species adapted to a low oxygen atmosphere plus neon rather than nitrogen.
4. A sinuous, limbless species, possessing fringed flippers, however, that are snakish in a way.
5. A small, winged species adapted to a thick atmosphere.
6. A strong, slow-moving, blocklike species with no appendages, and adapted to a gravity higher than Earth's.

The intelligences each control more than their native planets. They can be pictured as going through the Galaxy, colonizing and settling planets suitable to themselves. In general, a world suitable for one is not particularly desirable for any of the others, and with plenty of each variety, there is no push for going to the enormous expense of modifying a planet to suit one's own kind. The intelligences can therefore live together in the Galaxy without treading on each other's toes. There is nothing to fight over unless there is an inability to overcome the unreasoning dislike of one species for another because, of course, each appears incredibly ugly to all the others, and each may have social customs and ways of thought that are distasteful to the others.

Yet the various intelligences need to be in contact, since trade among them is useful for all, and since advances in technology by one species may be useful to others as well (and each intelligence has its own specialities in technology, some of which are unpalatable to the others for one reason or another), and since disputes may arise occasionally and there must be some form of political/social machinery to settle them. There are even occasional dangers that might require Galactic cooperation. What's more, each intelligence may be split up into several mutually hostile subcultures.

So, you see, the Universe I invented (and which I described in considerable detail to the publishers and to the writers who were willing to chance working within it) supplies plenty of problems, some of which would certainly be beyond my imagination to handle well, and has broad enough limits to allow the writer a great deal of personal room for his own visions.

You can see how it works out in the sampling of stories in this volume, which (we very much hope) will be but the first of a series. Good reading—and if you like it, write and say so. It will lower my level of guilt, and I can always use that.

Flying Saucers and Science Fiction

I am helping to edit a book on flying saucers? Isaac Asimov? Surely, I am a leading and vocal skeptic where flying saucers are concerned!

Have I changed my mind now? Do I believe in the existence of flying saucers?

That depends on what you mean by the question. Do I believe that many people have seen something in the sky that they can't explain?

Absolutely! Of course! You bet! Seeing something one can't explain is very common. Every time I watch a magician perform his act I see something I can't explain.

However, when I see something I can't explain, I assume there is a perfectly normal explanation, one that fits in with the structure of the universe as worked out by modern science. I don't instantly jump to the idea that there is no explanation short of the supernatural or of some far-out near-zero-probability hypothesis.

For that reason, I have no tendency to explain every appearance of a light in the sky by declaring it to be a spaceship manned by extraterrestrial beings.

Nowadays, in an effort to gain respectability, people who

accept the wilder hypotheses about flying saucers call them "unidentified flying objects" and abbreviate it UFO. On numerous occasions, I have been asked if I "believe" in UFOs.

My usual answer is, "I assume that by UFO you mean 'unidentified flying objects.' I certainly believe that many people have seen objects in the air or sky that they can't identify, and those are UFOs. But then, many people can't identify the planet Venus, or a mirage. If you are asking me whether I believe that some mysterious object reported is a spaceship manned by extraterrestrial beings, then I must say I am very skeptical. But that, you see, is an *identified* flying object, and that's not what you're asking about, is it?"

Mysterious objects have been reported in Earth's skies all through history. Usually they are interpreted according to the preoccupations of the day. In ancient and medieval times and in primitive societies, they would be interpreted as angels, demons, spirits, and so on. In technological societies, they would be interpreted as first balloons, then dirigibles, then airplanes, and then spaceships.

Of course, if they're spaceships *now*, then they've been spaceships all the time, and some people have indeed interpreted Ezekiel's vision in the Bible, for instance, as the sighting of spaceships manned by extraterrestrials.

The modern surge of flying saucer sightings began on June 24, 1947, when Kenneth Arnold, a salesman, claimed he saw bright disk-shaped objects flying rapidly through the air near Mount Rainier. From the shapes he described, the expression "flying saucers" came into being.

Nothing much might have happened in consequence, for wild reports about all sorts of things reach the news media every day and then fade out. In this case, though, the report attracted the attention of Raymond A. Palmer, who was then the editor of the science fiction magazine *Amazing Stories*.

Palmer may not himself have been a piece of broken pottery, but he was certainly not averse to building circulation by means of items that appealed to crackpots. He had shown this in his earlier work on something completely wacky that he called "The Great Shaver Mystery."

Now he took up flying saucers and single-handedly promoted them into an international mania. That is one connection (an important one) between flying saucers and science fiction.

Mind you, I have a soft spot in my heart for Ray Palmer. Way back in 1938, he bought the first science fiction story I ever sold, and sent me the very first check I ever earned as a professional writer. Nevertheless, candor compels me to state that for years after this noble deed of his I never had occasion to believe a word he said.

At the other extreme of the flying saucer spectrum is Professor J. Allen Hynek. He is a respectable and learned scientist who has spent decades examining the evidence and who remains firmly convinced that there is something there. He doesn't accept the extraterrestrial spacecraft hypothesis, but he thinks that something mysterious underlies the phenomenon, which, if understood, may revolutionize science.

However, in all the years he's been investigating the phenomenon, he's come up with—nothing! Far from revolutionizing science, his work has not added one even marginal item to the world of physical science.

Then what am I doing helping edit this anthology?

That brings us to the second connection between flying saucers and science fiction. The whole concept of flying saucers—the whole notion of thousands upon thousands of spaceships hovering about us without ever seeming to do anything or to affect us in any way—has supplied science fiction writers with an endless supply of story material.

All of us have written flying saucer stories. I have myself, and one of them is included in this book.

Generally, we have to deal with a situation in which extraterrestrial spacecraft visit us, but keep out of sight for some reason, or decide not to do anything for some reason, or try to do something and fail for some reason, or fail to manage to convince Earthpeople they are real for some reason.

You see, science fiction writers, being sane and rational, have to find some *reason* for so many spaceships doing *nothing*. Usually the results turn out to be funny, satiric or ironic; sometimes tragic. Very often, they prove to be stories that are entertaining and good—so what we have done is to collect a sizable number of them into one book for your delectation.

Come, see for yourself that every cloud has a silver lining, and that even the silliest notions can undergo a sea change into something rich and strange in the hands of skilled science fiction writers.

Invasion

Invasion is undoubtedly as old as humanity. Hunting groups must occasionally have encountered each other, if only by accident. Each side must have felt the other was invading. The obviously weaker side would have had to decamp. If the matter were not obvious, there might have been threats or even a brief struggle to settle the matter.

Once agriculture became a way of life and farmers were pinned in place by their farms and food stores, these same food stores became an overwhelming temptation to surrounding nomads; invasions were more terrible because farmers could not flee but had to stand and fight.

We begin to have records of early civilizations suddenly inundated and taken over by raiders. The Sumerians were taken over by Gutian invaders as early as 2200 B.C. The Egyptians fell under the grip of the Hyksos invaders soon after 1700 B.C. We can go through an endless list of such things.

Considering that those people who were invaded (until quite recent times) had little knowledge of the world outside the boundaries of their own cultures, the invasions must usually have come as unbelievable shocks, as a sudden influx of the unknown from the unknown. This would be especially so when the invaders spoke strange languages, wore strange clothes, had strange ways, and even, perhaps, have *looked* odd.

As the most recent example of our cultural ancestors being subjected to the horror of an unexpected invasion, we need only go back to 1240, when the Mongols (short, squat, slant-eyed) swept into Europe on their hardy desert mounts. Europe knew nothing about them, had no way of knowing they were on the way (they had been ravaging Asian kingdoms for twenty years). All they knew were that these terrible horsemen, moving with incredible speed and organization, winning every battle, smashed Russia, Poland, Hungary, and were penetrating Germany and reaching for Italy, all in a matter of a single year. And then they left and raced eastward again, smashing Bulgaria en route. (They left because their khan had died back in Mongolia and the army had to be there for the election of a successor. Nothing the Europeans could have done would have stopped them.)

But the Mongols were "the last of the barbarians." Partly because of the Mongolian empire that was set up, communications between China and Europe became smoother. Such things as printing, the magnetic compass, and (most of all) gunpowder, leaked westward from China, and these things—for some reason not exploited by the technologically more advanced Chinese—were put to amazing use by Europeans.

And beginning about 1420, the tide of invasion was reversed. The "civilized" Europeans, with their ships and their guns, fell upon the coastlines of all the continents and, eventually, penetrated the interiors until Europe dominated the world politically and militarily (and as it still does, even today, culturally).

But how did the non-Europeans feel about it? How about the Africans who watched the Portuguese ships come from nowhere and carry them off as slaves; the Asians who watched Portuguese, Dutch, and English ships come in, set up trading posts, skim off profits and treat them as inferiors; the Native Americans who watched the Spanish ships come in and take over and destroy their civilizations? There must have been the feeling of monsters arriving from some other world.

All invasions, however, at least of the kind I'm discussing, were by human beings. However strange they might have seemed—Mongols to Europeans, or Spaniards to Incas—they were clearly human beings. (There were also invasions of infestations of non-human types—rats, locusts, the plague bacterium of the Black Death, the AIDS virus—but these fall outside the subject matter of this introduction, and even they were forms of terrestrial life.)

What if, however, the invaders were intelligent beings who were not human and, in fact, not Earthly. The possibility did not seriously arise until the time when it was thoroughly recognized that the planets were other worlds and that the universe might be full of still other planets outside the domain of our own sun.

At first, other worlds were the subject of "travel tales." Human beings went to the moon (as early as the second century A.D. in fiction and more frequently as time went on), but there are no tales I can think of in which the inhabitants of the moon came to Earth.

In 1752, the French satirist Voltaire wrote *Micromegas*, in which visitors from Saturn and Sinus observe the Earth, but this cannot be taken literally. The visitors are merely Voltaire's device for having Earth viewed with apparent objectivity from without in order to have its follies and contradictions made plain.

But then in 1877, there was the discovery of thin, dark

markings on Mars. This was interpreted by some as "canals" and the American astronomer Percival Lowell was convinced that they were artificial waterways built by intelligent beings trying to use the ice of the polar caps to maintain agriculture on their increasingly desiccated planet. He wrote books on the subject in the 1890s that created quite a stir.

The British science fiction writer Herbert George Wells proceeded to make use of the notion and, in 1898, published *The War of the Worlds*, the first significant tale of the invasion and attempted conquest of Earth by more advanced intelligences from another world (in this case, Mars). I have always thought that Wells, in addition to wanting to write an exciting story with an unprecedented plot, was also bitterly satirizing Europe. At the time he wrote, Europeans (the British, particularly) had just completed dividing up Africa without any regard for the people living there. Why not show the British how it would feel to have advanced intelligences treat them as callously as they were treating the Africans?

Wells's novel created a new subgenre—tales of alien invasion. The manner in which Wells made the Martians unpitying exploiters of humanity (for the sake of excitement and, I believe, satire); the memory, perhaps, of the Mongol invasion; the feeling of guilt over the European despoliation of all the other continents; combined to make it conventional to have the alien invaders unfeeling conquerors, for the most part.

Actually, we have no reason to think this would be so. As far as we know, no invaders from without have ever reached Earth and, for a variety of reasons, it might be argued that none ever will. However, if they do come, there is no a priori reason to suspect they won't come in friendship and curiosity, to teach and to learn.

Yet such is the power of humanity's own shameful history and the conventions of fiction that very few people would be willing to consider alien invaders coming in peace as a real possibility. In fact, when plaques and recordings were placed on rocket probes designed to leave the solar system and go wandering off into interstellar space, in order that alien intelligences (if any) might find them someday, millions of years in the future, and that they might thus learn that Earthmen had once existed—there were those who thought it a dangerous process. Why advertise our existence? Why encourage ferocious aliens to come here in order to ravage and destroy?

Here, then, in this collection, are stories of alien invasion. We have selected a variety of contemporary treatments of the problem, some a matter of excitement, some thoughtfully philosophic, some even funny. They view the possibility from all angles and stretch our minds on the matter, as good science fiction should.

The Science Fiction Blowgun

In science fiction, experience seems to show that long stories have an advantage over short ones. The longer the story, all things being equal, the more memorable.

There is reason to this. The longer the story, the more the author can spread himself. If the story is long enough, he can indulge himself in plot and subplot with intricate interconnections. He can engage in leisurely description, in careful character delineation, in thoughtful homilies and philosophical discussions. He can play tricks on the reader, hiding important information, misleading and misdirecting, then bringing back forgotten themes and characters at the moment of greatest effect.

But in every worthwhile story, however long, there is a point. The writer may not consciously put it there, but it will be there. The reader may not consciously search for it, but he'll miss it if it isn't there. If the point is obtuse, blunt, trivial or non-existent, the story suffers and the reader will react with a deadly, "So what?"

Long, complicated stories can have the point well hidden under cloaking layers of material. Academic people, for whom the search for the point is particularly exciting, can whip their students to the hunt, and works of literature that are particularly deep and rich can elicit scholarly theses without number that will deal with the identification and explanations of points and subpoints.

But now let's work toward the other extreme. As a story grows shorter and shorter, all the fancy embroidery that length makes possible must go. In the short story, there can be no subplots; there is no time for philosophy; what description and character delineation there is must be accomplished with concision.

The point, however, must remain. Since it cannot be economized on, its weight looms more largely in the lesser overall bulk of the short story.

Finally, in the short short story, everything is eliminated *but* the point. The short short story reduces itself to the point alone and presents that point to you like a bare needle fired from a blowgun; a needle that can tickle or sting and leave its effect buried within you for a long time.

Here, then, are some points made against the background and with the technique of science fiction. A hundred of them, to be exact, each from the science fiction blowgun of a master (to be modest, there are *also* a couple of my own stories), and each with a one-line introductory blurb by myself.

Now, since it would make no sense to have an introduction longer than the stories it introduces, and having made *my* point—I'll stop.

The Robot Chronicles

What is a robot? We might define it most briefly and comprehensively as "an artificial object that resembles a human being."

When we think of resemblance, we think of it, first, in terms of appearance. A robot *looks* like a human being.

It could, for instance, be covered with a soft material that resembles human skin. It could have hair, and eyes, and a voice, and all the features and appurtenances of a human being, so that it would, as far as outward appearance is concerned, be indistinguishable from a human being.

This, however, is not really essential. In fact, the robot, as it appears in science fiction, is almost always constructed of metal, and has only a stylized resemblance to a human being.

Suppose, then, we forget about appearance and consider only what it can do. We think of robots as capable of performing tasks more rapidly or more efficiently than human beings. But in that case *any* machine is a robot. A sewing machine can sew faster than a human being, a pneumatic drill can penetrate a hard surface faster than an unaided human being can, a television set can detect and organize radio waves as we cannot, and so on.

We must apply the term robot, then, to a machine that is more specialized than an ordinary device. A robot is a *computerized* machine that is capable of performing tasks of a kind that are too complex for any living mind other than that of a man, and of a kind that no non-computerized machine is capable of performing.

In other words to put it as briefly as possible:

$$robot = machine + computer$$

Clearly, then, a true robot was impossible before the invention of the computer in the 1940s, and was not practical (in the sense of being compact enough and cheap enough to be put to everyday use) until the invention of the microchip in the 1970s.

Nevertheless, the *concept* of the robot—an artificial device that mimics the actions and, possibly, the appearance of a human being—is old, probably as old as the human imagination.

The ancients, lacking computers, had to think of some other way of instilling quasi-human abilities into artificial objects, and they made use of vague supernatural forces and depended on godlike abilities beyond the reach of mere men.

Thus, in the eighteenth book of Homer's *Iliad*, Hephaistos, the Greek god of the forge, is described as having for helpers, "a couple of maids . . . made of gold exactly like living girls; they have sense in their heads, they can speak and use their muscles, they can spin and weave and do their work." Surely, these are robots.

Again, the island of Crete, at the time of its greatest power, was supposed to possess a bronze giant named Talos that ceaselessly patrolled its shores to fight off the approach of any enemy.

Throughout ancient and medieval times, learned men

were supposed to have created artificially living things through the secret arts they had learned or uncovered—arts by which they made use of the powers of the divine or the demonic.

The medieval robot-story that is most familiar to us today is that of Rabbi Loew of sixteenth-century Prague. He is supposed to have formed an artificial human being—a robot—out of clay, just as God had formed Adam out of clay. A clay object, however much it might resemble a human being, is "an unformed substance" (the Hebrew word for it is "golem"), since it lacks the attributes of life. Rabbi Loew, however, gave his golem the attributes of life by making use of the sacred name of God, and set the robot to work protecting the lives of Jews against their persecutors.

There was, however, always a certain nervousness about human beings involving themselves with knowledge that properly belongs to gods or demons. There was the feeling that this was dangerous, that the forces might escape human control. This attitude is most familiar to us in the legend of the "sorcerer's apprentice," the young fellow who knew enough magic to start a process going but not enough to stop it when it had outlived its usefulness.

The ancients were intelligent enough to see this possibility and be frightened by it. In the Hebrew myth of Adam and Eve, the sin they commit is that of gaining knowledge (eating of the fruit of the tree of knowledge of good and evil; i.e., knowledge of everything) and for that they were ejected from Eden and, according to Christian theologians, infected all of humanity with that "original sin."

In the Greek myths, it was the Titan, or Prometheus, who supplied fire (and therefore technology) to human beings and for that he was dreadfully punished by the infuriated Zeus, who was the chief god.

*　　*　　*

In early modern times, mechanical clocks were perfected, and the small mechanisms that ran them ("clockwork")—the springs, gears, escapements, ratchets, and so on—could also be used to run other devices.

The 1700s was the golden age of "automatons." These were devices that could, given a source of power such as a wound spring or compressed air, carry out a complicated series of activities. Toy soldiers were built that would march; toy ducks that would quack, bathe, drink water, eat grain and void it; toy boys that could dip a pen into ink and write a letter (always the same letter, of course). Such automata were put on display and proved extremely popular (and, sometimes, profitable to the owners).

It was a dead-end sort of thing, of course, but it kept alive the thought of mechanical devices that might do more than clockwork tricks, that might be more nearly alive.

What's more, science was advancing rapidly, and in 1798, the Italian anatomist, Luigi Galvani, found that under the influence of an electric spark, dead muscles could be made to twitch and contract as though they were alive. Was it possible that electricity was the secret of life?

The thought naturally arose that artificial life could be brought into being by strictly scientific principles rather than by reliance on gods or demons. This thought led to a book that some people consider the first piece of modern science fiction—*Frankenstein*, by Mary Shelley, published in 1818.

In this book, Victor Frankenstein, an anatomist, collects fragments of freshly dead bodies and, by the use of new scientific discoveries (not specified in the book), brings the whole to life, creating something that is referred to only as the "Monster" in the book. (In the movie, the life principle was electricity.)

However, the switch from the supernatural to science did

not eliminate the fear of the danger inherent in knowledge. In the medieval legend of Rabbi Loew's golem, that monster went out of control and the rabbi had to withdraw the divine name and destroy him. In the modern tale of Frankenstein, the hero was not so lucky. He abandoned the Monster in fear, and the Monster—with an anger that the book all but justifies—in revenge killed those Frankenstein loved and, eventually, Frankenstein himself.

This proved a central theme in the science fiction stories that have appeared since *Frankenstein*. The creation of robots was looked upon as the prime example of the overweening arrogance of humanity, of its attempt to take on, through misdirected science, the mantle of the divine. The creation of human life, with a soul, was the sole prerogative of God. For a human being to attempt such a creation was to produce a soulless travesty that inevitably became as dangerous as the golem and as the Monster. The fashioning of a robot was, therefore, its own eventual punishment, and the lesson, "there are some things that humanity is not meant to know," was preached over and over again.

No one used the word "robot," however, until 1920 (the year, coincidentally, in which I was born). In that year, a Czech playwright, Karel Čapek, wrote the play *R.U.R.*, about an Englishman, Rossum, who manufactured artificial human beings in quantity. These were intended to do the arduous labor of the world so that real human beings could live lives of leisure and comfort.

Čapek called these artificial human beings "robots," which is a Czech word for "forced workers," or "slaves." In fact, the title of the play stands for "Rossum's Universal Robots," the name of the hero's firm.

In this play, however, what I call "the Frankenstein complex" was made several notches more intense. Where Mary

Shelley's Monster destroyed only Frankenstein and his family, Čapek's robots were presented as gaining emotion and then, resenting their slavery, wiping out the human species.

The play was produced in 1921 and was sufficiently popular (though when I read it, my purely personal opinion was that it was dreadful) to force the word "robot" into universal use. The name for an artificial human being is now "robot" in every language, as far as I know.

Through the 1920s and 1930s, *R.U.R.* helped reinforce the Frankenstein complex, and (with some notable exceptions such as Lester del Rey's "Helen O'Loy" and Eando Binder's "Adam Link" series) the hordes of clanking, murderous robots continued to be reproduced in story after story.

I was an ardent science fiction reader in the 1930s and I became tired of the ever-repeated robot plot. I didn't see robots that way. I saw them as machines—advanced machines—but machines. They might be dangerous but surely safety factors would be built in. The safety factors might be faulty or inadequate or might fail under unexpected types of stresses; but such failures could always yield experience that could be used to improve the models.

After all, all devices have their dangers. The discovery of speech introduced communication—and lies. The discovery of fire introduced cooking—and arson. The discovery of the compass improved navigation—and destroyed civilizations in Mexico and Peru. The automobile is marvelously useful—and kills Americans by the tens of thousands each year. Medical advances have saved lives by the millions—and intensified the population explosion.

In every case, the dangers and misuses could be used to demonstrate that "there are some things humanity was not meant to know," but surely we cannot be expected to divest ourselves of all knowledge and return to the status of the australopithecines. Even from the theological standpoint, one might argue that God would never have given human beings brains to reason with if He hadn't intended those brains to be used to devise new things, to make wise use of them, to install safety factors to prevent unwise use—and to do the best we can within the limitations of our imperfections.

So, in 1939, at the age of nineteen, I determined to write a robot story about a robot that was wisely used, that was not dangerous, and that did the job it was supposed to do. Since I needed a power source I introduced the "positronic brain." This was just gobbledy-gook but it represented some unknown power source that was useful, versatile, speedy, and compact—like the as-yet uninvented computer.

The story was eventually named "Robbie," and it did not appear immediately, but I proceeded to write other stories along the same line—in consultation with my editor, John W. Campbell, Jr., who was much taken with this idea of mine—and eventually they were all printed.

Campbell urged me to make my ideas as to the robot safeguards explicit rather than implicit, and I did this in my fourth robot story, "Runaround," which appeared in the March 1942 issue of *Astounding Science Fiction*. In that issue, on page 100, in the first column, about one-third of the way down (I just happen to remember) one of my characters says to another, "Now, look, let's start with the Three Fundamental Rules of Robotics."

This, as it turned out, was the very first known use of the word "robotics" in print, a word that is the now-accepted and widely used term for the science and technology of the construction, maintenance, and use of robots. The *Oxford English Dictionary*, in the 3rd Supplementary Volume, gives me credit for the invention of the word.

I did not know I was inventing the word, of course. In my

youthful innocence, I thought that *was* the word and hadn't the faintest notion it had never been used before.

"The Three Fundamental Rules of Robotics" mentioned at this point eventually became known as "Asimov's Three Laws of Robotics," and here they are:

1. A robot may not injure a human being, or, through inaction, allow a human being to come to harm.

2. A robot must obey the orders given it by human beings except where such orders would conflict with the First Law.

3. A robot must protect its own existence as long as such protection does not conflict with the First or Second Law.

Those laws, as it turned out (and as I could not possibly have foreseen), proved to be the most famous, the most frequently quoted, and the most influential sentences I ever wrote. (And I did it when I was twenty-one, which makes me wonder if I've done anything since to continue to justify my existence.)

My robot stories turned out to have a great effect on science fiction. I dealt with robots unemotionally—they were produced by engineers, they presented engineering problems that required solutions, and the solutions were found. The stories were rather convincing portrayals of a future technology and were not moral lessons. The robots were machines and not metaphors.

As a result, the old-fashioned robot story was virtually killed in all science fiction stories above the comic-strip level. Robots began to be viewed as machines rather than metaphors by other writers, too. They grew to be commonly seen as benevolent and useful except when something went wrong, and then as capable of correction and improvement. Other writers did not quote the Three Laws—they tended to be reserved for me—but they *assumed* them, and so did the readers.

Astonishingly enough, my robot stories also had an important effect on the world outside.

It is well known that the early rocket experimenters were strongly influenced by the science fiction stories of H. G. Wells. In the same way, early robot experimenters were strongly influenced by my robot stories, nine of which were collected in 1950 to make up a book called *I, Robot*. It was my second published book and it has remained in print in the four decades since.

Joseph F. Engelberger, studying at Columbia University in the 1950s, came across *I, Robot* and was sufficiently attracted by what he read to determine that he was going to devote his life to robots. About that time, he met George C. Devol, Jr., at a cocktail party. Devol was an inventor who was also interested in robots.

Together, they founded the firm of Unimation and set about working out schemes for making robots work. They patented many devices, and by the mid-1970s, they had worked out all kinds of practical robots. The trouble was that they needed computers that were compact and cheap—but once the microchip came in, they had it. From that moment on, Unimation became the foremost robot firm in the world and Engelberger grew rich beyond anything he could have dreamed of.

He has always been kind enough to give me much of the credit. I have met other roboticists such as Marvin Minsky and Shimon Y. Nof, who also admitted, cheerfully, the value of their early reading of my robot stories. Nof, who is an Israeli, had first read *I, Robot* in a Hebrew translation.

The roboticists take the Three Laws of Robotics seriously and they keep them as an ideal for robot safety. As yet, the types of industrial robots in use are so simple, essentially, that safety devices have to be built in externally. However, robots may confidently be expected to grow more versatile and capable and the Three Laws, or their equivalent, will surely be built into their programming eventually.

I myself have never actually worked with robots, never even as much as seen one, but I have never stopped thinking about them. I have to date written at least thirty-five short stories and five novels that involve robots, and I dare say that if I am spared, I will write more.

My robot stories and novels seem to have become classics in their own right and, with the advent of the "Robot City" series of novels, have become the wider literary universe of other writers as well. Under those circumstances, it might be useful to go over my robot stories and describe some of those which I think are particularly significant and to explain why I think they are.

1. "Robbie": This is the first robot story I wrote. I turned it out between May 10 and May 22 of 1939, when I was nineteen years old and was just about to graduate from college. I had a little trouble placing it, for John Campbell rejected it and so did *Amazing Stories*. However, Fred Pohl accepted it on March 25, 1940, and it appeared in the September 1940 issue of *Super Science Stories*, which he edited. Fred Pohl, being Fred Pohl, changed the title to "Strange Playfellow," but I changed it back when I included it in my book *I, Robot* and it has appeared as "Robbie" in every subsequent incarnation.

Aside from being, my first robot story, "Robbie" is significant because in it, George Weston says to his wife in defense of a robot that is fulfilling the role of nursemaid, "He just can't help being faithful and loving and kind. He's a machine—*made so.*" This is the first indication, in my first story, of what eventually became the "First Law of Robotics," and of the basic fact that robots were made with built-in safety rules.

2. "Reason": "Robbie" would have meant nothing in itself if I had written no more robot stories, particularly since it appeared in one of the minor magazines. However, I wrote a second robot story, "Reason," and that one John Campbell liked. After a bit of revision, it appeared in the April 1941 issue of *Astounding Science Fiction*, and there it attracted notice. Readers became aware that there were such things as "positronic robots," and so did Campbell. That made everything afterward possible.

3. "Liar!": In the very next issue of *Astounding*, that of May 1941, my third robot story, "Liar!" appeared. The importance of this story was that it introduced Susan Calvin, who became the central character in my early robot stories. This story was originally rather clumsily done, largely because it dealt with the relationship between the sexes at a time when I had not yet had my first date with a young lady. Fortunately, I'm a quick learner, and it is one story in which I made significant changes before allowing it to appear in *I, Robot*.

4. "Runaround": The next important robot story appeared in the March 1942 issue of *Astounding*. It was the first story in which I listed the Three Laws of Robotics explicitly instead of making them implicit. In it, I have one character, Gregory Powell, say, to another,

Michael Donovan: "Now, look, let's start with the Three Fundamental Rules of Robotics—the three rules that are built most deeply into a robot's positronic brain." He then recites them.

Later on, I called them the Laws of Robotics, and their importance to me was threefold:

A) They guided me in forming my plots and made it possible to write many short stories, as well as several novels, based on robots. In these, I constantly studied the consequences of the Three Laws.

B) It was by all odds my most famous literary invention, quoted in season and out by others. If all I have written is someday to be forgotten, the Three Laws of Robotics will surely be the last to go.

C) The passage in "Runaround" quoted above happens to be the very first time the word "robotics" was used in print in the English language. I am therefore credited, as I have said, with the invention of that word (as well as of "robotic," "positronic," and "psychohistory") by the *Oxford English Dictionary*, which takes the trouble—and the space—to quote the Three Laws. (All these things were created by my twenty-second birthday and I seem to have created nothing since, which gives rise to grievous thoughts within me.)

5. "Evidence": This was the one and only story I wrote while I spent eight months and twenty-six days in the Army. At one point I persuaded a kindly librarian to let me remain in the locked library over lunch so that I could work on the story. It is the first story in which I made use of a humanoid robot. Stephen Byerley, the humanoid robot in question (though in the story I don't make it absolutely clear whether he is a robot or not), represents my first approach toward R. Daneel Olivaw, the humaniform robot who appears in a number of my novels. "Evidence" appeared in the September 1946 issue of *Astounding Science Fiction*.

6. "Little Lost Robot": My robots tend to be benign entities. In fact, as the stories progressed, they gradually gained in moral and ethical qualities until they far surpassed human beings and, in the case of Daneel, approached the godlike. Nevertheless, I had no intention of limiting myself to robots as saviors. I followed wherever the wild winds of my imagination led me, and I was quite capable of seeing the uncomfortable sides of the robot phenomena.

It was only a few weeks ago (as I write this) that I received a letter from a reader who scolded me because, in a robot story of mine that had just been published, I showed the dangerous side of robots. He accused me of a failure of nerve.

That he was wrong is shown by "Little Lost Robot" in which a robot is the villain, even though it appeared nearly half a century ago. The seamy side of robots is *not* the result of a failure in nerve that comes of my advancing age and decrepitude. It has been a constant concern of mine all through my career.

7. "The Evitable Conflict": This was a sequel to "Evidence" and appeared in the June 1950 issue of *Astounding*. It was the first story I wrote that dealt primarily with computers (I called them "Machines" in the story) rather than with robots per se. The difference is not a great one. You might define a robot as a "computerized machine" or as a "mobile computer." You might consider a computer as an "immobile robot." In any case, I clearly did not distinguish between the two, and although the Machines, which don't make an actual physical appearance in the story, are clearly computers, I included the story, without hesitation, in my robot collection, *I, Robot*, and neither the publisher nor the readers objected. To be sure, Stephen Byerley is in the story, but the question of his roboticity plays no role.

8. "Franchise": This was the first story in which I dealt with computers *as computers*, and I had no thought in mind of their being robots. It appeared in the August 1955 issue of *If: Worlds of Science Fiction*, and by that time I had grown familiar with the existence of computers. My computer is "Multivac," designed as an obviously larger and more complex version of the actually existing "Univac." In this story, and in some others of the period that dealt with Multivac, I described it as an enormously large machine, missing the chance of predicting the miniaturization and etherealization of computers.

9. "The Last Question": My imagination didn't betray me for long, however. In "The Last Question," which appeared first in the November 1956 issue of *Science Fiction Quarterly*, I discussed the miniaturization and etherealization of computers and followed it through a trillion years of evolution (of both computer and man) to a logical conclusion that you will have to read the story to discover. It is, beyond question, my favorite among all the stories I have written in my career.

10. "The Feeling of Power": The miniaturization of computers played a small role as a side issue in this story. It appeared in the February 1958 issue of *If* and is also one of my favorites. In this story I dealt with pocket computers, which were not to make their appearance in the marketplace until ten to fifteen years after the story appeared. Moreover, it was one of the stories in which I foresaw accurately a social implication of technological advance rather than merely the technological advance itself.

The story deals with the possible loss of ability to do simple arithmetic through the perpetual use of computers. I wrote it as a satire that combined humor with passages of bitter irony, but I wrote more truly than I knew. These days I have a pocket computer and I begrudge the time and effort it would take me to subtract 182 from 854. I use the darned computer. "The Feeling of Power" is one of the most frequently anthologized of my stories.

In a way, this story shows the negative side of computers, and in this period I also wrote stories that showed the possible vengeful reactions of computers or robots that are mistreated. For computers, there is "Someday," which appeared in the August 1956 issue of *Infinity Science Fiction*, and for robots (in automobile form) see "Sally," which appeared in the May-June 1953 issue of *Fantastic*.

11. "Feminine Intuition": My robots are almost always masculine, though not necessarily in an actual sense of gender. After all, I give them masculine names and refer to them as "he." At the suggestion of a female editor, Judy-Lynn del Rey, I wrote "Feminine Intuition," which appeared in the October 1969 issue of

The Magazine of Fantasy and Science Fiction. It showed, for one thing, that I could do a feminine robot, too. She was still metal, but she had a narrower waistline than my usual robots and had a feminine voice, too. Later on, in my book *Robots and Empire*, there was a chapter in which a humanoid female robot made her appearance. She played a villainous role, which might surprise those who know of my frequently displayed admiration of the female half of humanity.

12. "The Bicentennial Man": This story, which first appeared in 1976 in a paperback anthology of original science fiction, *Stellar #2*, edited by Judy-Lynn del Rey, was my most thoughtful exposition of the development of robots. It followed them in an entirely different direction from that in "The Last Question." What it dealt with was the desire of a robot to become a man and the way in which he carried out that desire, step by step. Again, I carried the plot all the way to its logical conclusion. I had no intention of writing this story when I started it. It wrote itself, and turned and twisted in the typewriter. It ended as the third favorite of mine among all my stories. Ahead of it come only "The Last Question," mentioned above, and "The Ugly Little Boy," which is not a robot story.

13. *The Caves of Steel:* Meanwhile, at the suggestion of Horace L. Gold, editor of *Galaxy*, I had written a robot novel. I had resisted doing so at first for I felt that my robot ideas only fit the short story length. Gold, however, suggested I write a murder mystery dealing with a robot detective. I followed the suggestion partway. My detective was a thoroughly human Elijah Baley (perhaps the most attractive character I ever invented, in my opinion), but he had a robot side-kick, R. Daneel Olivaw. The book, I felt, was the perfect fusion of mystery and science fiction. It appeared as a three-part serial in the October, November, and December 1953 issues of *Galaxy*, and Doubleday published it as a novel in 1954.

What surprised me about the book was the reaction of the readers. While they approved of Lije Baley, their obvious interest was entirely with Daneel, whom I had viewed as a mere subsidiary character. The approval was particularly intense in the case of the women who wrote to me. (Thirteen years after I had invented Daneel, the television series *Star Trek* came out, with Mr. Spock resembling Daneel quite closely in character—something which did not bother me—and I noticed that women viewers were particularly interested in him, too. I won't pretend to analyze this.)

14. *The Naked Sun:* The popularity of Lije and Daneel led me to write a sequel, *The Naked Sun*, which appeared as a three-part serial in the October, November, and December 1956 issues of *Astounding* and was published as a novel by Doubleday in 1957. Naturally, the repetition of the success made a third novel seem the logical thing to do. I even started writing it in 1958, but things got in the way and, what with one thing and another, it didn't get written till 1983.

15. *The Robots of Dawn:* This, the third novel of the Lije Baley/R. Daneel series, was published by Doubleday in 1983. In it, I introduced a second robot, R. Giskard Reventlov, and this time I was not surprised when he turned out to be as popular as Daneel.

16. *Robots and Empire:* When it was necessary to allow Lije Baley to die (of old age), I felt I would have no problem in doing a fourth book in the series, provided I allowed Daneel to live. The fourth book, *Robots and Empire*, was published by Doubleday in 1985. Lije's death brought some reaction, but nothing at all compared to the storm of regretful letters I received when the exigencies of the plot made it necessary for R. Giskard to die.

Of the short stories I have listed as "notable" you may have noticed that three—"Franchise," "The Last Question," and "The Feeling of Power"—are not included in the collection you are now holding. This is not an oversight, nor is it any indication that they are not suitable for collection. The fact is that each of the three is to be found in an earlier collection, *Robot Dreams*, that is a companion piece for this one. It wouldn't be fair to the reader to have these stories in both collections.

To make up for that, I have included in *Robot Visions* nine robot stories that are not listed above as "notable." This is no way implies that these nine stories are inferior, merely that they broke no new ground.

Of these nine stories, "Galley Slave" is one of my favorites, not only because of the wordplay in the title, but because it deals with a job I earnestly wish a robot would take off my hands. Not many people have gone through more sets of galleys than I have.

"Lenny" shows a human side of Susan Calvin that appears in no other story, while "Someday" is my foray into pathos. "Christmas Without Rodney" is a humorous robot story, while "Think!" is a rather grim one. "Mirror Image" is the only short story I ever wrote that involves R. Daneel

Olivaw, the co-hero of my robot novels. "Too Bad!" and "Segregationist" are both robot stories based on medical themes. And, finally, "Robot Visions" is written specifically for this collection.

So it turns out that my robot stories have been almost as successful as my Foundation books, and if you want to know the truth (in a whisper, of course, and please keep this confidential), I like my robot stories better.

Finally, a word about the essays in this book. The first essay was written in 1956. All the others have appeared in 1974 and thereafter. Why the eighteen-year gap?

Easy. I wrote my first robot story when I was nineteen, and I wrote them, on and off, for over thirty years without really believing that robots would ever come into existence in any real sense—at least not in my lifetime. The result was that I never once wrote a serious essay on robotics. I might as well expect myself to have written serious essays on Galactic empires and psychohistory. In fact, my 1956 piece is not a serious discussion of robotics but merely a consideration of the use of robots in science fiction.

It was not till the mid-1970s, with the development of the microchip, that computers grew small enough, versatile enough, and cheap enough to allow computerized machinery to become practical for industrial use. Thus, the industrial robot arrived—extremely simple compared to my imaginary robots, but clearly en route.

And, as it happened, in 1974, just as robots were becoming real, I began to write essays on current developments in science, first for *American Way* magazine and then for the Los Angeles Times Syndicate. It became natural to write an occasional piece on real robotics. In addition, Byron Preiss Visual Publications, Inc., began to put out a remarkable series of books under the general title of *Isaac Asimov's*

Robot City, and I was asked to do essays on robotics for each of them. So it came about that before 1974, I wrote virtually no essays on robotics, and after 1974 quite a few. It's not my fault, after all, if science finally catches up to my simpler notions.

Golden Age Ahead

It seems to be an almost unvarying habit among human beings to find golden ages in the past, both in their own personal lives and in their societies.

That's only natural. In the first place, there's something to it—at least in our personal lives. To those of us who are elderly (or even in their late youth, as I am) there is no question but that there are memories of a time when we were younger and stronger and thinner and more vigorous and less creaky and could perform more frequently and grow tired less frequently and so on. And if that isn't golden, what is?

In general, this is naturally extrapolated to the point where whatever society was like in our teenage years is our view of what society *ought* to be like. Every change since then is viewed as a deterioration, a degeneration, an abomination.

Then, too, there are the falsities of memory, which cast a delicious haze over the past, eliminating the annoyances and frustrations and magnifying the joys. Add to that the falsities of history which inevitably produce a greater emphasis on heroism, on dogged determination, on civic virtue, while overlooking squalor, corruption, and injustice.

And in the sub-universe of science fiction, isn't this also

true? Doesn't every reader who has been reading for a decade or two remember a "golden age"? Doesn't he complain that science fiction stories aren't as good as they used to be? Doesn't he dream of the classics of the past?

Of course. We all do that. I do it, too.

There is one "Golden Age of Science Fiction" that has actually been institutionalized and frozen in place, and that is the period between 1938 and 1950, with its peak years from 1939 to 1942.

John W. Campbell, Jr. became editor of *Astounding Stories* in 1938, changed its name to *Astounding Science Fiction*, changed its style, and found new writers or encouraged older writers to expand their horizons. He helped develop me, L. Sprague de Camp, Lester del Rey, Theodore Sturgeon, Eric Frank Russell, Hal Clement, Arthur C. Clarke, and many others; and all produced stories that are among the great all-time classics of the genre. In particular, in 1939 Robert A. Heinlein and A. E. Van Vogt both burst on the scene with crackerjack stories.

Let's, however, take a closer and unimpassioned look at the Golden Age.

To begin with, how was it viewed in its own time? Did all the readers sit around, saying, "Golly, gee, wow, I'm living through a Golden Age!"?

You'd better not believe it. Sure, the young readers who had just come into the field were fascinated, but the older readers who had been reading since the late 1920s were not. Instead, they frequently talked of the "good old days" and longed for *their* golden age of the Tremaine *Astounding*, which ran from 1933 to 1938.

I was one of the old fossils, as a matter of fact. Much as I liked the stories of the Campbell era and much as I enjoyed contributing to them myself, it was of the earlier 1930s that *I* dreamed. It wasn't Heinlein that was the epitome to me of science fiction (though I recognized his worth)—it was Jack Williamson's "The Legion of Space"; it was E. E. Smith's "Galactic Patrol"; it was Nat Schachner's "Past, Present, and Future"; it was Charles R. Tanner's "Tumithak of the Corridors."

Even at this very day there is an organization called "First Fandom" (to which I belong), and only those can belong to it who were science fiction fans *before* 1938.

And if there were golden ages before the Golden Age, there were also golden ages to still-younger readers *after* the Golden Age. Indeed, Terry Carr has just published an excellent anthology of stories from 1939 through 1942 entitled *Classic Science Fiction: The First Golden Age*.

How many more have there been? I should guess that there has been one for every three-year interval since the first—to one group of readers or another.

Think again? Were the stories of your golden age really golden? Have you reread them lately?

I have reread the stories of my own golden age and found the results spotty indeed. Some of the stories I slavered over as a teenager turned out to be impenetrable and embarrassing when I tackled them again. A few ("Tumithak of the Corridors" for one) held up very well, in my opinion.

It was clear to me, though, that the general average of writing forty years ago was much lower than the general average later. That, in fact, seems to me to have been a general rule. Magazine science fiction over the last half-century has steadily risen above and away from its pulpish origins.

That means me, too. I imagine that many people who drooled over "Nightfall," *The Foundation Trilogy*, and *I, Robot* in their teens find some of the gloss gone when they reread them in their thirties. (Fortunately for myself, a substantial number do not—and there are always new teenagers entering the field and ready to be dazzled.)

Why has the quality of writing gone up?

For one thing, the competition to science fiction has gone. The pulp magazines are gone. The slick magazines scarcely publish fiction. Whereas, some decades back, science fiction magazines—with their small circulation and even smaller financial rewards—could not compete in the marketplace and could gain only raw enthusiasts, there is now comparatively little else for a beginning writer to do, few other places for him to go.

The competition for space in the science fiction magazines is therefore keener, so that better natural talents reach their pages—and set higher standards for other novices to shoot at.

I doubt, for instance, that I could possibly have broken into science fiction in 1979 with nothing more than the talent I had when I broke into the field in 1939. (Nor need this discourage new writers—they are learning in a better school in 1979 than I did in 1939.)

There is also greater knowledge of science today.

The writers of my own golden age knew very little science that they didn't pick up from the lurid newspaper stories of the day (equivalent to learning about sex in the gutter).

Nowadays, on the other hand, even those science fiction writers who are not particularly educated in science and who don't particularly use science in their stories nevertheless know much more about science and use it far more skillfully (when they do) than did the creaky old giants of the past. The new writers can't help it. We now live in a society in which science saturates every medium of communication and the very air we breathe—and the growing ranks of capable science writers see to it that the communications are of high quality.

What do we face then?

We will have stories by better writers, dealing with more exciting and more subtle themes in a more intelligently scientific manner.

Need we worry that it will all come to an end, that science is outpacing science fiction and putting us all out of a job?

No! What the scientists are doing is exactly the reverse. They are providing us with fresh, new gimmicks daily: new ideas, new possibilities.

In just the last few days, I have read about the discovery of gases in Venus's atmosphere which seem to show that Venus could not have been formed in the same way Earth was. I have read about the possibility of setting up a modulated beam of neutrinos that could allow communication *through* the Earth instead of around it. I have read that the Sun may have a steadily ticking internal clock with the irregularities of the sunspots a superficial modification—but what the clock is and why the modification, we do not know.

Each of these items can serve as the starting point for a story that might not have been possible to write last year, let alone thirty years ago. And they will be written with the skill and expertise of today.

These are exciting times for society, for science, for science fiction, for science fiction writers, for science fiction readers. George, Joel, and I are having more fun putting this magazine together all the time; and, we hope, you are having more fun reading it all the time.

Why not? There's a Golden Age ahead!

The All-Human Galaxy

In 1928, "The Skylark of Space" by Edward E. Smith appeared in *Amazing Stories*, and was instantly recognized as an important milestone in science fiction.

Until then, stories involving space travel dealt almost exclusively with the solar system. Trips to the Moon and to Mars were the staples. Visitors from other stellar systems may have been mentioned (as in the case of the visitor from Sirius in Voltaire's "Micromegas") but these were trivial instances.

Smith, however, introduced interstellar travel as a commonplace thing and placed his heroes and villains within a space-frame that included the entire galaxy. It was the first time this had happened and the readers devoured it and demanded more. The "superscience story" became the hit of the decade. Smith held the lead in this respect for twenty years, although during the first half of his career, John W. Campbell was a close second.

Smith and Campbell viewed the galaxy as including many, many intelligent species. Almost every planet possessed them and Smith, in particular, was most inventive in dreaming up unearthly shapes and characteristics for his alien beings.

This "many-intelligence galaxy" is not as prominent in science fiction as it once was, but you may find it in contemporary television. In *Star Trek* and its lesser imitations, it sometimes seemed as though a spaceship could not travel in any direction at random, for a week, without coming across an intelligent species (usually inimical in one way or another). The visual media are hampered in their ability to represent these aliens imaginatively, for somehow an actor usually exists under the makeup or plastic. The extraterrestrial creatures, therefore, if not human, were nevertheless clearly primate.

In this connection, though, the science fiction writer, Hal Clement raised an interesting question, which I think of as "Clement's Paradox."

The universe has existed for perhaps fifteen billion years, and if there are many civilizations that have risen here and there among its stars, these must have appeared at any time in the past twelve billion years (allowing three billion for the first to arise).

It should follow, therefore, that human explorers, when locating an extraterrestrial civilization, would be quite apt to find them anywhere from one to twelve billion years old in the vast majority of cases (assuming them to be very long-lived). If they were not very long-lived, but only endured, say, a million years or less before coming to a natural or a violent end, then almost all planets bearing such civilizations would show signs of the ruins of a long-dead one, or possibly a series of two or more sets of ruins.

To a lesser extent, in relatively young planetary systems, the civilization might not be ready to arise for anywhere from a million to a billion years.

The chance of encountering a civilization, then, that is at some level near our own would have to be very small.

And yet (and this is Clement's Paradox), science fiction

writers consistently show alien civilizations to be fairly close in technological level to Earth's. They might be a little more primitive or a little more advanced, but considering the rate at which technology advances on Earth these days, it would seem that the aliens are not more than a few thousand years behind us at most, or a few hundred years ahead of us at best.

How enormous the odds are against that!

As far as I know, however, science fiction writers didn't worry about this. Certainly, I didn't.

Since I began publishing in 1939, when Edward E. Smith was at the very height of his success (though John Campbell had just retired to the job of editing *Astounding*), I naturally tried my hand at the "many-intelligence" galaxy myself.

For instance, there was my eighth published story, "Homo Sol," which appeared in the September 1940 *Astounding*. It dealt with a galactic empire consisting of the civilized beings from many, many planetary systems—each planetary system containing a different type of intelligent being. Each bore the name of the native star in the species name, so that there would be "Homo Arcturus," "Homo Canopus" and so on. The plot dealt with Earth's coming of technological age and the possible entry of Earthmen ("Homo Sol," you see) into the empire.

And now there came a struggle between John Campbell and myself. John could not help but feel that people of northwest European descent (like himself) were in the forefront of human civilization and that all other people lagged behind. Expanding this view to a galactic scale, he viewed Earthmen as the "northwest Europeans" of the galaxy. He did not like to see Earthmen lose out to aliens, or to have Earthmen pictured as in any way inferior. Even if Earthmen were behind technologically, they should win anyway because they invariably were smarter, or braver, or had a superior sense of humor, or *something*.

I, however, was not of northwest European stock, and, as a matter of fact (this was 1940, remember, and the Nazis were in the process of wiping out the European Jews), I was no great admirer of them. I felt that Earthmen, if they symbolized these northwest Europeans according to the Campbellian outlook, might well prove inferior in many vital ways to other civilized races; that Earthmen might lose out to the aliens; that they might even *deserve* to lose out.

However, John Campbell won out. He was a charismatic and overwhelming person, and I was barely twenty years old, very much in awe of him, and very anxious to sell stories to him. So I gave in, adjusted the story to suit his prejudices and have been ashamed of that ever since.

Nevertheless, I didn't plan to have that happen again, *ever.* I wrote a sequel to "Homo Sol," which I called "The Imaginary," in which I evaded the issue by having Earthmen not appear (and Campbell rejected it). I wrote another story in which Earthmen fought villainous extraterrestrial overlords, and felt that would be all right, for the overlords were transparent symbols of the Nazis (and, as it happened, Campbell rejected that, too).

I continued to want to write "superscience stories" *my* way, however, and continued to probe for strategies that would allow me to do so without encountering Campbellian resistance.

I arrived at the answer when I first thought of my story "Foundation." For it, I needed a galactic empire, as in "Homo Sol," and I wanted a free hand to have it develop as I wished. The answer, when it came to me, was so simple, I can only wonder why it took me so long to reach it. Instead of having an empire with no human beings as in "The

Imaginary," I would have an empire with nothing but human beings. I would not even have robots in it.

Thus was born the "all-human galaxy."

It worked remarkably well for me. Campbell never raised any objections; never suggested that I ought to insert a few alien races; never asked why they were missing. He threw himself into the spirit of the stories and accepted my galactic empire on my terms, and I never had to take up the problem of racial superiority/inferiority.

Nor did I spend time worrying about the rationale behind the all-human galaxy myself. I had what I wanted, and I was satisfied.

I did not ask myself, for instance, why it was that human beings were the only intelligent species in the galaxy. As it happens, it is possible that though planets are extremely numerous, relatively few are habitable; or that though many planets may be habitable, few may develop life; or that though many planets may be life-bearing, few indeed may develop intelligent life or civilizations. Nevertheless, I made no effort whatsoever to state any of this explicitly as explanation for what I was describing. It is only with my new novel *Foundation's Edge*, written forty years after the series had begun, that I have started to explore the rationale behind it.

Nor did I ask myself, at the start, if the idea were a novel one. Years later, I began to think that no one before myself had ever postulated an all-human galaxy. It seems to have been my invention (though I stand ready to be corrected in this by some SF-historian more knowledgeable than myself).

If I did indeed invent the concept, it is a useful one, quite apart from the role it played in the duel between Campbell and myself (a duel which Campbell never knew existed). By removing the alien element, the play and interplay of human beings can be followed on an enormous canvas. Writers can deal with human interactions (only) on different worlds and within different societies and it gives rise to interesting opportunities of all sorts.

And, what is more, the all-human galaxy offers a way of getting around Clement's Paradox—perhaps the *only* way of doing so.

Psychohistory

Psychohistory" is one of three words (that I know of) that I get early-use credit for in *The Oxford English Dictionary*. The other two, for the record, are "positronic" and "robotics."

This is not at all unusual. Every science fiction writer makes up words and sometimes they actually penetrate the language (but then English is notoriously hospitable to neologisms—which is one of its strengths, in my opinion).

The more unimaginative and inevitable a word is, the more likely it is to be adopted, and I am not prone to making up words wildly. Thus, once the positron was discovered and named in 1935, and once "robot" became accepted as a term for a humaniform automaton in the 1920s, it was simply a matter of time before the words "positronic" and "robotics" appeared in print. That I seem to have been the first in each case is purely accidental.

In fact, when I first used the word "positronic" in print (in my story "Reason," which appeared in the April 1941 issue of *Astounding Science Fiction*) as a natural analogue of "electronic," I thought the word already existed. The same was true when I first used the word "robotics," in my story

"Runaround," which appeared in the March 1942 issue of *Astounding Science Fiction*.

In the case of "psychohistory," however, I suspected that the word was not in common use, and might even never have been used before. (Actually, the *O.E.D.* cites one example of its use as early as 1934.) I first used it in my story "Foundation," which appeared in the May 1942 issue of *Astounding Science Fiction*.

I came up with the word because John Campbell and I were discussing the course I was to take in the Foundation series once I came to him with my initial idea on the subject. I was quite frank in my intention of using Edward Gibbon's *Decline and Fall of the Roman Empire* as my model and as a basic guide for plot ideas, but I needed something that would make science fiction out of it. I couldn't simply call it the Galactic Empire and then just treat it as a hypertrophied Roman Empire.

So I suggested we add the fact that a mathematical treatment existed whereby the future could be predicted in a statistical fashion, and I called it "psychohistory." Actually, it was a poor word and did not represent what I truly meant. I should have called it "psychosociology" (a word which the *O.E.D.* lists as having first been used in 1928). However, I was so intent on history, thanks to Gibbon, that I could think of nothing but psychohistory. In any case, Campbell was enthusiastic about the idea and we were off and running.

I modeled my concept of psychohistory on the kinetic theory of gases, which I had been beat over the head with in my physical chemistry classes. The molecules making up gases moved in an absolutely random fashion in any direction in three dimensions and in a wide range of speeds. Nevertheless, one could fairly describe what those motions would be *on the average* and work out the gas laws from those average motions with an enormous degree of precision.

In other words, although one couldn't possibly predict what a single molecule would do, one could accurately predict what umptillions of them would do.

So I applied that notion to human beings. Each individual human being might have "free will," but a huge mob of them should behave with some sort of predictability, and the analysis of "mob behavior" was my psychohistory.

There were two conditions that I had to set up in order to make it work, and they were not chosen carelessly. I picked them in order to make psychohistory more like kinetic theory. First, I had to deal with a large number of human beings, as kinetic theory worked with a large number of molecules. Neither would work for small numbers. It is for that reason that I had the Galactic Empire consist of twenty-five million worlds, each with an average population of four billion. That meant a total human population of one hundred quadrillion. (In my heart, I didn't think that was enough, but I didn't want to place any greater strain on the suspension of disbelief than I absolutely had to.)

Second, I had to retain the "randomness" factor. I couldn't expect human beings to behave as randomly as molecules, but they might approach such behavior if they had no idea as to what was expected of them. So it was necessary to suppose that human beings in general did not know what the predictions of psychohistory were and therefore would not tailor their activities to suit.

Much later in the game, I thought of a third condition that I didn't think of earlier simply because I had taken it so completely for granted. The kinetic theory assumes that gases are made up of nothing *but* molecules, and psychohistory will only work if the hosts of intelligence are made up of nothing *but* human beings. In other words, the presence of aliens with non-human intelligence might well bollix the works. This situation may actually develop in future books of the Foundation series, but so far I have stayed clear of non-human intelligences in my Galactic Empire (partly because Campbell and I disagreed fundamentally on what their role would be if they existed and since neither of us would give in).

Eventually, I thought that *my* psychohistory would fade out of human consciousness because the term came to be used by psychiatrists for the study of the psychiatric background of *individuals* (such as Woodrow Wilson, Sigmund Freud, or Adolf Hitler) who had some pronounced effect on history. Naturally, since I felt a proprietary interest in the term psychohistory as a predictive study of large faceless masses of human beings, I resented the new use of the word.

But then as time went on, I grew more philosophical. After all, it might well be that there could be no analogy drawn between molecules and human beings and that there could be no way of predicting human behavior. As mathematicians began to be interested in the details of what is now called "chaos," it seemed to me that human history might prove to be essentially "chaotic" so that there could be no psychohistory. Indeed, the question of whether psychohistory can be worked out or not lies at the center of the novel I have recently completed, *Prelude to Foundation*, in which Hari Seldon (the founder of psychohistory) is portrayed as a young man who is in the process of trying to devise the science.

Imagine, then, how exciting it is for me to see that scientists are increasingly interested in *my* psychohistory, even though they may not be aware that that's what the study is called and may never have read any of my Foundation novels, and thus may not know of my involvement. (Who cares? The concept is more important than I am.)

Some months ago, a reader, Tom Wilsdon of Arden, North Carolina, sent me a clipping from the April 23, 1987, issue of *Machine Design*. It reads as follows, in full:

> *"A computer model originally intended to simulate liquid turbulence has been used to model group behavior. Researchers at Los Alamos National Laboratories have found that there is a similarity between group behavior and certain physical phenomena. To do the analysis, they assigned certain physical characteristics such as level of excitement, fear, and size of the crowd to model parameters. The interaction of the crowd closely paralleled the turbulent flow equations. Although the analysis cannot predict exactly what a group will do, it reportedly does help determine the most probable consequence of a given event."*

Then, too, Roger N. Shepard, a professor of psychology at Stanford University, has published an article in the September 11, 1987 issue of *Science* entitled "Toward a Universal Law of Generalization for Psychological Science."

Unfortunately, although I made a valiant effort to read it, the mathematics was too tough for me and even the nonmathematical portions produced only a rather dim and hazy understanding within me. However, here is the summary of the article as given at the beginning:

> *"A psychological space is established for any set of stimuli by determining metric distances between the stimuli such that the probability that a response learned to any stimulus will generalize to any other is an invariant monotonic function of the distance between them. To a good approximation, this probability of generalization (i) decays exponentially with this distance, and (ii) does so in accordance with one of two metrics, depending on the relation between the dimensions*

*along with the stimuli vary. These empirical regularities
are mathematically derivable from universal principles of
natural kinds and probabilistic geometry that may, through
evolutionary internalization, tend to govern the behaviors
of all sentient organisms."*

As I said, I don't really understand this but I have the
feeling that Hari Seldon would understand it without trouble. I am also concerned, suddenly, that psychohistory may
be developed within the next century. I placed its development 20,000 years in the future. Is this going to be another
case of my science-fictional imagination falling ludicrously
short?

Science Fiction Series

I have received a letter from Nancy Bykowski of Boling-brook, Illinois, which says, in part, "I have noticed the trend in recent years towards trilogies and serial volumes. I enjoy reading a series of books set in the same background, but it can be frustrating when the books do not stand alone. . . . But there are some authors out there that seem to be writing serials so that we will be forced to buy their next book. I believe I read somewhere that the publishers tend to encourage that kind of thinking. So my question to you is, did you write your Foundation trilogy in response to a request from a publisher, or was it simply the result of an idea that was too big for one volume?"

As it happens, I, too, have noticed the tendency for novels to come in clumps these days. (It's true of movies, also. Someday, we will have a motion picture called *Rocky XVII Meets Superman XI*.)

But why is that? Why are so many writers turning out a series of connected novels?

One very obvious reason is that it makes life simpler for them. Instead of having to invent a new social background for each story, they can make use of one that they have already devised. The writer can thus begin a new novel with a ready-made background and sometimes with ready-made characters. If you're not a writer yourself, you have no idea how much mental agony and psychic wear-and-tear that saves.

Then, too, readers who have enjoyed a book often welcome a return of the same characters and background. As a result, the pressure for a sequel and even for a continuing series is likely to come, at least to begin with, from those readers rather than from the author or publisher.

Publishers naturally welcome any book in which the chance of success and profitability is high. They are always more eager to receive a manuscript from an established writer than from a newcomer because they can usually be sure that the former will be profitable, while the latter always represents a risk. By similar reasoning publishers would prefer to have an established writer do another book of a popular series than venture in a new direction altogether. The series book is more nearly a sure thing, and publishers are almost as fond of a sure thing as you and I are.

However, are these series of novels written simply to force readers to buy the next book against his will? Of course not. If readers don't like a particular book, they are not likely to buy a sequel. If they like the first three books of a series and find the fourth disappointing, they are less likely to buy the fifth.

In short, a maintained popularity and profitability will tend to keep a series going indefinitely. Non-popularity or declining popularity will bring an end to the series quickly.

As a matter of fact, far from a series of books continuing just to lure reluctant readers into purchasing volumes that they don't really want to read, it is the reverse that is likely to be true. It is the writer, not the reader, who is likely to be victimized. After all, writing a long series of related books can grow awfully tiresome for a writer. He may have sucked the juice out of his characters and background and may long to go in other directions, thus stretching and resting his cramped and aching mind.

The writer therefore quits and goes about his business—and then a storm arises. Readers express loud disappointment and make demands for another book in the series. Publishers, becoming aware of this, and seeing no reason to allow profitability to go glimmering, then proceed to put pressure on the writer, who is often far less enthusiastic about his series than anyone else is—and, in the end, he *must* write. In that case, anyone who says to him, "You're turning out endless reams of this junk just to con the reader into buying your books," is likely to get a punch in the mouth if the writer is of the violent persuasion, or a sad look if the writer is as gentle and lovable as I am.

I'm talking from personal experience. The first three books of the Foundation series are compilations of separate pieces written for *Astounding Science Fiction* between 1942 and 1950. They were written at editorial insistence, but, for a while, I was eager to comply.

I had had enough of them after eight years, however, and, in 1950, determined to write no more. I resisted all entreaties for additions to the Foundation series and ignored all threats for thirty-two years! And then, finally, Doubleday began snarling and foaming at the mouth so I agreed to write *Foundation's Edge* and *Foundation and Earth*, the fourth and fifth books of the series.

So there you are, Ms. Bykowski. My Foundation series was written, at least in part, as a result of publisher's (and readers') pressures, but they also deal with a theme too large to be contained in one story or one novel, and each portion of the series, whether a short story or a novel, stands on its own.

But is this business of stories and novels in series an invention of science fiction? It certainly is not. It is not even a modern phenomenon. The same pressures that lead to sequelization today were operative in ancient times as well so that sequels and series must surely be as old as writing.

The *Iliad* had the *Odyssey* as its sequel, and other Greek writers capitalized on the unparalleled popularity of these two epics by writing other epics concerning events preceding, succeeding, and in between these two (none of which have survived).

The great Greek dramatists tended to write trilogies of plays. Aeschylus built a trilogy around Agamemnon, Sophocles built a trilogy about Oedipus, and so on.

Coming closer to home, Mark Twain wrote *Tom Sawyer* and when that proved successful, he wrote a sequel, *Huckleberry Finn*, and when that proved even more successful, he wrote a couple of other tales of Tom and Huck, and when those were *not* successful, he stopped.

Of course, a series need not concentrate on "continuing the plot." It may consist of a series of independent stories, which, however, share a common background and a continuing character. An enormously successful series of this sort was A. Conan Doyle's Sherlock Holmes stories. So compelling a character did Doyle create in Sherlock Holmes that the public could never get enough of him.

Doyle quickly began to grow tired of writing the stories and, indeed, began to hate Sherlock Holmes who had grown so large in public consciousness as to totally overshadow Doyle himself. In desperation, Doyle *killed* Sherlock Holmes—and was then forced to bring him back to life. Here is an extreme example of the victimization of an author (though it did make Doyle extremely wealthy). Other mystery novel series featuring a continuing detective (Hercule Poirot, Nero Wolfe, etc.) followed as a matter of course.

When I was young, series of independent stories featuring continuing characters were extremely common. There were the Nick Carter books, the Frank Merriwell books, and others, too. There were magazines which, in each issue, carried a novella featuring some character such as the Shadow, the Spider, Doc Savage, Secret Agent X, Operator 5, and so on.

Naturally, science fiction was influenced by such things. During the 1930s and 1940s, Neil R. Jones wrote some twenty stories featuring Professor Jameson and a group of companion robots with human brains; Eando Binder wrote ten stories about another robot, Adam Link; Nelson Bond wrote ten stories about a lovable bumbler named Lancelot Biggs.

However, the first successful series of *novels* in science fiction were by E. E. Smith. Between 1928 and 1934, he turned out three Skylark novels, and between 1934 and 1947, he turned out five Lensman novels.

In the 1940s, Robert A. Heinlein produced something new in his Future History series. Here the plots seemed independent and were set at widely different times, but they all fit into a consistent historical development of the solar system, so that there were references in stories set later in time to events in stories set earlier in time.

I began another series of this sort with *Foundation* in 1942. I expanded the background to the galaxy as a whole and proceeded to trace the history methodically from story to story, without jumping about. Later, I tied in my Robot series and my Empire series so that my own future history series now consists of thirteen novels—with others to come, I suppose.

Other series of the Foundation type followed, the most successful being Frank Herbert's Dune series.

In fantasy, the great success was J. R. R. Tolkien's Lord of the Rings trilogy, which inspired a host of imitations. The late Judy-Lynn del Rey, and her husband, Lester, with their marvelous ability to spot trends, encouraged the writing of novel series and put them out under their publishing imprint of "Del Rey books," so that we now have a virtual inundation of book series.

The fashion may pass, but while it is here, it seems to be bringing us a considerable number of good things to enjoy.

Survivors

Martin H. Greenberg and I have co-edited a series of anthologies for Daw Books, which include the best stories of a given year. We began with the best of 1939 (a book that appeared in 1979), and proceeded year by year until in 1986, the fifteenth volume appeared with the best of 1953. In press (as I write this) is volume sixteen which deals with the best of 1954, and in preparation is volume seventeen which deals with the best of 1955.

For each of these books, Marty writes a general introduction outlining the events of the year, both in the real world of science fiction, and in the imaginary world of the great outside. We then each supply a headnote for each of the stories in the volume. Marty's headnotes deal with the science fiction writer's career, while I write on some subject or other that either the author or the story has inspired in my weird brain.

I read Marty's headnotes with avidity for they always tell me more about the writer than I know, but not more than I want to know, of course.

One thing that I've noticed, with some curiosity, is that science fiction writers tend to have a ten-year lifespan, or, if anything, less.

That is, they will write science fiction, sometimes copiously, for ten years or less, and then they will dwindle off and fade to a halt. Sometimes, they don't even dwindle, they simply stop dead. It leaves me wondering why.

One explanation, of course, is that they find other and more lucrative markets. John D. MacDonald wrote science fiction in his early years and then made the big time in mystery thrillers. John Jakes wrote science fiction in *his* early years and then made the big time in historical fiction.

Another explanation is that they die—even science fiction writers die. Back in the 1950s, Cyril Kornbluth and Henry Kuttner died while each was at the peak of his career, and more recently the same was true for Philip K. Dick and Frank Herbert.

But there are those who simply stop and end what seems a fruitful career without switching to other fields and while remaining vigorously alive. I can even think of names of fresh young writers who graced the pages of this magazine in its early issues whom we (or anyone else) don't hear from much anymore.

Why is that? Do they run out of ideas? Do they simply get tired of writing? Does science fiction change into new channels with which they are out of sympathy?

I simply don't know.

Perhaps this is something that is true of all forms of writing and not of science fiction alone. Perhaps it is true of all forms of creative endeavor. Perhaps "burnout" is a common phenomenon which ought to be studied more than it is—by psychologists, not by me.

But if burnout is common, then what about those cases in which burnout does *not* occur? It may be just as useful to study those who are burnout-immune, and who have been writing high-quality science fiction steadily, prolifically, and successfully for, say, forty years and more, and who show no signs of breaking under the strain.

Lately, I have noticed that such people are termed "dinosaurs" by some observers in the field. I suspect that the term is used pejoratively; that is, it is *not* used as a compliment. From the things they have to say about the writers they call dinosaurs, I gather that, like the *real* dinosaurs, these writers are considered to be ancient, clumsy, and outmoded.

The term, however, is particularly inappropriate because the characteristic that we most associate with the real dinosaurs is that they are extinct, while the characteristic most noticeable about the writing dinosaurs is that they are *not* extinct. As a matter of fact, I gather from the nature of the comments made about these dinosaurs that those who use the term are rather aggrieved at them for *not* being extinct and for hogging too much of the spotlight for far too much time.

Well, that's *their* problem. For myself, I prefer to use the term "survivors," which is neither pejorative nor complimentary, but merely factual.

What are the characteristics that would qualify a science fiction writer to be a survivor?

To begin with, since I talked about a successful and steady and prolific writing life of at least forty years, a survivor would have to be at least sixty years old, and alive, and working. Naturally, he would have had to have started at quite a young age and been swatting away at it steadily since then.

I can think, offhand, of nine writers who fulfill these qualifications, and here they are:

1) Jack Williamson. His first story was published in 1928, when he was twenty years old. He has been writing steadily for fifty-nine years, and he is now eighty years old. To me, he is the undoubted and well-beloved dean of science fiction. His "The Legion of Space," which bounced me off the wall when I was a teenager, appeared fifty-three years ago.

2) Clifford D. Simak. His first story was published in 1931, when he was twenty-seven years old. He has been writing steadily for fifty-six years and he is now eighty-two years old. His "City" appeared forty-three years ago, and "Cosmic Engineers" forty-eight years ago.

3) L. Sprague de Camp. His first story was published in 1937, when he was thirty years old. He has been writing steadily for forty-nine years and is now seventy-nine years old. His "Lest Darkness Fall" which I read in preference to studying for an all-important test in physical chemistry (without ever re-gretting it) appeared forty-eight years ago.

4) Isaac Asimov. (You didn't think I'd leave myself out through some perverted notion of modesty, did you?) My first story was published in March, 1939, when I was nineteen. I have been writing steadily for forty-eight years, and I am now sixty-seven years old. My story "Nightfall" appeared forty-six years ago.

5) Robert Heinlein. His first story was published in August, 1939, when he was thirty-two. He has been writing steadily for forty-eight years and he is now eighty years old. His "Blowups Happen" appeared forty-seven years ago.

6) Fritz Leiber. His first story was published in August, 1939, when he was twenty-nine. He has been writing steadily for forty-eight years and he is now seventy-six years old. His "Conjure Wife" appeared forty-four years ago.

7) Frederik Pohl. It's hard to say because so much of his early stuff appeared under pseudonyms of one sort or another, but an undoubted story of his appeared in 1941 when he was twenty-one. He has been writing steadily for forty-six years, and he is now sixty-seven years old. His "Gravy Planet" ("Space Merchants") appeared thirty-five years ago.

8) Arthur C. Clarke. His first story appeared in 1946, when he was twenty-nine. He has been writing steadily for forty-one years, and he is now seventy years old. His "Rescue Party" appeared forty-one years ago.

9) Poul Anderson. His first story appeared in 1947, when he was twenty-one. He has been writing steadily for forty years, and is now sixty-one years old. His "The Helping Hand" appeared thirty-seven years ago.

I don't pretend that this list is necessarily definitive. Off-hand, I can think of three other possible survivors. Lester del Rey's first story was published in 1938, while A. E. van Vogt and Alfred Bester were each first published in 1939. In recent decades, however, they have not published much, so I can't honestly deny burnout in their cases.

If we look at the list, we can come to some conclusions, I think. In the first place the survivors were all science fiction fans from a very early age, and gained a life-long fascination with the field. That *must* be so.

Secondly, each must be a nonsuffering writer. Lots of good writers, even great writers, don't necessarily like to write, and must force themselves to do so. This doesn't prevent them from writing well, you understand, but it does prevent them from writing a *lot*, and my qualification for being a survivor is that one writes steadily and prolifically.

Thirdly, each resists the notion of abandoning science fiction. It is not likely that survivors can write only SF and nothing else. To my knowledge, Simak, Pohl, and Anderson have written good nonfiction; Clarke and de Camp have written quite a bit of good nonfiction; and I have written a thundering lot of it. In addition, Pohl has written mainstream fiction (he has a new novel entitled *Chernobyl* that's coming out—very unusual and *not* science fiction). De Camp has written excellent historical novels. As for me, I have written a great deal of mystery fiction. In every case, however, no matter how they stray, these survivors always return to science fiction.

There you are. "Dinosaurs"? I think not. I think the survivors (even I) are the great pillars of science fiction. I wonder how many more of them will appear in the future.

Nowhere!

In 1516, the English scholar Thomas More (1478–1535) published a book (in Latin), with a long title—as was the fashion in those days—that was also in Latin. When it finally appeared in its first English edition in 1551, the title was given as "A fruteful and pleasant Worke of the beste State of a publyque Weale, and of the newe yle, called Utopia." We refer to the book simply as *Utopia*.

In the book, More described the workings of what he considered an ideal human society, as found on the island nation of Utopia, one that was governed entirely by the dictates of reason. His description of such a society is *so* noble and rational that it would seem enviable even today.

More was under no illusions as to the real world, however. The word "utopia" is from the Greek "ou" ("not") and "topos" ("place") so that it means "nowhere." More realized, in other words, that his ideal existed nowhere on Earth (and still doesn't). In fact, his book, in describing his ideal society, served also by clear contrast to excoriate the actual governments of his day, particularly that of his native England which, of course, he knew the best.

An easy mistake was made, however. Since Utopia, as described, was such a wonderful place, it could easily be imagined that the first syllable was from the Greek prefix "eu-" meaning "good" so that Utopia became not "nowhere" but the "good place."

The word "utopia" entered the English language, and the other European languages as well, as meaning an ideal society. The adjective "utopian" refers to any scheme that has what seems a good end in view, but that is not practical, and cannot be carried through in any realistic sense.

We might speak of utopian literature—written accounts in which ideal societies are described, with More's as the classic, but not the earliest, example. Plato's *Republic* was a description, nineteen centuries earlier than *Utopia*, of an ideal state dependent upon reason. Earlier still, were accounts of ideal states in mythological or religious literature, in the form of past golden ages or of future messianic ones. The Garden of Eden is a well-known example of the former, and the eleventh chapter of Isaiah of the latter.

The production of utopian accounts has not fallen off since the time of More, either. The most influential recent examples have been *Looking Backward*, published in 1888 by Edward Bellamy (1850–1898), which described the United States of 2000 under an ideal Socialist government, and *Walden Two*, published in 1948 by B. F. Skinner (1904–), which described an ideal society based on Skinner's own theories of social engineering.

All such utopias are not convincing, however. Unless one accepts the conventions of religion, it is difficult to believe in golden or messianic ages. Nor can one easily suppose that sweet reason will at any time dominate humanity.

In the course of the nineteenth century, however, something new entered the field of utopianism. The possibility arose that scientific and technological advance might impose a utopia from without, so to speak. In other words, while human beings remained as irrational and imperfect as ever, the advance of science might supply plenty of food, cure disease and mental ailments, track down and abort irrational impulses, and so on. A perfect technology would cancel out an imperfect humanity. The tendency to take this attitude and to paint the future in glowing technological colors reached the point where what we call science fiction is called, in Germany, "utopian stories."

As a matter of fact, however, it isn't at all likely that the average writer is going to try to write a truly utopian story. There's no percentage in it. All you can do is describe such a society and explain, at great length, how good it is, and how well it works, and how it manages not to break down. There can't be any drama in it, no problems, no risks, no threat of catastrophe, no pulling through by the merest squeak. Clearly, if such things were possible, the utopia would be no utopia. It follows that utopian stories are, by their very nature, dreadfully dull. The one utopian novel I've actually managed to read was *Looking Backward*, and although it was a best-seller in its times and still has its enthusiasts, I tell you right now that if dullness could kill, reading it would be a death sentence.

So dull are utopian books that they fail to fulfill their function of pointing out the errors and faults of the societies that really exist. You can't grow indignant over these faults if you fall asleep in the process.

There developed, therefore, the habit of attacking societies in a more direct fashion. Instead of describing the good opposite, one described the evil reality, but exaggerated it past bearing. Instead of a society in which everything was ideally good, one described a society in which everything was ideally bad.

The word coined for a totally bad society is "dystopia," where the first syllable is from the Greek prefix "dys-"

meaning "abnormal" or "defective." Dystopia is the "bad place." Thus, you can figure out what "dystopian literature" would be.

Dystopias are intrinsically more interesting than utopias. Milton's description of his dystopian Hell in the first two books of *Paradise Lost* is far more interesting than his description of utopian Hell in the third book. And in *The Lord of the Rings*, not much can be told about the stay of the Fellowship in the utopian elfland of Lorien, but how the story intensifies and grows more interesting as we approach the dystopian Morder.

But can there be dystopias today with science and technology advancing as they do?

Certainly! You need only view science and technology as *contributing* to the evil (which is not difficult to do).

And yet *pure* dystopian tales are as dull and as unbearable as pure utopian ones. Consider the most famous pure dystopian tale of modern times, *1984*, by George Orwell (1903–1950), published in 1948 (the same year in which *Walden Two* was published). I consider it an abominably poor book. It made a big hit (in my opinion) only because it rode the tidal wave of cold war sentiment in the United States.

The pure utopian tale can only hit the single note of "Isn't it wonderful—wonderful—wonderful." The pure dystopian tale can only hit the single note of "Isn't it awful—awful—awful." And one cannot build a melody on the basis of a single note.

Well, then, what is a science fiction writer supposed to do if both utopian and dystopian stories are dull?

Remember, they are poor only if they are pure, so avoid the extremes. Milton's Hell was made interesting because of his portrait of Satan, courageous even in the ultimate adversity, feeling pangs of remorse even when immersed in ultimate evil. Milton's Heaven was without interest because there was no way of introducing danger in the face of an omnipotent, omniscient God. His dystopia was not pure, his utopia was.

The evil of Mordor was made bearable by the courage and humanity of Frodo and the story would have remained interesting and successful even if Frodo had failed in the end. It was his courage and humanity, not his victory, that really counted.

The essence of a story is the struggle of one thing against another: a living thing against the impersonal universe; a living thing against another living thing; one aspect of a living thing against another aspect of himself.

In each case, you have to make it possible for the reader to identify with at least one side of the struggle, so that his interest and sympathy is engaged. I say "at least" one side, because if you are skillful, you can cause him to identify with both sides and be emotionally torn.

The side or sides with whom you identify must carry on the struggle with courage, intelligence, and decency—or, at least, learn to do so. The story won't be effective if you are ashamed of the side you make your own.

Both sides must have a fair chance to win. It is tempting to pile the odds up against your side, so as to make your hero's ultimate victory the more unexpected, exciting, and triumphant, but in that case you must be sure that your side *does* end up victorious. You can't make it David versus Goliath unless David wins, and as one becomes more and more experienced and sophisticated in reading, that may come to seem too obvious and even too unrealistic.

It seems to me, then, that the best one can do is to present one's story as a struggle between sides which are both mixtures of good and evil (thus placing it somewhere between the extremes of utopia and dystopia), and don't make the odds overwhelming in either direction. One can then proceed to make one's point without being *forced* into a happy ending and under conditions of maximum excitement and reader uncertainty. The reader will not only be uncertain as to how his side will win, but *if* it will win, or even, perhaps, which is truly his side.

I don't say this is easy, of course.

Outsiders, Insiders

I am a great booster of "the brotherhood of science fiction." I wrote an editorial on the subject, with just that title, in the fifth issue of *IASFM* (January–February, 1978). I delight in thinking of us ardent writers and readers of science fiction as a band of brothers (and sisters, of course) fond of each other, and supporting each other.

Unfortunately, there are aspects of such a situation that are not entirely delightful. Let's consider these unfavorable aspects, because if the field of science fiction is to remain as ideal as we all want it to be, we have to see the dangers. We may not be able to defeat those dangers even if we see them, but we certainly can't, if we *don't* see them.

For instance, if we are truly a small and intimate band (as I remember us being in the Golden Age of Campbell, though perhaps that may only be the consequence of nostalgia) then there is a danger that we might close our ranks, unfairly and petty-mindedly, against outsiders.

I remember, for instance, when Michael Crichton wrote *The Andromeda Strain* and it hit the best-seller lists. In those days, it had not yet become common for science fiction and fantasy to be actual best-sellers, and here was an "outsider" who had accomplished it. What made him an outsider? Well, he hadn't sold to the magazines. He didn't show up at conventions. He wasn't one of *us*.

There followed reviews in various science fiction prozines and fanzines and it seemed to me, at the time, that they were uniformly unfavorable. I can't judge how justified those reviews might have been for I never read the book (perhaps because I, too, felt he was an outsider) but there did appear, in my opinion, an extra helping of venom beyond what I usually notice in unfavorable reviews.

Was that fair? No, it wasn't. Crichton, a person of great talent, went on to be very successful, both in his later books (some of them not science fiction) and in movies as well. Our objections to him did not hurt him and he doesn't need us. In retrospect, we might conclude that some of us were petty.

Nor am I trying to preach from some high moral position, implying that I am myself above such things. Not at all.

I went through a period soon after World War II, in which I reacted badly (though entirely within myself), and I look back on that period in shame.

When one is part of a small and comparatively insignificant clique, warming one's self in its closeness and camaraderie, what happens if one of the clique suddenly rises and becomes famous in the wild world outside?

Thus, in the 1940s, Robert Heinlein was quickly accepted as the best science fiction writer of us all (and in the opinion of many, he still is *the* grand master) and I accepted that, too. I was not envious, for I was just a beginner and I knew that many writers were better than I was. Besides, I liked Bob's writing a great deal. And most of all, he was one of *us*, writing for the same magazines, going to the same conventions, corresponding with us, first-naming me and expecting me to first-name him, and so on.

But then, soon after World War II, Bob Heinlein was involved with a motion picture, *Destination: Moon*. It wasn't a very good motion picture; it didn't make the hit that the later *2001: A Space Odyssey* or *Star Wars* did. But it was the first motion picture involving one of *us*, and while I said not a word, I was secretly unhappy. Bob had left our group and become famous in the land of the infidels.

To make it worse, he had published "The Green Hills of Earth" in *The Saturday Evening Post* and it had created a stir. It was a real science fiction story and it was in the slicks; not only in the slicks, but in the greatest and slickest slick of them all. We all dreamed of publishing in the *SEP* (I, also) but that was like dreaming of taking out Marilyn Monroe on a date. You knew it was just a dream and you had no intention of even *trying* to make it come true. And now Bob had done it. He hadn't just tried, he had *done* it.

I don't know whether I simply mourned his loss, because I thought that now he would never come back to us; or whether I was simply and greenly envious. All I knew was that I felt more and more uncomfortable. It was like having a stomachache in the mind, and it seemed to spoil all my fun in being a science fiction writer.

So I argued it out with myself—not because I am a noble person but because I hated feeling the way I did, and I wanted to feel better. I said to myself that Bob had blazed new trails, and that it didn't matter *who* did it, as long as it was done. Those new trails had been opened not for Robert Heinlein, but for *science fiction*, and all of us who were in the business of writing or reading science fiction could be grateful and thankful for we would sooner or later experience the benefit of Bob's pioneering.

And that was true. Because Bob made science fiction look good to people who did not ordinarily read science fiction, and who despised it when they thought of it at all, it became more possible for the rest of us to have our stuff published outside the genre magazines—even in the *SEP*. (I had a two-part serial published in that magazine myself eventually, but that was when it was long past its great days.)

The result of my working this out meant I was free of sickness on later occasions. When my first book, *Pebble in the Sky*, appeared under the Doubleday imprint, it was followed in a matter of months by *The Martian Chronicles* by Ray Bradbury. I don't have to tell you that Ray's book far outshone mine. It didn't bother me, for it seemed to me that the better Ray's book did, the more people would read science fiction in book form, and some of them would be sure to look for more of the same and stumble over mine. And they did. *Pebble* is still earning money, thirty-six years later.

And however annoying it might be that Michael Crichton could enter our field straight out of medical school, move right up to the novel level, and land on the best-seller list, and have everyone drooling over him, where's the harm? He did it (unintentionally, perhaps) for *us*. He added to the respectability of science fiction among those who found us unrespectable, and made it easier for the rest of us to get on the best-seller list occasionally.

Far from snarling, we should have been cheering.

Another point. A band of brothers (and sisters) is at its best when there is nothing much to compete for. As long as we were all getting no more than one and two cents a word (as we did in that wonderful Golden Age of Campbell) with no chance at book publication, foreign sales and movies; as long as the only kudos we could get was first place in the "Analytical Laboratory" which meant a half-cent-a-word bonus; as long as no one outside our small field had ever heard of any of us under any circumstances—what was there to compete over? The most successful of us were almost as permanently impecunious as the least so there was no reason to snarl and bite.

Now, however, times have changed. There are many more of us, and some of us write best-sellers. In fact, the greatest best-seller of the 1980s, Stephen King, is, after a fashion, one of us. It's no longer a few thousand bucks that's at stake; it's a few million. And that brother bit fades, bends, and crumples under the strain.

I don't write reviews, but I do read them, and I'm beginning to see the venom again as one writer discusses the work of another member of the brotherhood. What's more, the annual award of the Nebulas, which are determined by vote among the members of the Science Fiction Writers of America, seems to rouse hard feeling and contentiousness every year. The stakes are simply too high.

Thus, a young member of the brotherhood (to *me* he seemed a child) complained to me the other day that the "young writers" (young to *him*) were ferocious in their competitiveness. There was none of the friendliness, he said, that there was in *our* day (meaning his and mine, though I was a published writer when he was born).

I suppose he's right, though.

In a way, I can't ache to return to the good old days when we were all impoverished together. It seems a glamorous time in my mind now, but I remember Sophie Tucker's immortal dictum: "I've tried poor, and I've tried rich, and rich is better."

But is there a price we must pay for it? Must the camaraderie be gone? Must the friendly back-and-forth be over?

Why not remember that science fiction is still a relatively specialized field; that SF writers have to know a great deal more, and develop more unusual skill, than ordinary writers; that SF readers, too, demand more because they need more? Can we remember that we're all in this together?

That those in front pave the way for those behind? That at any time someone can appear from the strange land of outside, or the stranger land of youth, and carve out new territory for all of us, and that they should be welcomed gladly?

Let's be friends. There are endless worlds of the mind and emotions to conquer, and we can advance more surely, if we support—not fight—each other.

Science Fiction Anthologies

I hear it said now and then that the short story is a lost literary art form, that the magazines and various outlets that fostered the short story are dead and gone, that fiction today concentrates on the novel.

That would be too bad if it were true; but, of course, it isn't entirely true. In the field of science fiction, at least, the short story absolutely flourishes and the readers simply can't get enough of it. Indeed, any good science fiction story can count on periodic resurrection in the form of items in single-author collections and in multi-author anthologies. Some of my stories have been anthologized up to thirty times, and I by no means hold the record for such things. I suspect that both Ray Bradbury and Harlan Ellison (to name but two) can cite stories of their own that have seen far more repetitions than any of mine have.

And there you have something that is oddly characteristic of science fiction—the vast number and varying nature of anthologies in the field. I have the impression that there is no precedent in literature for this.

Why is it so? Why should science fiction, rather than

some other subsection of popular literature, spawn an unending series of anthologies of enormous variety?

I suspect that, in part at least, what is responsible is the
unusual fervor of the devoted science fiction reader. Particular stories strike such a reader with the force of a sledgehammer. Combine this with the fact that magazine science
fiction tends to be ephemeral. Few young readers save the
magazines for long. Even if they start a collection, after a few
years there comes college or marriage or other interests generally; and the collection falls apart, drifts away, vanishes.

Yet the memory of those particularly good stories lingers,
and a glow of glory builds about them. I have long lost
count of the number of letters I have received from readers
who tell me that once, when the world was young, they read
a story about thus-and-so. They can't remember the title,
the author, where it appeared or anything more than thus-
and-so; but could I tell them what the story was and how
they could go about finding it again?

Sometimes I remember the story from the small clues
they present and can give them the missing information.
More often I cannot.

You see, then, that anthologies offer a second chance.
They sometimes bring back for readers stories once loved
and then lost. Once I deliberately devised an anthology (*Before the Golden Age*, Doubleday, 1974) in order to present
some stories that I myself had loved and lost.

Sometimes such stories are better not found, for they
don't, in actual fact, bear the prismatic colors that fond
memory lends them; but sometimes they do. When I reread
"Tumithak of the Corridors" during the preparation of my
1974 anthology, I found it to be a time machine that restored me to my teenage years for an hour or two.

The first anthology of magazine science fiction appeared

in 1943. It was *The Pocket Book of Science Fiction*, edited by Donald A. Wollheim. Among the stories it contained was Stanley G. Weinbaum's "A Martian Odyssey," which I had never read, having missed the issue in which it first appeared. I was able to enjoy it for the first time when I bought the anthology. And there is another service such books offer. They allow you to recover stories you never knew you had lost.

In 1946, there appeared the first *hardcover* anthology of magazine science fiction, *The Best of Science Fiction*, edited by Groff Conklin. It was an anthology of almost painfully intense interest to me for it was the first to contain a story of mine—"Blind Alley." That was never one of my own favorites; in fact, I considered it then, and now, too, as rather second-rate. Still, I discovered eventually that Groff's opinions of quality could usually be relied on, so perhaps I underestimate "Blind Alley."

In any case, *Astounding*, the magazine in which "Blind Alley" had originally appeared, retained all rights in those days; but John Campbell insisted that anthology income go to the authors involved. It was in this way that I made the great discovery that the same story could be paid for twice and, therefore, by extension, any number of times. (It is only that which makes it possible for a science fiction writer to earn a living, so this was by no means a non-significant discovery.)

Later in that same year, the most successful science fiction anthology ever to appear was published. It was *Adventures in Time and Space*, edited by Raymond J. Healy and J. Francis McComas. It was a large, thick volume, with stories drawn almost entirely from the Golden Age of *Astounding*, and it contained my story "Nightfall." That was my introduction to the strange notion that one of my own stories was already considered a classic.

The success of the Healy-McComas anthology opened the floodgates. I haven't the faintest idea how many anthologies have been published since, but I am quite certain that there isn't an issue of any science fiction magazine that hasn't been carefully picked over to see if any gems have remained undiscovered—nor any gem or even semi-gem that hasn't been discovered and rediscovered and rediscovered.

Lately, I myself have joined the parade. I'm not entirely a novice at the anthologists' game, for I edited *The Hugo Winners* (Doubleday, 1962) along with successor volumes in 1971 and 1977, all of which were quite successful.

However, I never let myself get too involved in such matters because every anthology entails a great deal of tedious scutwork—selection, obtaining of permissions, the making out of payments and so on. The result was that through 1978, I edited only nine anthologies, which is very few for a person of my own wholesale proclivities who considers nothing worth doing that isn't worth doing *a lot.*

With my ninth anthology, however, *One Hundred Great Science Fiction Short-Short Stories* (Doubleday, 1978), I made the marvelous discovery that my friend, Martin Harry Greenberg—tall, a little plump, intelligent, conscientious, hard-working, and good-humored—found a peculiar perverted pleasure in doing all those things, like getting permissions and taking care of payments, that I hated to do.

Then the two of us discovered Charles G. Waugh, also tall, hard-working, intelligent, and conscientious, but less plump and much more grave than either Martin or I. It turned out, he knew every science fiction story ever published, remembered all the statistics and plots, and could put his hand on any of them instantly. Ask him for a story about extraterrestrials from Uranus who reproduce by binary fission and I imagine he would have three different sets of xeroxes in your hand the next day.

That changed everything. In 1979 and 1980, I helped edit no less than twelve anthologies and, at the moment of writing, there are six in press and more in preparation. (Not all are with Martin and Charles: a couple are with Alice Laurance, who has an attribute that the first two lack to an enormous degree—beauty; and one is with J. O. Jeppson, to whom I am closely related by marriage.)

Very often these recent anthologies have had my name blown out of proportion on the covers for crass commercial reasons, and over my protests, since I contribute no more than my fair share.

On the other hand I contribute no less than my fair share either, and it chafes a little when someone takes it for granted that I am merely collecting money for the use of my name. I would overlook the slur on my integrity involved in this, since all great men suffer calumny; but I hate to lose credit for all the work I do.

Charles, Martin, and I constantly consult each other by mail and phone; and we each dabble in every part of the work; but there is division of labor, too. Charles works particularly hard at locating stories and making photocopies. Martin works particularly hard at the business details.

And as for me—Well, all the stories descend on me; and I read them all and do the final judging (what I throw out is thrown out). I then write the introduction or the headnotes or (usually) both. And since I'm the one who lives in New York, I tend to do the trotting round to various publishers when that is necessary.

The net result is that each of the three of us does what he best likes to do so that preparing the anthologies becomes fun for all of us. To be sure, I labor under the steady anxiety that something might happen to Martin or Charles; but, under my shrewd questioning, both Sally Greenberg and Carol-Lynn Waugh have made it clear that each entirely understands the importance of keeping her husband functioning; and I rely on them with all confidence.

The Influence of Science Fiction

I suppose it's only natural that those of us who are devotees of science fiction would like to find in it something more than a matter of idle amusement. It ought to have important significance.

On many occasions in the past I have advanced arguments for supposing such significance to exist. Here is how it goes:

The human way of life has always been subject to drastic and more or less irreversible change, usually (or, as I believe, always) mediated by some advance in science and/or technology. Thus, life is forever changed with the invention of fire—or the wheel—or agriculture—or metallurgy—or printing.

The rate of change has been continually increasing, too; for as these changes are introduced, they tend to increase the security of the human species and therefore increase its number, thus in turn increasing the number of those capable of conceiving, introducing, and developing additional advances in science and technology. Besides that, each advance serves as a base for further advance so that the effect is cumulative.

During the last two centuries, the rate of change has become so great as to be visible in the course of the individual lifetime. This has put a strain on the capacity of individuals, and societies, too, to adapt to such change, since the natural feeling always is that there should be no change. One is used to things as they are.

During the last thirty years, the rate of change has become so great as to induce a kind of social vertigo. There seems no way in which we can plan any longer, for plans become outdated as fast as they are implemented. By the time we recognize a problem, action must be taken at once; and by the time we take action, however quickly, it is too late; the problem has changed its nature and gotten away from us.

What makes it worse is that, in the course of scientific and technological advance we have reached the stage where we dispose of enough power to destroy civilization (if it is misused), or to advance it to unheard-of heights (if we use it correctly).

With stakes so high and the situation so vertiginous, what can we do?

We must learn to anticipate fairly correctly and, in making our plans, take into account not what now exists, but what is likely to exist five years hence—or ten—or twenty—whenever the solution is likely to come into effect.

But how can one take change into account correctly, when the vast mass of the population stolidly refuses to take into account the existence of any change at all? (Thus, most Americans, far from planning now for 1990, have shown by their recent actions that what they want is to see 1955 restored.)

That is where science fiction comes in. Science fiction is the one branch of literature that accepts the fact of change, the inevitability of change. Without the initial assumption that there will be change, there is no such thing as science fiction, for nothing is science fiction unless it includes events played out against a social or physical background significantly different from our own. Science fiction is at its best if the events described could not be played out at all *except* in a social or physical background significantly different from our own.

That doesn't mean that a science fiction story should be predictive, or that it should portray something that is going to happen, before it can be important. It doesn't even have to portray something that might conceivably happen.

The existence of change, the acceptance of change, is enough. People who read science fiction come, in time, to know that *things will be different*. Maybe better, maybe worse, but *different*. Maybe this way, maybe that way, but *different*.

If enough people read science fiction or are, at least, sufficiently influenced by people who read science fiction, enough of the population may come to accept change (even if only with resignation and grief) so that government leaders can plan for change in the hope of meeting something other than stolid resistance from the public. And then, who knows, civilization might survive.

And yet this is highly tenuous; and while I accept the line of reasoning thoroughly (having, as far as I know, made it up), I can see that others might dismiss it as special pleading by someone who doesn't want the stuff he writes to be dismissed as just . . . stuff.

Well, then, has science fiction already influenced the world? Has anything that science fiction writers have written so influenced real scientists, or engineers, or politicians, or industrialists as to introduce important changes?

What about the case of space flight, of trips to the Moon? This has been a staple of imaginative literature since

Roman times; and both Jules Verne and H. G. Wells wrote highly popular stories about trips to the Moon in the nineteenth and early twentieth centuries.

Certainly, those scientists and engineers who began to deal with rocketry realistically had read science fiction; and there is no question that men such as Robert Goddard and Werner von Braun had been exposed to such things.

This is not to say that science fiction taught them any rocketry. As a matter of fact, Wells used an anti-gravity device to get to the Moon, and Verne used a gigantic gun, and both of these devices can be dismissed out of hand as ways of reaching the Moon.

Nevertheless, they stirred the imagination, as did all the other science fiction writers who flooded into the field as the twentieth century wore on, and who began to write material in large masses (if not always in high quality). All of this prepared the minds of more and more people for the notion of such trips.

It followed that when rockets were developed as war weapons during World War II, there were not lacking engineers who saw them as devices for scientific exploration, for orbital flights, for trips to the Moon and beyond. And all this would not be laughed out of court by the general public, all the way down to the rock-bottom of the average Congressman—because science fiction had paved the way.

Even this may not seem enough—too general—too broad.

How about specific influence? How about something a specific writer has done that has influenced a specific person in such a way that the world has been changed?

That has been done, too. Consider the Hungarian physicist, Leo Szilard, who—in the middle 1930s—began thinking of the possibility of a nuclear chain reaction that might produce a nuclear bomb, who recognized that his thought had become a very real possibility when uranium fission was discovered in 1939, who moved heaven and earth to persuade Allied scientists to censor themselves voluntarily in order to keep information from reaching the Nazi enemy, who persuaded Einstein to persuade President Roosevelt to initiate a vast project for developing a nuclear bomb.

We know how that changed the world (whether for better or for worse is beside the point right now, but I certainly would not have wanted Hitler to have gotten the first nuclear bomb in the early 1940s), so we can say that Leo Szilard changed it.

And how did Szilard come to have his original idea? According to Szilard himself, that idea came to him because he read a story by H. G. Wells (originally published in 1902) in which an "atomic bomb"—the phrase H. G. Wells himself used—had been featured.

Here's another case. At the present moment, industrial robots are appearing on the assembly line with increasing frequency. In Japan, whole factories are being roboticized. What's more, the robots themselves are being made more versatile, more capable, and more "intelligent" very rapidly. It isn't far-fetched to say that in a couple of decades this roboticization will be seen to have changed the face of society permanently (assuming that civilization continues to survive).

Is there anyone we can credit for this? It is difficult to place that credit on a single pair of shoulders, but perhaps the pair most likely to deserve it belongs to a man named Joseph F. Engelberger, who is the president of Unimation, which manufactures one-third of all the robots in use and has installed more of them than anybody else.

Engelberger founded his company in the late 1950s, and how do you suppose he came to found it?

Some years before, according to his own account, when he was still a college undergraduate, he became enthusiastic about the possibility of robots when he read *I, Robot* by Isaac Asimov.

I assure you that when I was writing my positronic robot stories back in the 1940s, my intentions were clear and simple. I just wanted to write some stories, sell them to a magazine, make a little money to pay my college tuition, and see my name in print. If I had been writing anything but science fiction, that's all that would have happened.

But I was writing science fiction—so I'm now changing the world.

Women and Science Fiction

My early science fiction stories had no women in them for the most part. There were two reasons for this, one social, one personal. The social reason first.

Prior to public recognition in the United States that babies are not brought by the stork, there was simply no sex in the science fiction magazines. This was not a matter of taste, it was a matter of custom that had the force of law. In most places, non-recognition of the existence of sex was treated as though it was the law, and for all I know, maybe it was indeed local law. In any case, words or actions that could bring a blush to the leathery cheek of the local censor were strictly out.

But if there's no sex, what do you do with female characters? They can't have passions and feelings. They can't participate on equal terms with male characters because that would introduce too many complications where some sort of sex might creep in. The best thing to do was to keep them around in the background, allowing them to scream in terror, to be caught and then rescued, and, at the end, to smile prettily at the hero. (It can be done safely then because THE END is the universal rescue.)

Yet it must be admitted that science fiction magazines showed no guts whatsoever in fighting this situation. That brings us to the personal reason. In the 1930s and 1940s, the readership of the science fiction magazines was heavily (almost exclusively, in fact) masculine. What's more it was young-and-intellectual masculine. The stereotypical science fiction reader was a skinny kid with glasses and acne, introverted and scapegoated by the tough kids who surrounded him and were rightly suspicious of anyone who knew how to read.

It stands to reason these youngsters knew nothing about girls. By and large, I imagine they didn't dare approach them, and if they did, were rejected by them scornfully, and if they weren't, didn't know what to do next. So why on Earth should they want this strange sub-species in the stories they read? They had not yet gotten out of the "I hate (translation: "I'm scared of") girls" stage.

This is an exaggeration, perhaps, and no doubt there were a number of tough young men and girl-chasing young men who read science fiction, but by and large, I suspect it was the stereotypical "skinny intellectual" who wrote letters to the magazines and denounced any intrusion of femininity. I know. I wrote such letters myself. And in the days when I was reading and rating every science fiction story written, I routinely deducted many points for any intrusion of romance, however sanitized it might be.

At the time I wrote and sold my first few stories, I had not yet had a date with a young woman. I knew nothing about them except what I could guess by surreptitious glances from a distance. Naturally, there were no women in my stories.

(I once received a letter from a woman who denounced me for this lack. Humbly, I wrote back to explain the reason, stating that I was, very literally, an innocent as far as women were concerned at the beginning of my writing career. She had a good answer for that, too. She wrote back in letters of flame, "That's no excuse!")

But times change!

For one thing, society changed. The breath of liberty brought on by all the talk about it during World War II weakened the censor, who retreated, muttering sourly under his breath. The coming of the pill heralded the liberation of women from unwanted pregnancy, and marked the weakening of the double standard.

For another, people *will* grow up. Even *I* didn't remain innocent. I actually went out on a date on my twentieth birthday. I met a particular woman two years later, fell in love at first sight, and all trace of fear suddenly left me. I was married five months later and you'd be *surprised* how I changed! I have in my proud possession a plaque handed me by a science fiction convention. On the brass plate is inscribed that quality of mine that had earned me the plaque. It reads "Lovable Lecher."

And yet science fiction lagged a bit, I think. Old habits didn't change easily. My own stories, for instance, remained free of sex except where it was an integral part of the development and then only to that extent, and *still* so remain. I have gotten rid of my fear (witness my five volumes of naughty limericks), but not of my sense of decorum.

What, then, really brought on the change and brought science fiction more nearly into the mainstream of contemporary literature?

In my opinion, it was not chiefly social evolution; it was not the daring new writers; not the Russes and LeGuins.

It was the coming of women into the science fiction readership!

If science fiction readers had remained almost entirely masculine—even had the acne cleared up and the youth withered—I think science fiction would have remained male chauvinist in the crudest possible way.

Nowadays, I honestly think that at least a third, and possibly nearly half the science fiction readers are women. When that is so, and when it is recognized that women are at least as articulate as men and (these days) quite ready to denounce male chauvinism and to demand treatment as human beings, it becomes impossible to continue villainy.

Even *I* have to bow to the breath of decency. In my new novel, *Foundation's Edge*, of my seven central characters, four are women—all different, all perfectly able to take care of themselves, and all formidable. (For that matter, I introduced Susan Calvin in 1940, and she strode through a man's world, asking no quarter, and certainly giving none. I just thought I'd mention that.)

And what brought in the women readers? I suppose there are a large number of reasons, but I have one that I favor. It's Mr. Spock's ears.

There is no question in my mind that the first example of decent science fiction that gained a mass following was the television show *Star Trek*, nearly twenty years ago. For a wonder, it attracted as many women as men. I don't suppose there is room to doubt that what chiefly served to attract those women was the unflappable Mr. Spock. And for some reason I won't pretend to guess at, they were intrigued by his ears.

Very few of the "Trekkies" leaked over into print science fiction (or all the magazines would have grown rich), but a minor percentage did and that was enough to feminize the readership of the science fiction magazines. And I think that was all to the good, too.

With so many women thumbing the magazines, women writers were naturally more welcome and their viewpoints greeted with greater reader sympathy—and women editors made more sense, too.

Don't get me wrong. There were women writers even in the early days of magazine science fiction, and women editors, too. When I was young, some of my favorite stories were by A. R. Long and by Leslie F. Stone. I didn't know they were women, but they were. In addition, Mary Gnaedinger, Bea Mahaffey, and Cele Goldsmith were excellent editors. I never met Ms. Gnaedinger, but I did meet Bea and Cele and I hereby testify that in addition to lots of brains, character, and personality, they each happened to be beautiful. (Irrelevant, I know, but I thought I would mention it.)

Consequently, when George Scithers left us, I found it delightful that Kathleen Moloney agreed to be the new editor. It never occurred to me for an instant that a woman couldn't handle the job just because she was a woman and, as a matter of fact, Kathleen took to it with a kind of rabid delight. She introduced interesting changes and stamped her personality on the magazine.

But then, there came along the all-too-frequent villain in such cases, the offer-one-can't-refuse. It may have been Kathleen's performance here that aroused interest in other publishing houses and—well, one can't turn down a chance to advance in one's chosen profession, so we lost Kathleen.

And yet all is not lost, either. I have on numerous occasions mentioned the charming Shawna McCarthy, who is as sharp as a scalpel, and who is universally liked for the excellent reason that she is universally likable. *I* like her.

Shawna served faithfully as right-hand person first to George, and then to Kathleen. In the process, she learned every facet of the editing business and developed (thank goodness) the ambition to hold the top position.

So when Kathleen left, I said, "It has to be Shawna" and everyone agreed with me, especially Shawna.

And here she is. Readers—female and male—I give you Shawna!

Religion and Science Fiction

In the November 1983 issue of *Asimov's*, the cover story was "The Gospel According to Gamaliel Crucis," by that excellent writer, Michael Bishop. It dealt with a sensitive subject—the coming of a savior, or, in effect, the second coming of Christ.

What makes it even more effective as a science fiction story is that the savior is an extraterrestrial, and not a particularly attractive one to our human eyes since she (!) is a giant mantis. This is entirely legitimate, it seems to me, since if there is other life in the universe, especially intelligent life, one would expect that a truly universal God would be as concerned for them as for us, and would totally disregard physical shape since it is only the "soul," that inner intellectual and moral identity, that counts.

What is more, Bishop decided to make the story more powerful by casting it into a biblical shape, dividing it into chapters and verses and making use of a touch of suitable biblical wording.

The result was a *tour de force* which we obviously considered quite successful, or we would not have published it. Still we were prepared for the fact that some readers might feel uneasy with, or even offended by, the subject matter and/or style.

One letter was quite angry, indeed. The writer was "strongly displeased" and considered it "a burlesque of the scriptures" and, finding no other value to the story, considered it to have been written and published only for the sake of the burlesque.

This can be argued with, of course, but never entirely settled. If a reader sees in it only burlesque, he or she can scarcely be argued out of it. There will always be differences of opinion, often based upon emotion rather than reason, with regard to the value of any work of art.

But there is something more general here. There is the matter of how science fiction ought to deal with religion, especially *our* religion. (Few people worry very much about how some other religion is handled, since only our own is the true one.)

No one wants to offend people unnecessarily, and religion is a touchy subject, as we all know. In that case, might it not be best simply to avoid religious angles altogether in writing science fiction? As our angry correspondent says, "I suggest . . . that offending any substantial religious group is not the way to win friends or sell magazines."

Yes, we know that, and since we *do* want to win friends and sell magazines, we would not knowingly go out of our way to embarrass and humiliate even non-substantial groups of our readers just for the fun of it.

But we are also editing a serious science fiction magazine that, we earnestly hope, includes stories of literary value, and it is the very essence of literature that it consider the great ideas and concerns of human history. Surely that complex of ideas that goes under the head of "religion" is one of the most central and essential, and it would be rather a shame to have it declared out of bounds. In fact, for a magazine to self-censor itself out of discussing religion would be to bow to those forces that don't really believe in our constitutional guarantee of freedom of speech and press. If we were to do so, we would be, in a very deep sense, un-American.

Besides, if we were to try to avoid this very touchy subject where do we stop? I tend to ignore religion in my own stories altogether, except when I absolutely have to have it. Well, I absolutely had to have it in some of my early Foundation stories and in "Nightfall," and so I made use of it. And, whenever I bring in a religious motif, that religion is bound to seem vaguely Christian because that is the only religion I know anything about, even though it is not mine. An unsympathetic reader might think I am "burlesquing" Christianity, but I am not.

Then, too, it is impossible to write science fiction and *really* ignore religion. What if we find intelligent beings on other worlds. Do *they* have a religion? Is our God universal, and is he/she/it their God as well? What do we do about it? What do they do about it?

This point is almost never taken up but, since it would certainly arise if such beings were discovered in actual fact, science fiction loses touch with reality in taking the easy way out and pretending religion doesn't exist.

Or, consider time-travel. I don't know how many stories have been written about people going back in time to keep Lincoln from being assassinated, but how about people going back in time to keep Jesus from being crucified? Surely that greater feat would occur to someone in actual fact, if time-travel were possible.

Think of the changes that could be rung on such a theme. If Jesus were rescued while on his way to the site of crucifixion, and if the rescue were made by modern technology—a helicopter or something more advanced, while the

Roman soldiers were held off by rifle-fire at the very least—would it not seem to the people of the time that supernatural forces were rescuing Jesus? Would it not seem that angels were coming to the aid of a true savior? Would it not establish Christianity as the true religion at once?

Or would it? Clearly, it was God's divine purpose (assuming the God of the Bible exists) to have the crucifixion take place in order that Jesus serve as a divine atonement for Adam's sin. Would the subversion of this plan be allowed to take place?

It's a nice dilemma, and it is within the province of legitimate science fiction. Yet who has ever considered writing such a story, even though it would give us a chance to deal with what many consider the central event of history? The story would be an extremely difficult one to write, and I wouldn't feel up to it myself, but I think it is primarily self-censorship that keeps it from being written.

For that matter, what if we went back in time and found that the biblical Jesus never existed?

The mere existence of time-travel makes all these speculations irresistible, so is it possible that very religious people might object to time-travel themes, and call them blasphemous, simply because of the possibilities they give rise to?

The correspondent says in his letter, "Dr. Asimov, I know that you are an atheist—" and there may be the implication that because of this I am insensitive to the feelings of religionists, or perhaps even anxious to make them seem ridiculous.

As a matter of fact, I have frequently, in my writings, made it clear that I have never encountered any convincing evidence of the existence of the biblical God, and that I am incapable of accepting that existence on faith alone. That makes me an atheist, but, although this may surprise some Americans, the Constitution safeguards my right to be one and to proclaim myself one.

Nevertheless, although I am an atheist, I am not a prose-lytizing one; I am not a missionary; I do not treat atheism as a kind of true faith that I must force on everyone. After all, I have published more than almost anyone, about 20,000,000 words so far, and I have frequently discussed controversial problems. You are free to go through my writings and search for any sign that I ridicule religion as such. I have opposed those people who attack legitimate scientific findings (evolution, as an example) in the name of religion, and who do so without evidence, or (worse yet) with distorted and false evidence. I don't consider them true religionists, however, and I am careful to point out that they disgrace religion, and are a greater danger to honest religion than to science.

And suppose I weren't an atheist. My parents were Jewish and I might have been brought up an Orthodox Jew, or become one of my own volition. Might it then be argued that I would naturally favor any story burlesquing Christianity?

Or suppose I were a Methodist; would I therefore look for stories that burlesqued Judaism, or Catholicism—or atheism?

If I were in the mood to run this magazine in such a way as to offend "any substantial religious group" I wouldn't have to be an atheist. I could do it if I were anything at all, provided only that I were a bigot, or an idiot, or both.

In actual fact, I am neither and again, I offer my collected writings as evidence. As for Shawna, she doesn't have a similar body of written works to cite but, if I may serve as character witness, I can tell you right now she is certainly not a bigot, and a hundred times certainly not an idiot.

Needless to say, I am sorry that our correspondent was upset by "The Gospel According to Gamaliel Crucis." If we lived in an ideal world, we would never publish any story that upset *anyone*. In this case, though, we had to choose. On the one hand, we had a remarkable story that considered, quite fearlessly, an important idea, and we felt that most readers would recognize this point—if not at once then upon mature consideration. On the other hand, we had a story that might offend some of our readers.

We made the choice. We put quality and importance ahead of the chance of some offence. We hope that our angry correspondent will consider the matter again and see that the story is far more than a burlesque. He might even give Bishop points for skill and courage.

Time-Travel

I have often said, in speaking and in writing, that the qualified science fiction writer avoids the scientifically impossible. Yet I can't bring myself to make that rule an absolute one, because there are some plot devices that offer such dramatic possibilities that we are forced to overlook the utter implausibilities that are involved. The most glaring example of this is time-travel.

There are infinite tortuosities one can bring to plot development if only you allow your characters to move along the time axis, and I, for one, can't resist them, so that I have written a number of time-travel stories, including one novel, *The End of Eternity*.

You can get away with a kind of diluted time-travel story, if you have your character move in the direction we all move—from present to future—and suspend the usual consciousness that accompanies the move by having him (please understand that, for conciseness I am using "him" as a shorthand symbol for "him or her") sleep away a long period of time, as Rip van Winkle did, or, better, having him frozen for an indefinite period at liquid nitrogen temperatures. Better still, you might make use of relativistic notions and have your character move into the future by having his subjective-time slowed through motion at speeds close to that of light, or motion through an enormously intense gravitational field.

These are plausible devices that do not do damage to the structure of the Universe, but they are one-way motions, with no return possible. I did it in *Pebble in the Sky* although I made use of an unknown (and unspecified) natural law involving nuclear fission, which was then quite new. This was a weakness in the plot, but I got past it in the first couple of pages and never brought it up again so I hoped no one would notice it. (Alas, many did.)

The same device can be used to make repeated jumps, always into the future, or to bring someone from the past into the present.

Once you have a device that sends someone into the future, however, it is asking too much of writer-nature not to use some device—such as a blow on the head—to send a person into the past. (Mark Twain does it in "A Connecticut Yankee at King Arthur's Court.") For that, there is some scientific justification at the subatomic level, where individual particles are involved and entropy considerations are absent. For ordinary objects, where entropy *is* involved, there is none.

But all one-shot changes in either direction are only devices to start the story, which then usually proceeds in a completely time-bound fashion. That's not the true, or pure, time-travel story. In true time-travel, the characters can move, at will, back and forth in time. Nor is it fair if this is done through supernatural intervention as in Charles Dickens's *A Christmas Carol*. It must be done by an artificial device under the control of a human being.

The first true time-travel story was H. G. Wells's *The Time Machine*, published in 1895. Wells, who was probably the best science fiction writer of all time,[1] carefully explained the rationale behind it. It requires four dimensions to locate an object: it is somewhere on the north-south axis, somewhere on the east-west axis, somewhere on the up-down axis, and somewhere on the past-future axis. It exists not only in a certain point of three-dimensional space but at a certain instant of time. A merely three-dimensional object is as much a mathematical abstraction as is a two-dimensional plane, or a one-dimensional line, or a zero-dimensional point. Suppose you considered the Great Wall of China as existing for zero time and therefore consisting of three dimensions only. It would then not exist at all and you could walk through its supposed position at any time.

Since duration is a dimension like height, width, and thickness, and since we can travel at will north and south, east and west, and (if only by jumping) up and down, why shouldn't we also travel yesterward and tomorrowward as soon as we work out a device for the purpose?

That was 1895, remember, and Wells's analysis at that time had some shadow of justification. But then, in 1905, came Einstein's special theory of relativity, and it became clear that time is a dimension but it is *not* like the three spatial dimensions, and it can't be treated as though it were.

And yet Wells's argument was so winning and the plots it made possible so enticing that science fiction writers generally just ignore Einstein and follow Wells. (I do so myself in *The End of Eternity*.)

The dead giveaway that true time-travel is flatly impossible arises from the well-known "paradoxes" it entails. The classic example is "What if you go back into the past and kill your grandfather when he was still a little boy?" In that case,

[1] If others, since, seem to have reached greater heights, it is only because they stand on Wells's shoulders.

you see, the murderer was never born, so who killed the little boy?

But you don't need anything so drastic. What if you go back and change any of the many small items that made it possible for your father and mother to meet, or to fall in love after they met, or to marry after they fall in love. Suppose you merely interfered with *the* crucial moment of sex and had it happen the next evening, or perhaps just five minutes later than it did, so that another sperm fertilized the ovum rather than the one that should have. That, too, would mean the person committing the act would never come into existence, so who would commit the act?

In fact, to go into the past and do *anything* would change a great deal of what followed, perhaps everything that followed. So complex and hopeless are the paradoxes that follow, so wholesale is the annihilation of any reasonable concept of causality, that the easiest way out of the irrational chaos that results is to suppose that true time-travel is, and forever will be, impossible.

However, any discussion of this gets so philosophical that I lose patience and would rather consider something simpler.

Suppose you get into a time machine and travel twenty-four hours into the future. The assumption is that you are traveling only in the time dimension, and that the three spatial dimensions are unchanged. However, as is perfectly obvious, Earth is moving through the three dimensions in a very complex way. The point on the surface on which the time-machine is located is moving about the Earth's axis. The Earth is moving about the center of gravity of the Earth-Moon system, and also about the center of gravity of the Earth-Sun system; is accompanying the Sun in its motion about the center of the galaxy, and the galaxy in its undefined motion relative to the center of gravity of the Local

Group and to the center of gravity of the universe as a whole if there is one.

You might, of course, say that the time-machine partakes of the motion of the Earth, and wherever Earth goes, the time-machine goes, too. Suppose, though, we consider the Earth's motion (with the solar system generally) around the galactic center. Its speed relative to that center is estimated to be about 220 kilometers per second. If the time-machine travels twenty-four hours into the future in one second, it travels 220 kilometers x 86,400 (the number of seconds in a day), or 19,008,000 kilometers in one second. That's over sixty-three times the speed of light. If we don't want to break the speed-of-light limit, then we must take not less than twenty-three minutes to travel one day forward (or backward) in time.

What's more, I suspect that considerations of acceleration would have to be involved. The time-machine would have to accelerate to light speed and then decelerate from it, and perhaps the human body could only stand so much acceleration in the time direction. Considering that the human body has never in all its evolution accelerated at all in the time direction, the amount of acceleration it ought to be able to endure might be very little indeed, so that the time-machine would have to take considerably more than an hour to make a one-day journey—say, at a guess, twelve hours.

That would mean we could only gain half a day per day, at most, in traveling through time. Spending ten years to go twenty years into the future, would not be in the least palatable. (Can a time machine carry a life-support system of that order of magnitude?)

And, on top of that, I don't see that having to chase after the Earth would fail to cost the usual amount of energy just because we're doing it by way of the time dimension. Without calculating the energy, I am positive time-travel is insu-

perably difficult, quite apart from the theoretical considerations that make it totally impossible. So let's eliminate it
from serious consideration.

But not from science fiction! Time-travel stories are too
much fun for them to be eliminated merely out of mundane
considerations of impracticability, or even impossibility.

Part Three

ON WRITING
SCIENCE FICTION

Plotting

Every once in a while, an article about me appears in a newspaper, usually in the form of an interview. I don't go looking for these things, because I hate the hassle of being photographed (which, these days, invariably goes with interviews) and I hate the risk of being misquoted or misinterpreted.

Nevertheless, I can't always turn these things down because I'm not really a misanthrope, and because I do like to talk about myself. (Oh, you noticed?)

As a result of one such interview, an article about me appeared in the *Miami Herald* of August 20, 1988. It was a long article and quite favorable (the headline read "The Amazing Asimov") and it had very few inaccuracies in it. It did quote me, to be sure, as saying that my book *The Sensuous Dirty Old Man* was "nauseating." That is wrong. I said that the books it satirized, *The Sensuous Woman* and *The Sensuous Man*, were nauseating. *My* book was funny.

It also quoted me as saying that I considered "Nightfall" to be my best story. I don't, not by a long shot. I said it was my "best-known" story, a different thing altogether.

Usually any reporter who interviews me is willing to let

it go at that, but the *Miami Herald* reporter was more enterprising. She asked questions of my dear wife, Janet, and of my brother, Stan, who's a vice-president at the Long Island *Newsday*. Both said nice things, but then they both like me.

However, she also consulted someone who teaches a course in science fiction at Rutgers University. Her name is Julia Sullivan, and I don't think I know her, though it is clear from what she is quoted as saying that she is a woman of luminous intelligence and impeccable taste.

She praised my clarity and wit, for instance, but I'm used to that. The thing is, she is also quoted as saying about me that "he surprises me. Sometimes I think he's written himself out, and then he comes up with something really good. . . . He has the greatest mind for plot of any science fiction writer."

That's nice!

I can't recall anyone praising me for my plots before, and so, of course, it got me to thinking about the whole process of plotting.

A plot is an outline of the events of a story. You might say, for instance, "There's this prince, see? His father has recently died and his mother has married his uncle, who becomes the new king. This upsets the prince who hoped to be king himself and who doesn't like the uncle anyway. Then he hears that the ghost of his dead father has been seen—"

The first thing you have to understand is that a plot is not a story, any more than a skeleton is a living animal. It's simply a guide to the writer, in the same way that a skeleton is a guide to a paleontologist as to what a long-extinct animal must have looked like. The paleontologist has to fill in the organs, muscles, skin, etc. all around the skeleton, and that's not feasible except for a trained person. Hence, if you give the plot of *Hamlet* to a non-writer, that will *not* help him produce *Hamlet* or anything even readable.

Well, then, how do you go about building a story around the plot?

1) You can, if you wish, make the plot so detailed and so complex that you don't have to do much in the way of "building." Events follow one another in rapid succession and the reader (or viewer) is hurried from one suspense-filled situation to another. You get this at a low level in comic strips and in the old movie serials of the silent days. This is recognized as being suitable mainly for children, who don't mind being rushed along without regard for logic or realism or any form of subtlety. In fact children are apt to be annoyed with anything that impedes the bare bones of the plot, so that a few minutes of love interest is denounced as "mush." Of course, if it is done well enough, you have something like *Raiders of the Lost Ark*, which I enjoyed tremendously, even if there were parts that made no sense at all.

2) You can go to the other extreme, if you wish, and virtually eliminate the plot. There need be no sense of connected events. You might simply have a series of vignettes as in Woody Allen's *Radio Days*. Or you might tell a story that is designed merely to create a mood or evoke an emotion or illuminate a facet of the human condition. This, too, is not for everyone, although, done well, it is satisfying to the sophisticated end of the reader (or viewer) spectrum. The less sophisticated may complain that the story is not a story and ask "But what does it *mean?*" or "What happened?" The plotless story is rather like free verse, or abstract art, or atonal music. Something is given up that most people imagine to be inseparable from the art form, but which, if done well (and my goodness, is it hard to do it well), transcends the form and gives enormous satisfaction to those who can follow the writer into the more rarefied realms of the art.

3) What pleases the great middle—people who are not children or semi-literate adults, but who are not cultivated esthetes, either—are stories that have distinct plots, plots that are filled-out successfully, one way or another, with non-plot elements of various types. I'll mention a few.

3a) You can use the plot as a way of bringing in humor or satire. Read books by P. G. Wodehouse, or Mark Twain's *Tom Sawyer*, or Charles Dickens's *Nicholas Nickleby*.

3b) You can use the plot to develop an insight into the characters of the individuals who people the story. The great literary giants, such as Homer, Shakespeare, Goethe, Tolstoy, Dostoyevksy, do this supremely well. Since human beings and their relationships with each other and with the universe are far more complex and unpredictable than are simple events, the ability to deal with "characterization" successfully is often used as a way of defining "great literature."

3c) You can use the plot to develop ideas. The individuals who people the story may champion alternate views of life and the universe, and the struggle may be one in which each side tries to persuade or force the other into adopting its own world-view. To do this properly, each side must present its view (ostensibly to each other, but really to the reader) and the reader must be enticed into favoring one side or another so that he can feel suspense over which side will win. Done perfectly, the two opposing views should represent not white and black, but two grays of slightly different shades so that the reader cannot make a clear-cut decision but must *think* and come to conclusions of his own. I go into greater detail on this version than on the other two, because this is what *I* do.

There are many other ways of dealing with plot, but the important thing to remember is that they are not necessarily mutually exclusive. A humorous novel can be full of quite serious ideas and develop interesting characters, for instance.

On the other hand, writers can, more or less deliberately, sacrifice some elements of plot buildups in their anxiety to do, *in great detail*, what it is they want to do. I am so intent on presenting my opposing ideas, for instance, that I make no serious attempt to characterize brilliantly or to drench the tale in humor. As a result, much is made of my "cardboard characters" and I am frequently accused of being "talky." But these accusations usually come from critics who don't see (or perhaps lack the intelligence to see) what it is that I am trying to do.

But I'm sure that this is not what Ms. Sullivan meant when she said I had "the greatest mind for plot."

I rather think she means that my stories (especially my novels) have very complicated plots that hang together and have no loose ends, that don't get in the way of the ideas I present in my stories, and that are not obscured by those ideas, either.

Now, how is that done?

I wish I could tell you. All I'm aware of is that it takes a great deal of hard thinking, and that between the thinking and the writing that I must do, there is little time for me to do anything else. Fortunately, I both think and write very quickly and with almost no dithering, so I can get a great deal done.

Which brings me to another part of the interview. The reporter speaks of my apartment as "filled with eclectic, utilitarian furniture chosen more for comfort than for style, much like Asimov's wardrobe. For a recent speaking engagement, he wore a Western tie, a too-big jacket, and a striped shirt with the kind of long wide collar that was popular in the 1970s."

She's absolutely right. As far as style is concerned, I'm a shambles. It doesn't bother me, though. To learn to live and dress with full attention to style would require hours upon umpteen hours of thought, of education, of decision-making, and so on. And that takes time I don't want to subtract from my writing.

What would *you* rather have? Asimov, the prolific writer, or Asimov, the fashion plate? I warn you. You can't have them both.

Metaphor

I received a letter from a fan the other day, one who had bought a copy of *Agent of Byzantium*, by Harry Turtledove, which appeared in a series entitled "Isaac Asimov Presents." (That's why he wrote to me.)

The cover shows a man dressed, says my correspondent, "in a Romanesque military uniform, holding a Roman helmet in his left hand." He also carried "a very large, very modern, very lethal looking blaster rifle" and "an electronic scanning device."

My correspondent was intrigued by the anachronism, bought the book, read it, and "enjoyed the book." However, he found no place in the story where a man was holding such a rifle and scanning device, and he felt cheated. He had been lured into buying and reading the book by an inaccurate piece of cover art, and he wrote to complain.

So I thought about it. Now my knowledge of art is so small as to be beneath contempt, so naturally, I can't be learned about it. There is, however, nothing I don't understand about the word trade (fifty years of intimate, continuous and successful practice at it gives me the right to say that), and so I will approach matters from that angle.

I see the reader's complaint as the protest of the "literalist" against "metaphor." The literalist wants a piece of art (whether word or picture) to be precise and exact with all its information in plain view on the surface. Metaphor, however, (from a Greek word meaning "transfer") converts one piece of information into another analogous one, because the second one is more easily visualizable, more dramatic, more (in short) poetic. However, you have to realize there is a transfer involved and if you're a "born-again literalist," if I may use the phrase, you miss the whole point.

Let's try the Bible, for instance. The children of Israel are wandering in the desert and come to the borders of Canaan. Spies are sent in to see what the situation is and their hearts fail them. They find a people with strong, walled cities; with many elaborate chariots and skilled armies; and with a high technology. They come back and report "all the people we saw in it are men of a great stature. And there we saw the giants. . . . and we were in our own sight as grasshoppers and so we were in their sight."

Right! They were of "great stature" in the sense that they had a high technology. They were "giants" of technology and the Israelites were "grasshoppers" in comparison. There was as much chance, the spies felt, of the Israelites defeating the Canaanites as of a grasshopper defeating a man.

It makes perfect metaphoric sense. The use of "giants" and "grasshoppers" is *dramatic* and gets across the idea. However, both Jewish and Christian fundamentalists get the vague notion that the Canaanites were two hundred feet tall, so that ordinary human beings were as grasshoppers in comparison. The infliction of literalism on us by fundamentalists who read the Bible without seeing anything but words is one of the great tragedies of history.

Or let's turn to Shakespeare and the tragedy of *Macbeth*.

Macbeth has just killed Duncan and his hands are bloody and he is himself horror-struck at the deed. Lady Macbeth is concerned over her husband's having been unmanned and gives him some practical advice. "Go," she says, "get some water and wash this filthy witness from your hand."

And Macbeth, his whole mind in disarray, says, "Will all great Neptune's ocean wash this blood clean from my hand? No. This my hand will rather the multitudinous seas incarnadine, making the green one red."

It's a powerful figure, as you see a bloody hand dipped into the ocean and all the vast sea turning red in response, but, literally, it makes no sense. How can a few drops of blood turn the ocean red? All the blood in all the human beings on Earth if poured into the ocean would not change its overall color perceptibly. Macbeth might seem to be indulging in "hyperbole" (an extravagant exaggeration which sometimes makes its point, but usually reduces it to ridicule).

This, however, is not hyperbole, but metaphor. Consider! Macbeth has killed a man who had loved him and loaded him with honors, so he commits the terrible sin of ingratitude. Furthermore, the man he murdered was a guest in his house, so that Macbeth has violated the hallowed and civilized rules of hospitality. Finally, the man he murdered was his king and in Shakespeare's time, a king was looked upon as the visible representative of God on Earth. This triple crime has loaded Macbeth's soul with infinite guilt.

The blood cannot redden the ocean, but the blood is not blood, it is used here as a metaphor for guilt. The picture of the ocean turning red gives you a violently dramatic notion of the infinite blackness that now burdens Macbeth's soul, something you couldn't get if he had merely said, "Oh, my guilt is infinite."

A literalist who sets about calculating the effect on the

ocean of a bloody hand is getting no value out of what he reads.

One more example. Consider Coleridge's "Rime of the Ancient Mariner." In the fourteenth verse of the third part, there come the lines: "Till clomb above the eastern bar the horned Moon, with one bright star within the nether tip."

The "horned Moon" is the crescent moon, of course, and there *can't* be a bright star within the nether tip. The crescent is the lighted portion of the moon, but the rest of it, though out of the sunlight and dark, is still there. For a bright star to be within the nether tip is to have it shining through hundreds of miles of lunar substance. It is an impossibility, and I don't know how many readers have snickered at Coleridge's naïveté in this.

But is it naïveté? The poem begins very simply and naturally till the Ancient Mariner kills the albatross, a lovable and unoffending bird. This itself is a metaphor. After all, human beings have killed lovable and unoffending birds since time immemorial. In this case, though, the killing represents all the callous and indifferent cruelty of the human species, and, as a result, the ship with its crew (who approved the Mariner's deed) enters a strange world in which natural law is suspended and chaos is come again as God removes himself. The atmosphere of the poem becomes weird and unearthly and normality begins to return only after the Mariner involuntarily blesses all the living things in the ocean in a gush of love.

I have a feeling that Coleridge knew that a star could not shine within the nether tip of the crescent but merely used it as one more example of the chaos of a world in which human cruelty denies love, order, and God's presence. It is only fitting that a star shine where no star could possibly shine.

To miss that point is to miss the point of the poem and to

understand only its jigging meter and its clever rhyming—
which is plenty, but far from enough. A literalist deprives
himself of the best part of art.

Suppose we apply this way of looking at things to visual
art. If you ask an artist to illustrate a piece of writing *precisely*, you make of him a slave to the literal word. You sup-
press his creativity and impugn the independence of his
mind and ability. The better the artist, the less likely he is
(barring an absolute need for money) to accept such a job.

An artist worth his salt does not illustrate the literal
words, but the mood of a story. He tries, by virtue of his art
and ability, to deepen and reinforce the meaning of a story
and the intent of the writer.

Thus, in the mid-December 1988 issue, the cover of *Asimov's* illustrates my story "Christmas Without Rodney." It
does not illustrate any incident in the story. Instead it shows
in the foreground a boy with a sullen and self-absorbed expression. What's more, the predominant color is red, which
to my way of thinking symbolizes anger (a metaphor for the
flushed face of a person in rage). This demonstrates the
anger of a spoiled brat who does not instantly have his own
way, and the anger he inspires in the narrator of the story.
Behind the boy is an elaborate robot, with one metal hand
to his cheek as though uncertain as to his course of action,
something that fulfills one of the underlying themes of the
story. The artist, Gary Freeman, does not illustrate the
story, but adds to it and gives it a visual dimension. That is
what he is supposed to do and what he is paid to do.

This brings us to the cover illustration of *Agent of Byzantium*. It is clearly the intent of the artist to illustrate the *nature* of the story, not the story itself. Constantinople is in the
background, identified by the gilded dome of Hagia Sophia.
In the foreground is a soldier who has Byzantine characteristics. So far we have an historical novel. But he also pos-

sesses objects of high technology associated with modern western culture. Clearly it is an historical novel set in an alternate reality. And that is what the book deals with. The cover is precise, it tells us what we need to know, it satisfies the artist's own cravings, and if the *details* of the technology are not precisely met in any incident in the book, that matters not a whit.

Ideas

Someone once asked Isaac Newton how he managed to reach solutions to problems that others found impenetrable. He answered, "By thinking and thinking and thinking about it."

I don't know what other answer people can possibly expect. There is the romantic notion that there is such a thing as "inspiration," that a heavenly Muse comes down and plunks her harp over your head and, presto, the job is done. Like all romantic notions, however, this is just a romantic notion.

Some people may be better at solving problems and getting ideas than others are; they may have a livelier imagination, a more efficient way of grasping at distant consequences; but it all comes down to thinking in the end. What counts is how well you can think, and even more, how long and persistently you can think without breaking down. There are brilliant people, I imagine, who produce little, if anything, because their attention span to their own thoughts is so short; and there are less brilliant people who can plug away at their thoughts until they wrench something out of them.

All this comes up in my mind now because a friend of mine, a science fiction writer whose work I admire enormously, in the course of a conversation asked, in a very embarrassed manner, "How do you get your ideas?"

I could see what the problem was. He had been having a little trouble coming up with something and he thought that perhaps he had lost the knack of getting ideas, or had never really had it, and he turned to me. After all, I write so *much* that I must have no trouble getting ideas and I might even have some special system that others could use, too.

But I answered, very earnestly, "How do I get my ideas? By thinking and thinking and thinking till I'm ready to jump out the window."

"You, too?" he said, quite obviously relieved.

"Of course," I said. "If you're having trouble, all it means is that you're one of us. After all, if getting ideas were easy, everyone in the world would be writing."

After that, I put some serious thought into the matter of getting ideas. Was there any way I could spot my own system? Was there, in fact, any system at all, or did one simply think at random?

I went back over what happened in my mind before I wrote my most recent novel, *Nemesis*, which Doubleday published in October 1989, and I thought it might be helpful to aspiring writers, or even just to readers, if I described the preliminary thinking that went into the novel.

It started when my Doubleday editor, Jennifer Brehl, said to me, "I'd like your next novel not to be part of a series, Isaac. I don't want it to be a Foundation novel or a Robot novel or an Empire novel. Write one that's completely independent."

So I started thinking, and this is the way it went, in brief. (I'll cut out all the false starts and dead ends and mooning about and try to trace a sensible pathway through it all.)

The Foundation novels, Robot novels, and Empire novels are all interconnected and all deal with a background in which interstellar travel at superluminal speeds is well established. Of my previous independent novels, *The End of Eternity* deals with time-travel; *The Gods Themselves* with communication between universes; and *Fantastic Voyage II* with miniaturization. In none of these is there interstellar travel.

Very well, then, let me have a new novel which exploits an entirely new background. Let it deal with the *establishment* of interstellar travel, with the first interstellar voyages. Immediately I imagined a settled solar system, an Earth in decay, large numbers of space settlements in lunar orbit and in the asteroids. I imagined the space settlements as hostile to Earth and vice versa.

That gave me a reason for the drive to develop interstellar travel. Naturally, technological advances may be made for their own sake (as mountains are climbed "because they're there") but it helps to have a less exalted reason. A settlement might want to get away from the solar system to create a completely new society, profiting by past experience to avoid some of humanity's earlier mistakes.

Good, but where do they go? If they have true interstellar flight, as in my Foundation novels, they can go anywhere, but that's too much freedom. It introduces too many possibilities and not enough difficulties. If humanity is just *developing* interstellar flight, it might not be a very efficient process at first and a settlement trying to escape might find itself with a very limited range.

Now where do they go? The logical place is Alpha Centauri, the nearest star, but that is *so* logical that there's no fun to it. Well, then, what if there's another star only half as far as Alpha Centauri? That would be easier to reach.

But why haven't we seen it, if it exists? Well, it's a red-dwarf star and very dim, and besides there's a patch of interstellar dust between it and ourselves and that dims it further so that it just hasn't been noticed.

At that point, I remembered that a few years ago there was some speculation that the Sun might have a very distant red-dwarf companion that once in every revolution penetrated the comet cloud and sent some comets whizzing into the inner solar system where one or two might occasionally collide with Earth and produce the periodic waves of life-extinction. The red dwarf was called Nemesis.

The suggestion seems to have died down, but I made use of it. My characters would go to the nearby red dwarf, which I would call Nemesis, and then use that as the name for my novel. Of course, you can't very well have a habitable planet circling a red-dwarf star, but I wanted one. It would give me greater flexibility than simply to have the settlement go into orbit about the red dwarf. That meant I had to think up a set of conditions that (if you don't question things too closely) would make it sound as though a habitable planet could exist. For that I had to invent a gas giant, with an Earth-sized satellite, and it would be the satellite that would be habitable.

Now I needed a problem. The obvious one would be that Nemesis was circling the Sun and would eventually pass through the comet cloud. I rejected that because it had been well discussed in the media and I wanted something a little less expected. So I decided that Nemesis was an independent star that happened to be en route to a relatively near miss of the solar system, with possibly dangerous gravitational effects.

That was a good problem, but I needed a plausible solution. That took some time but I finally thought one up. (Sorry, I won't tell you what it is. For that you'll have to read the book.)

What I needed next was a good character that would serve as the spinal column of the book, around whom everything would revolve. I chose a fourteen-year-old girl, with certain characteristics that I thought would make her interesting.

Then I needed a place to start the book. I would begin with my main character and have her do or say something that starts the chain of events that will take up the rest of the book. I made the choice and then waited no longer. I sat down and started the book.

But, you might point out that I didn't yet have the novel. All I had was the social framework, a problem, a solution, a character and a beginning. When do I make up all the details that go into the characteristically involved plot of one of my novels (and *Nemesis* is *quite* involved).

I'm afraid that I make that up as I go along, but not without thought. Having worked out the first scene, I find that by the time I've finished that, I have the second scene in mind, at the conclusion of which I have the third scene, and so on all the way through to the ninety-fifth scene or so, which ends the novel.

To do that, I have to keep on thinking, on a smaller and more detailed scale all the time that I'm doing the book (which takes me nine months, perhaps). I do it at the cost of lots of lost sleep and lots of lack of attention to people and things about me (including an occasional blank stare even at my dear wife, Janet, who never fails to get the alarmed notion that "something's wrong" each time I go into a spasm of thought).

But then isn't it possible that two-thirds of the way through the book I realize that toward the beginning I made a wrong turn and am now beating my way down a blind alley? It *is* possible, but it's never happened to me yet, and I don't expect it to. I always build the next scenes on whatever it is I have already done and never consider any possible alternatives. I simply have no time to start over again.

However, I don't mean to make the process sound simpler than it really is. You must take into account, in the first place, that I have a natural aptitude for this sort of thing, and, also, that I have been doing it for over half a century now, and experience counts.

Anyway, this is the closest I can come to explaining where I get my ideas.

Suspense

I have said over and over again that I write by instinct only and that there is nothing purposeful or deliberate in what I do. Consequently, I am always more or less puzzled by people who analyze my writing and find all sorts of subtle details in it that I don't recall ever putting in but that I suppose must be there or the critic wouldn't find them and pull them out.

Still, I have never been so puzzled as recently when I read a discussion of science fiction (where and by whom I do not remember for I threw it out in annoyance as soon as I came across the passage I'm about to tell you of). Getting to me, the essayist mentioned the fact that my style was clumsy, my dialog stilted, my characterization non-existent, but that there was no question that my books were "page-turners." In fact, he said, I was the most reliable producer of "page-turning" writing in science fiction.

It was only after I had thrown out the material and sworn a bit that I began to think of what I had read. What the essayist had said seemed to make no sense. Of course, he might be mad, but suppose, for the sake of argument, that he wasn't. In that case, if I were utterly deficient in style, dialog, and characterization, how could my writings be "page-turners"? Why should any reader want to turn the page (that is, keep on reading) when what he read had nothing to recommend it?

What made a person want to keep on reading anything? The most obvious reason was "suspense," which comes from Latin words meaning "to be hanging"; that is, "to be suspended." The reader finds himself in a painful situation where he is uncertain as to what will happen next in his reading matter, and he wants desperately to find out.

Mind you, suspense is not an inalienable part of literature. No one reads Shakespeare's sonnets in order to experience suspense. Nor do you read a P. G. Wodehouse novel for the sake of suspense. You know that Bertie Wooster will get out of the ridiculous fix in which he finds himself, and you don't really care whether he does or not. You read on only because you enjoy laughing.

Most writing, however, especially in the less exalted realms of literature, is kept going by suspense. The simplest form of suspense is to put your protagonist into constant danger, and make it seem certain that he can't possibly get out of it. Then get him out of it just so that you can plunge him into something even worse, and so on. Then, having carried it on as long as you can, you let him emerge victorious.

You get this in its purest simplicity in something like the Flash Gordon comic strip, where, for years, Flash ricocheted from crisis to crisis without ever getting time to wipe his brow (let alone go to the bathroom). Or consider the kind of movie serial typified by *The Perils of Pauline*, in which the perils continued for fifteen installments, each ending in a cliffhanger. (This was so-called because the protagonist was left hanging from a cliff or caught in some equally dangerous situation until the next episode of the serial a week later—a week spent by the kid-viewers in delicious agony—resolved the situation.)

This sort of suspense is ultra-simple. Whether Flash or Pauline survives matters really only to Flash or Pauline. Nothing of greater moment hinges on their survival.

We take a step forward in crime novels whereupon success or failure may hinge the smooth functioning of justice; or in spy novels whereupon success or failure may hinge the survival of the nation; or in science fiction whereupon success or failure may hinge the survival of the Earth itself, or even of the universe.

If we consider Jack Williamson's *The Legion of Space*, which I read as a teenager with the same emotions that I viewed the movie serials half a decade earlier, we find the same unending danger about to destroy our beloved heroes *and* the security of Earth along with them. That gives more meaning and more tension to the story.

Moving still farther up, then, we come to tales of unending danger that involve the great battle between good and evil, almost in the abstract. Surely the best example of this is J. R. R. Tolkien's *The Lord of the Rings*, in which the forces of good, crystallized in the end into the person of brave, suffering little Frodo, must somehow defeat the all-but-omnipotent Satan-figure of Sauron.

Mind you, suspense is not all that is required to make a piece of writing totally effective. In most cases, it suffices only for one reading. Once you have seen *The Perils of Pauline* once, there is no need ever to see it again, because you know how she overcomes all her perils. That removes the suspense, and once the suspense is gone, nothing else remains.

Yet there are suspense-filled items you read over and over again long after the suspense has been knocked out of them. I suppose that it is possible for a person who is reading (or seeing) *Hamlet* for the first time to be caught up most of all in whether Hamlet will defeat his wicked uncle or not. But I have read and seen *Hamlet* dozens of times and I know every word of the play and yet I always enjoy it, because the beauty of the language is sufficient in itself, and the texture of the plot is so thick that one never runs out of different methods of producing the play.

In the same way, I have read *The Lord of the Rings* five times and enjoyed it more each time, because getting the suspense out of the way actually allows me to enjoy the writing and the texture of the book all the more.

Now I come to my own writing, but I can only discuss it if you who are reading it understand that I never did anything of what I am about to describe *purposely*. It all got done, every bit of it, instinctively, and I only understand it now after the fact.

I was interested, apparently, in going beyond the rather simplistic balance between good and evil; I didn't want the hero adventuring with the reader always certain that he *ought* to win over the nasty villains, so that the nation or the society or the Earth or the universe could be saved.

I wanted a situation in which the reader could not be certain which side was good and which evil, or in which he might wonder if perhaps both sides contained mixtures of good and evil. I wanted a situation where the problem and the danger was itself uncertain, and where the resolution was not necessarily a true resolution because it might conceivably make things worse in the long run.

In short, I wanted to write fictional *history* in which there are no true endings, no true "they lived happily ever after," but in which, even when a problem is apparently solved, a new one arises to take its place.

To this end, I sacrificed everything else. I made no attempt to indulge in anything but necessary description, so

that I worked always on a "bare stage." I forced the dialog
to serve nothing more than as an indication of the progress
of the problem (if there was one) toward the resolution (if
there was one). I wasted no time on action for its own sake,
or on characterization or on poetic writing. I made everything just as clear and as straightforward as I could, so that
the reader could concentrate on (and drive himself mad
over) all the ambiguities I would introduce.

(As you see, then, critics who complain that my books are
too talky, and that they contain little or no action, miss the
point completely.)

I do my best to present a number of characters, each of
whom has a different world view and each of whom argues
his case as cogently as possible. *Each* of them thinks he is
doing the sensible thing, working for the good of humanity,
or his part of it. There is no general agreement on what the
problem might be, or even, sometimes, whether there is one
at all, and when the story ends even the hero himself may
not be satisfied with what he has done.

I worked this out little by little in my stories and novels,
and it reached its peak in the Foundation series.

There is indeed suspense in the series on a simple scale.
Will the small world of the First Foundation hold its own
against the surrounding mightier kingdoms and, if so, how?
Will it survive the onslaught of the Empire and of a mutant
emotion-controller, and of the Second Foundation?

But that is not the *prime* suspense. *Should* the First Foundation survive? *Should* there be a Second Empire? Will the
Second Empire just be a repetition of the miseries of the
First? Are the Traders or the Mayors correct in their view
of what the First Foundation ought to do?

In the two later volumes, the hero Golan Trevize spends
the first in coming to an agonized decision, and the second
in an agonized wonder as to whether his decision was right.

In short, I try to introduce all the uncertainties of history, instead of the implausible certainties of an unrealistic fictional world.

And apparently it works, and my novels are "page-turners."

But I have more to say and I will continue my discussion of suspense in next month's editorial.

Serials

When is a writer not a writer?

When he is asked to write outside his specialty.

Writing is not a unitary matter. A person who is a skilled science writer, or who can turn out fascinating popular histories, may be hopeless when it comes to writing fiction. The reverse is also true.

Even a person like myself who is adept at both fiction and nonfiction and ranges over considerable variety in both subdivisions is not a universal writer. I can't and won't write plays, whether for the theater, motion pictures, or television. I don't have the talent for it.

It is surprising, in fact, how thinly talent can be subdivided. The functions, advantages, and disadvantages of fiction differ so with subject matter that every writer is more at home in one kind of fiction than in another. I can do science fiction and mysteries, but I would be madly misjudging myself if I tried to do "mainstream" fiction or even "new-wave" science fiction.

Oddly enough, even length counts. You might think that if someone is writing a story, it can be any length. If it finishes itself quickly, it is a short story; if it goes on for a long time, it is a novel; if it is something in between, it is a novelette or a novella.

That's just not so. Length is not the sole difference. A novel is not a lengthy short story. A short story is not a brief novel. They are two different species of writing.

A novel has space in which to develop a plot leisurely, with ample room for subplots, for detailed background, for description, for character development, for comic relief.

A short story must make its point directly and without side issues. Every sentence must contribute directly to the plot development.

A novel is a plane; a short story is a line.

A novel which is too short and thus abbreviates the richness of its development would be perceived by the reader as skimpy and therefore unsatisfactory. A short story which is too long and allows the reader's attention to wander from the plot is diffuse and therefore unsatisfactory.

There are writers who are at home with the broad swing of the novel and are not comfortable within the confinement of the short story. There are writers who are clever at driving home points in short stories and who are lost in the echoing chambers of the novel. And of course there are writers who can do both.

A magazine such as ours is primarily a vehicle in which the short story is displayed. It is important we fulfill this function for a variety of reasons:

1. Short stories are worth doing and worth reading. They can make concise points that novels cannot, in ways that novels cannot.

2. A group of short stories which, in length, take up the room of one novel, offers far more variety than a novel can; and there is something very pleasant about variety.

3. Those writers who are adept at the short story need a vehicle.

4. Beginning writers need a vehicle, too; and beginners are well-advised to concentrate on short stories at the start. Even if their true skill turns out to be in the novel, initial training had better be in the short story, which requires a smaller investment in time and effort. A dozen short stories will take no more time than a novel and offer much more scope for experimentation and "finding one's self."

When George, Joel, and I began this magazine, we were aware of all these points and were determined to make it a magazine devoted to the short story exclusively. And we are still so determined.

Yet it is not easy to be rigid. It is perhaps not even desirable to be rigid under all circumstances. There are times when the best of rules ought to be bent a little.

What are the forces, for instance, that drag us in the direction of length?

To begin with, there are (rightly or wrongly) more literary honors and monetary rewards for novels than for short stories, so that if a writer can handle any length, he usually finds himself gravitating toward the novel.

Naturally, since a novel requires a great investment of time and effort, it is the experienced writers of tried quality who are most likely to move in that direction. And once they've done that, they're not likely to want to let go. It becomes difficult, in fact, to persuade them to take time out from their current novel in order to write a short story.

As long as we stick rigidly to short stories, therefore, we tend to lose the chance at picking up the work of some of the best practitioners in the field. Newcomers, however worthy, tend to have lesser experience and their writing tends to be less polished.

For the most part, this does not dismay us. We *want* the newcomers, and the freshness of concept and approach is quite likely to make up for what clumsiness of technique is brought about through inexperience. The clumsiness, after all, will smooth out with time—and at that point, the new talent will almost inevitably begin to write novels.

Occasionally, then, we bend. If a story comes along by an established writer that is unusually good but is rather long, we are tempted to run it. We have indeed run stories as long as 40,000 words in a single issue.

There are advantages to this. If you like the story, you can get deeply immersed in it and savor the qualities that length makes possible and that you can't get otherwise. And there are disadvantages. If you don't like the story and quit reading it, you have only half a magazine left and you may feel cheated.

George must judge the risk and decide when a long story is likely to be so generally approved of that the advantage will far outweigh the disadvantage.

But what do we do about novels? Ignore them?

Most novelists do not object to making extra money by allowing a magazine to publish part or all of the novel prior to its publication *as* a novel. And most magazines welcome the chance of running a novel in installments.

Consider the advantages to the magazine. If the first part of a serial is exciting, well written and grabs the reader, it is to be expected that a great many readers will then haunt the newsstands waiting for the next issue. If many serials prove to have this grabbing quality, readers will subscribe rather than take the chance of missing installments.

Magazine publishers do not object to this. Even Joel wouldn't.

There are, however, disadvantages. Some readers actively dislike novels. Others may like novels but bitterly resent being stopped short and asked to wait a month for a continuation, and may also resent having to run the risk of missing installments.

We are aware of these disadvantages and also of our own responsibility for encouraging the short story, so we have sought a middle ground.

These days there are so many novels and so few magazines that there isn't room to serialize them all. Many good novels are therefore available for the prior publication of only a chunk of themselves—some chunk that stands by itself. We have been deliberately keeping our eyes open for these.

It's not always easy to find a novel-chunk that stands by itself. The fact that something goes afterward, or comes before, or both, is likely to give the reader a vague feeling of incompleteness. Sometimes, then, we try to run several chunks, each of which stands by itself, or almost does. This comes close to serialization, but if the second piece can be read comfortably without reference to the first, then it's not. Again, George must use his judgment in such cases.

But then, every once in a long while, we are trapped by our own admiration of a novel and find ourselves with a chunk we would desperately like to publish, but that is too long to fit into a single issue and that can't conveniently be divided into two independent chunks.

Then, with a deep breath, if we can think of no way out, we serialize. We hate to do this, and we hardly ever will. But hardly ever isn't never!

When there's no other way out, rather than lose out on something really first-class, we will have to ask you to wait a month.

But hardly ever.

The Name of Our Field

In last issue's editorial, I talked of Jules Verne's "extraordinary voyages" and that brings up the point of how difficult it was to find a name for the land of items that are published in this magazine and others like it.

This magazine contains "stories"; and "story" is simply a shortened form of "history," a recounting of events in orderly detail. The recounting could, in either case, be of real incidents or of made-up ones, but we have become used to thinking of a "history" as real and of a "story" as made-up.

A "tale" is something that is "told" (from the Anglo-Saxon) and a "narrative" is something that is "narrated" (from the Latin). Either "tale" or "narrative" can be used for either a real or a made-up account. "Narrative" is the less common of the two simply because it is the longer word and therefore has an air of pretentiousness about it.

A word which is used exclusively for made-up items and never for real ones is "fiction," from a Latin word meaning "to invent."

What this magazine contains, then, are stories—or tales—or, most precisely, fiction. Naturally, fiction can be of different varieties, depending on the nature of the content.

If the events recounted deal mainly with love, we have "love stories" or "love tales" or "love fiction." Similarly, we can have "detective stories," or "terror tales," or "mystery fiction," or "confession stories," or "western tales," or "jungle fiction." The items that appear in this magazine deal, in one fashion or another, with future changes in the level of science, or of science-derived technology. Doesn't it make sense, then, to consider the items to be "science stories," or "science tales," or, most precisely, "science fiction"?

And yet "science fiction," which is so obvious a name when you come to think of it, is a late development.

Jules Verne's extraordinary voyages were called "scientific fantasies" in Great Britain, and the term "science fantasy" is still sometimes used today. "Fantasy" is from a Greek word meaning "imagination" so it isn't completely inappropriate, but it implies the minimal existence of constraints. When we speak of "fantasy" nowadays, we generally refer to stories that are not bound by the laws of science, whereas science fiction stories *are* so bound.

Another term used in the 1920s was "scientific romance." Romance was originally used for anything published in the "Romance languages," that is, in the popular tongues of western Europe, so that it was applied to material meant to be read for amusement. More serious works were written in Latin, of course. The trouble is that "romance" has come to be applied to love stories in particular so "science romance" has a wrong feel to it.

"Pseudo-science stories" was sometimes used, but that is insulting. "Pseudo" is from a Greek word meaning "false," and while the kind of extrapolations of science used in science fiction are not true science, they are not false science either. They are "might-be-true" science.

"Super-science stories," still another name, is childish.

In 1926, when Hugo Gernsback published the first magazine ever to be devoted exclusively to science fiction, he called it *Amazing Stories*.

This caught on. When other magazines appeared, synonyms for "amazing" were frequently used. We had *Astounding Stories, Astonishing Stories, Wonder Stories, Marvel Stories*, and *Startling Stories* all on the stands, when the world and I were young.

Such names, however, do not describe the nature of the stories but their effect on the reader, and that is insufficient. A story can amaze, astound, astonish, and startle you; it can cause you to marvel and wonder; and yet it need not be science fiction. It need not even be fiction. Something better was needed.

Gernsback knew that. He had originally thought of calling his magazine "Scientific Fiction." That is hard to pronounce quickly, though, chiefly because of the repetition of the syllable "fic." Why not combine the words and eliminate one of those syllables? We then have "scientifiction."

"Scientifiction," though, is an ugly word, hard to understand and, if understood, likely to scare off those potential readers who equate the "scientific" with the "difficult." Gernsback therefore used the word only in a subtitle: *Amazing Stories: the Magazine of Scientifiction*. He introduced "stf" as the abbreviation of "scientifiction." Both abbreviation and word are still sometimes used.

When Gernsback was forced to give up *Amazing Stories* he published a competing magazine, *Science Wonder Stories*. In its first issue (June, 1929), he used the term "science fiction" and the abbreviation "S.F."—or "SF" without periods—became popular. Occasionally, the word has been hyphenated as "science-fiction," but that is only done rarely. The story, however, doesn't end there.

As I said last issue, there is a feeling among some that the phrase "science fiction" unfairly stresses the science content of the stories. Since 1960 in particular, science fiction has tended to shift at least some of its emphasis from science to society, from gadgets to people. It still deals with changes in the level of science and technology, but those changes move farther into the background.

I believe it was Robert Heinlein who first suggested that we ought to speak of "speculative fiction" instead; and some, like Harlan Ellison, strongly support that move now. To me, though, "speculative" seems a weak word. It is four syllables long and is not too easy to pronounce quickly. Besides, almost anything can be speculative fiction. A historical romance can be speculative; a true-crime story can be speculative. "Speculative fiction" is not a precise description of our field and I don't think it will work. In fact, I think "speculative fiction" has been introduced only to get rid of "science" but to keep "s.f."

This brings us to Forrest J. Ackerman, a wonderful guy whom I love dearly. He is a devotee of puns and word-play and so am I, but Forry has never learned that some things are sacred. He couldn't resist coining "sci-fi" as an analog, in appearance and pronunciation, to "hi-fi," the well-known abbreviation for "high fidelity." "Sci-fi" is now widely used by people who don't read science fiction. It is used particularly by people who work in movies and television. This makes it, perhaps, a useful term.

We can define "sci-fi" as trashy material sometimes confused, by ignorant people, with SF. Thus, *Star Trek* is SF while *Godzilla Meets Mothra* is sci-fi.

Hints

Every once in a short while I get a letter from some eager young would-be writer asking me for some "hints" on the art of writing science fiction.

The feeling I have is that my correspondents think there is some magic formula jealously guarded by the professionals, but that since I'm such a nice guy I will spill the beans if properly approached.

Alas, there's no such thing, no magic formula, no secret tricks, no hidden short-cuts.

I'm sorry to have to tell you that it's a matter of hard work over a long period of time. If you know of any exceptions to this, that's exactly what they are—exceptions.

There are, however, some general principles that could be useful, to my way of thinking, and here they are:

1) You have to prepare for a career as a successful science fiction writer—as you would for any other highly specialized calling.

First, you have to learn to use your tools, just as a surgeon has to learn to use his.

The basic tool for any writer is the English language, which means you must develop a good vocabulary and brush up on such prosaic things as spelling and grammar.

There can be little argument about vocabulary, but it may occur to you that spelling and grammar are just frills. After all, if you write great and gorgeous stories, surely the editor will be delighted to correct your spelling and grammar.

Not so! He (or she) won't be.

Besides, take it from an old war-horse, if your spelling and grammar are rotten, you won't be writing a great and gorgeous story. Someone who can't use a saw and hammer doesn't turn out stately furniture.

Even if you've been diligent at school, have developed a vocabulary, can spell "sacrilege" and "supersede" and never say "between you and I" or "I ain't never done nothing," that's still not enough. There's the subtle structure of the English sentence and the artful construction of the English paragraph. There is the clever interweaving of plot, the handling of dialog, and a thousand other intricacies.

How do you learn that? Do you read books on how to write, or attend classes on writing, or go to writing conferences? These are all of inspirational value, I'm sure, but they won't teach you what you really want to know.

What *will* teach you is the careful reading of the masters of English prose. This does not mean condemning yourself to years of falling asleep over dull classics. Good writers are invariably fascinating writers—the two go together. In my opinion, the English writers who most clearly use the correct word every time and who most artfully and deftly put together their sentences and paragraphs are Charles Dickens, Mark Twain, and P. G. Wodehouse.

Read them, and others, but with attention. They represent your schoolroom. Observe what they do and try to figure out why they do it. It's no use other people explaining it to you; until you see it for yourself and it becomes part of you, nothing will help.

But suppose that no matter how you try, you can't seem to absorb the lesson. Well, it may be that you're not a writer. It's no disgrace. You can always go on to take up some slightly inferior profession like surgery or the presidency of the United States. It won't be as good, of course; but we can't all scale the heights.

Second, for a science fiction writing career, it is not enough to know the English language; you also have to know science. You may not want to use much science in your stories; but you'll have to know it anyway, so that what you do use, you don't misuse.

This does not mean you have to be a professional scientist, or a science major at college. You don't even have to go to college. It does mean, though, that you have to be willing to study science on your own, if your formal education has been weak in that direction.

It's not impossible. One of the best writers of hard science fiction is Fred Pohl, and he never even finished high school. Of course, there are very few people who are as bright as Fred, but you can write considerably less well than he does and still be pretty good.

Fortunately, there is more good, popular-science writing these days than there was in previous generations, and you can learn a great deal, rather painlessly, if you read such science fiction writers as L. Sprague de Camp, Ben Bova, and Poul Anderson in their non-fictional moods—or even Isaac Asimov.

What's more, professional scientists are also writing effectively for the public these days, as witness Carl Sagan's magnificent books. And there's always *Scientific American*.

Third, even if you know your science and your writing, it is still not likely that you will be able to put them together from scratch. You will have to be a diligent reader of science fiction itself to learn the conventions and the tricks of the trade—how to interweave background and plot, for instance.

2) You have to work at the job.

The final bit of schooling is writing itself. Nor must you wait till your preparation is complete. The act of writing is itself part of the preparation.

You can't completely understand what good writers do until you try it yourself. You learn a great deal when you find your story breaking apart in your hands—or beginning to hang together. Write from the very beginning, then, and keep on writing.

3) You have to be patient.

Since writing is itself a schooling, you can't very well expect to sell the first story you write. (Yes, I know Bob Heinlein did it, but he was Bob Heinlein. You are only you.)

But then, why should that discourage you? After you finished the first grade at school, you weren't through, were you? You went on to the second grade, then the third, then the fourth, and so on.

If each story you write is one more step in your literary education, a rejection shouldn't matter. [Editors don't reject writers; they reject pieces of paper that have been typed on. Ed.] The next story will be better, and the next one after that still better, and eventually—

But then why bother to submit the stories? If you don't, how can you possibly know when you graduate? After all, you don't know which story you'll sell.

You might even sell the first. You almost certainly won't, but you just might.

Of course, even after you sell a story, you may fail to place the next dozen, but having done it once, it is quite likely that you will eventually do it again, if you persevere.

But what if you write and write and write and you don't seem to be getting any better and all you collect are printed rejection slips? Once again, it may be that you are not a writer and will have to settle for a lesser post such as that of chief justice of the Supreme Court.

4) You have to be reasonable.

Writing is the most wonderful and satisfying task in the world, but it does have one or two insignificant flaws. Among those flaws is the fact that a writer can almost never make a living at it.

Oh, a few writers make a lot of money—they're the ones we all hear about. But for every writer who rakes it in, there are a thousand who dread the monthly rent bill. It shouldn't be like that, but it is.

Take my case. Three years after I sold my first story, I reached the stage of selling everything I wrote, so that I had become a successful writer. Nevertheless, it took me seventeen more years as a *successful* writer before I could actually support myself in comfort on my earnings as a writer.

So while you're trying to be a writer, make sure you find another way of making a decent living—and don't quit your job after you make your first sale.

Writing for Young People

There is an exceedingly useful volume entitled *The Science Fiction Encyclopedia*, edited by Peter Nicholls (Doubleday, 1979), to which I frequently refer. Recently, as I leafed through its pages en route to looking up something, I came across the following passage:

"The intellectual level of a book is not necessarily expressed by a marketing label. Much adult sf, the works of . . . Isaac Asimov, for example, is of great appeal to older children, and is to some extent directed at them."

The line of three dots in the above quotation signals the omission of a few words in which the writer specifies two other science fiction writers. I omit them because they may resent the original statement and may not feel I ought to give the remark further circulation.

As for me, I don't object to the comment because, for one thing, I consider it true. I write my "adult" novels for adults, but I have no objection whatsoever to young people reading them, and I try to write in such a way that my novels are accessible to them.

Why?

First, it is the way I like to write. I like to have the ideas in my novels sufficiently interesting and subtle to catch at the attention and thinking of intelligent adults, and, at the same time, to have the writing clear enough so as to raise no difficulties for the intelligent youngster. To manage the combination I consider a challenge, and I like challenges.

Second, it is good business. Attract an adult and you may well have someone who is here today and gone tomorrow. Attract a youngster and you have a faithful reader for life.

Mind you, I don't write as I do with the second reason in mind; I write as I do for the first reason I gave you. Nevertheless, I have discovered that the second reason exists, and I have long lost count of the number of people who tell me they have an astronomical number of my books and that they "were at once hooked after reading my book, so-and-so, when they were ten years old."

But if the same books can be read by both adults and youngsters, what is the distinction between truly adult books (ones that the writer of the item in *The Science Fiction Encyclopedia* would judge as possessing a high "intellectual level") and truly juvenile books?

Let's see. Can it be vocabulary? Do adult books have "hard words" while juvenile books have "easy words"?

To some extent, I suppose that might be so. If an author makes a fetish of using unusual words, as William Buckley does (or Clark Ashton Smith, to mention someone in our own line), then the writing grows opaque for youngsters and adults alike, for it is my experience that the average adult does not have a vocabulary much larger, if any, than a bright youngster does.

On the other hand, if an author uses the *correct* words, hard or easy, then the bright youngster will guess the meaning from the context or look it up in a dictionary. I think the bright youngster enjoys having his mind stretched and welcomes the chance of learning a new word. I don't worry about my vocabulary, for that reason, even when I am writing my science books for grade school youngsters. I may give the pronunciation of scientific terms they are not likely to have encountered before, and I sometimes define them, but I don't avoid them, and after having given pronunciation and definition I use them freely.

Well, then, is it the difference between long sentences and short sentences?

That is true only in this sense: It is more difficult to make a long sentence clear than it is to make a short one clear. If, then, you are a poor writer and want to make sure that youngsters understand you, stick to short sentences. Unfortunately, a long series of short sentences, like a long stretch of writing with no "hard" words, is irritating to anyone intelligent, young or old. A youngster is particularly offended because he thinks (sometimes with justice) that the writer thinks that because the youngster is young, he is therefore stupid. The book is at once discarded. (This is called "writing down," by the way, something I try never to do.)

The trick is to write clearly. If you write clearly enough, a long sentence will hold no terrors. If you hit the proper mix of long and short, and hard and easy, and make everything clear, then, believe me, the youngster will have no trouble. Of course, he has to be an intelligent youngster, but there are a larger percentage of those than of intelligent oldsters, for life hasn't had a chance yet to dull the youngsters' wits.

Is it a matter of subject matter? Do adult novels deal with death and torture and mayhem and sex (natural and unnatural) and all kinds of unpleasantness, while juvenile novels deal with sweetness and niceness?

You *know* that's not so. Think of the current rash of "horror" films, which fill the screen with blood and murder and torture and are designed to frighten. Youngsters flock to them, and the gorier they are, the more they enjoy them.

Even censors don't seem to mind the mayhem. When there are loud squawks from the righteous who want to kick books out of school libraries, the objections are most often to the use of "dirty" words and to sex. However, I have, in my time, lived half a block from a junior high school and listened to the youngsters going there and coming back. I picked up a lot of colorful obscenity, both sexual and scatological, in that way, for I had forgotten some of what I had learned as a youngster. I think the youngsters themselves would have no objection to books containing gutter language and sexual detail—or fail to understand them, either. *That* distinction between adult books and juvenile books is not a natural one but is enforced by adult fiat.

(I admit that I use no gutter language or sex in my juvenile books, but then I use no gutter language and very little sex in my adult books.)

How about action, then? Adult books can pause for sensitive description of all kinds, or for a skillful and painstaking dissection of motivation, and so on. Juvenile books tend to deal entirely with action. Is that right?

Actually, the distinction is not between adults and juveniles, but between a few people (both adult and juvenile) and most people (both adult and juvenile). Most people, of whatever age, are impatient with anything but action. Watch the popular adventure programs on television, subtract the action, and find out what you have left, and then remember that it is adults, for the most part, who are watching them.

On the other hand, my books contain very little "action" (hence no movie sales) and deal largely with the interplay of ideas in rather cerebral dialog (as many critics point out, sometimes with irritation) and yet, says the *Encyclopedia*, I appeal to youngsters. Clarity, not action, is the key.

Can it be a question of style? Are adult books written in a complicated and experimental style, while juvenile books are not?

To be sure, a juvenile book written in a complicated and experimental style is more apt to be a commercial failure than one written in a straightforward style. On the other hand, this is also true of adult books. The difference is that tortuous style is frequently admired by critics in adult books, but never in juvenile books. This means that many adults, who are guided by critics, or who merely wish to appear chic, buy opaque and experimental books, and then, possibly, don't read them, aside from any "dirty parts" they might have. Proust's *Remembrance of Things Past* springs to mind. My dear wife, Janet, is reading it, every word, for the *second* time but there are moments when I see the perspiration standing out, in great drops, on her forehead.

How about rhetorical tricks? Metaphors, allusions, and all the rest of it, depend upon experience, and youngsters, however bright they are, have not yet had time to gather experience.

For instance, my George and Azazel stories are pure fluff, but they are the most nearly adult stories I write. I use my full vocabulary, together with involved sentence structure, and never hesitate to rely on the reader to fill in what I leave out. I can refer to "the elusive promise of nocturnal Elysium" without any indication of what I mean. I can speak of the Eiffel Tower as a "stupid building still under construction" and depend on the reader to know what the Tower looks like and therefore see why the remark is wrong, but apt. Nevertheless, the stories are meant to be humorous and all the rhetorical devices contribute to that. The young person who misses some of the allusions nevertheless should get much of the humor and enjoy the story anyway.

In short, I maintain there is no hard and fast distinction between "adult" writing and "juvenile" writing. A good book is a good book and can be enjoyed by both adults and youngsters. If my books appeal to both, that is to my credit.

Names

We received an interesting letter some time ago from Greg Cox of Washington State. It is short and I will take the liberty of quoting its one sentence in full:

"I enjoyed very much the Good Doctor's story in the May issue ("The Evil Drink Does"), but I *have* to ask: How did a young lady from such an allegedly puritanical background end up with the unlikely (if appealing) name of 'Ishtar Mistik'???"

It's a good question, but it makes an assumption. In the story, Ishtar remarks, "I was brought up in the strictest possible way. It is impossible for me to behave in anything but the most correct manner."

From that you may suppose that Ishtar's family were rigidly doctrinaire Presbyterians, or superlatively moral Catholics, or tradition-bound Orthodox Jews, but if you do, it's an assumption. I say nothing about Ishtar's religious background.

To be sure, Ishtar is the Babylonian goddess of love, the analog of the Greek Aphrodite, and it is therefore odd that such a name should be given a child by puritanical parents, if the puritanism is Christian or Jewish in origin. But who says it is? The family may be a group of puritanical Druids (even Druids may have strict moral codes, and probably do) who chose "Ishtar" for its sound.

But let's go into the matter of names more systematically. Every writer has to give his characters names. There are occasional exceptions as when a writer may refer to a limited number of characters, in Puckish fashion, as "the Young Man," "the Doctor," "the Skeptic," and so on. P. G. Wodehouse, for example, in his golf stories, refers to the narrator as "the Oldest Member" and never gives him a name. He only need be referred to for a few paragraphs at the start, however, and then remains in the background as a disembodied voice. In my own George and Azazel stories, the first-person character to whom George speaks in the introduction and whom he regularly insults, has no name. He is merely "I." Of course, the perceptive reader may think (from the nature of George's insults) that I's name is Isaac Asimov, but again that is only an assumption.

Allowing for such minor exceptions then, writers need names.

You might think that this is not something that bothers anyone but apparently it does. I have received numerous letters (usually from young teenagers) who seem to be totally unimpressed by the ease with which I work up complex plots and ingenious gimmicks and socko endings but who say, "How do you manage to decide what names to give your characters?" *That* is what puzzles them.

In my attempts to answer, I have had to think about the subject.

In popular fiction intended for wide consumption, especially among the young, names are frequently chosen for blandness. You don't want the kids to stumble over the pronunciation of strange names or to be distracted by them. Your characters, therefore, are named Jack Armstrong or

Pat Reilly or Sam Jones. Such stories are filled with Bills and Franks and Joes coupled with Harpers and Andersons and Jacksons. That is also part of the comforting assumption that all decent characters, heroes especially, are of northwest European extraction.

Naturally, you may have comic characters or villains, and *they* can be drawn from among the "inferior" races, with names to suit. The villainous Mexican can be Pablo; the comic black, Rastus; the shrewd Jew, Abie; and so on.

Aside from the wearisome sameness of such things, the world changed after the 1930s. Hitler gave racism a bad name, and all over the world, people who had till then been patronized as "natives" began asserting themselves. It became necessary to choose names with a little more imagination and to avoid seeming to reserve heroism for your kind and villainy for the other kind.

On top of this science fiction writers had a special problem. What names do you use for non-human characters—robots, extraterrestrials, and so on?

There have been a variety of solutions to this problem. For instance, you might deliberately give extraterrestrials unpronounceable names, thus indicating that they speak an utterly strange language designed for sound-producing organs other than human vocal cords. The name Xlbnushk, for instance.

That, however, is not a solution that can long be sustained. No reader is going to read a story in which he periodically encounters Xlbnushk without eventually losing his temper. After all, he has to look at the letter-combination and he's bound to try to pronounce it every time he sees it.

Besides, in real life, a difficult name is automatically simplified. In geology, there is something called "the Mohorovicic discontinuity" named for its Yugoslavian discoverer. It is usually referred to by non-Yugoslavians as

"the Moho discontinuity." In the same way, Xlbnushk
would probably become "Nush."

Another way out is to give non-human characters (or
even human characters living in a far future in which messy
emotionalism has been eliminated) codes instead of names.
You can have a character called "21MM792," for instance.
That sort of thing certainly gives a story a science-fictional
ambience. And it can work. In Neil Jones' Professor Jameson stories of half a century ago, the characters were organic
brains in metallic bodies, all of whom had letter-number
names. Eventually, one could tell them apart, and didn't
even notice the absence of ordinary names. This system,
however, will work only if it rarely occurs. If all, or even
most, stories numbered their characters, there would be rebellion in the ranks.

My own system, when dealing with the far future, or with
extraterrestrials, is to use names, not codes, and easily pro-
nounceable names, too; but names that don't resemble any
real ones, or any recognizable ethnic group.

For one thing that gives the impression of "alienism"
without annoying the reader. For another, it minimizes the
chance of offending someone by using his or her name.

This is a real danger. The most amusing example was one
that was encountered by L. Sprague de Camp when he
wrote "The Merman" back in 1938. The hero was one Vernon Brock (not a common name) and he was an ichthyolo-
gist (not a common profession). After the story appeared in
the December 1938 *Astounding*, a thunderstruck Sprague
heard from a real Vernon Brock who was really an ichthy-
ologist. Fortunately, the real Brock was merely amused and
didn't mind at all, but if he had been a nasty person, he
might have sued. Sprague would certainly have won out, but
he would have been stuck with legal fees, lost time, and
much annoyance.

Sometimes I get away with slight misspellings: Baley instead of Bailey; Hari instead of Harry; Daneel instead of Daniel. At other times, I make the names considerably different, especially the first name: Salvor Hardin, Gaal Dornick, Golan Trevize, Stor Gendibal, Janov Pelorat. (I hope I'm getting them right; I'm not bothering to look them up.)

My feminine characters also receive that treatment, though the names I choose tend to be faintly classical because I like the sound: Callia, Artemisia, Noÿs, Arcadia, Gladia, and so on.

I must admit that when I started doing this, I expected to get irritated letters from readers, but, you know, I never got one. It began in wholesale manner in 1942 with the first Foundation story and in the forty-plus years since, not one such letter arrived. Well, Damon Knight once referred to Noÿs in a review of *The End of Eternity* as "the woman with the funny name," but that's as close as it got.

Which brings me to the George and Azazel stories again. There I use a different system. The George and Azazel stories are intended to be humorous. In fact, they are farces, with no attempt at or pretense of realism. The stories are outrageously overwritten on purpose. My ordinary writing style is so (deliberately) plain that every once in a while, I enjoy showing that I can be florid and rococo if I choose.

Well, then, in a rococo story, how on Earth can I be expected to have characters with ordinary names, even though the stories are set in the present and (except for Azazel) deal only with Earth people, so that I can't use nonexistent names?

Instead I use real names, but choose very unusual and pretentious first names. In my George and Azazel stories, characters have been named Mordecai Sims, Gottlieb Jones, Menander Block, Hannibal West, and so on. By associating the outlandish first name with a sober last name, I heighten the oddness of the first. (On second thought, I should have made Ishtar Mistik, Ishtar Smith.)

None of this is, of course, intended as a universal rule. It's just what *I* do. If you want to write an SF story, by all means make up a system of your own.

Originality

Having published an editorial entitled "Plagiarism" in the August 1985 issue of the magazine, it occurs to me to look at the other side of the coin. After all, if plagiarism is reprehensible, total originality is just about impossible.

The thing is that there exists an incredible number of books in which an enormous variety of ideas and an even more enormous variety of phrases and ways of putting things have been included. Anyone literate enough to write well has, as a matter of course, read a huge miscellany of printed material and, the human brain being what it is, a great deal of it remains in the memory at least unconsciously, and will be regurgitated onto the manuscript page at odd moments.

In 1927, for instance, John Livingston Lowes (an English professor at Harvard) published a six-hundred-page book entitled *The Road to Xanadu*, in which he traced nearly every phrase in "The Rime of the Ancient Mariner" to various travel books that were available to the poet, Samuel Taylor Coleridge.

I tried reading the book in my youth, but gave up. It could only interest another Coleridge scholar. Besides, I saw no point to it. Granted that the phrases already existed scattered through a dozen books, they existed for everybody. It was only Coleridge who thought of putting them together, with the necessary modifications, to form one of the great poems of the English language. Coleridge might not have been a hundred percent original but he was original *enough* to make the poem a work of genius. You can't overrate the skills involved in selection and arrangement.

It was this that was in my own mind, once, when I was busily working on a book of mine called *Words of Science* back in the days when I was actively teaching at Boston University School of Medicine. The book consisted of 250 one-page essays on various scientific terms, giving derivations, meanings and various historical points of interest. For the purpose, I had an unabridged dictionary spread out on my desk, for I couldn't very well make up the derivations, nor could I rely on my memory to present them to me in all correct detail. (My memory is good, but not *that* good.)

A fellow faculty member happened by and looked over my shoulder. He read what I was writing at the moment, stared at the unabridged and said, "Why, you're just copying the dictionary."

I stopped dead, sighed, closed the dictionary, lifted it with an effort and handed it to my friend. "Here," I said. "The dictionary is yours. Now go write the book."

He shrugged his shoulders and walked away without offering to take the dictionary. He was bright enough to get the point.

There are times, though, when I wonder how well any story of mine would survive what one might call the "Road to Xanadu" test. (There's no point in offending fellow writers by analyzing *their* originality, so I'll just stick to my own stuff.)

The most original story I ever wrote in my opinion was "Nightfall," which appeared back in 1941. I had not quite reached my twenty-first birthday when I wrote it and I have always been inordinately proud of the plot. "It was a brand-new plot," I said, "and I killed it as I wrote it, for no one else would dare write a variation of it."

To be sure, it was John Campbell who presented me with the Emerson quote that began the story: "If the stars would appear one night in a thousand years, how would men believe and adore; and preserve for many generations the remembrance of the City of God—" and it was Campbell who sent me home to write the reverse of Emerson's thesis.

Allowing for that, the development and details of the story were mine—or were they?

In 1973, I was preparing an anthology of my favorite stories of the 1930s (the years, that is, before John Campbell's editorship, so that I named the book *Before the Golden Age*) and I included, of course, Jack Williamson's "Born of the Sun," which had been published in 1934 and had, at that time, fascinated my fourteen-year-old self. I reread it, naturally, before including it and was horrified.

You see, it dealt in part with a cult whose members were furious at scientists for rationalizing the mystic tenets of the believers. In an exciting scene, the cultists attacked the scientists' citadel at a very crucial moment and the scientists tried to hold them off long enough to get their task done.

I can't deny having read that story. After all, I still remembered it with pleasure forty years later. Yet only six and a half years after reading it, I wrote "Nightfall" which dealt in part with a cult whose members were furious at scientists for rationalizing the mystic tenets of the believers. In an exciting scene, the cultists attacked the scientists' citadel at a very crucial moment and the scientists tried to hold them off long enough to get their task done.

No, it wasn't plagiarism. For one thing I wrote it entirely differently. However, the scene fit both stories and having been impressed by it in Jack's story, I drew from memory, and used it in my own story automatically—never for one moment considering that I wasn't making it up out of nothing but had earlier read something very like that scene.

I suppose that any thoroughgoing scholar who was willing to spend several years at the task could trace almost every quirk in "Nightfall" to one story or another that appeared in the science fiction magazines in the 1930s. (Yes, I read them all.) Naturally, he could do the same for any other story written by any other author.

Here's something even more curious. In a note dated June 27, 1985, a reader sent me an enclosure—a photocopy of a short article from the October 1937 issue of the magazine *Sky* (now known as *Sky and Telescope*, I believe).

The article is entitled "If the Stars Appeared Only One Night in a Thousand Years." It begins with the Emerson quotation and it is by M. T. Brackbill. The author describes what it might be like if *the* night on which the stars appear were coming. There might be "prostellarists" who believe the stars are coming; and "anti-stellarists" who dismiss the whole thing as a fable. And then the night comes and everyone stares entranced at the stars and finally watches them disappear with the dawn, sadly realizing that for a thousand years they will never be seen again.

It's rather touching, and about the only thing Brackbill misses, that I could see, was the certainty that on that particular night there was bound to be a heavy night-long overcast in various parts of the world, so that millions of people would invariably be disappointed.

The person who sent me the photocopy accompanied it with this note: "Dear Mr. Asimov—I happened to spot this article. I wonder if it was an inspiration for one of the greatest short stories ever written!"

Just an "inspiration"? If the article and "Nightfall" were carefully studied and compared, how many events and phrases in the story might seem to have been inspired or hinted at in the article. I haven't the heart to do this myself and I hope no one else does.

Unfortunately, neither the name nor address of the person who sent me the article was on the note, and the envelope the whole thing had come in had not been saved. (Please, everyone, if you want an answer, put your name and return address *on your letter* and not just on the envelope. I frequently discard envelopes without glancing at them except to make sure they are addressed to me.)

In any case, I couldn't answer him. So I must use this editorial as the only way of reaching him.

The truth is that I never saw the article; never had a hint that it existed until the day I received the note and enclosure from my unknown correspondent. It had not the slightest iota of direct influence on my story.

But John Campbell presented me with the Emerson quote and the request that I reverse it, only three years after the article had appeared. Had *he* seen it?

I wouldn't be surprised if he had, and if, as soon as he had come across it or had had it drawn to his attention, copied down the quote and then waited for the first unwary science fiction writer to cross his threshold. (How thankful I am that it was I.)

Were he still alive (he would only be seventy-five today, if he were), I would ask him about it. I am quite sure, though, what his answer would be. It would be, "What difference does it make?"

So there arises the question: "If it is impossible to be

completely original, how can you tell permissible influence from plagiarism?"

Well, it depends on the extent and detail of the borrowing. Based on that, it is possible to tell! It may not always be provable in a court of law, but, believe me, it is possible to tell!

Book Reviews

I have never made any secret of the fact that I dislike the concept of reviews and the profession of reviewing. It is a purely emotional reaction because, for reasons that are all too easy to work out, I strongly dislike having anyone criticize my stuff adversely.

I don't think I'm alone in this. From my close observation of writers (almost all my friends are writers) they fall into two groups: 1) those who bleed copiously and visibly at any bad review, and 2) those who bleed copiously and secretly at any bad review.

I'm class one. Most of my friends aim at class two and don't quite make it and aren't quite aware that they don't make it.

Unfortunately, there's no way in which one can get back at a reviewer. I have sometimes had the urge to do some fancy horse-whipping in the form of a mordant letter designed to flay the reptilian hide off the sub-moron involved; but, except in my very early days, I have always resisted. This is not out of idealism but out of the bitter knowledge that the writer always loses in such a confrontation.

Instead, then, I take to muttering derogatory comments about reviewing and reviewers in general.

But I'm in a bad spot here. This magazine (which is the apple of my eye) not only has a regular book review column, but has other items, less regularly included, that review one or another of the facets of the science fiction field. If I really despise reviewing so, why is it I allow reviewing in the magazine?

Because I *don't* really despise reviewing and reviewers. That is an emotional reaction that I recognize as emotional, and therefore discount. I am a rational man; I like to think; and in any disagreement between my emotions and my rationality, I should hope it is rationality that wins out every time.

Now let's get down to cases.

A publisher to whom I was beholden asked me to read a book by an important writer and to give them a quote that could be used on the cover. I tried to beg off, but they insisted that I at least read it, and give it a chance.

So I did. I *tried* to read it—and the gears locked tight long before I finished. It seemed to me so unsuccessful a book that there was no way in which I could give it the quote that was wanted. I felt awful, but I had to call the publisher and beg off.

Now, then, assuming my judgment was correct, should that book be reviewed? Why say unkind things about it?

In the case of an ordinary bad book, one might wonder. At the most, it might only be necessary to say, "This is a bad book because—" with a few unemotional sentences added. You don't crack a peanut with a sledgehammer.

An unsatisfactory book written by an important writer, however, requires a detailed review to explain *why* it seems to have gone wrong and *where* and *how*. This is not so much to warn off readers, who will probably have bought the book in great numbers anyway by the time the review comes out. It is because even a flawed book by a good writer can be an important educational experience.

Its failure can be used as a way of sharpening the general taste for the literary good. It will educate (properly reviewed) not only the reader, but the writer as well, the veteran as well as the neophyte.

And yet despite the value of such a review, I could not in a million years review the book myself.

There are emotional objections. How can I say unkind things about someone else when I detest having someone say unkind things about me? If I can't take it, I have no right to dish it out. Then, too, how can I review a book by a friend (or, possibly, a rival) and be sure of being objective?

If that isn't enough, there are technical objections. Even if everyone were to grant that I am a whizz at writing science fiction, that does *not* necessarily mean that I'm a whizz at understanding what makes science fiction good and bad. Even when I feel a story to be bad I don't necessarily have the ability to point out just where and how and why the badness exists.

So we have Baird Searles reviewing books for us. He has the talent for saying what needs to be said and I am grateful that he has.

Now consider what a reviewer must do, if he is to be good at his job.

1) A reviewer must read the book carefully; every word of it, if possible; even if it seems to be very bad. This is an extraordinarily difficult job. It is the mark of an unsuccessful book if it is hard to read; if it is clumsy, wearying, uninteresting, dull, monotonous, insulting to the intelligence, predictable, repetitious, infelicitous—any or all of these things. When you and I read a book of this sort, we stop reading. A competent reviewer mustn't. He must stick to it to give the book an utterly fair shake.

2) A reviewer must read with attention, marking passages perhaps, taking notes perhaps, so that he won't have to work from memory alone in writing his review, so that he won't make factual errors or unreasonable criticisms.

3) A reviewer must read with detachment and not allow his judgment of the book to be twisted by his judgment of the writer. He may know a writer to be an irritating boor and yet realize the writer's book may be great. He may know a writer to be a saint, and yet realize the writer's book may be awful. He must concentrate on the book and only on the book.

4) A reviewer must not only be a person of literary judgment, but he must have a wide knowledge of the field, so that he can exert his judgment of the book against the context of other books by the author, of books by other authors of similar experience or similar intent, and of the field in general.

5) A reviewer must be a competent writer himself, for the most literarily penetrating review ever written loses its point if it, itself, is so badly written that any reader grows bored, irritated, or confused.

6) Finally—and this is the point where even the cleverest reviewer (perhaps *especially* the cleverest reviewer) can come a cropper—the review must not be a showcase for the reviewer himself. The purpose of the review is not to demonstrate the superior erudition of the reviewer or to make it seem that the reviewer, if he but took the trouble, could write the book better than the author did. (Why the devil doesn't he do it, then?)

Nor must it seem to be a hatchet job in which the reviewer is carrying out some private vengeance. (This may not be so, you understand, but it mustn't even *seem* to be so.)

These are not easy conditions to meet; and the fact is that though there are many reviewers, there are not many good reviewers.

And why not? Probably all reviewers will gladly accept Sturgeon's Law (that ninety percent of everything is crud) with respect to the books they review—and it holds just as solidly for the reviews they write.

And is there anything a good book reviewer must receive from the editor for all that is expected of him? Certainly! In a word, independence.

When an editor hires a book reviewer, he doesn't (or shouldn't) buy a scribbler who has agreed to put the boss's opinions into words. No, it is the book reviewer *and his opinions* that have been hired. The book reviews in this magazine do not necessarily express the opinions of George, Shawna, or myself—although they might. In fact, George, Shawna, and myself do not necessarily agree among ourselves as to the worth of a particular piece of writing.

But it is the reviewer's opinions you want, not ours; and it is his you will get. He is the professional in this respect.

Baird Searles, in my opinion, is one of the good reviewers, and we are glad we have him, and we hope he stays with us a long time. He does not ask us for our views before he writes his column and if (inconceivably) he asked us, we wouldn't tell him.

And it's because reviewers can be like Baird Searles that we have a review column.

What Writers Go Through

Every once in a while I get a letter that strikes a chord. Jeanne S. King of Marietta, Georgia, suggested that I write an editorial on what writers go through. Her tender heart bled for writers and I think she has a point.

First, let me make it clear what I mean by "writers." I don't want to confine the word only to those who are successful, who have published bestselling books, or who crank out reams of published material every year (if not every day), or who make a lavish living out of their pens, typewriters, or word processors, or who have gained fame and adulation.

I also mean those writers who just sell an occasional item, who make only a bit of pin money to eke out incomes earned mainly in other fashions, whose names are not household words, and who are not recognized in the street.

In fact, let me go farther and say I even mean those writers who never sell anything, who are writers only in the sense that they work doggedly at it, sending out story after story, and living in a hope that is not yet fulfilled.

We can't dismiss this last classification as "failures" and not "real" writers. For one thing, they are not necessarily failures forever. Almost every writer, before he becomes a success, even a runaway supernova success, goes through an apprentice period when he's a "failure."

Secondly, even if a writer is destined always to be a failure, and even if he is never going to sell, he remains a human being for whom all the difficulties and frustration of a writer's life exist and, in fact, exist without the palliation of even an occasional and minor triumph.

If we go to the other extreme and consider the writer whose every product is an apparently sure sale, we find that the difficulties and frustrations have not disappeared. For one thing, no number of triumphs, no amount of approval, seem to have any carrying power at the crucial moment.

When even the most successful writer sits down before a blank piece of paper, he is bound to feel that he is starting from scratch and, indeed, that the Damoclean sword of rejection hangs over him. (By the way, when I say "he" and "him," I mean to add "she" and "her" every time.)

If I may use myself as an example, I always wince a little when anyone, however sincerely and honestly, assumes that I am never rejected. I admit that I am rarely rejected, but between "rarely" and "never" is a vast gulf. Even though I no longer work on spec and write only when a particular item is requested, I *still* run the risk. The year doesn't pass without at least one failure. It was only a couple of months ago that *Esquire* ordered a specific article from me. I duly delivered it; and they, just as duly, handed it back.

That is the possibility all of us live with. We sit there alone, pounding out the words, with our heart pounding in time. Each sentence brings with it a sickening sensation of not being right. Each page keeps us wondering if we are moving in the wrong direction.

Even if, for some reason, we feel we *are* getting it right and that the whole thing is singing with operatic clarity, we are going to come back to it the next day and reread it and hear only a duck's quacking.

It's torture for every one of us.

Then comes the matter of rewriting and polishing; of removing obvious flaws (at least, they seem obvious, but are they really?) and replacing them with improvements (or are we just making things worse?). There's simply no way of telling if the story is being made better or is just being pushed deeper into the muck until the time finally comes when we either tear it up as hopeless, or risk the humiliation of rejection by sending it off to an editor.

Once the story is sent off, no amount of steeling one's self, no amount of telling one's self over and over that it is sure to be rejected, can prevent one from harboring that one wan little spark of hope. Maybe—Maybe—

The period of waiting is refined torture in itself. Is the editor simply not getting round to it, or has he read it and is he suspended in uncertainty? Is he going to read it again and *maybe* decide to use it, or has it been lost, or has it been tossed aside to be mailed back at some convenient time and been forgotten?

How long do you wait before you write a query letter? And if you do write a letter, is it subservient enough? Sycophantic enough? Grovelling enough? After all, you don't want to offend him. He might be just on the point of accepting; and if an offensive letter from you comes along, he may snarl and rip your manuscript in two, sending you the halves.

And when the day comes that the manila envelope appears in the mail, all your mumbling to yourself that it is sure to come will not avail you. The sun will go into eclipse.

It's been over forty years since I've gone through all this in its full hellishness, but I remember it with undiminished clarity.

And then even if you make a sale, you have to withstand the editor's suggestions which, at the very least, mean you have to turn back to the manuscript, work again, add or change or subtract material, and perhaps produce a finished product that will be so much worse than what had gone before that you lose the sale you thought you had made. At the worst, the changes requested are so misbegotten from your standpoint that they ruin the whole story in your eyes; and yet you may be in a position where you dare not refuse, so that you must maim your brainchild rather than see it die. (Or ought you to take back the story haughtily and try another editor? And will the first editor then blacklist you?)

Even after the item is sold and paid for and published, the triumph is rarely unalloyed. The number of miseries that might still take place are countless. A book can be produced in a slipshod manner or it can have a repulsive book jacket, or include blurbs that give away the plot or clearly indicate that the blurb writer didn't follow the plot.

A book can be nonpromoted, treated with indifference by the publisher and therefore found in no bookstores, and sell no more than a few hundred copies. Even if it begins to sell well, that can be aborted when it is reviewed unsympathetically or even viciously by someone with no particular talent or qualifications in criticism.

If you sell a story to a magazine you may feel it is incompetently illustrated, or dislike the blurb, or worry about misprints. You are even liable to face the unsympathetic comments of individual readers who will wax merry, sardonic, or contemptuous at your expense—and what are *their* qualifications for doing so?

You will bleed as a result. I never met a writer who didn't bleed at the slightest unfavorable comment, and no number of favorable or even ecstatic remarks will serve as a styptic pencil.

In fact, even total success has its discomforts and inconveniences. There are, for instance:

People who send you books to autograph and return, but don't bother sending postage or return envelopes, reducing you to impounding their books or (if you can't bring yourself to do that) getting envelopes, making the package, expending stamps, and possibly even going to the post office.

People who send you manuscripts to read and criticize (Nothing much, just a page-by-page analysis, and if you think it's all right, would you get it published with a generous advance, please? Thank you.).

People who dash off two dozen questions, starting with a simple one like: What in your opinion is the function of science fiction and in what ways does it contribute to the welfare of the world, illustrating your thesis with citations from the classic works of various authors. (Please use additional pages, if necessary.)

People who send you a form letter, with your name filled in (misspelled), asking for an autographed photograph, and with no envelope or postage supplied.

Teachers who flog a class of thirty into each sending you a letter telling you how they liked a story of yours, and sending you a sweet letter of her own asking you to send a nice answer to each one of the little dears.

And so on—

Well, then, why write?

A seventeenth-century German chemist, Johann Joachim Becher, once wrote: "The chemists are a strange class of mortals, impelled by an almost insane impulse to seek their pleasure among smoke and vapor, soot and flame, poisOns and poverty; yet among all these evils I seem to live so sweetly, that may I die if I would change places with the Persian King."

Well, what goes for chemistry, goes for writing. I know

all the miseries, but somewhere among them is happiness. I can't easily explain where it is or what it consists of, but it is there. I know the happiness and I experience it, and I will not stop writing while I live—and may I die if I would change places with the President of the United States.

Revisions

When it comes to writing, I am a "primitive." I had had no instruction when I began to write, or even by the time I had begun to publish. I took no courses. I read no books on the subject.

This was not bravado on my part, or any sense of arrogance. I just didn't know that there *were* courses or books on the subject. In all innocence, I just thought you sat down and wrote. Naturally, I have picked up a great deal about writing in the days since I began; but in certain important respects, my early habits imprinted me and I find I can't change.

Some of these imprinted habits are trivial. For instance, I cannot leave a decent margin. Editors have tried begging and they have tried ordering, and my only response is a firm "Never!"

When I was a kid, you see, getting typewriting paper was a hard thing to do for it required m-o-n-e-y, of which I had none. Therefore what I had, I saved—single-spaced, both sides, and typing to the very edge of the page, all four edges. Well, I learned that one could not submit a manuscript unless it was double-spaced on one side of the page only; and

I was *forced*, unwillingly, to adopt that wasteful procedure. I also learned about margins and established them—but not wide enough. Nor could I ever make them wide enough. My sense of economy had gone as far as it would go and it would go no farther.

More important was the fact that I had never learned about revisions. My routine was (and still is) to write a story in first draft as fast as I can. Then I go over it, and correct errors in spelling, grammar, and word order. Then I prepare my second draft, making minor changes as I go and as they occur to me. My second draft is my final draft. No more changes except under direct editorial order and then with rebellion in my heart.

I didn't know there was anything wrong with this. I thought it was the way you were *supposed* to write. In fact when Bob Heinlein and I were working together at the Navy Yard in Philadelphia during World War II, Bob asked me how I went about writing a story and I told him. He said, "You type it *twice?* Why don't you type it correctly the first time?"

I felt bitterly ashamed; and the very next story I wrote, I tried my level best to get it right the first time. I failed. No matter how carefully I wrote, there were always things that had to be changed. I decided I just wasn't as good as Heinlein.

But then, in 1950, I attended the Breadloaf Writers' Conference at the invitation of Fletcher Pratt. There I listened in astonishment to some of the things said by the lecturers. "The secret of writing," said one of them, "is rewriting."

Fletcher Pratt himself said, "If you ever write a paragraph that seems to you to *sing*, to be the best thing you've ever written, to be full of wonder and poetry and greatness—cross it out, it stinks!"

Over and over again, we were told about the importance
of polishing, of revising, of tearing up and rewriting. I got
the bewildered notion that, far from being expected to type
it right the first time, as Heinlein had advised me, I was expected to type it all wrong, and get it right only by the
thirty-second time, if at all.

I went home immersed in gloom; and the very next time
I wrote a story, I tried to tear it up. I couldn't make myself
do it. So I went over it to see all the terrible things I had
done, in order to revise them. To my chagrin, everything
sounded great to me. (My own writing always sounds great
to me.) Eventually, after wasting hours and hours—to say
nothing of spiritual agony—I gave it up. My stories would
have to be written the way they always were—and still are.

What is it I am saying, then? That it is wrong to revise?
No, of course not—any more than it is wrong not to revise.

You don't do *anything* automatically, simply because some
"authority" (including me) says you should. Each writer is
an individual, with his or her own way of thinking, and
doing, and writing. Some writers are not happy unless they
polish and polish, unless they try a paragraph this way and
that way and the other way.

Once Oscar Wilde, coming down to lunch, was asked
how he had spent his morning. "I was hard at work," he
said.

"Oh?" he was asked. "Did you accomplish much?"

"Yes, indeed," said Wilde. "I inserted a comma."

At dinner, he was asked how he had spent the afternoon.
"More work," he said.

"Inserted another comma?" was the rather sardonic question.

"No," said Wilde, unperturbed. "I removed the one I had
inserted in the morning."

Well, if you're Oscar Wilde, or some other great stylist,

polishing may succeed in imparting an ever-higher gloss to your writing and you *should* revise and revise. If, on the other hand, you're not much of a stylist (like me, for instance) and are only interested in straightforward story-telling and clarity, then a small amount of revision is probably all you need. Beyond that small amount you may merely be shaking up the rubble.

I was told last night, for instance, that Daniel Keyes (author of the classic "Flowers for Algernon") is supposed to have said, "The author's best friend is the person who shoots him just before he makes one change too many."

Let's try the other extreme. William Shakespeare is reported by Ben Jonson to have boasted that he "never blotted a word." The Bard of Avon, in other words, would have us believe that, like Heinlein, he got it right the first time, and that what he handed in to the producers at the Globe Theatre was first draft. (He may have been twisting the truth a bit. Prolific writers tend to exaggerate the amount of nonrevision they do.)

Well, if you happen to be another Will Shakespeare, or another Bob Heinlein,[1] maybe you can get away without revising at all. But if you're just an ordinary writer (like me) maybe you'd better do *some*. (As a matter of fact, Ben Jonson commented that he wished Will had "blotted out a thousand," and there are indeed places where Will might have been—ssh!—improved on.)

Let's pass on to a slightly different topic.

I am sometimes asked if I prepare an outline first before writing a story or a book.

The answer is: No, I don't.

To begin with, this was another one of those cases of ini-

---

[1]Mr. Heinlein now admits to two or three drafts on his longer works.—Ed.

tial ignorance. I didn't know at the start of my career that such things as outlines existed. I just wrote a story and stopped when I finished, and if it happened to be one length it was a short story, and if it happened to be another it was a novelette.

When I wrote my first novel, Doubleday told me to make it 70,000 words long. So I wrote until I had 70,000 words and then stopped—and by the greatest good luck, it turned out to be the end of the novel.

When I began my second novel, I realized that such an amazing coincidence was not likely to happen twice in a row, so I prepared an outline. I quickly discovered two things. One, an outline constricted me so that I could not breathe. Two, there was no way I could force my characters to adhere to the outline; even if I wanted to do so, they refused. I never tried an outline again. In even my most complicated novels, I merely fix the ending firmly in my mind; decide on a beginning; and then, from that beginning, charge toward the ending, making up the details as I go along.

On the other hand, P. G. Wodehouse, for whose writings I have an idolatrous admiration, always prepared outlines, spending more time on them than on the book and getting every event, however small, firmly in place before begininning.

There's something to be said on both sides of course.

If you are a structured and rigid person who likes everything under control, you will be uneasy without an outline. On the other hand, if you are an undisciplined person with a tendency to wander all over the landscape, you will be better off with an outline even if you feel you wouldn't like one.

On the third hand, if you are quick-thinking and ingenious, but with a strong sense of the whole, you will be better off without an outline.

How do you decide which you are? Well, try an outline, or try writing without one, and find out for yourself.

The thing is: Don't feel that any rule of writing must be hard and fast, and handed down from Sinai. Try them all out by all means; but in the last analysis, stick to that which makes you comfortable. You are, after all, an individual.

Irony

It is well known that I know nothing about the craft of writing in any formal way. I say so myself—constantly. Being an editorial director, however, has its demands and duties. I must answer letters from readers, for instance, and take into account any unhappiness they may have with stories and editorial policy. And that means I am sometimes forced to think about writing techniques.

That brings me to the subject at hand, the matter of the use of irony by writers.

In the March 1984 issue, I discussed satire. The two are often lumped together, and, in fact, sometimes confused and treated as though they were synonymous. They are not!

Satire, as I explained, achieves its purpose of castigating the evils of humanity and society by exaggeration. It puts those evils under a magnifying glass with the intention of making them clearly visible.

Irony does it differently. You can get a hint from the fact that "irony" is from a Greek word meaning "dissimulation." An ironist must pretend, and the classic ironist was Socrates, who in his discussions with others would relentlessly pretend ignorance and ask all kinds of naive questions designed to trap an overconfident adversary into rashly taking positions that then proved to be indefensible under further naive questioning by Socrates.

Naturally, Socrates was *not* ignorant and the questions were *not* naive, and his method of procedure is known as "Socratic irony." You may well believe that those who suffered under his bland lash did not grow to love him, and I suspect he fully earned his final draught of hemlock.

Socrates set the fashion for irony for all time. He pretended to be ignorant when he was actually piercingly intelligent, and ever since then, ironists have pretended to believe and say the opposite of what they wanted the reader to understand. Instead of exaggerating the evils they are denouncing, they reverse them and call them good.

The satirist induces laughter by his exaggeration, the ironist induces indignation by his reversal. The satirist is often good-natured, the ironist tends to be savage and bitter. Satire is a comparatively mild technique whose purpose is easily grasped. Irony is a difficult technique whose point is frequently missed, and the ironist may find he is holding a two-edged sword and is himself badly gashed.

Most satirists find themselves indulging in irony sometimes, and I know exactly where I first encountered irony. I was reading Charles Dickens's *Pickwick Papers* for the first time (as a pre-teener) and in chapter two, I encountered Dickens's description of Tracy Tupman's zeal at "general benevolence." Said Dickens, "The number of instances . . . in which that excellent man referred objects of charity to the houses of other members for left-off garments or pecuniary relief is almost incredible."

I was astonished. I thought to myself that it wasn't very kind of Mr. Tupman to send poor people to other members instead of giving them something himself, so how could he be benevolent? And after a while, the light dawned. He *wasn't* benevolent. In fact, I decided indignantly, he was a stingy bum, and my liking for him was strictly limited for the rest of the book and ever since. I did not know that what I had just read was irony, but I understood the concept from that time on, and I eventually learned the word.

If you want a savage and prolonged bit of writing with a great deal of irony in it, I refer you to Mark Twain's *The Mysterious Stranger,* which was not published till after he was safely dead. I warn you, though, it's not pleasant reading. It certainly makes plain, however, Twain's bitter feelings about humanity and the assorted evils that seemed (to Twain, at any rate) to be inextricably bound up with it. And it may, for a time at least, embitter you with humanity, too.

Even that, however, must take second place to the all-time high in caustic irony—a pamphlet by Jonathan Swift, published about 1730, entitled "A Modest Proposal for Preventing the Children of Poor People in Ireland from being a Burden to their Parents or Country and for Making them Beneficial to the Public." Swift served in Ireland and could see first-hand, and with enormous indignation, the manner in which the English brutally and callously ground the Irish into helpless and hopeless poverty.

He therefore pointed out that since the only thing the Irish were allowed to produce and keep for their own use were their children, it would supply them with needed money, and others with needed food, if those Irish children were sold in order to be fattened and slaughtered for sale at the butcher's. With an absolutely straight face, and with incredible ingenuity, he pointed out all the advantages that would accrue from such cannibalism.

If anything could possibly have evoked shame and even reform from those responsible for the Irish plight, that pamphlet would have done it. Undoubtedly, many of those who read the pamphlet *were* shamed; some may even have altered their attitudes and behavior. By and large, however, the exploitation of the Irish continued unchanged for nearly two more centuries and the light that casts on humanity is not a good one.

And yet, you know, not everyone has a "sense of irony," which is by no means the same as a "sense of humor." I firmly believe that one can have one and not the other. It is possible to be confused by a pretense to believe the opposite of what you believe, as I was for a few minutes by Dickens's description of Tupman as benevolent. Of course, I caught on, but if I had lacked a sense of irony, I suppose I wouldn't have.

There were, actually, good and kindly people who read Swift's pamphlet with indignation, not at the mistreatment of the Irish, but at Swift's apparently callous and immoral advocacy of cannibalism. They thought he *meant* it, and denounced him with immeasurable vehemence.

And that finally brings me to *Asimov's* for sometimes what we publish contains irony, and if irony is hard to handle even for the absolute master of the art, good old Swift, you can understand that it is a slippery tool for lesser mortals.

In the February 1984 issue, Tom Rainbow wrote a "Viewpoint" article entitled, "Sentience and the Single Extraterrestrial," that dealt with the requirements for such things as intelligence, sentience, and self-awareness. He described the kind of extraterrestrials that might, or might not, possess such things.

From the title alone, you can tell that he is writing in the humorous mode, and indeed, when you read his essay, you will find that he is saying perfectly serious things in a deliberately funny way.

In one place, he uses irony. Having talked of the requirements of self-awareness in terms of brain/body ratios, he points out that women's brains are smaller than men's but so are their bodies, leaving the brain/body ratio nearly the same in both sexes. (Actually, if there's an advantage it's on the side of women.) With heavy irony, he says, "this reasoning leads to the somewhat startling conclusion that women must be *self-aware*."

How can one believe that Rainbow really thinks the conclusion is "startling"? He's using ironic dissimulation. He's *pretending* to think it's startling (and italicizing "self-aware" as a typographical indication of astonishment) in order for you to understand thoroughly that this is *not* startling and that people who consider women inferior beings are ignorant, and even stupid.

And to make it even plainer, he puts himself in the ironic position of these ignoramuses and says in the next sentence, "Heck, guys, if even *girls* can be self-aware, then there's hope for Giant Dill Pickles."

The use of the adolescent term "Heck," and the equally adolescent "guys," and the shift from "women" to italicized "girls" all show that he is not speaking in his own persona and that he has nothing but contempt for the attitude. He is relying, poor fellow, on his readers having a sense of irony.

Well, they do—by and large.

But there are always exceptions, and a few women have written indignant letters to point out that this was insulting. One said that it wasn't funny or cute.

No, indeed, Swift's advocacy of cannibalism wasn't funny or cute, either, but he was trying for something else.

To be sure, Swift's entire pamphlet was aimed at his target and Rainbow was merely bringing in the matter of women's brains as a side issue, and perhaps if he were doing it again, he might decide it would be more judicious not to indulge. But please, women, the man is on your side and tried to show it by the use of that two-edged sword, irony. You may think the irony didn't work, but that doesn't make Rainbow any enemy of womankind.

Plagiarism

To the ancient Romans, a "plagiarius" was what we call a kidnapper, and to steal children is certainly a heinous crime. It appears to those who work with their minds and imagination, however, that to steal one's brainchildren is almost as heinous a crime, and so "plagiarism," in English, has come to mean the stealing of the ideas, forms, or words by someone who then puts them forth as his or her own.

A scientist's formulas, an artist's paintings, an inventor's models, a philosopher's thoughts, might all be the subject of plagiarism, but common usage has come to apply the term, specifically, to the theft of a writer's production.

Plagiarism is a horrid nightmare to writers in several different ways; and it is much more serious than non-writers may realize.

If a writer, for any reason, commits plagiarism, copying some already published material, and if he gets away with it to the extent of getting the plagiarized material republished, he is bound to be caught sooner or later. Some reader, somewhere, will notice the theft. In that case, even if the plagiarist isn't sued or punished in any way, you can be sure that no editor who knows of the plagiarism will buy anything from that writer again. If the plagiarist has a career, it is permanently ruined.

You may think that such a literary thief deserves a ruined career, and certainly I think so, but copying an already published item word for word is such a surefire failure that only an idiot or a complete novice would do it. What about the case where someone simply makes use of the central idea of the story, the series of events it contains, the climax, the emotional milieu, and so on, but does *not* repeat it word for word? What if he uses his (or her) own words entirely, changes the incidents in nonessential details, puts it in a different setting and so on?

In that case, it becomes more difficult to decide whether plagiarism has taken place. After all, it is possible to have the same ideas someone else has had.

Thus, Ted Sturgeon once wrote a story which he sent to Horace Gold of *Galaxy* and which was accepted. I wrote a story which I sent to Horace Gold while Ted's story was still unpublished. There was no communication between us; we lived in different cities and had not exchanged phone calls or letters in months, nor had either of us discussed our stories with anyone. Nevertheless, not only did we both center our stories about a double meaning in the word "hostess," but two of my characters were Drake and Vera, and two of his were Derek and Verna.

It was the purest of coincidences, for except for the double meaning and the character names that we shared, the stories were miles apart. Nevertheless, even the *appearance* of plagiarism must be avoided. I had to make enough changes in my story (because it was the later one received) to destroy the appearance. To do so spoiled the story in my opinion, but it had to be done anyway.

In the same way, when I am writing a story, I must be conscious that there have been other stories dealing with similar ideas or similar characters or similar events, and I must make every effort to dilute that similarity. When I wrote a story once called "Each an Explorer," I never for a moment forgot John Campbell's "Who Goes There?" and spent more time trying to avoid his story than trying to write my own. In the same way, when I wrote "Lest We Remember" (published in this magazine), I had to steer a mile wide of Keyes's "Flowers for Algernon." It's part of the game.

But I haven't read every story ever written and many that I have read, I have completely forgotten, at least consciously. What if I duplicate important elements of stories I have never read, or have forgotten? It's possible. I once wrote a short-short that ended with a certain dramatic climax in the last sentence. Eventually, I received a letter from another writer whose story had been published before I wrote my story and who had made use of the same dramatic climax in his last sentence. What's more, I had his story in an anthology in my library. I did not remember reading it, but I had had the opportunity to do so. The two stories, except for the climaxes, were completely different, but I promptly wrote the other author and told him that although he had my word that there was no conscious imitation, I would withdraw the story from circulation and it would never again appear in any anthology, any collection, any form whatever—and it never has.

Fortunately, the other writer accepted this, but what protection do I (or any other writer) have against the accusation of plagiarism over what is a bit of unconscious recall, or, for that matter, an outright coincidence?

Actually, very little. I rely, to a large extent, on my prolificity and my unblemished record. No one as prolific as I would seem to have to depend on someone else's ideas, and my own mental fertility is obvious to all. Secondly, I am cautious enough never to discuss my stories before they are published, nor will I listen to others who might want to discuss *their* stories. In fact, I won't even read unsolicited manuscripts sent me by strangers. They go back at once, unread.

Even so, every established writer lives under an eternal Damocles's sword of possible accusation of plagiarism. A casual reference, a small similarity, a nonessential duplication may be enough to produce such a suit. Such a suit, however unjustified, however certain of being thrown out of court, can be hurtful to an innocent writer. It is, after all, an expense. Lawyers must be paid, time must be lost and, invariably, one is urged to "pay off the kook."

But what if *you*, the established writer, have been plagiarized? That has never happened to me to the extent of publication—that I know of. To be sure, there have been pastiches of me, deliberate imitations of my robot stories, or my Black Widowers mystery stories, and so on. These come under the heading of fun. The writer who turns them out makes no secret of it, and the editor knows that it's a pastiche. Sometimes, they send the manuscript to me to ask if I have any objection. I have always given permission. Then, too, there are stories that are bound to be similar to mine in some benign way. The *Star Wars* movies have some distant similarities to my Foundation stories, but, what the heck, you can't make a fuss about such things.

Unpublished plagiarism is more common. An English professor once sent me a story written by a student in first-year English. It didn't seem to her likely that the kid could have written that good a story and there were things in it that seemed reminiscent of me—like the Three Laws of Robotics. I went over the story and it was my "Galley Slave" word for word. I returned it to the professor and told her to (a) punish the student appropriately, and (b) not let me know anything about it. (I'm soft-hearted.)

And what if you're an editor and get stuck with some material that might conceivably be plagiarized. In the first place—is it? A completely original, nonreminiscent story is possible, but very rarely met up with. Similarities with some particular published story are almost unavoidable. However, the more similarities there are, with the same previously published story, the greater the possibility of plagiarism. Nevertheless, it is difficult to establish certainty if the copying isn't word for word.

Should an editor refuse a story, however good, if there are too many similarities? Of course! Remember that I said even the appearance of plagiarism must be strictly avoided.

There is, however, a catch. An editor has not read every story that has been published. Sometimes an editor, being human, has not even read every *famous* story ever published. Or an editor has read many stories but some of them have completely gone from her mind. Such an editor may, in all innocence, therefore publish a doubtful story. He (or she) is then a *victim* and not an accomplice.

Just as honest, established writers must live, constantly, with the fear of being accused of plagiarism, or of themselves being plagiarized, so must honest, established editors live, constantly, with the fear of being victimized into publishing a doubtful story.

What does one do in such a case? One can't entirely ignore the matter. For one thing, the similarity between the new story and an older story is sure to be seen by some readers. Even if the older story is very obscure, someone will have read it and remembered it. If it is a well-known story, letters will come in heaps.

One can ask the writer of the doubtful story for an explanation. If the explanation seems unconvincing, one can avoid buying stories from the writer again. One might warn other editors in the field to be careful. And one can try hard not to let it happen again—knowing full well that there is no way of stopping *every* piece of literary prestidigitation.

It is comforting to know, however, that if an editor lets something suspicious get into print, the fact will not remain unreported for long. We can be sure, then, that if no indignant reader has written within two weeks of the appearance of an issue, we have probably committed no ghastly mistakes of this nature in that issue.

Symbolism

To a child, a story is a story, and to many of us, as we grow older, a story remains a story. The good guy wins, the bad guy loses. Boy meets girl, boy loses girl, boy gets girl. We don't want anything beyond that—at least to begin with.

The trouble is that if that's all there is, one is likely to grow weary eventually. Children love to play tick-tack-toe, for instance, but it's such a limited game that, after a while, most children don't want to play it any more. In the same way, children, as they grow older, may stop wanting to read stories that are only stories.

Since writers get as tired writing stories that are only stories, as readers get tired reading them, it is only natural that writers begin to search for new and different ways to tell a story—for their own mental health, if nothing else.

A writer can try to find a new kind of plot, or he can indulge in stylistic experimentation, or he can strive for events that are ambiguous and conclusions that are inconclusive, or he can blur the distinction between good and evil, or between dream and reality. There are many, many things he can do and the one thing all these attempts have in common is that they annoy those readers who still are in the stage of wanting stories that are only stories.

Mind you, I don't sneer at such readers. For one thing, I myself still write stories that are primarily stories, because that's what *I* like. In my stories, there is a clear beginning, a clear middle, and a clear end, the good guy usually wins, and so on.

Nevertheless, you can't blame writers and readers for wanting something more than that, and those of us (I include myself, please note) who are suspicious of experimentation and fancy tricks ought to make some effort to understand what's going on. We may fail to grasp it entirely, but we may at least see just enough to avoid an explosion of unreasonable anger.

One game that writers very commonly play is the one called "symbolism." A story can be written on two levels. On the surface, it is simply a story, and anyone can read it as such and be satisfied. Even children can read it.

But the simple characters and events of the surface may stand for (or symbolize) other subtler things. Below the surface, therefore, there may be hidden and deeper meanings that children and unsophisticated adults don't see. Those who can see the inner structure, however, can get a double pleasure out of it. First, since the inner structure is usually cleverer and more convoluted than the surface, it exercises the mind more pleasantly. Second, since it is not easy to detect, the reader has the excitement of discovery and the pleasure of admiring his own cleverness. (You can easily imagine what fun the writer has constructing such symbolic significance.)

I suppose the best example of something written on two levels is the pair of books popularly known as *Alice in Wonderland*. On the surface, it's a simply written fantasy, and children love it. Some adults reading it, however, find themselves in an intricate maze of puns, paradoxes, and inside jokes. (Read Martin Gardner's *The Annotated Alice*, if you want to increase your pleasure in the book.)

Or take J. R. R. Tolkien's *The Lord of the Rings*. On the surface, it is a simple tale of a dangerous quest. The small hobbit, Frodo, must take a dangerous ring into the very teeth of an all-powerful enemy and destroy it—and, of course, he succeeds. On a second, deeper level, it is an allegory of good and evil, leading us to accept the possibility that the small and weak can triumph where the (equally good) large and powerful might not; that even evil has its uses that contribute to the victory of the good, and so on.

But there is a third level, too. What *is* the ring that is so powerful and yet so evil? Why is it that those who possess it are corrupted by it and cannot give it up? Is such a thing pure fantasy or does it have an analogue in reality?

My own feeling is that the ring represents modern technology. This corrupts and destroys society (in Tolkien's view) and, yet, those societies who gain it and who are aware of its evils simply cannot give it up. I have read *The Lord of the Rings* five times, so far, and I have not yet exhausted my own symbolic reading of it. I do not agree with, and I resent, Tolkien's attitude and yet I get pleasure out of the intricacy and skill of the structure.

There is another important point to be made concerning symbolism.

A writer may insert it, without knowing he has done so; or else, a clever interpreter can find significance in various parts of a story that a writer will swear he had no intention of inserting.

This has happened to me, for instance. The middle portion of my novel *The Gods Themselves*, with its intricate picture of a trisexual society, has been interpreted psychiatrically and philosophically in ways that I *know* I didn't intend, and in terms that I literally don't understand. My Foundation series has been shown, by apparently careful analysis, to be thoroughly Marxist in inspiration, except that I had never read one word by Marx, or about Marx either, at the time the stories were written, or since.

When I complained once to someone who worked up a symbolic meaning of my story "Nightfall" that made no sense to me at all, he said to me, haughtily, "What makes you think you understand the story just because you've written it?"

And when I published an essay in which I maintained that Tolkien's ring symbolized modern technology, and a reader wrote to tell me that Tolkien himself had denied it, I responded with, "That doesn't matter. The ring nevertheless symbolizes modern technology."

Sometimes it is quite demonstrable that an author inserts a deeper symbolism than he knows—or even understands. I have almost never read a layman's explanation of relativity that didn't succumb to the temptation of quoting *Alice* because Lewis Carroll included paradoxes that are unmistakably relativistic in nature. He did not know that, of course; he just happened to be a genius at paradox.

Well, sometimes this magazine publishes stories that must not be read only on the surface, and, as is almost inevitable, this riles a number of readers.

I am thinking, for instance, of the novella "Statues" by Jim Aikin, which appeared in our November 1984 issue, and which some readers objected to strenuously. There were statements to the effect that it wasn't science fiction or even fantasy, that it had no point, that it was anti-Christian, and so on.

To begin with, the story, taken simply as a story, is undoubtedly unpleasant in spots. I winced several times when

I read it, and I tell you, right now, that I wouldn't, and couldn't, write such a story. But I'm not the be-all and the end-all. The story, however difficult to stomach some of its passages may be, was skillfully and powerfully written. Even some of those who objected had to admit that.

And it was indeed a fantasy. Aikin made it clear toward the end that the statues were not pushed about, and that their apparent movement was not a delusion. They were on the side of the heroine and were cooperating with her, trying to rescue her from her unhappy life.

But that is only the surface. A little deeper and we see that it is a case of the old gods trying to save the young woman from the new. It is a rebellion against the rigid Pharisaic morality of some aspects of the Judeo-Christian tradition and a harking back to the greater freedom of some aspects of paganism. The story is in the spirit of that powerful line of A. C. Swinburne in his "Hymn to Proserpine": "Thou has conquered, O pale Galilean; the world has grown gray from thy breath."

Looked at this way, the story is not anti-Christian (surely the "Christian" characters in the story are not all there is to Christianity), but is against hypocrisy-in-the-name-of-religion, which I imagine no one favors, least of all Christians. The great French dramatist Molière took up his cudgels against that same foe in his masterpiece *Tartuffe* and you can't imagine the trouble he got into as a result.

But if you go deeper still, you will find the story is one more expression of the longing for the old. In this story it is expressed by contrasting the frowning new god with the kindly old ones. In *The Lord of the Rings* it is expressed by contrasting the evil technology of the Dark Lord, Sauron, with the pastoral life of the simple hobbits. (Of course, it is much safer to make of the enemy a Devil-figure than a God-figure, so Tolkien got into no trouble at all.)

You can see the value of symbolism when you compare either of these with Jack Finney's famous "The Third Level," where he demonstrates his longing for the old by a straightforward contrast between 1950 and 1880. It leaves nothing to discover and, in my opinion, therefore, is a weak story.

But "Statues"—like it or not—is a *strong* story that makes an important point with great skill.

Prediction

There is a general myth among laymen that, somehow, the chief function of a science fiction writer is to make predictions that eventually come true.

Thus, I am frequently asked, "How does it feel to see all the predictions you have made coming true?"

To which I can only reply, "It feels great—in those very few cases in which something I have said actually came to pass."

At other times, I am asked with utter confidence, "Can you give us a few of your predictions that have come true?"

I would love to be able to say, "Well, to name just a few: airplanes, radios, television, skyscrapers, and, in my early days, the wheel and fire."

But I can't bring myself to do that. The interviewers might actually print it, and they might try to give me a medal for predicting fire.

However, I came across a prediction I made once that I didn't know I had made—that actually I didn't know was a prediction. Nor did I discover it myself. Someone pointed it out to me.

In order to explain this, I'll have to take the long way round. Please bear with me.

Back in 1952, I began to write a novel called *The Caves of Steel*. It was finished in 1953, was published in the October, November, and December 1953 issues of *Galaxy* as a three-part serial, and was published in book form by Doubleday in 1954.

It was a science fiction murder mystery that introduced my characters Elijah Baley and R. Daneel Olivaw, whom some of you may have come across in your reading. Toward the end of *The Caves of Steel*, I needed a second murder for the sake of the plot, and that bothered me, for I don't like murders and I rarely have them in my mysteries. When I do, there is only one and it is committed offstage, usually before the story begins. (I'm funny that way.)

The first murder in *The Caves of Steel* had been offstage before the story began, and the second murder would be offstage, also, but I didn't want to kill a human being, so, instead, I killed a rather simple robot. But, again, I didn't want to kill him brutally by smashing in his cranium or throwing him into a vat of melted lead. I preferred something more science fictional.

So here is a character in the story, a Dr. Gerrigel, describing the dead robot:

" 'In the robot's partly clenched right fist,' said Dr. Gerrigel, 'was a shiny ovoid about two inches long and half an inch wide with a mica window at one end. The fist was in contact with his skull as though the robot's last act had been to touch his head. The thing he was holding was an alpha-sprayer. You know what they are, I suppose?' "

The nature of the alpha-sprayer was then explained for the sake of the reader. It was described as a device that sends out a beam of alpha particles through the mica window. The impingement of the alpha particles on the robot's positronic brain was drastic. Or, as I put it: "Dr. Gerrigel said, 'Yes, and his positronic brain paths were immediately randomized. Instant death, so to speak.' "

Well, why not? Alpha particles are capable of knocking electrons out of atoms. It is because they do so, leaving electrically charged ions behind, that it was discovered, in 1911, that they could be detected in cloud chambers. The ions, with their electric charge, served as nuclei for tiny water droplets and those droplets marked out the path of the particle.

Positrons, which I use in robotic brain paths in order to make them sound science fictional, are precisely like electrons except for possessing a positive charge rather than a negative one. Alpha particles should shove them out of the way with equal ease, and if positrons make up the brain paths, shoving them away disrupts the brain paths and inactivates the robots.

There's nothing ingenious about it at all. Perfectly humdrum.

And then a short time ago, I received a letter from a gentleman working with a corporation that deals with computers. It begins as follows:

"This letter is to inform you and congratulate you on another remarkable scientific prediction of the future; namely your foreseeing of the dynamic random-access memory (DRAM) logic upset problem caused by alpha particle emission, first observed in 1977, but written about by you in Caves of Steel in 1957." [Note: Actually, 1952.]

Apparently the corporation tracked down failures in memory devices and finally decided that:

"These failures are caused by trace amounts of radioactive elements present in the packaging material used to encapsulate the silicon devices which, upon radioactive decay, emit high energy alpha particles that upset the logic states of the semiconductor memory. . . .

"I am writing you about this topic because in your book, Caves of Steel, published in the 1950s, you use an alpha particle emitter to 'murder' one of the robots in the story, by destroying ('randomizing') its positronic brain. This is, of course, as good a way of describing a logic upset as any I've heard.

"I get a great big kick out of finding out that our millions of dollars of research, culminating in several international awards for the most important scientific contribution in the field of reliability of semiconductor devices in 1978 and 1979, was predicted in substantially accurate form twenty years [Note: twenty-five years, actually] before the events took place! You may certainly with great pride add this phenomenon to your collection of scientific predictions."

Well, you can easily imagine that I was delighted, but truth is mighty and will prevail. I instantly wrote to the gentleman who was so pleased at my prediction that I honestly was not aware that I was making a prediction, and that the whole thing was a tribute, not to my ingenuity, but to the good luck that constantly dogs my footsteps.

A much more intuitive and remarkable prediction was made by the science-fictional father of us all, H. G. Wells. First, a little background.

In 1913, the British chemist Frederick Soddy (1877–1956), advanced the "isotope concept" based on his studies of the elements produced in the course of radioactive decay. He proposed that a particular element might be made up of atoms identical in chemical properties but differing somewhat in atomic weight. Elements, then, instead of necessarily being made up of absolutely identical elements were actually mixtures of several almost identical "isotopes" differing in atomic weight.

This made so much sense, it was quickly accepted and has remained a cornerstone of chemistry and of atomic physics ever since.

But just the other day, I received a reprint of a paper by H. G. Wells, written on September 5, 1896 (seventeen years *before* Soddy's suggestion), in which he refers to some work done by a chemist the previous year, before radioactivity had even been discovered, and suggests that to explain that work, it is possible to suppose that "there are two kinds of oxygen, one with an atom a little heavier than the other." By saying that, he is anticipating and predicting the existence of isotopes.

Furthermore, he points out that "the electric spark traversing the gas has a . . . selective action. Your heavier atoms or molecules get driven this or that way with slightly more force." This is a pretty good description of a phenomenon first noted by the British physicist Joseph John Thomson (1856–1940), in 1912, sixteen years after Wells's suggestion.

How's that!

Naturally, I would like to point to something of my own that contained a bit of nice intuitive insight, and here it is. In 1966, I wrote a scientific essay, "I'm Looking Over a Four-Leaf Clover," which eventually appeared in the September 1966 issue of *The Magazine of Fantasy and Science Fiction*.

In it I wanted to speculate about the origin of the universe and I was anxious to rebut the favorite comment of some who would ask, "If the universe started as a 'cosmic egg,' where did the cosmic egg come from?" The hope was that if I were faced with that question I would have to admit the existence of a supernatural agency of creation.

I therefore postulated the existence of "negative energy" and supposed that energy was created in both negative and positive form so that there was no *net* creation. I went on to advance what I called "Asimov's Cosmogonic Principle" and wrote, "The most economical way of expressing the principle is 'In the Beginning, there was Nothing.' "

Well, some ten years later, the theory of the "inflationary universe" was advanced. It was altogether different from anything I had suggested, but in one respect it was identical. The universe was pictured as starting as a quantum fluctuation in a vacuum, so that "In the Beginning, there was Nothing."

That piece of insight I am really proud of.

Best-seller

In the December 1982 issue of this magazine, you may recall that the first two chapters of my novel *Foundation's Edge* were presented as an excerpt, together with an essay of my own on the novel's genesis and some pleasant comments from my friends and colleagues. I agreed to all this under strong pressure from the editorial staff, who thought it would be a Good Thing and who overrode my own objections that readers would complain that I was using the magazine for personal aggrandizement.

As it happened, my fears were groundless. Readers' comments were generally friendly, and a gratifying number indicated their determination to get the book and finish reading it.

It may be that you are curious to know what happened after the book was published. (For those of you interested in Asimovian trivia, it was published on October 8, 1982.) I'd like to tell you, because what happened astonished me totally. The book proved to be a best-seller!

I don't mean it was a "best-seller" in the usual publisher's-promotion way of indicating that it didn't actually sink without a trace on publication day. I mean it appeared on the national best-seller lists and as I write, it is in third place on both *The New York Times* and on the *Publishers Weekly* list of hardcover fiction. Maybe by the time this editorial appears, it will have disappeared from the lists, but *right now* it's there.

In the past, in these editorials, I have promised to keep you up to date on my endeavors and I will do it now in the form of an invented interview:

Q. *Dr. Asimov, is this your first best-seller?*

A. For some reason, people find that hard to believe, perhaps because I'm so assiduous at publicizing myself, but *Foundation's Edge* is my first best-seller. It is my 262nd book and I have been a professional writer for forty-four years, so I guess this qualifies me as something less than an overnight success.

Mind you, this is not my first successful book. Very few of my books have actually lost money for the publisher and many of them have done very well indeed over the years. The earlier books of the Foundation trilogy have sold in the millions over the thirty years they have been in print. Again, if you group all my books together and total the number of sales of "Asimov" (never mind the titles) then I have a best-seller every year.

However, *Foundation's Edge* is the first time a *single* book of mine has sold enough copies in a *single* week to make the best-seller lists, and in the eight weeks since publication (as I write), it has done it in each of eight weeks.

Q. *And how do you feel about that, Dr. A.?*

A. Actually, I have no room for any feeling but that of astonishment. After publishing two hundred and sixty-one books without any hint of best-sellerdom, no matter how many of them might have been praised, I came to think of that as a law of nature. As for *Foundation's Edge* in particular, it has no sex in it, no violence, no sensationalism of any kind, and I had come to suppose that this was a perfect recipe for respectable non-best-sellerdom.

Once I get over the astonishment, though (if ever), I suppose I will have room for feeling great. After all, *Foundation's Edge* will earn more money than I expected, and it will help my other books to sell more copies, and it may mean that future novels of mine may do better than I would otherwise expect, and I can't very well complain about any of that.

Then, too, think of the boost to my ego! (Yes, I know! You think that's the last thing it needs.) People who till now have known I was a writer and accepted it with noticeable lack of excitement even over the number of books I have committed, now stop me in order to congratulate me, and do so with pronounced respect. Personally, I don't think that being on the best-seller lists makes a book any the higher in quality and, all too often, it might indicate the reverse, but I must admit I enjoy the congratulations and all that goes with it.

Q. *Are there any disadvantages to all this great stuff, Isaac?*

A. Oddly enough, there are. For one thing, my esteemed publishers, Doubleday and Company, would like me to travel all over the United States pushing the book. (It is, at the moment, their only fiction best-seller and they are as eager as I am to have it stay on the lists forever.) They are putting considerable money into advertising and promotion and it would only be fair that I do my bit as well. However, I don't like to travel, and so I have to refuse their suggestions that I go to Chicago, for instance. And it makes me feel guilty, and a traitor both to my publisher and my book. I *have* made a trip to Philadelphia, though.

There is also a higher than normal demand for interviews through visits or on the telephone. This doesn't demand traveling on my part and I try to oblige (telling myself it's good publicity for the book), but it does cut into my writing time, and I can't allow too much of that.

Then, too, there's an extraordinary demand for free copies. This is a common disease among writers' friends and relations, who feel that there is no purpose in knowing a writer if you have to help support him. My dear wife (J. O. Jeppson), who is a shrewd questioner, has discovered the astonishing fact that some people think writers get unlimited numbers of free copies to give out. They don't! Except for a certain very small number, they have to *buy* copies just as anyone else does. (Even if they did have unlimited numbers of free copies, giving them rather than selling them would ruin a writer, just as giving meat rather than selling it would ruin a butcher.)

What I have done is to resist firmly any temptation to hand out *Foundation's Edge*. I have told everyone they must buy copies at a bookstore. If they insist, I will give them copies of other books, but those sales of *Foundation's Edge* must be registered. Every little bit helps.

Q. *Do you see any importance in this situation aside from personal profit and gratification?*

A. I do, indeed. Soon after *Foundation's Edge* was published, Arthur C. Clarke's new novel, *2010: Odyssey Two* was published, and it hit the bestseller lists, too. At the moment of writing it is in fifth place on *The New York Times* list. Earlier this year, Robert A. Heinlein made the list with *Friday* and Frank Herbert did so with *White Plague*.

I think this is the first year in which four different science fiction writers made the lists with straight science fiction books. I also think that in the case of Clarke and myself, this is the first time straight science fiction has landed so high on the lists.

This is gratifying to me as a long time science fiction fan. It indicates to me that, finally, science fiction is coming to be of interest to the general public and not simply to those few who inhabit the SF "ghetto."

In fact, I wish to point this out to those SF writers who are bitter and resentful because they feel that their books are shoved into the background and disregarded merely because they have the SF label on them. Neither *Foundation's Edge* nor *2010: Odyssey Two* makes any effort to hide the fact that it is science fiction. The publishers' promotion in each case utterly fails to obscure that fact. In the case of *Foundation's Edge*, *The New York Times* carefully describes it as "science fiction" each week in its best-seller listing. And yet it continues to sell.

To be sure, there is a trace of the "ghetto" just the same. There is one thing that Arthur and I have in common, aside from bestselling books. As of the moment of writing, neither *Foundation's Edge* nor *2010: Odyssey Two* has been reviewed in *The New York Times*. I presume the paper hesitates to bestow that accolade on mere science fiction. Oh, well!

Q. *And what are your present projects, Isaac?*

A. Well, Doubleday has informed me, in no uncertain terms, that I am condemned to write one novel after another for life, and that I am not permitted to consider dying.

So I am working on another novel. This one is to be the third novel of the robot series. Both Lije Baley and R. Daneel will reappear, and will complete the trilogy that began with *The Caves of Steel* and *The Naked Sun*. The third novel is called *World of the Dawn*.

After that, I am afraid that Doubleday expects me to do a fifth Foundation novel; and, apparently, so do the readers.

For three decades they badgered me for a sequel to the Foundation trilogy and when I gave that to them, the ungrateful dogs responded by badgering me for a sequel to the sequel.

I'd complain, except that I love it.

NOTE:

On December 19, 1982, *The New York Times* finally reviewed *Foundation's Edge*, and very favorably too. On that day, the book had slipped to sixth place in the best-seller list (still not bad) but Clarke had climbed to second place.

Pseudonyms

It was quite fashionable, in earlier times, to refrain from putting one's name to things one had written. The writer could leave himself unnamed ("anonymous"—from Greek words meaning "no name"), or else he could use a false name ("pseudonym"—from Greek words meaning "false name"). So common was the practice that a pseudonym is often referred to as a "pen-name," or, to give it greater elegance by placing it in French, a "nom de plume."

There were a variety of reasons for this. In most places in the world and at most times, it was all too easy to write something that would get you in trouble. The corruption, venality, and cruelty of those in power cried out for exposure, and those in power had the strongest objections to being exposed. For that reason, writers had to expect all sorts of governmental correction if caught—anywhere from a fine to death by torture.

The best-known example of this type of pseudonym was Voltaire, the eighteenth century French satirist, whose real name was Francois-Marie Arouet.

A second major reason was that any nonscholarly writing was looked upon as rather frivolous, and a decent person guilty of concocting such material might well be looked upon askance by society, and considered as having lost caste. A pseudonym, therefore, preserved respectability. This was especially true of women who were widely considered sub-human in mentality (by men) and who would have shocked the world by a too-open demonstration of the possession of brains. Mary Ann Evans, therefore, wrote under the name of George Eliot, and Charlotte Brontë at first wrote under the name of Currer Bell.

One would think that neither reason would hold for the world of modern American science fiction. Why should anyone fear punishment for writing science fiction in our free land, or why should anyone fear the loss of respectability if convicted of the deed. And yet—

It is conceivable, particularly in the early days of maga-zine science fiction, that people in the more sensitive pro-fessions, such as teaching, would not have cared to have it known that they wrote "pseudo-scientific trash" and so would protect themselves from lack of promotion, or out-right dismissal, by the use of a pseudonym. I don't know of such cases definitely, but I suspect some.

It is even more likely that in the bad old days before the women's movement became strong, women who wrote sci-ence fiction concealed their sex from the readers (and even, sometimes, from the editors). Science fiction was thought to be a very masculine pursuit at the time and I know two editors (no names, please, even though both are now dead) who insisted on believing that women *could not* write good science fiction. Pseudonyms were therefore necessary if they were to sell anything at all.

Sometimes, women did not have to use pseudonyms. Their first names might be epicene, and that would be pro-tection enough. Thus, Leslie F. Stone and Leigh Brackett were women but, as far as one could tell from their names, they might be as masculine as Leslie Fiedler and Leigh Hunt. Editors and readers at first believed they were.

Or women might simply convert names to initials. Could you tell that A. R. Long owned up to the name of Amelia, or that C. L. Moore was Catherine to her friends?

There were other reasons for pseudonyms in science fiction. In the early days of the magazine many of the successful writers could only make a living by writing a great deal just as fast as they could, for a variety of pulp markets. They might use different names for different markets, creating separate personalities, so to speak, that wouldn't compete with each other. Thus Will Jenkins wrote for the slicks under his own name, but adopted the pseudonym Murray Leinster when he wrote science fiction.

Sometimes, even within the single field of science fiction, particular writers wrote too many stories. They were so good that editors would cheerfully buy, let us say, eighteen stories from them in a particular year in which they only published twelve issues of their magazines. This meant (if you work out the arithmetic carefully) that it would be necessary to run more than one story by them in a single issue now and then, and editors generally have a prejudice against that. Readers would feel they were cheated of variety, or suspect that editors were showing undue favoritism, or who knows what. Therefore some of the stories would be put under a pseudonym.

The pseudonyms might be transparent enough. For instance, Robert A. Heinlein at the height of his magazine popularity wrote half his stories under the name of Anson MacDonald, but Bob's middle initial A. stood for Anson, and MacDonald was the maiden name of his then-wife. Similarly, L. Ron Hubbard wrote under the name of Rene Lafayette, but the initial L. in Hubbard's name was Lafayette, and Rene was a not-too-distant version of Ron. Still, as long as the readers were led to believe that not too many stories of one author were included in the inventory, all was well.

Sometimes, an author is so identified with a particular type of story, that when he writes another type of story, he doesn't want to confuse the reader by false associations—so he adopts a new name. Thus, John W. Campbell was a writer of super-science stories of cosmic scope, and one day he wrote a story called "Twilight" which was altogether different. He put it under the name of Don A. Stuart (his then-wife's maiden name was Dona Stuart, you see) and rapidly made that name even more popular than his own.

Sometimes, an author simply wants to separate his writing activities from his nonwriting activities, if they are of equal importance to him. Thus, a talented teacher at Milton Academy, who is named Harry C. Stubbs, writes under the name of Hal Clement. He's not hiding. Hal is short for Harry, as all Shakespearian devotees know, and the C. in his full name stands for Clement.

Again, my dear wife has practiced medicine for over thirty years as Janet Jeppson, M.D. As a writer she prefers J. O. Jeppson. The earnings fall into two different slots as far as the I.R.S. is concerned and that makes it convenient for her bookkeeping.

In my own case, I have eschewed pseudonyms almost entirely; I am far too fond of my own name, and far too proud of my writing to want to sail under false colors for *any* reason. And yet, in one or two cases . . .

Thus in 1951, I was persuaded to write a juvenile science fiction novel in the hope that it would be sold as the beginning of a long-lived television series. (Those were early days, and no one understood how television was going to work.) I objected, very correctly I think, that TV might ruin the stuff and make me ashamed of having my name associated with it. My editor said, "Then use a pseudonym."

I did, plucking Paul French out of the air for the purpose, and eventually wrote six novels under that name. (Some people, with little knowledge of science fiction, assumed from this that *all* my SF was written under Paul French, a suggestion that simply horrified me.)

As soon as it was clear that TV was not interested in my juveniles, I dropped all pretense, and made use of the Three Laws of Robotics, for instance, which was a dead giveaway. Eventually, when it was time for new printings, I had my own name put upon it.

Again, in 1942, I wrote a short story for an editor who wanted it done under a pseudonym in order to give the impression that it was by a brand-new author. (The reason is complicated and I won't bore you with it. You'll find it in my autobiography.) I wrote it, reluctantly, under the name George E. Dale, but eventually included it in my book *The Early Asimov* as a story of my own.

Also, in 1942, I sold a story to the magazine *Super Science Stories* which printed it under the pseudonym H. B. Ogden, for reasons I no longer remember. (Even *my* memory has its limits.) So little did I care for the story, and so unhappy was I over the nonuse of my name that I totally forgot about it, until nearly forty years later when I was going over my diary carefully in order to prepare my autobiography.

I was shocked to find there was a story of mine that I had forgotten and didn't own in printed form. Fortunately, with the help of Forrest J. Ackerman I got the issue and reprinted the story in the first volume of my autobiography, *In Memory Yet Green*, acknowledging it as my own.

In 1971, I was persuaded to write a book entitled *The Sensuous Dirty Old Man*, in which I gently satirized sexual how-to books such as *The Sensuous Woman*. Since the latter book was written by a writer identified only as "J," my editor felt the joke should be carried on by having my book written by "Dr. A." Even before publication day, however, it was announced that I was the author and my identity was never a secret.

At the present moment, then, absolutely none of my writing appears under anything but my own name.

Which brings up one puzzle. The early pulps occasionally made use of "house names." A particular magazine would use a pseudonym that was never used except in that magazine, but that pseudonym might be used by any number of *different* writers. I have never really understood why this was done and if any reader knows I would appreciate being told.

Dialog

Most stories deal with people and one of the surefire activities of people is that of talking and of making conversation. It follows that in most stories there is dialog. Sometimes stories are largely dialog; my own stories almost always are. For that reason, when I think of the art of writing (which isn't often, I must admit) I tend to think of dialog.

In the romantic period of literature in the first part of the nineteenth century, the style of dialog tended to be elaborate and adorned. Authors used their full vocabulary and had their characters speak ornately.

I remember when I was very young and first read Charles Dickens's *Nicholas Nickleby*. How I loved the conversation. The funny passages were very funny to me, though I had trouble with John Browdie's thick Yorshire accent (something his beloved Matilda, brought up under similar conditions, lacked, for some reason). What I loved even more though was the ornamentation—the way everyone "spoke like a book."

Thus, consider the scene in which Nicholas Nickleby confronts his villainous Uncle Ralph. Nicholas's virtuous and beautiful sister, Kate, who has been listening to Ralph's false version of events, which make out Nicholas to have been doing wrong, cried out wildly to her brother, "Refute these calumnies."

Of course, I had to look up "refute" and "calumny" in the dictionary, but that meant I had learned two useful words. I also had never heard any seventeen-year-old girl of my acquaintance use those words but that just showed me how superior the characters in the book were, and that filled me with satisfaction.

It's easy to laugh at the books of that era and to point out that no one *really* talks that way. But then, do you suppose people in Shakespeare's time went around casually speaking in iambic pentameter?

Still, don't you want literature to improve on nature? Sure you do. When you go to the movies, the hero and heroine don't look like the people you see in the streets, do they? Of course not. They look like movie stars. The characters in fiction are better looking, stronger, braver, more ingenious and clever than anyone you are likely to meet, so why shouldn't they speak better, too?

And yet there are values in realism—in making people look, and sound, and act like real people.

For instance, back in 1919, some of the players on the pennant-winning Chicago White Sox were accused of accepting money from gamblers to throw the World Series (the so-called "Black Sox" scandal) and were barred from baseball for life as a result. At the trial, a young lad is supposed to have followed his idol, the greatest of the accused, "Shoeless" Joe Jackson, and to have cried out in anguish, "Say it ain't so, Joe."

That is a deathless cry that can't be tampered with. It is unthinkable to have the boy say "Refute these calumnies, Joseph," even though that's what he means. Any writer who tried to improve matters in that fashion would, and should, be lynched at once. I doubt that anyone would, or should, even change it to "Say it isn't so, Joe."

For that matter, you couldn't possibly have had Kate Nickleby cry out to her brother, "Say it ain't so, Nick."

Of course, during much of history most people were illiterate and the reading of books was very much confined to the few who were educated and scholarly. Such books of fiction as existed were supposed to "improve the mind," or risk being regarded as works of the devil.

It was only gradually, as mass education began to flourish, that books began to deal with ordinary people. Of course, Shakespeare had his clowns and Dickens had his Sam Wellers, and in both cases, dialog was used that mangled the English language to some extent—but that was intended as humor. The audience was expected to laugh uproariously at these representatives of the lower classes.

As far as I know the first great book which was written entirely and seriously in substandard English and which was a great work of literature nevertheless (or even, possibly, to some extent *because* of it) was Mark Twain's *Huckleberry Finn*, which was published in 1884. Huck Finn is himself the narrator, and he is made to speak as an uneducated backwoods boy *would* speak—if he happened to be a literary genius. That is, he used the dialect of an uneducated boy, but he put together sentences and paragraphs like a master.

The book was extremely popular when it came out because its realism made it incredibly effective—but it was also extremely controversial as all sorts of fatheads inveighed against it because it didn't use proper English.

And yet, at that, Mark Twain had to draw the line, too, as did all writers until the present generation.

People, all sorts of people, use vulgarisms as a matter of course. I remember my days in the army when it was impossible to hear a single sentence in which the common word for sexual intercourse was not used as an all-purpose adjective. Later, after I had gotten out of the army, I lived on a street along which young boys and girls walked to the local junior high school in the morning, and back again in the evening, and their shouted conversations brought back memories of my barracks days with nauseating clarity.

Yet could writers reproduce that aspect of common speech? Of course not. For that reason, Huck Finn was always saying that something was "blamed" annoying, "blamed" this, "blamed" that. You can bet that the *least* he was really saying was "damned."

A whole set of euphemisms was developed and placed in the mouths of characters who wouldn't, in real life, have been caught dead saying them. Think of the all the "dad-blameds," and "gol-darneds," and "consarneds" we have seen in print and heard in the movies. To be sure, youngsters say them as a matter of caution for they would probably be punished (if of "good family") by their parents if caught using the terms they had heard said parents use. (Don't let your hearts bleed for the kids for when they grow up they will beat up *their* kids for the same crime.)

For the last few decades, however, it has become permissible to use all the vulgarisms freely and many writers have availed themselves of the new freedom to lend an air of further realism to their dialog. What's more, they are apt to resent bitterly any suggestion that this habit be modified or that some nonvulgar expression be substituted.

In fact, one sees a curious reversal now. A writer must withstand a certain criticism if he does *not* make use of said vulgarisms.

Once when I read a series of letters by science fiction writers in which such terms were used freely and frequently,

I wrote a response that made what seemed to me to be an obvious point. In it, I said something like this:

"Ordinary people, who are not well educated and who lack a large working vocabulary, are limited in their ability to lend force to their statements. In their search for force, they must therefore make use of vulgarisms which serve, through their shock value, but which, through overuse, quickly lose whatever force they have, so that the purpose of the use is defeated.

"Writers, on the other hand, have (it is to be presumed) the full and magnificent vocabulary of the English language at their disposal. They can say anything they want with whatever intensity of invective they require in a thousand different ways without ever once deviating from full re-spectability of utterance. They have, therefore, no need to trespass upon the usages of the ignorant and forlorn, and to steal their tattered expressions as substitutes for the lan-guage of Shakespeare and Milton."

All I got for my pains were a few comments to the effect that there must be something seriously wrong with me.

Nevertheless, it is my contention that dialog is realistic when, and only when, it reflects the situation as you de-scribe it and when it produces the effect you wish to pro-duce.

At rather rare intervals, I will make use of dialect. I will have someone speak as a Brooklyn-bred person would (that is, as I myself do, in my hours of ease), or insert Yiddishisms here and there, if it serves a purpose. I may even try to make up a dialect, as I did in *Foundation's Edge*, if it plays an im-portant part in the development of the story.

Mostly, however, I do not.

The characters in my stories (almost without exception) are pictured as being well educated and highly intelligent. It is natural, therefore, for them to make use of a wide vocabulary and to speak precisely and grammatically, even though I try not to fall into the ornateness of the Romantic Ear.

And, as a matter of quixotic principle, I try to avoid expletives, even mild ones, when I can. But other writers, of course, may do as they please.

Acknowledgments

To list his honors, as to list his books, would be obsessive. Let it simply be noted that ISAAC ASIMOV was the most famous, most honored, most widely read, and most beloved science fiction author of all time. In his five decades as an author, he wrote more than four hundred books, won every award his readers and colleagues could contrive to give him, and provided pleasure and insight to millions.

He died in 1992, still at work.